THE WAVE

AN EGYPTIAN AFTERMATH

THE WAVE

AN EGYPTIAN AFTERMATH

ALGERNON BLACKWOOD

WILDSIDE PRESS

THE WAVE: AN EGYPTIAN AFTERMATH

Originally published in 1916.

Published by Wildside Press LLC.
www.wildsidebooks.com

CHAPTER I

Since childhood days he had been haunted by a Wave.

It appeared with the very dawn of thought, and was his earliest recollection of any vividness. It was also his first experience of nightmare: a wave of an odd, dun colour, almost tawny, that rose behind him, advanced, curled over in the act of toppling, and then stood still. It threatened, but it did not fall. It paused, hovering in a position contrary to nature; it waited.

Something prevented; it was not meant to fall; the right moment had not yet arrived.

If only it would fall! It swept across the skyline in a huge, long curve far overhead, hanging dreadfully suspended. Beneath his feet he felt the roots of it withdrawing; he shuffled furiously and made violent efforts; but the suction undermined him where he stood. The ground yielded and dropped away. He only sank in deeper. His entire weight became that of a feather against the gigantic tension of the mass that any moment, it seemed, must lift him in its rising curve, bend, break, and twist him, then fling him crashing forward to his smothering fate.

Yet the moment never came. The Wave hung balanced between him and the sky, poised in mid-air. It did not fall. And the torture of that infinite pause contained the essence of the nightmare.

The Wave invariably came up behind him, stealthily, from what seemed interminable distance. He never met it. It overtook him from the rear. The horizon hid it till it rose.

There were stages in its history, moreover, and in the effect it produced upon his early mind. Usually he woke up the moment he realised it was there. For it invariably announced its presence. He heard no sound, but knew that it was coming—there was a feeling in the atmosphere not unlike the heavy brooding that precedes a thunderstorm, only so different from anything he had yet known in life that his heart sank into his boots. He looked up. There, above his head was the huge, curved monster, hanging in mid-air. The mood had justified itself. He called it the 'wavy feeling.' He was never wrong about it.

The second stage was reached when, instead of trying to escape shorewards, where there were tufts of coarse grass upon a sandy bank, he turned and faced the thing. He looked straight into the main underbody of the poised billow. He saw the opaque mass out of which this line rose up and curved. He stared against the dull, dun-coloured parent body whence it came—the sea. Terrified yet fascinated, he examined it in detail, as a man about to be executed might examine the grain of the wooden block close against his eyes. A little higher, some dozen feet above the level of his head, it became transparent; sunlight shot through the glassy curve. He saw what appeared to be streaks and bubbles and transverse lines of foam that yet did not shine quite as water shines. It moved suddenly; it curled a little towards the crest; it was about to topple over, to break—yet did not break.

About this time he noticed another thing: there was a curious faint sweetness in the air beneath the bend of it, a delicate and indescribable odour that was almost perfume. It was sweet; it choked him. He called it, in his boyish way, a whiff. The 'whiff' and the 'wavy feeling' impressed themselves so vividly upon his mind that if ever he met them in his ordinary life—out of dream, that is—he was sure that he would know them. In another sense he felt he knew them already. They were familiar.

But another stage went further than all the others put together. It amounted to a discovery. He was perhaps ten years old at this time, for he was still addressed as 'Tommy,' and it was not till the age of fifteen that his solid type of character made 'Tom' seem more appropriate. He had just told the dream to his mother for the hundredth time, and she, after listening with sympathy, had made her ever-green suggestion—'If you dream of water, Tommy, it means you're thirsty in your sleep,'—when he turned and stared straight into her eyes with such intentness that she gave an involuntary start.

'But, mother, it isn't water!'

'Well, darling, if it isn't water, what is it, then?' She asked the question quietly enough, but she felt, apparently, something of the queer dismay that her boy felt too. It seemed the mother-sense was touched. The instinct to protect her offspring stirred uneasily in her heart. She repeated the question, interested in the old, familiar dream for the first time since she heard it several years before: 'If it isn't water, Tommy, what is it? What can it be?' His eyes, his voice, his manner— something she could not properly name—had startled her.

But Tommy noticed her slight perturbation, and knowing that a boy of his age did not frighten his mother without reason, or even with it, turned his eyes aside and answered:

'I couldn't tell. There wasn't time. You see, I woke up then.'

'How curious, Tommy,' she rejoined. 'A wave is a wave, isn't it?'

And he answered thoughtfully: 'Yes, mother; but there are lots of things besides water, aren't there?'

She assented with a nod, and a searching look at him which he purposely avoided. The subject dropped; no more was said; yet somehow from that moment his mother knew that this idea of a wave, whether it was nightmare or only dream, had to do with her boy's life in a way that touched the protective thing in her, almost to the point of positive defence. She could not explain it; she did not like it; instinct warned her—that was all she knew. And Tommy said no more. The truth was, indeed, that he did not know himself of what the Wave was composed. He could not have told his mother even had he considered it permissible. He would have loved to speculate and talk about it with her, but, having divined her nervousness, he knew he must not feed it. No boy should do such a thing.

Moreover, the interest he felt in the Wave was of such a deep, enormous character—the adjectives were his own—that he could not talk about it lightly. Unless to some one who showed genuine interest, he could not even mention it. To his brothers and sister, both older and younger than himself, he never spoke of it at all. It had to do with something so fundamental in him that it was sacred. The realisation of it, moreover, came and went, and often remained buried for weeks together; months passed without a hint of it; the nightmare disappeared. Then, suddenly, the feeling would surge over him, perhaps just as he was getting into bed, or saying his prayers, or thinking of quite other things. In the middle of a discussion with his brother about their air-guns and the water-rat they hadn't hit—up would steal the 'wavy' feeling with its dim, familiar menace. It stole in across his brother's excited words about the size and speed of the rat; interest in sport entirely vanished; he stared at Tim, not hearing a word he said; he dived into bed; he had to be alone with the great mood of wonder and terror that was rising. The approach was unmistakable; he cuddled beneath the sheets, fighting-angry if Tim tried to win him back to the original interest. The dream was coming; and, sure enough, a little later in his sleep, it came.

For even at this stage of his development he recognised instinctively this special quality about it—that it could not, was not meant to be avoided. It was inevitable and right. It hurt, yet he must face it. It was as necessary to his well-being as having a tooth out. Nor did he ever seek to dodge it. His character was not the kind that flinched. The one thing he did ask was—to understand. Some day, he felt, this full understanding would come.

There arrived then a new and startling development in this curious obsession, the very night, Tommy claims, that there had been the fuss about the gun and water-rat, on the day before the conversation with his mother. His brother had plagued him to come out from beneath the sheets and go on with the discussion, and Tommy, furious at being disturbed in the 'wavy' mood he both loved and dreaded, had felt himself roused uncommonly. He silenced Tim easily enough with a smashing blow from a pillow, then, with a more determined effort than usual, buried himself to face the advent of the Wave. He fell asleep in the attempt, but the attempt bore fruit. He felt the great thing coming up behind him; he turned; he saw it with greater distinctness than ever before; almost he discovered of what it was composed.

That it was not water established itself finally in his mind; but more— he got very close to deciding its exact composition. He stared hard into the threatening mass of it; there was a certain transparency about the substance, yet this transparency was not clear enough for water: there were particles, and these particles went drifting by the thousand, by the million, through the mass of it. They rose and fell, they swept along, they were very minute indeed, they whirled. They glistened, shimmered, flashed. He made a guess; he was just on the point of guessing right, in fact, when he saw another thing that for the moment obliterated all his faculties. There was both cold and heat in the sensation, fear and delight. It transfixed him. He saw eyes.

Steady, behind the millions of minute particles that whirled and drifted, he distinctly saw a pair of eyes of light-blue colour, and hardly had he registered this new discovery, when another pair, but of quite different kind, became visible beyond the first pair—dark, with a fringe of long, thick lashes. They were—he decided afterwards—what is called Eastern eyes, and they smiled into his own through half-closed lids. He thinks he made out a face that was dimly sketched behind them, but the whirling particles glinted and shimmered in such a confusing way that he could not swear to this. Of one thing only, or rather of two, did he feel quite positive: that the dark eyes were those of a woman, and that they were kind and beautiful and true: but that the pale-blue eyes were false, unkind, and treacherous, and that the face to which they belonged, although he could not see it, was a man's. Dimly his boyish heart was aware of happiness and suffering. The heat and cold he felt, the joy and terror, were half explained. He stared. The whirling particles drifted past and hid them. He woke.

That day, however, the 'wavy' feeling hovered over him more or less continuously. The impression of the night held sway over all he did and thought. There was a kind of guidance in it somewhere. He obeyed this guidance as by an instinct he could not, dared not disregard, and towards dusk it led him into the quiet room overlooking the small Gardens at the back of the house, his father's study. The room was empty; he approached the big mahogany cupboard; he opened one of the deep drawers where he knew his father kept gold and private things, and birthday or Christmas presents. But there was no dishonourable intention in him anywhere; indeed, he hardly knew exactly why he did this thing. The drawer, though moving easily, was heavy; he pulled hard; it slid out with a rush; and at that moment a stern voice sounded in the room behind him: 'What are you doing at my Eastern drawer?'

Tommy, one hand still on the knob, turned as if he had been struck. He gazed at his father, but without a trace of guilt upon his face.

'I wanted to see, Daddy.'

'I'll show you,' said the stern-faced man, yet with kindness and humour in the tone. 'It's full of wonderful things. I've nothing secret from you; but another time you'd better ask first—Tommy.'

'I wanted to see,' faltered the boy. 'I don't know why I did it. I just had a feeling. It's the first time—really.'

The man watched him searchingly a moment, but without appearing to do so. A look of interest and understanding, wholly missed by the culprit, stole into his fine grey eyes. He smiled, then drew Tommy towards him, and gave him a kiss on the top of his curly head. He also smacked him playfully. 'Curiosity,' he said with pretended disapproval, 'is divine, and at your age it is right that you should feel curiosity about everything in the world. But another time just ask me—and I'll show you all I possess.' He lifted his son in his arms, so that for the first time the boy could overlook the contents of the opened drawer. 'So you just had a feeling, eh——?' he continued, when Tommy wriggled in his arms, uttered a curious exclamation, and half collapsed. He seemed upon the verge of tears. An ordinary father must have held him guilty there and then. The boy cried out excitedly:

'The whiff! Oh, Daddy, it's my whiff!'

The tears, no longer to be denied, came freely then; after them came confession too, and confused though it was, the man made something approaching sense out of the jumbled utterance. It was not mere patient kindness on his part, for an older person would have seen that genuine interest lay behind the half-playful, half-serious cross-examination. He watched the boy's eager, excited face out of the corner of his eyes; he put discerning questions to him, he assisted his faltering replies, and he obtained in the end the entire story of the dream—the eyes, the wavy feeling, and the whiff. How much coherent meaning he discovered in it all is hard to say, or whether the story he managed to disentangle held together. There was this strange deep feeling in the boy, this strong emotion, this odd conviction amounting to an obsession; and so far as could be discovered, it was not traceable to any definite cause that Tommy could name—a fright, a shock, a vivid impression of one kind or another upon a sensitive young imagination. It lay so deeply in his being that its roots were utterly concealed; but it was real.

Dr. Kelverdon established the existence in his second boy of an unalterable premonition, and, being a famous nerve specialist, and a disciple of Freud into the bargain, he believed that a premonition has a cause, however primitive, however carefully concealed that cause may be. He put the boy to bed himself and tucked him up, told Tim that if he teased his brother too much he would smack him with his best Burmese slipper which had tiny nails in it, and then whispered into Tommy's ear as he cuddled down, happy and comforted, among the blankets: 'Don't make a special effort to dream, my boy; but if you do dream, try to remember it next morning, and tell me exactly what you see and feel.' He used the Freudian method.

Then, going down to his study again, he looked at the open drawer and sniffed the faint perfume of things—chiefly from Egypt—that lay inside it. But there was nothing of special interest in the drawer; indeed, it was one he had not touched for years.

He went over one by one a few of the articles, collected from various points of travel long ago. There were bead necklaces from Memphis, some trash from a mummy of doubtful authenticity, including several amulets and a crumbling fragment of old papyrus, and, among all this, a tiny packet of incense mixed from a recipe said to have been found in a Theban tomb. All these, jumbled together in pieces of tissue-paper, had lain undisturbed since the day he wrapped them up some dozen years before— indeed he heard the dry rattle of the falling sand as he undid the tissue-paper. But a strong perfume rose from the parcel to his nostrils. 'That's what Tommy means by his whiff,' he said to himself. 'That's Tommy's whiff beyond all question. I wonder how he got it first?'

He remembered, then, that he had made a note of the story connected with the incense, and after some rummaging he found the envelope and read the account jotted down at the time. He had meant to hand it over to a literary friend—the tale was so poignantly human—then had forgotten all about it. The papyrus, dating over 3000 B.C., had many gaps. The Egyptologist had admittedly filled in considerable blanks in the afflicting story:—

A victorious Theban General, Prince of the blood, brought back a Syrian youth from one of his foreign conquests and presented him to his young wife who, first mothering him for his beauty, then made him her personal slave, and ended by caring deeply for him. The slave, in return, loved her with passionate adoration he was unable to conceal. As a Lady of the Court, her quasi-adoption of the youth caused comment. Her husband ordered his dismissal. But she still made his welfare her especial object, finding frequent reasons for their meeting. One day, however, her husband caught them together, though their meeting was in innocence. He half strangled the youth, till the blood poured down upon his own hands, then had him flogged and sent away to On, the City of the Sun.

The Syrian found his way back again, vengeance in his fiery blood. The clandestine yet innocent meetings were renewed. Rank was forgotten. They met among the sand-dunes in the desert behind the city where a pleasure tent among a grove of palms provided shelter, and the slave losing his head, urged the Princess to fly with him. Yet the wife, true to her profligate and brutal husband, refused his plea, saying she could only give a mother's love, a mother's care. This he rejected bitterly, accusing her of trifling with him. He grew bolder and more insistent. To divert her husband's violent suspicions she became purposely cruel, even ordering him punishments. But the slave misinterpreted. Finally, warning him that if caught he would be killed, she devised a plan to convince him of her sincerity. Hiding him behind the curtains of her tent, she pleaded with her husband for the youth's recall, swearing that she meant no wrong. But the soldier, in his fury, abused and struck her, and the slave, unable to contain himself, rushed out of his hiding-place and stabbed him, though not mortally. He was condemned to death by torture. She was to be chief witness against him.

Meanwhile, having extracted a promise from her husband that the torture should not be carried to the point of death, she conveyed word to the victim that he should endure bravely, knowing that he would not die. She now realised that she loved. She promised to fly with him.

The sentence was duly carried out, the slave only half believing in her truth. It was a public holiday in Thebes. She was compelled to see the punishment inflicted before the crowd. There were a thousand drums. A sand-storm hid the sun.

Seated beside her husband on a terrace above the Nile, she watched the torture—then knew she had been tricked. But the Syrian did not know; he believed her false. As he expired, casting his last glance of anguish and reproach at her, she rose, leaped the parapet, flung herself into the river, and was drowned. The husband had their bodies thrown into the sea, unburied. The same wave took them both. Later, however, they were recovered by influential friends; they were embalmed, and secretly laid to rest in his ancestral Tomb in the Valley of the Kings among the Theban Hills. In due course the husband, unwittingly, was buried with them.

Nearly five thousand years later all three mummies were discovered lying side by side, their story inscribed upon a papyrus inside the great sarcophagus.

Dr. Kelverdon glanced through the story he had forgotten, then tore it into little pieces and threw them into the fireplace. For a moment longer, however, he stood beside the open drawer reflectingly. Had he ever told the tale to Tommy? No; it was hardly likely; indeed it was impossible. The boy was not born even when first he heard it. To his wife, then? Less likely still. He could not remember, anyhow. The faint suggestion in his mind—a story communicated pre-natally—was not worth following up.

He dismissed the matter from his thoughts. He closed the drawer and turned away. The little packet of incense, however, taken from the Tomb, he did not destroy. 'I'll give it to Tommy,' he decided. 'Its whiff may possibly stimulate him into explanation!'

CHAPTER II

As a result of having told everything to his father, Tommy's nightmare, however, largely ceased to trouble him. He had found the relief of expression, which is confession, and had laid upon the older mind the burden of his terror. Once a month, once a week, or even daily if he wanted to, he could repeat the expression as the need for it accumulated, and the load which decency forbade being laid upon his mother, the stern-faced man could carry easily for him.

The comfortable sensation that forgiveness is the completion of confession invaded his awakening mind, and had he been older this thin end of a religious wedge might have persuaded him to join what his mother called that 'vast conspiracy.' But even at this early stage there was something stalwart and self-reliant in his cast of character that resisted the cunning sophistry; vicarious relief woke resentment in him; he meant to face his troubles alone. So far as he knew, he had not sinned, yet the Wave, the Whiff, the Eyes were symptoms of some fate that threatened him, a premonition of something coming that he must meet with his own strength, something that he could only deal with effectively alone, since it was deserved and just. One day the Wave would fall; his father could not help him then. This instinct in him remained unassailable. He even began to look forward to the time when it should come—to have done with it and get it over, conquering or conquered.

The premonition, that is, while remaining an obsession as before, transferred itself from his inner to his outer life. The nightmare, therefore, ceased. The menacing interest, however, held unchanged. Though the name had not hitherto occurred to him, he became a fatalist. 'It's got to come; I've got to meet it. I will.'

'Well, Tommy,' his father would ask from time to time, 'been dreaming anything lately?'

'Nothing, Daddy. It's all stopped.'

'Wave, eyes, and whiff all forgotten, eh?'

Tommy shook his head. 'They're still there,' he answered slowly, 'but——' He seemed unable to complete the sentence. His father helped him at a venture.

'But they can't catch you—is that it?'

The boy looked up with a dogged expression in his big grey eyes. 'I'm ready for them,' he replied. And his father laughed and said, 'Of course. That's half the battle.'

He gave him a present then—one of the packets of tissue-paper—and Tommy took it in triumph to his room. He opened it in private, but the contents seemed to him without especial interest. Only the Whiff was, somehow, sweet and precious; and he kept the packet in a drawer apart where the fossils and catapult and air-gun ammunition could not interfere with it, hiding the key so that Tim and the servants could not find it. And on rare occasions, when the rest of the household was asleep, he performed a little ritual of his own that, for a boy of his years, was distinctly singular.

When the room was dark, lit in winter by the dying fire, or in summer by the stars, he would creep out of bed, make quite sure that Tim was asleep, stand on a chair to reach the key from the top of the big cupboard, and carefully unlock the drawer. He had oiled the wood with butter, so that it was silent. The tissue-paper gleamed dimly pink; the Whiff came out to meet him. He lifted the packet, soft and crackling, and set it on the window-sill; he did not open it; its contents had no interest for him, it was the perfume he was after. And the moment the perfume reached his nostrils there came a trembling over him that he could not understand. He both loved and dreaded it. This manly, wholesome-minded, plucky little boy, the basis of whose steady character was common sense, became the prey of a strange, unreasonable fantasy. A faintness stole upon him; he lost the sense of kneeling on a solid chair; something immense and irresistible came piling up behind him; there was nothing firm he could push against to save himself; he began shuffling with his bare feet, struggling to escape from something that was coming, something that would probably overwhelm him yet must positively be faced and battled with. The Wave was rising. It was the wavy feeling.

He did not turn to look, because he knew quite well there was nothing in the room but beds, a fender, furniture, vague shadows and his brother Tim. That kind of childish fear had no place in what he felt. But the Wave was piled and curving over none the less; it hung between him and the shadowed ceiling, above the roof of the house; it came from beyond the world, far overhead against the crowding stars. It would not break, for the time had not yet come. But it was there. It waited. He knelt beneath its mighty shadow of advance; it was still arrested, poised above his eager life, competent to engulf him when the time arrived. The sweep of its curved mass was mountainous. He knelt inside this curve, small, helpless, but not too afraid to fight. The perfume stole about him. The Whiff was in his nostrils. There was a strange, rich pain—oddly remote, yet oddly poignant....

And it was with this perfume that the ritual chiefly had to do. He loved the extraordinary sensations that came with it, and tried to probe their meaning in his boyish way. Meaning there was, but it escaped him. The sweetness clouded something in his brain, and made his muscles weak; it robbed him of that resistance which is fighting strength. It was this battle that he loved, this sense of shoving against something that might so easily crush and finish him. There was a way to beat it, a way to win—could he but discover it. As yet he could not. Victory, he felt, lay more in yielding and going-with than in violent resistance.

And, meanwhile, in an ecstasy of this half yielding, half resisting, he lent himself fully to the overmastering tide. He was conscious of attraction and repulsion, something that enticed, yet thrust him backwards. Some final test of manhood, character, value, lay in the way he faced it. The strange, rich pain stole marvellously into his blood and nerves. His heart beat faster. There was this exquisite seduction that contained delicious danger. It rose upon him out of some inner depth he could not possibly get at. He trembled with mingled terror and delight. And it invariably ended with a kind of inexpressible yearning that choked him, crumpled him inwardly, as he described it, brought the moisture, hot and smarting, into his burning eyes, and—each time to his bitter shame— left his cheeks wet with scalding tears.

He cried silently; there was no heaving, gulping, audible sobbing, just a relieving gush of heartfelt tears that took away the strange, rich pain and brought the singular ritual to a finish. He replaced the tissue-paper, blotted with his tears; locked the drawer carefully; hid the key on the top of the cupboard again, and tumbled back into bed.

Downstairs, meanwhile, a conversation was in progress concerning the welfare of the growing hero.

'I'm glad that dream has left him anyhow. It used to frighten me rather. I did not like it,' observed his mother.

'He doesn't speak to you about it any more?' the father asked.

For months, she told him, Tommy had not mentioned it. They went on to discuss his future together. The other children presented fewer problems, but Tommy, apparently, felt no particular call to any profession.

'It will come with a jump,' the doctor inclined to think. 'He's been on the level for some time now. Suddenly he'll grow up and declare his mighty mind.'

Father liked humour in the gravest talk; indeed the weightier the subject, the more he valued a humorous light upon it. The best judgment, he held, was shaped by humour, sense of proportion lost without it. His wife, however, thought 'it a pity.' Grave things she liked grave.

'There's something very deep in Tommy,' she observed, as though he were developing a hidden malady.

'Hum,' agreed her husband. 'His subconscious content is unusual, both in kind and quantity.' His eyes twinkled. 'It's possible he may turn out an artist, or a preacher. If the former, I'll bet his output will be original; and, as for the latter,'—he paused a second—'he's too logical and too fearless to be orthodox. Already he thinks things out for himself.'

'I should like to see him in the Church, though,' said Mother. 'He would do a lot of good. But he is uncompromising, rather.'

'His honesty certainly is against him,' sighed his father. 'What do you think he asked me the other day?'

'I'm sure I don't know, John.' The answer completed itself with the unspoken 'He never asks me anything now.'

'He came straight up to me and said, 'Father, is it good to feel pain? To let it come, I mean, or try to dodge it?''

'Had he hurt himself?' the woman asked quickly. It seemed she winced.

'Not physically. He had been feeling something inside. He wanted to know how 'a man' should meet the case.'

'And what did you tell him, dear?'

'That pain was usually a sign of growth, to be understood, accepted, faced. That most pain was cured in that way——'

'He didn't tell you what had hurt him?' she interrupted.

'Oh, I didn't ask him. He'd have shut up like a clam. Tommy likes to deal with things alone in his own way. He just wanted to know if his way was—well, my way.'

There fell a pause between them; then Mother, without looking up, enquired: 'Have you noticed Lettice lately? She's here a good deal now.'

But her husband only smiled, making no direct reply. 'Tommy will have a hard time of it when he falls in love,' he remarked presently. 'He'll know the real thing and won't stand any nonsense—just as I did.' Whereupon his wife informed him that if he was not careful he would simply ruin the boy—and the brief conversation died away of its own accord. As she was leaving the room a little later, unsatisfied but unaggressive, he asked her: 'Have you left the picture books, my dear?' and she pointed to an ominous heap upon the table in the window, with the remark that Jane had 'unearthed every book that Tommy had set eyes upon since he was three. You'll find everything that's ever interested him,' she added as she went out, 'every picture, that is—and I suppose it is the pictures that you want.'

For an hour and a half the great specialist turned pages without ceasing— well-thumbed pages; torn, crumpled, blotted, painted pages. It was easy to discover the boy's favourite pictures; and all were commonplace enough, the sort that any normal, adventure-loving boy would find delightful. But nothing of special significance resulted from the search; nothing that might account for the recurrent nightmare, nothing in the way of eyes or wave. He had already questioned Jane as to what stories she told him, and which among them he liked best. 'Hunting or travel or collecting,' Jane had answered, and it was about 'collecting that he asks most questions. What kind of collecting, sir? Oh, treasure or rare beetles mostly, and sometimes—just bones.'

'Bones! What kind of bones?'

'The villin's, sir,' explained the frightened Jane. 'He always likes the villin to get lost, and for the jackals to pick his bones in the desert——'

'Any particular desert?'

'No, sir; just desert.'

'Ah—just desert! Any old desert, eh?'

'I think so, sir—as long as it is desert.'

Dr. Kelverdon put the woman at her ease with the humorous smile that made all the household love—and respect—him; then asked another question, as if casually: Had she ever told him a story in which a wave or a pair of eyes were in any way conspicuous?

'No, never, sir,' replied the honest Jane, after careful reflection. 'Nor I wouldn't,' she added, 'because my father he was drowned in a tidal wave; and as for eyes, I know that's wrong for children, and I wouldn't tell Master Tommy such a thing for all the world——'

'Because?' enquired the doctor kindly, seeing her hesitation.

'I'd be frightening myself, sir, and he'd make such fun of me,' she finally confessed.

No, it was clear that the nurse was not responsible for the vivid impression in Tommy's mind which bore fruit in so strange a complex of emotions. Nor were other lines of enquiry more successful. There was a cause, of course, but it would remain unascertainable unless some clue offered itself by chance. Both the doctor and the father in him were pledged to a persistent search that was prolonged over several months, but without result. The most perplexing element in the problem seemed to him the whiff. The association of terror with a wave needed little explanation; the introduction of the eyes, however, was puzzling, unless some story of a drowning man was possibly the clue; but the addition of a definite odour, an Eastern odour, moreover, with which the boy could hardly have become yet acquainted,—this combination of the three accounted for the peculiar interest in the doctor's mind.

Of one thing alone did he feel reasonably certain: the impression had been printed upon the deepest part of Tommy's being, the very deepest; it arose from those unplumbed profundities—though a scientist, he considered them unfathomable—of character and temperament whence emerge the most primitive of instincts,—the generative and creative instinct, choice of a mate, natural likes and dislikes,—the bed-rock of the nature. A girl was in it somewhere, somehow....

Midnight had sounded from the stable clock in the mews when he stole up into the boys' room and cautiously approached the yellow iron bed where Tommy lay. The reflection of a street electric light just edged his face. He was sound asleep—with tear-stains marked clearly on the cheek not pressed into the pillow. Dr. Kelverdon paused a moment, looked round the room, shading the candle with one hand. He saw no photograph, no pictures anywhere. Then he sniffed. There was a faint and delicate perfume in the air. He recognised it. He stood there, thinking deeply.

'Lettice Aylmer,' he said to himself presently as he went softly out again to seek his own bed; 'I'll try Lettice. It's just possible.... Next time I see her I'll have a little talk.' For he suddenly remembered that Lettice Aylmer, his daughter's friend and playmate, had very large and beautiful dark eyes.

CHAPTER III

Lettice Aylmer, daughter of the Irish Member of Parliament, did not provide the little talk that he anticipated, however, because she went back to her Finishing School abroad. Dr. Kelverdon was sorry when he heard it. So was Tommy. She was to be away a year at least. 'I must remember to have a word with her when she comes back,' thought the father, and made a note of it in his diary twelve months ahead. 'Three hundred and sixty-five days,' thought Tommy, and made a private calendar of his own.

It seemed an endless, zodiacal kind of period; he counted the days, a sheet of foolscap paper for each month, and at the bottom of each sheet two columns showing the balance of days gone and days to come. Tuesday, when he had first seen her, was underlined, and each Tuesday had a number attached to it, giving the total number of weeks since that wonderful occasion. But Saturdays were printed. On Saturday Lettice had spoken to him; she had smiled, and the words were, 'Don't forget me, Tommy!' And Tommy, looking straight into her great dark eyes, that seemed to him more tender even than his mother's, had stammered a reply that he meant with literal honesty: 'I won't—never...'; and she was gone... to France... across the sea.

She took his soul away with her, leaving him behind to pore over his father's big atlas and learn French sentences by heart. It seemed the only way. Life had begun, and he must be prepared. Also, his career was chosen. For Lettice had said another thing—one other thing. When Mary, his sister, introduced him, 'This is Tommy,' Lettice looked down and asked: 'Are you going to be an engineer?' adding proudly, 'My brother is.' Before he could answer she was scampering away with Mary, the dark hair flying in a cloud, the bright bow upon it twinkling like a star in heaven—and Tommy, hating his ridiculous boyish name with an intense hatred, stood there trembling, but aware that the die was cast—he was going to be an engineer.

Trembling, yes; for he felt dazed and helpless, caught in a mist of fire and gold, the furniture whirling round him, and something singing wildly in his heart. Two things, each containing in them the essence of genuine shock, had fallen upon him: shock, because there was impetus in them as of a blow. They had been coming; they had reached him. There was no doubt or question possible. He staggered from the impact. Joy and terror touched him; at one and the same moment he felt the enticement and the shrinking of his dream.... He longed to seize her and prevent her ever going away, yet also he wanted to push her from him as though she somehow caused him pain.

For, on the two occasions when speech had taken place between himself and Lettice, the dream had transferred itself boldly into his objective life— yet not entirely. Two characteristics only had been thus transferred. When his sister first came into the hall with 'This is Tommy,' the wavy feeling had already preceded her by a definite interval that was perhaps a second by the watch. He was aware of it behind him, curved and risen—not curving, rising—from the open fireplace, but also from the woods behind the house, from the whole of the country right back to the coast, from across the world, it seemed, towering overhead against the wintry sky. And when Lettice smiled and asked that question of childish admiration about being an engineer, he was already shuffling furiously with his feet upon the Indian rug. She was gone again, luckily, he hoped, before the ridiculous pantomime was noticeable.

He saw her once or twice. He was invariably speechless when she came into his presence, and his silence and awkwardness made him appear at great disadvantage. He seemed intentionally rude. Nervous self-consciousness caused him to bridle over nothing. Even to answer her was a torture. He dreaded a snub appallingly, and bridled in anticipation. Furious with himself for his inability to use each precious opportunity, he pretended he didn't care. The consequence was that when she once spoke to him sweetly, he was too overpowered to respond as he might have done. That she had not even noticed his anguished attitude never occurred to him.

'We're always friends, aren't we, Tommy?'

'Rather,' he blurted, before he could regain his composure for a longer sentence.

'And always will be, won't we?'

'Rather,' he repeated, cursing himself later for thinking of nothing better to say. Then, just as she flew off in that dancing way of hers, he found his tongue. Out of the jumbled mass of phrases in his head three words got loose and offered themselves: 'We'll always be!' he flung at her retreating figure of intolerable beauty. And she turned her head over her shoulder, waved her hand without stopping her career, and shouted 'Rather!'

That was the Tuesday in his calendar. But on Saturday, the printed Saturday following it, the second characteristic of his dream announced itself: he recognised the Eyes. Why he had not recognised them on the Tuesday lay beyond explanation; he only knew it was so. And afterwards, when he tried to think it over, it struck him that she had scampered out of the hall with peculiar speed and hurry; had made her escape without the extra word or two the occasion naturally demanded—almost as though she, too, felt something that uneasily surprised her.

Tommy wondered about it till his head spun round. She, too, had received an impact that was shock. He was as thorough about it as an instinctive scientist. He also registered this further fact—that the dream-details had not entirely reproduced themselves in the affair. There was no trace of the Whiff or of the other pair of Eyes. Some day the three would come together; but then....

The main thing, however, undoubtedly was this: Lettice felt some-thing too: she was aware of feelings similar to his own. He was too hon-est to assume that she felt exactly what he felt; he only knew that her eyes betrayed familiar intimacy when she said 'Don't forget me, Tommy,' and that when she rushed out of the hall with that unnecessary abruptness it was because—well, he could only transfer to her some degree of the 'wavy' feeling in himself.

And he fell in love with abandonment and a delicious, infinite yearn-ing. From that moment he thought of himself as Tom instead of Tommy.

It was an entire, sweeping love that left no atom or corner of his being untouched. Lettice was real; she hid below the horizon of distant France, yet could not, did not, hide from him. She also waited.

He knew the difference between real and unreal people. The latter wavered about his life and were uncertain; sometimes he liked them, sometimes he did not; but the former—remained fixed quantities: he could not alter towards them. Even at this stage he knew when a person came into his life to stay, or merely to pass out again. Lettice, though seen but twice, belonged to this first category. His feeling for her had the Wave in it; it gathered weight and mass, it was irresistible. From the dim, invisible foundations of his life it came, out of the foundations of the world, out of that inexhaustible sea-foundation that lay below ev-erything. It was real; it was not to be avoided. He knew. He persuaded himself that she knew too.

And it was then, realising for the first time the searching pain of be-ing separated from something that seemed part of his being by natural right, he spoke to his father and asked if pain should be avoided. This conversation has been already sufficiently recorded; but he asked other things as well. From being so long on the level he had made a sudden jump that his father had foretold; he grew up; his mind began to think; he had peered into certain books; he analysed. Out of the nonsense of his speculative reflections the doctor pounced on certain points that puzzled him completely. Probing for the repressed elements in the boy's psychic life that caused the triple complex of Wave and Eyes and Whiff, he only saw the cause receding further and further from his grasp until it finally lost itself in ultimate obscurity. The disciple of Freud was baffled hope-lessly....

Tom, meanwhile, bathed in a sea of new sensations. Distance held meaning for him, separation was a kind of keen starvation. He made discoveries— watched the moon rise, heard the wind, and knew the stars shone over the meadows below the house, things that before had been merely commonplace. He pictured these details as they might occur in France, and once when he saw a Swallow Tail butterfly, knowing that the few English specimens were said to have crossed the Channel, he had a touch of ecstasy, as though the proud insect brought him a message from the fields below the Finishing School. Also he read French books and found the language difficult but exquisite. All sweet and lovely things came from France, and at school he attempted violent friendships with three French boys and the Foreign Language masters, friendships that were not appreciated because they were not understood. But he made progress with the language, and it stood him in good stead in his examinations. He was aiming now at an Engineering College. He passed in—eventually—brilliantly enough.

Before that satisfactory moment, however, he knew difficult times. His inner life was in a splendid tumult. From the books he purloined he read a good many facts concerning waves and wave-formation. He learned, among other things, that all sensory impressions reached the nerves by impact of force in various wave-lengths; heat, light and sound broke upon the skin and eyes and ears in vibrations of æther or air that advanced in steady series of wavy formations which, though not quite similar to his dream-wave, were akin to it. Sensation, which is life, was thus linked on to his deepest, earliest memory.

A wave, however, instantly rejoined the parent stock and formed again. And perhaps it was the repetition of the wave—its forming again and breaking again—that impressed him most. For he imagined his impulses, emotions, tendencies all taking this wave-form, sweeping his moods up to a certain point, then dropping back into his centre—the Sea, he called it— which held steady below all temporary fluctuations—only to form once more and happen all over again.

With his moral and spiritual life it was similar: a wind came, wind of desire, wind of yearning, wind of hope, and he felt his strength accumulating, rising, bending with power upon the object that he had in view. To take that object exactly at the top of the wave was to achieve success; to miss that moment was to act with a receding and diminishing power, to dissipate himself in foam and spray before he could retire for a second rise. He saw existence as a wave. Life itself was a wave that rose, swept, curved, and finally—must break.

He merely visualised these feelings into pictures; he did not think them out, nor get them into words. The wave became symbolic to him of all life's energies. It was the way in which all sensation expressed itself. Lettice was the high-water mark on shore he longed to reach and sweep back into his own tumultuous being. In that great underneath, the Sea, they belonged eternally together....

One thing, however, troubled him exceedingly: he read that a wave was a segment of a circle, the perfect form, yet that it never completed itself. The ground on which it broke prevented the achievement of the circle. That, he felt, was a pity, and might be serious; there was always that sinister retirement for another effort that yet never did, and never could, result in complete achievement. He watched the waves a good deal on the shore, when occasion offered in the holidays—they came from France!—and made a discovery on his own account that was not mentioned in any of the books. And it was this: that the top of the wave, owing to its curve, was reflected in the under part. Its end, that is, was foretold in its beginning.

There was a want of scientific accuracy here, a confusion of time and space, perhaps, yet he noticed the idea and registered the thrill. At the moment when the wave was poised to fall its crest shone reflected in the base from which it rose.

But the more he watched the waves on the shore, the more puzzled he became. They seemed merely a movement of the sea itself. They endlessly repeated themselves. They had no true, separate existence until they— broke. Nor could he determine whether the crest or the base was the beginning, for the two ran along together, and what was above one minute was below the minute after. Which part started first he never could decide. The head kept chasing the tail in an effort to join up. Only when a wave broke and fell was it really—a wave. It had to 'happen' to earn its name.

There were ripples too. These indicated the direction of the parent wave upon whose side they happened, but not its purpose. Moods were ripples: they varied the surface of life but did not influence its general direction.

His own life followed a similar behaviour; he was full of ripples that were for ever trying to complete themselves by happening in acts. But the main Wave was the thing—end and beginning sweeping along together, both at the same time somehow. That is, he knew the end and could foretell it. It rose from the great 'beneath' which was the sea in him. It must topple over in the end and complete itself. He knew it would; he knew it would hurt; he knew also that he would not shirk it when it came. For it was a repetition somehow.

'I jolly well mean to enjoy the smash,' he felt. 'I know one pair of Eyes already; there's only the Whiff and the other Eyes to come. The moment I find them, I'll go bang into it.' He experienced a delicious shiver at the prospect.

One thing, however, remained uncertain: the stuff the Wave was made of. Once he discovered that, he would discover also—where the smash would come.

CHAPTER IV

'Can a chap feel things coming?' he asked his father. He was perhaps fifteen or sixteen then. 'I mean, when you feel them coming, does that mean they must come?'

His father listened warily. There had been many similar questions lately.

'You can feel ordinary things coming,' he replied; 'things due to association of ideas.'

Tom looked up. 'Association?' he queried uncertainly.

'If you feel hungry,' explained the doctor, 'you know that dinner's coming; you associate the hunger with the idea of eating. You recognise them because you've felt them both together before.'

'They ought to come, then?'

'Dinner does come—ordinarily speaking. You've learned to expect it from the hunger. You could, of course, prevent it coming,' he added dryly, 'only that would be bad for you. You need it.'

Tom reflected a moment with a puckered face. His father waited for him to ask more, hoping he would. The boy felt the sympathy and invitation.

'Before,' he repeated, picking out the word with sudden emphasis, his mind evidently breaking against a problem. 'But if I felt hungry for something I hadn't had before——?'

'In that case you wouldn't call it hunger. You wouldn't know what to call it. You'd feel a longing of some kind and would wonder what it meant.'

Tom's next words surprised him considerably. They came promptly, but with slow and thoughtful emphasis.

'So that if I know what I want, and call it dinner, or pain, or—love, or something,' he exclaimed, 'it means that I've had it before? And that's why I know it.' The last five words were not a question but a statement of fact apparently.

The doctor pretended not to notice the variants of dinner. At least he did not draw attention to them.

'Not necessarily,' he answered. 'The things you feel you want may be the things that everybody wants—things common to the race. Such wants are naturally in your blood; you feel them because your parents, your grandparents, and all humanity in turn behind your own particular family have always wanted them.'

'They come out of the sea, you mean?'

'That's very well expressed, Tom. They come out of the sea of human nature, which is everywhere the same, yes.'

The compliment seemed to annoy the boy.

'Of course,' he said bluntly. 'But—if it hurts?' The words were sharply emphasised.

'Association of ideas again. Toothache suggests the pincers. You want to get rid of the pain, but the pain has to get worse before it can get better. You know that, so you face it gladly—to get it over.'

'You face it, yes,' said Tom. 'It makes you better in the end.'

It suddenly dawned upon him that his learned father knew nothing, nothing at least that could help him. He knew only what other people knew. He turned then, and asked the ridiculous question that lay at the back of his mind all the time. It cost him an effort, for his father would certainly deem it foolish.

'Can a thing happen before it really happens?'

Dr. Kelverdon may or may not have thought the question foolish; his face was hidden a moment as he bent down to put the Indian rug straight with his hand. There was no impatience in the movement, nor was there mockery in his expression, when he resumed his normal position. He had gained an appreciable interval of time—some fifteen seconds. 'Tom, you've got good ideas in that head of yours,' he said calmly; 'but what is it that you mean exactly?'

Tom was quite ready to amplify. He knew what he meant:

'If I know something is going to happen, doesn't that mean that it has already happened—and that I remember it?'

'You're a psychologist as well as engineer, Tom,' was the approving reply. 'It's like this, you see: In emotion, with desire in it, can predict the fulfilment of that desire. In great hunger you imagine you're eating all sorts of good things.'

'But that's looking forward,'; the boy pounced on the mistake. 'It's not remembering.'

'That is the difficulty,' explained his father; 'to decide whether you're anticipating only—or actually remembering.'

'I see,' Tom said politely.

All this analysis concealed merely: it did not reveal. The thing itself dived deeper out of sight with every phrase. He knew quite well the difference between anticipating and remembering. With the latter there was the sensation of having been through it. Each time he remembered seeing Lettice the sensation was the same, but when he looked forward to seeing her again the sensation varied with his mood.

'For instance, Tom—between ourselves this—we're going to send Mary to that Finishing School in France where Lettice is.' The doctor, it seemed, spoke carelessly while he gathered his papers together with a view to going out. He did not look at the boy; he said it walking about the room. 'Mary will look forward to it and think about it so much that when she gets there it will seem a little familiar to her, as if—almost as if she remembered it.'

'Thank you, father; I see, yes,' murmured Tom. But in his mind a voice said so distinctly 'Rot!' that he was half afraid the word was audible.

'You see the difficulty, eh? And the difference?'

'Rather,' exclaimed the boy with decision.

And thereupon, without the slightest warning, he looked out of the window and asked certain other questions. Evidently they cost him effort; his will forced them out. Since his back was turned he did not see his father's understanding smile, but neither did the latter see the lad's crimson cheeks, though possibly he divined them.

'Father—is Miss Aylmer older than me?'

'Ask Mary, Tom. She'll know. Or, stay—I'll ask her for you—if you like.'

'Oh, that's all right. I just wanted to know,' with an assumed indifference that barely concealed the tremor in the voice.

'I suppose,' came a moment later, 'a Member of Parliament is a grander thing than a doctor, is it?'

'That depends,' replied his father, 'upon the man himself. Some M.P.'s vote as they're told, and never open their mouths in the House. Some doctors, again——'

But the boy interrupted him. He quite understood the point.

'It's fine to be an engineer, though, isn't it?' he asked. 'It's a real profession?'

'The world couldn't get along without them, or the Government either. It's a most important profession indeed.'

Tom, playing idly with the swinging tassel of the window-blind, asked one more question. His voice and manner were admirably under control, but there was a gulp, and his father heard and noted it.

'Shall I have—shall I be rich enough—to marry—some day?'

Dr. Kelverdon crossed the room and put his hand on his son's shoulder, but did not try to make him show his face. 'Yes,' he said quietly, 'you will, my boy—when the time comes.' He paused a moment, then added: 'But money will not make you a distinguished man, whereas if you become a famous engineer, you'll have money of your own and—any nice girl would be proud to have you.'

'I see,' said Tom, tying the strings of the tassel into knots, then untying them again with a visible excess of energy—and the conversation came somewhat abruptly to an end. He was aware of the invitation to talk further about Lettice Aylmer, but he resisted and declined it. What was the use? He knew his own mind already about that.

Yet, strictly speaking, Tom was not imaginative. It was as if an instinct taught him. More and more, the Wave, with its accompanying details of Eyes and Whiff, seemed to him the ghost of some dim memory that brought a forgotten warning in its train—something missed, something to be repeated, something to be faced and learned and—mastered....

* * * *

His father, meanwhile, went forth upon his rounds that day, much preoccupied about the character of his eldest boy. He felt a particular interest in the peculiar obsession that he knew overshadowed the young, growing life. It puzzled him; he found no clue to it; in his thought he was aware of a faint uneasiness, although he did not give it a definite name—something akin to what the mother felt. Admitting he was baffled, he fell back, however, upon such generalities as prenatal influence, ancestral, racial, and so eventually dismissed it from his active mind.

Tom, meanwhile, for his part, also went along his steep, predestined path. The nightmare had entirely deserted him, he now rarely dreamed; and his outer life shaped bravely, as with a boy of will, honesty, and healthy ambition might be expected. Neither Wavy feeling, Eyes, nor Whiff obtruded themselves: they left him alone and waited: he never forgot them, but he did not seek them out. Things once firmly realised remained in his consciousness; he knew that his life was rising like a wave, that all his energies worked in the form of waves, his moods and wishes, his passions, emotions, yearnings—all expressed themselves by means of this unalterable formula, yet all contributed finally to the one big important Wave whose climax would be reached only when it fell. He distinguished between Wave and Ripples. He, therefore, did not trouble himself with imaginary details; he did not search; he waited. This steady strength was his. His firm, square jaw and the fearless eyes of grey beneath the shock of straight dark hair told plainly enough the kind of stuff behind them. No one at school took unnecessary liberties with Tom Kelverdon.

But, having discovered one pair of Eyes, he did not let them go. In his earnest, dull, inflexible way he loved their owner with a belief in her truth and loyalty that admitted of no slightest question. Had his mother divined the strength and value of his passion, she would surely have asked herself with painful misgiving: 'Is she—can she be— worthy of my boy?' But his mother guessed it as little as any one else; even the doctor had forgotten those early signs of its existence; and Tom was not the kind to make unnecessary confidences, nor to need sympathy in any matter he was sure about.

There was down now upon his upper lip, for he was close upon seventeen and the Entrance Examination was rising to the crest of its particular minor wave, yet during the two years' interval nothing—no single fact—had occurred to justify his faith or to confirm its amazing certainty within his heart. Mary, his sister, had not gone after all to the Finishing School in France; other girl friends came to spend the holidays with her; the Irish member of Parliament had either died or sunk into another kind of oblivion; the paths of the Kelverdons and the Aylmer family had gone apart; and the name of Lettice no longer thrilled the air across the tea-table, nor chance reports of her doings filled the London house with sudden light.

Yet for Tom she existed more potently than ever. His yearning never lessened; he was sure she remembered him as he remembered her; he persuaded himself that she thought about him; she doubtless knew that he was going to be an engineer. He had cut a thread from the carpet in the hall—from the exact spot her flying foot had touched that Tuesday when she scampered off from him—and kept it in the drawer beside the Eastern packet that enshrined the Whiff. Occasionally he took it out and touched it, fingered it, even caressed it; the thread and the perfume belonged together; the ritual of the childish years altered a little—worship raised it to a higher level.

He saw her with her hair done up now, long skirts, and a softer expression in the tender, faithful eyes; the tomboy in her had disappeared; she gazed at him with admiration. The face was oddly real, it came very close to his own; once or twice, indeed, their cheeks almost touched: 'almost,' because he withdrew instantly, uneasily aware that he had gone too far— not that the intimacy was unwelcome, but that it was somehow premature. And the instant he drew back, a kind of lightning distance came between them; he saw her eyes across an immense and curious interval, though whether of time or space he could not tell. There was strange heat and radiance in it—as of some blazing atmosphere that was not England.

The eyes, moreover, held a new expression when this happened— pity. And with this pity came also pain: the strange, rich pain broke over all the other happier feelings in him and swamped them utterly....

But at that point instinct failed him; he could not understand why she should pity him, why pain should come to him through her, nor why it was necessary for him to feel and face it. He only felt sure of one thing— that it was essential to the formation of the Wave which was his life. The Wave must 'happen,' or he would miss an important object of his being—and she would somehow miss it too. The Wave would one day fall, but when it fell she would be with him, by his side, under the mighty curve, involved in the crash and tumult—with himself.

CHAPTER V

Then, without any warning, he received a second shock—it fell upon him from the blue and came direct from Lettice.

The occasion was a tennis party in the garden by the sea where the family had come to spend the summer holidays. Tom was already at College, doing brilliantly, and rapidly growing up. The August afternoon was very hot; no wind ruffled the quiet blue-green water; there were no waves; the leaves of the privet hedge upon the side of the cliffs were motionless. A couple of Chalk-Blues danced round and round each other as though a wire connected them, and Tom, walking in to tea with his partner after a victorious game, found himself watching the butterflies and making a remark about them—a chance observation merely to fill an empty pause. He felt as little interest in the insects as he did in his partner, an uncommonly pretty, sunburned girl, whose bare arms and hatless light hair became her admirably. She, however, approved of the remark and by no means despised the opportunity to linger a moment by the side of her companion. They stood together, perhaps a dozen seconds, watching the capricious scraps of colour rise, float over the privet hedge on balanced wings, dip abruptly down and vanish on the farther side below the cliff. The girl said something—an intentional something that was meant to be heard and answered: but no answer was forthcoming. She repeated the remark with emphasis; then, as still no answer came, she laughed brightly to make his silence appear natural.

But Tom had no word to say. He had not noticed the manœuvre of the girl, nor the manœuvre of the two Chalk-Blues; neither had he heard the words, although conscious that she spoke. For in that brief instant when the insects floated over the hedge, his eyes had wandered beyond them to the sea, and on the sea, far off against the cloudless horizon, he had seen— the Wave.

Thinking it over afterwards, however, he realised that it was not actually a wave he saw, for the surface of the blue-green sea was smooth as the tennis lawn itself: it was the sudden appearance of the 'wavy feeling' that made him think he saw the old, familiar outline of his early dream. He had objectified his emotion. His father perhaps would have called it association of ideas.

Abruptly, out of nothing obvious, the feeling rose and mastered him: and, after its quiescence—its absence—for so long an interval, this revival without hint or warning of any kind was disconcerting. The feeling was vivid and unmistakable. The joy and terror swept him as of old. He braced himself. Almost—he began shuffling with his feet....

'Tea's waiting for you,'; his mother's voice floated to his ears across the lawn, as he turned with an effort from the sea and made towards the group about the tables. The Wave, he knew, was coming up behind him, growing, rising, curving high against the evening sky. Beside him walked the sunburned girl, wondering doubtless at his silence, but happy enough, it seemed, in her own interpretation of its cause. Scarcely aware of her presence, however, Tom was searching almost fiercely in his thoughts, searching for the clue. He knew there was a clue, he felt sure of it; the 'wavy feeling' had not come with this overwhelming suddenness without a reason. Something had brought it back. But what? Was there any recent factor in his life that might explain it? He stole a swift glance at the girl beside him: had she, perhaps, to do with it? They had played tennis together for the first time that afternoon: he had never seen her before, was not even quite sure of her name; to him, so far, she was only 'a very pretty girl who played a ripping game.' Had this girl to do with it?

Feeling his questioning look, she glanced up at him and smiled. 'You're very absent-minded,' she observed with mischief in her manner. 'You took so many of my balls, it's tired you out!' She had beautiful blue eyes, and her voice, he noticed for the first time, was very pleasant. Her figure was slim, her ankles neat, she had nice, even teeth. But, even as he registered the charming details, he knew quite well that he registered them, one and all, as belonging merely to a member of the sex, and not to this girl in particular. For all he cared, she might follow the two Chalk-Blues and disappear below the edge of the cliff into the sea. This 'pretty girl' left him as untroubled as she found him. The wavy feeling was not brought by her.

He drank his tea, keeping his back to the sea, and as the talk was lively, his silence was not noticed. The Wave, meanwhile, he knew, had come up closer. It towered above him. Its presence would shortly be ex- plained. Then, suddenly, in the middle of a discussion as to partners for the games to follow, a further detail presented itself—also apparently out of nothing. He smelt the Whiff. He knew then that the Wave was poised immediately above his head, and that he stood underneath its threatening great curve. The clue, therefore, was at hand.

And at this moment his father came into view, moving across the lawn towards them from the French window. No one guessed how Tom welcomed the slight diversion, for the movement was already in his legs and in another moment must have set his feet upon that dreadful shuf- fling. As from a distance, he heard the formal talk and introductions, his father's statement that he had won his round of golf with 'the Dean,' praise of the weather, and something or other about the strange stillness of the sea— but then, with a sudden, hollow crash against his very ear, the appalling words: '. . . broke his mashie into splinters, yes. And, by the by, the Dean knows the Aylmers. They were staying here earlier in the summer, he told me. Lettice, the girl,—Mary's friend, you remember—is going to be married this week....'

Tom clutched the back of the wicker-chair in front of him. The sun went out. An icy air passed Up his spine. The blood drained from his face. The tennis courts, and the group of white figures moving towards them, swung up into the sky. He gripped the chair till the rods of wicker pressed through the flesh into the bone. For a moment he felt that the sensation of actual sickness was more than he could master; his legs bent like paper beneath his weight.

'You remember Lettice, Tom, don't you?' his father was saying somewhere in mid-air above him.

'Yes, rather.' Apparently he said these words; the air at any rate went through his teeth and lips, and the same minute, with a superhuman effort that only just escaped a stagger, he moved away towards the tennis courts. His feet carried him, that is, across the lawn, where some figures dressed in white were calling his name loudly; his legs went automatically. 'Hold steady!' he remembers saying somewhere deep inside him. 'Don't make an ass of yourself,'; whereupon another voice—or was it still his own?— joined in quickly, 'She's gone from me, Lettice has gone. She's dead.' And the words, for the first time in his life, had meaning: for the first time in his life, rather, he realised what their meaning was. The Wave had fallen. Moreover—this also for the first time in the history of the Wave—there was something audible. He heard a Sound.

Shivering in the hot summer sunshine, as though icy water drenched him, he knew the same instant that he was wrong about the falling: the Wave, indeed, had curled lower over him than ever before, had even toppled—but it had not broken. As a whole, it had not broken. It was a smaller wave, upon the parent side, that had formed and fallen. The sound he heard was the soft crash of this lesser wave that grew out of the greater mass of the original monster, broke upon the rising volume of it, and returned into the greater body. It was a ripple only. The shock and terror he felt were a foretaste of what the final smothering crash would be. Yet the Sound he had heard was not the sound of water. There was a sharp, odd rattling in it that he had never consciously heard before. And it was—dry.

He reached the group of figures on the tennis-courts: he played: a violent energy had replaced the sudden physical weakness. His skill, it seemed, astonished everybody; he drove and smashed and volleyed with a recklessness that was always accurate: but when, at the end of the amazing game, he heard voices praising him, as from a distance, he knew only that there was a taste of gall and ashes in his mouth, and that he had but one desire—to get to his room alone and open the drawer. Even to himself he would not admit that he wished for the relief of tears. He put it, rather, that he must see and feel the one real thing that still connected him with Lettice—the thread of carpet she had trodden on. That—and the 'whiff'—alone could comfort him.

The comedy, that is, of all big events lay in it; no one must see, no one must know: no one must guess the existence of this sweet, rich pain that ravaged the heart in him until from very numbness it ceased aching. He double-locked the bedroom door. He had waited till darkness folded away the staring day, till the long dinner was over, and the drawn-out evening afterwards. None, fortunately, had noticed the change in his demeanour, his silence, his absentmindedness when spoken to, his want of appetite. 'She is going to be married… this week,' were the only words he heard; they kept ringing in his brain. To his immense relief the family had not referred to it again.

And at last he had said good-night and was in his room—alone. The drawer was open. The morsel of green thread lay in his hand. The faint eastern perfume floated on the air. 'I am not a sentimental ass,' he said to himself aloud, but in a low, steady tone. 'She touched it, therefore it has part of her life about it still.' Three years and a half ago! He examined the diary too; lived over in thought every detail of their so-slight acquaintance together; they were few enough; he remembered every one.... Prolonging the backward effort, he reviewed the history of the Wave. His mind stretched back to his earliest recollections of the nightmare. He faced the situation, tried to force its inner meaning from it, but without success.

He did not linger uselessly upon any detail, nor did he return upon his traces as a sentimental youth might do, prolonging the vanished sweetness of recollection in order to taste the pain more vividly. He merely 'read up,' so to speak, the history of the Wave to get a bird's-eye view of it. And in the end he obtained a certain satisfaction from the process—a certain strength. That is to say, he did not understand, but he accepted. 'Lettice has gone from me—but she hasn't gone for good.' The deep reflection of hours condensed itself into this.

Whatever might happen 'temporarily,' the girl was loyal and true: and she was—his. It never once occurred to him to blame or chide her. All that she did sincerely, she had a right to do. They were in the 'underneath' together for ever and ever. They were in the sea.

The pain, nevertheless, was acute and agonising; the temporary separation of 'France' was nothing compared to this temporary separation of her marrying. There were alternate intervals of numbness and of acute sensation; for each time thought and feeling collapsed from the long strain of their own tension, the relief that followed proved false and vain. Up sprang the aching pain again, the hungry longing, the dull, sweet yearning—and the whole sensation started afresh as at the first, yet with a vividness that increased with each new realisation of it. 'Wish I could cry it out,' he thought. 'I wouldn't be a bit ashamed to cry.' But he had no tears to spill....

Midnight passed towards the small hours of the morning, and the small hours slipped on towards the dawn before he put away the parcel of tissue-paper, closed the drawer and locked it. And when at length he dropped exhausted into bed, the eastern sky was already tinged with the crimson of another summer's day. He dreaded it, and closed his eyes. It had tennis parties and engagements in its wearisome, long hours of heat and utter emptiness....

Just before actual sleep took him, however, he was aware of one other singular reflection. It rose of its own accord out of that moment's calm when thought and feeling sank away and deliberate effort ceased: the fact namely that, with the arrival of the Sound, all his five senses had been now affected. His entire being, through the only channels of perception it possessed, had responded to the existence of the Wave and all it might portend. Here was no case of a single sense being tricked by some illusion: all five supported each other, taste being, of course, a modification of smell.

And the strange reflection brought to his aching mind and weary body a measure of relief. The Wave was real: being real, it was also well worth facing when it—fell.

CHAPTER VI

Between twenty and thirty a man rises through years reckless of power and spendthrift of easy promises. The wave of life is rising, and every force tends upwards in a steady rush. At thirty comes a pause upon the level, but with thirty-five there are signs of the droop downhill. Age is first realised when, instead of looking forward only, he surprises thought in the act of looking—behind.

Of the physical, at any rate, this is true; for the mental and emotional wave is still ripening towards its higher curve, while the spiritual crest hangs hiding in the sky far overhead, beckoning beyond towards unvistaed reaches.

Tom Kelverdon climbed through these crowded years with the usual scars and bruises, but steadily, and without the shame of any considerable disaster. His father's influence having procured him an opening in an engineering firm of the first importance, his own talent and application maintained the original momentum bravely. He justified his choice of a profession. Also, staring eagerly into life's marvellous shop-window, he entered, hand in pocket, and made the customary purchases of the enchantress behind the counter. If worthless, well,—everybody bought them; the things had been consummately advertised; he paid his money, found out their value, threw them away or kept them accordingly. A certain good taste made his choice not too foolish: and there was this wholesome soundness in him, that he rarely repeated a purchase that had furnished him cheap goods. Slowly he began to find himself.

From learning what it meant to be well thrashed by a boy he loathed, and to apply a similar treatment himself—he passed on to the pleasure of being told he had nice eyes, that his voice was pleasant, his presence interesting. He fell in love—and out again. But he went straight. Moreover, beyond a given point in any affair of the heart he seemed unable to advance: some secret, inner tension held him back. While believing he loved various adorable girls the years offered him, he found it impossible to open his lips and tell them so. And the mysterious instinct invariably justified itself: they faded, one and all, soon after separation. There was no wave in them; they were ripples only....

And, meanwhile, as the years rushed up towards the crest of thirty, he did well in his profession, worked for the firm in many lands, obtained the confidence of his principals, and proved his steady judgment if not his brilliance. He became, too, a good, if generous, judge of other men, seeing all sorts, both good and bad, and in every kind of situation that proves character. His nature found excuses too easily, perhaps, for the unworthy ones. It is not a bad plan, wiser companions hinted, to realise that a man has dark behaviour in him, while yet believing that he need not necessarily prove it. The other view has something childlike in it; Tom Kelverdon kept, possibly, this simpler attitude alive in him, trusting overmuch, because suspicion was abhorrent to his soul. The man of ideals had never become the man of the world. Some high, gentle instinct had preserved him from the infliction that so often results in this regrettable conversion. Slow to dislike, he saw the best in everybody. 'Not a bad fellow,' he would say of some one quite obviously detestable. 'I admit his face and voice and manner are against him; but that's not his fault exactly. He didn't make himself, you know.'

* * * *

The idea of a tide in the affairs of men is obvious, familiar enough. Nations rise and fall, equally with the fortunes of a family. History repeats itself, so does the tree, the rose: and if a man live long enough he recovers the state of early childhood. There is repetition everywhere. But while some think evolution moves in a straight line forward, others speculate fancifully that it has a spiral twist upwards. At any given moment, that is, the soul looks down upon a passage made before—but from a point a little higher. Without living through events already experienced, it literally lives them over; it sees them mapped out below, and with the bird's-eye view it understands them.

And in regard to his memory of Lettice Aylmer—the fact that he was still waiting for her and she for him—this was somewhat the fanciful conception that lodged itself, subconsciously perhaps, in the mind of Tom Kelverdon, grown now to man's estate. He was dimly aware of a curious familiarity with his present situation, a sense of repetition—yet with a difference. Something he had experienced before was coming to him again. It was waiting for him. Its wave was rising. When it happened before it had not happened properly somehow—had left a sense of defeat, of dissatisfaction behind. He had taken it, perhaps, at the period of receding momentum, and so had failed towards it. This time he meant to face it. His own phrase, as has been seen, was simple: 'I'll let it all come.' It was something his character needed. Deep down within him hid this attitude, and with the passage of the years it remained—though remained an attitude merely.

But the attitude, being subconscious in him, developed into a definite point of view that came, more and more, to influence the way he felt towards life in general. Life was too active to allow of much introspection, yet whenever pauses came—pauses in thought and feeling, still backwaters in which he lay without positive direction—there, banked up, unchanging in the background, stood the enduring thing: his love for

Lettice Aylmer. And this background was 'the sea' of his boyhood days, the 'underneath' in which they remained unalterably together. There, too, hid the four signs that haunted his impressionable youth: the Wave, the other Eyes, the Whiff, the Sound. In due course, and at their appointed time, they would combine and 'happen' in his outward life. The Wave would—fall.

Meanwhile his sense of humour had long ago persuaded him that, so far as any claim upon the girl existed, or that she reciprocated his own deep passion, his love-dream was of questionable security. The man in him that built bridges and cut tunnels laughed at it; the man that devised these first in imagination, however, believed in it, and waited. Behind thought and reason, suspected of none with whom he daily came in contact, and surprised only by himself when he floated in these silent, tideless backwaters—it persisted with an amazing conviction that seemed deathless. In these calm deeps of his being, securely anchored, hid what he called the 'spiral' attitude. The thing that was coming, a tragedy whereof that childish nightmare was both a memory and a premonition, clung and haunted still with its sense of dim familiarity. Something he had known before would eventually repeat itself. But—with a difference; that he would see it from above—from a higher curve of the ascending spiral.

There lay the enticing wonder of the situation. With his present English temperament, stolid rather, he would meet it differently, treat it otherwise, learn and understand. He would see it from another—higher—point of view. He would know great pain, yet some part of him would look on, compare, accept the pain—and smile. The words that offered themselves were that he had 'suffered blindly,' but suffered with fierce and bitter resentment, savagely, even with murder in his heart; suffered, moreover, somehow or other, at the hands of Lettice Aylmer.

Lettice, of course,—he clung to it absurdly still—was true and loyal to him, though married to another. Her name was changed. But Lettice Aylmer was not changed. And this mad assurance, though he kept it deliberately from his conscious thoughts, persisted with the rest of the curious business, for nothing, apparently, could destroy it in him. It was part of the situation, as he called it, part of the 'sea,' out of which would rise eventually—the Wave.

Outwardly, meanwhile, much had happened to him, each experience contributing its modifying touch to the character as he realised it, instead of merely knowing that it came to others. His sister married; Tim, following his father's trade, became a doctor with a provincial practice, buried in the country. His father died suddenly while he was away in Canada, busy with a prairie railway across the wheat fields of Assiniboia.

He met the usual disillusions in a series, savoured and mastered them more or less in turn.

He was in England when his mother died; and, while his other experiences were ripples only, her going had the wave in it. The enormous mother-tie came also out of the 'sea'; its dislocation was a shock of fundamental kind, and he felt it in the foundations of his life. It was one of the things he could not quite realise. He still felt her always close and near. He had just been made a junior partner in the firm; the love and pride in her eyes, before they faded from the world of partnerships, were unmistakable: 'Of course,' she murmured, her thin hand clinging to his own, 'they had to do it... if only your father knew...' and she was gone. The wave of her life sank back into the sea whence it arose. And her going somehow strengthened him, added to his own foundations, as though her wave had merged in his.

With her departure, he felt vaguely the desire to settle down, to marry. Unconsciously he caught himself thinking of women in a new light, appraising them as possible wives. It was a dangerous attitude rather; for a man then seeks to persuade himself that such and such a woman may do, instead of awaiting the inevitable draw of love which alone can justify a life-long union.

In Tom's case, however, as with the smaller fires of his younger days, he never came to a decision, much less to a positive confession. His immense idealism concerning women preserved him from being caught by mere outward beauty. While aware that Lettice was an impossible dream of boyhood, he yet clung to an ideal she somehow foreshadowed and typified. He never relinquished this standard of his dream; a mysterious woman waited for him somewhere, a woman with all the fairy qualities he had built about her personality; a woman he could not possibly mistake when at last he met her. Only he did not meet her. He waited.

And so it was, as time passed onwards, that he found himself standing upon the little level platform of his life at a stage nearer to thirty-five than thirty, conscious that a pause surrounded him. There was a lull. The rush of the years slowed down. He looked about him. He looked—back.

CHAPTER VII

The particular moment when this happened, suitable, too, in a chance, odd way, was upon a mountain ridge in winter, a level platform of icy snow to which he had climbed with some hotel acquaintances on a skiing expedition. It was on the Polish side of the Hohe Tatra.

Why, at this special moment, pausing for breath and admiring the immense wintry scene about him, he should have realised that he reached a similar position in his life, is hard to say. There is always a particular moment when big changes claim attention. They have been coming slowly; but at a given moment they announce themselves. Tom associated that icy ridge above Zakopané with a pause in the rushing of the years: 'I'm getting on towards middle age; the first swift climb—impetuous youth—lies now behind me.' The physical parallel doubtless suggested it; he had felt his legs and wind a trifle less willing, perhaps; there was still a steep, laborious slope of snow beyond; he discovered that he was no longer twenty-five.

He drew breath and watched the rest of the party as they slowly came nearer in the track he had made through the deep snow below. Each man made this track in his turn, it was hard work, his share was done. 'Nagorsky will tackle the next bit,' he thought with relief, watching a young Pole of twenty-three in the ascending line, and glancing at the summit beyond where the run home was to begin. And then the wonder of the white silent scene invaded him, the exhilarating thrill of the vast wintry heights swept over him, he forgot the toil, he regained his wind and felt his muscles taut and vigorous once more. It was pleasant, standing upon this level ridge, to inspect the long ascent below, and to know the heavy yet enjoyable exertion was nearly over.

But he had felt—older. That ridge remained in his memory as the occasion of its first realisation; a door opened behind him; he looked back. He envied the other's twenty-three years. It is curious that, about thirty, a man feels he is getting old, whereas at forty he feels himself young again. At thirty he judges by the standard of eighteen, at the later age by that of sixty. But this particular occasion remained vivid for another reason—it was accompanied by a strange sensation he had almost forgotten; and so long an interval had elapsed since its last manifestation that for a moment a kind of confusion dropped upon him, as from the cloudless sky. Something was gathering behind him, something was about to fall. He recognised the familiar feeling that he knew of old, the subterranean thrill, the rich, sweet pain, the power, the reality. It was the wavy feeling.

Balanced on his ski, the sealskin strips gripping the icy ridge securely, he turned instinctively to seek the reason, if any were visible, of the abrupt revival. His mind, helped by the stimulating air and sunshine, worked swiftly. The odd confusion clouded his faculties still, as in a dream state, but he pierced it in several directions simultaneously.

Was it that, envying another's youth, he had re-entered imaginatively his own youthful feelings? He looked down at the rest of the party climbing towards him. And doing so, he picked out the slim figure of Nagorsky's sister, a girl whose winter costume became her marvellously, and whom the happy intimacy of the hotel life had made so desirable that an expedition without her seemed a lost, blank day. Unless she was of the party there was no sunshine. He watched her now, looking adorable in her big gauntlet gloves, her short skirt, her tasselled cap of black and gold, a fairy figure on the big snowfield, filling the world with sunshine—and knew abruptly that she meant to him just exactly—nothing. The intensity of the wavy feeling reduced her to an unreality.

It was not she who brought the great emotion.

The confusion in him deepened. Another scale of measurement appeared. The crowded intervening years now seemed but a pause, a brief delay; he had run down a side track and returned. He had not grown older. Seen by the grand scale to which the Wave and 'sea' belonged, he had scarcely moved from the old starting-point, where, far away in some unassailable recess of life, still waiting for him, stood—Lettice Aylmer.

Turning his eyes, then, from the approaching climbers, he glanced at the steep slope above him, and saw—as once before on the English coast— something that took his breath away and made his muscles weak. He stared up at it. It looked down at him.

Five hundred feet above, outlined against the sky of crystal clearness, ran a colossal wave of solid snow. At the highest point it was, of course, a cornice, but towards the east, whence came the prevailing weather, the wind had so manipulated the mass that it formed a curling billow, twenty or thirty feet in depth, leaping over in the very act of breaking, yet arrested just before it fell. It hung waiting in mid-air, perfectly moulded, a wave—but a wave of snow.

It swung along the ridge for half a mile and more: it seemed to fill the sky; it rose out of the sea of eternal snow below it, poised between the earth and heavens. In the hollow beneath its curve lay purple shadows the eye could not pierce. And the similarity to the earlier episode struck him vividly; in each case Nature assisted with a visible wave as by way of counterpart; each time, too, there was a girl—as though some significance of sex hid in the 'wavy feeling.' He was profoundly puzzled.

The same second, in this wintry world where movement, sound, and perfume have no place, there stole to his nostrils across the desolate ranges another detail. It was more intimate in its appeal even than the wavy feeling, yet was part of it. He recognised the Whiff. And the joint attack, both by its suddenness and by its intensity, overwhelmed him. Only the Sound was lacking, but that, too, he felt, was on the way. Already a sharp instinctive movement was running down his legs. He began to shuffle on his ski....

A chorus of voices, as from far away, broke round him, disturbing the intense stillness; and he knew that the others had reached the ridge. With a violent effort he mastered the ridiculous movement of his disobedient legs, but what really saved him from embarrassing notice was the breathless state of his companions, and the fact that his action looked after all quite natural—he seemed merely rubbing his ski along the snow to clean their under-surface.

Exclamations in French, English, Polish rose on all sides, as the view into the deep opposing valley caught the eye, and a shower of questions all delivered at once, drew attention from himself. What scenery, what a sky, what masses of untrodden snow! Should they lunch on the ridge or continue to the summit? What were the names of all these peaks, and was the Danube visible? How lucky there was no wind, and how they pitied the people who stayed behind in the hotels! Sweaters and woollen waistcoats emerged from half a dozen knapsacks, cooking apparatus was produced, one chose a spot to make a fire, while another broke the dead branches from a stunted pine, and in five minutes had made a blaze behind a little wall of piled-up snow. The Polish girl came up and asked Tom for his Zeiss glasses, examined the soaring slope beyond, then obediently put on the extra sweater he held out for her. He hardly saw her face, and certainly did not notice the expression in her eyes. All took off their ski and plunged them upright in the nearest drift. The sun blazed everywhere, the snow crystals sparkled. They settled down for lunch, a small dark clot of busy life upon the vast expanse of desolate snow... and anything unusual about Tom Kelverdon, muffled to the throat against the freezing cold, his eyes, moreover, concealed by green snow-spectacles, was certainly not noticed.

Another party, besides, was discovered climbing upwards along their own laborious track: in the absorbing business of satisfying big appetites, tending the fire, and speculating who these other skiers might be, Tom's silence caused no comment. His self-control, for the rest, was soon recovered. But his interest in the expedition had oddly waned; he was still searching furiously in his thoughts for an explanation of the unexpected 'attack,' waiting for the Sound, but chiefly wondering why his boyhood's nightmare had never revealed that the Wave was of snow instead of water—and, at the same time, oddly convinced that he had moved but one stage nearer to its final elucidation. That it was solid he had already discovered, but that it was actually of snow left a curious doubt in him.

Of all this he was thinking as he devoured his eggs and sandwiches, something still trembling in him, nerves keenly sensitive, but not quite persuaded that this wave of snow was the sufficient cause of what he had just experienced—when at length the other climbers, moving swiftly, came close enough to be inspected. The customary remarks and criticisms passed from mouth to mouth, with warnings to lower voices since sound carried too easily in the rarefied air. One of the party was soon recognised as the hotel doctor, and the other, first set down as a Norwegian owing to his light hair, shining hatless in the sunlight, proved on closer approach to be an Englishman—both men evidently experienced and accomplished 'runners.'

In any other place the two parties would hardly have spoken, settling down into opposing camps of hostile silence; but in the lonely winter mountains human relationship becomes more natural; the time of day was quickly passed, and details of the route exchanged; the doctor and his friend mingled easily with the first arrivals; all agreed spontaneously to take the run home together; and finally, when names were produced with laughing introductions, the Englishman—by one of those coincidences people pretend to think strange, but that actually ought to occur more often than they do—turned out to be known to Tom, and after considerable explanations was proved to be more than that—a cousin.

Welcoming the diversion, making the most of it in fact, Kelverdon presented Anthony Winslowe to his Polish companions with a certain zeal to which the new arrival responded with equal pleasure. The light-haired blue-eyed Englishman, young and skilful on his ski, formed a distinct addition to the party. He was tall, with a slight stoop about the shoulders that suggested study; he was gay and very easy-going too. It was 'Tom' and 'Tony' before lunch was over; they recalled their private school, a fight, an eternal friendship vowed after it, and the twenty intervening years melted as though they had not been.

'Of course,' Tom said, proud of his new-found cousin, 'and I've read your bird books, what's more. By Jove, you're quite an authority on natural history, aren't you?'

The other modestly denied any notoriety, but the girls, especially Nagorsky's sister, piqued by Tom's want of notice, pressed for details in their pretty broken English. It became a merry and familiar party, as the way is with easy foreigners, particularly when they meet in such wild and unconventional surroundings. Winslowe had lantern slides in his trunk: that night he promised to show them: they chattered and paid compliments and laughed, Tony explaining that he was on his way to

Egypt to study the bird-life along the Nile. Natural history was his passion; he talked delightfully; he made the bird and animal life seem real and interesting; there was imagination, humour, lightness in him. There was a fascination, too, not due to looks alone. It was in his atmosphere, what is currently, perhaps, called magnetism.

'No animals here for you,' said a girl, pointing to the world of white death about them.

'There's something better,' he said quickly in quite decent Polish. 'We're all in the animal kingdom, you know.' And he glanced with a bow of admiration at the speaker, whom the others instantly began to tease. It was Irena, Nagorsky's sister; she flushed and laughed. 'We thought,' she said, 'you were Norwegian, because of your light hair, and the way you moved on your ski.'

'A great compliment,' he rejoined, 'but I saw you long ago on the ridge, and I knew at once that you were—Polish.'

The girl returned his bow. 'The largest compliment,' she answered gaily, 'I had ever in my life.'

Tom had only arrived two days before, bringing a letter of introduction to the doctor, and that night he changed his hotel, joining his new friends and his cousin at the Grand. An obvious flirtation, possibly something more, sprung up spontaneously between him and the Polish girl, but Kelverdon welcomed it and felt no jealousy. 'Not trespassing, old chap, am I?' Tony asked jokingly, having divined on the mountains that the girl was piqued. 'On the contrary,' was the honest assurance given frankly, 'I'm relieved. A delightful girl, though, isn't she? And fascinatingly pretty!'

For the existence of Nagorsky's sister had become suddenly to him of no importance whatsoever. It was strange enough, but the vivid recurrence of long-forgotten symbols that afternoon upon the heights had restored to him something he had curiously forgotten, something he had shamefully neglected, almost, it seemed, had been in danger of losing altogether. It came back upon him now. He clung desperately to it as to a real, a vital, a necessary thing. It was a genuine relief that the relationship between him and the girl might be ended thus. In any case, he reflected, it would have 'ended thus' a little later—like all the others. No trace or sign of envy stayed in him. Irena and Tony, anyhow, seemed admirably suited to one another; he noticed on the long run home how naturally they came together. And even his own indifference would not bring her back to him. He felt quite pleased and satisfied. He had a long talk with Tony before going to bed. He felt drawn to him. There was a spontaneous innate sympathy between them.

They had many other talks together, and Tom liked his interesting, brilliant cousin. A week passed; dances, ski-ing trips, skating, and the usual programme of wintry enjoyments filled the time too quickly; companionship became intimacy; all sat at the same table: Tony became a general favourite. He had just that combination of reserve and abandon which—provided something genuine lies behind—attracts the majority of people who, being dull, have neither. Most are reserved, through emptiness, or else abandoned—also through emptiness. Tony Winslowe, full of experience and ideas, vivid experience and original ideas, combined the two in rarest equipoise. It was spontaneous, and not calculated in him. There was a stimulating quality in his personality. Like those tiny, exciting Japanese tales that lead to the edge of a precipice, then end with unexpected abruptness that is their purpose, he led all who liked him to the brink of a delightful revelation—then paused, stopped, vanished. And all did like him. He was light and gay, for all the depth in him. Something of the child peeped out. He won Tom Kelverdon's confidence without an effort. He also won the affectionate confidence of the Polish girl.

'You're not married, Tony, are you?' Tom asked him.

'Married!' Tony answered with a flush—he flushed so easily when teased— 'I love my wild life and animals far too much.' He stammered slightly. Then he looked up quickly into his cousin's eyes with frankness. Tom, without knowing why, almost felt ashamed of having asked it. 'I—I never can go beyond a certain point,' he said, 'with girls. Something always holds me back. Odd—isn't it?' He hesitated. Then this flashed from him: 'Bees never sip the last, the sweetest drop of honey from the rose, you know. The sunset always leaves one golden cloud adrift—eh?' So there was poetry in him too!

And Tom, simpler, as well as more rigidly moulded, felt a curious touch of passionate sympathy as he heard it. His heart went out to the other suddenly with a burst of confidence. Some barrier melted in him and disappeared. For the first time in his life he knew the inclination, even the desire, to speak of things hidden deep within his heart. His cousin would understand.

And Tony's sudden, wistful silence invited the confession. They had already been talking of their forgotten youthful days together. The ground was well prepared. They had even talked of his sister, Mary, and her marriage. Tony remembered her distinctly. He spoke of it, leaning forward and putting a hand on his cousin's knee. Tom noticed vaguely the size of the palm, the wrist, the fingers—they seemed disproportionate. They were ugly hands. But it was subconscious notice. His mind was on another thing.

'I say,' Tom began with a sudden plunge, 'you know a lot about birds and natural history—biology too, I suppose. Have you ever heard of the spiral movement?'

'Spinal, did you say?' queried the other, turning the stem of his glass and looking up.

'No—spiral,' Tom repeated, laughing dryly in spite of himself. 'I mean the idea—that evolution, whether individually in men and animals, or with nations—historically, that is—is not in a straight line ahead, but moves upwards—in a spiral?'

'It's in the air,' replied Tony vaguely, yet somehow as if he knew a great deal more about it. 'The movement of the race, you mean?'

'And of the individual too. We're here, I mean, for the purpose of development—whatever one's particular belief may be—and that this development, instead of going forwards in a straight line, has a kind of— spiral movement—upwards?'

Tony looked wonderfully wise. 'I've heard of it,' he said. 'The spiral movement, as you say, is full of suggestion. It's common among plants. But I don't think science—biology, at any rate—takes much account of it.'

Tom interrupted eagerly, and with a certain grave enthusiasm that evidently intrigued his companion. 'I mean—a movement that is always upwards, always getting higher, and always looking down upon what has gone before. That, if it's true, a soul can look back—look down upon what it has been through before, but from a higher point—do you see?'

Tony emptied his glass and then lit a cigarette. 'I see right enough,' he said at length, quick and facile to appropriate any and every idea he came across, yet obviously astonished by his companion's sudden seriousness. 'Only the other day I read that humanity, for instance, is just now above the superstitious period—of the Middle Ages, say—going over it again— but that the recrudescence everywhere of psychic interests— fortune-telling, palmistry, magic, and the rest—has become quasi-scientific. It's going through the same period, but seeks to explain and understand. It's above it—one stage or so. Is that what you mean, perhaps?'

Tom drew in his horns, though for the life of him he could not say why. Tony appropriated his own idea too easily somehow—had almost read his thoughts. Vaguely he resented it. Tony had stolen from him—offended against some schoolboy meum and tuum standard.

'That's it—the idea, at any rate,' he said, wondering why confidence had frozen in him. 'Interesting, rather, isn't it?'

And then abruptly he found that he was staring at his cousin's hands, spread on the table palm downwards. He had been staring at them for some time, but unconsciously. Now he saw them. And there was something about them that he did not like. Absurd as it seemed, his change of mood had to do with those big, ungainly hands, tanned a deep brown-black by the sun. A faint shiver ran through him. He looked away.

'Extraordinary,' Tony went chattering on. 'It explains these new wild dances perhaps. Anything more spiral and twisty than these modern gyrations I never saw!' He turned it off in his light amusing way, yet as though quite familiar with the deeper aspects of the question—if he cared. 'And what the body does,' he added, 'the mind has already done a little time before!'

He laughed, but whether he was in earnest, or merely playing with the idea, was uncertain. What had stopped Tom was, perhaps, that they were not in the same key together; Tom had used a word he rarely cared to use— soul—it had cost him a certain effort—but his cousin had not responded. That, and the hands, explained his change of mood. For the first time it occurred to his honest, simple mind that Tony was of other stuff, perhaps, than he had thought. That remark about the bees and sunset jarred a little. The lightness suggested insincerity almost.

He shook the notion off, for it was disagreeable, ungenerous as well. This was holiday-time, and serious discussion was out of place. The airy lightness in his cousin was just suited to the conditions of a winter-sport hotel; it was what made him so attractive to all and sundry, so easy to get on with. Yet Tom would have liked to confide in him, to have told him more, asked further questions and heard the answers; stranger still, he would have liked to lead from the spiral to the wave, to his own wavy feeling, and, further even—almost to speak of Lettice and his boyhood nightmare. He had never met a man in regard to whom he felt so forthcoming in this way. Tony surely had seriousness and depth in him; this irresponsibility was on the surface only.... There was a queer confusion in his mind—several incongruous things trying to combine....

'I knew a princess once—the widow of a Russian,' Tony was saying. He had been talking on, gaily, lightly, for some time, but Tom, busy with these reflections, had not listened properly. He now looked up sharply, something suddenly alert in him. 'They're all princes in Russia,' Tony laughed; 'it means less than Count in France or von in Germany.' He stopped and drained his glass. 'But you know,' he went on, his thoughts half elsewhere, it seemed, 'it's bad for a country when titles are too common, it lowers the aristocratic ideal. In the Caucasus— Batoum, for instance—every Georgian is a noble, your hotel porter a prince.' He broke off abruptly as though reminded of something. 'Of course!' he exclaimed, 'I was going to tell you about the Russian woman I knew who had something of that idea of yours.' He stopped as his eye caught his cousin's empty glass. 'Let's have another,' he said, beckoning to the waitress, 'it's very light stuff, this beer. These long ski-trips give one an endless thirst, don't they?' Tom didn't know whether he said yes or no. 'What idea?' he asked quickly. 'What do you mean exactly?' A curious feeling of familiarity stirred in him. This conversation had happened before.

'Eh?' Tony glanced up as though he had again forgotten what he was going to say. 'Oh yes,' he went on, 'the Russian woman, the Princess I met in Egypt. She talked a bit like that once... I remember now.'

'Like what?' Tom felt a sudden, breathless curiosity in him: he was afraid the other would change his mind, or pass to something else, or forget what he was going to say. It would prove another Japanese tale— disappear before it satisfied.

But Tony went on at last, noticing, perhaps, his cousin's interest.

'I was up at Edfu after birds,' he said, 'and she had a dahabieh on the river. Some friends took me there to tea, or something. It was nothing particular. Only it occurred to me just now when you talked of spirals and things.'

'You talked about the spiral?' Tom asked. 'Talked with her about it, I mean?' He was slow, almost stupid compared to the other, who seemed to flash lightly and quickly over a dozen ideas at once. But there was this real, natural sympathy between them both again. It seemed he knew exactly what his cousin was going to say.

Tony, blowing the foam off his beer glass, proceeded to quench his wholesome thirst. 'Not exactly,' he said at length, 'but we talked, I remember, along that line. I was explaining about the flight of birds— that all wild animal life moves in a spontaneous sort of natural rhythm— with an unconscious grace, I mean, we've lost because we think too much. Birds in particular rise and fall with a swoop, the simplest, freest movement in the world—like a wave——'

'Yes?' interrupted Tom, leaning over the table a little and nearly upsetting his untouched glass. 'I like that idea. It's true.'

'And—oh, that all the forces known to science move in a similar way—by wave-form, don't you see? Something like that it was.' He took another draught of the nectar his day's exertions had certainly earned.

'She said that?' asked Tom, watching his cousin's face buried in the enormous mug.

Tony set it down with a sigh of intense satisfaction, 'I said it,' he exclaimed with a frank egoism. 'You're too tired after all your falls this afternoon to listen properly. I was the teacher on that occasion, she the adoring listener! But if you want to know what she said too, I'll tell you.'

Tom waited; he raised his glass, pretending to drink; if he showed too much interest, the other might swerve off again to something else. He knew what was coming, yet could not have actually foretold it. He recognised it only the instant afterwards.

'She talked about water,' Tony went on, as though he had difficulty in recalling what she really had said, 'and I think she had water on the brain,' he added lightly. 'The Nile had bewitched her probably; it affects most of 'em out there—the women, that is. She said life moved in a stream— that she moved down a stream, or something, and that only things going down the stream with her were real. Anything on the banks— stationary, that is—was not real. Oh, she said a lot. I've really forgotten now—it was a year or two ago—but I remember her mentioning shells and the spiral twist of shells. In fact,' he added, as if there was no more to tell, 'I suppose that's what made me think of her just now—your mentioning the spiral movement.'

The door of the room, half café and half bar, where the peasants sat at wooden tables about them, opened, and the pretty head of Irena Nagorsky appeared. A burst of music came in with her. 'We dance,' she said, a note of reproach as well as invitation in her voice—then vanished. Tony, leaving his beer unfinished, laughed at his cousin and went after her. 'My last night,' he said cheerily. 'Must be gay and jolly. I'm off to Trieste tomorrow for Alexandria. See you later, Tom—unless you're coming to dance too.'

But, though they saw each other many a time again that evening, there was no further conversation. Next day the party broke up, Tom returning to the Water Works his firm was constructing outside Warsaw, and Tony taking the train for Budapesth en route for Trieste and Egypt. He urged Tom to follow him as soon as his work was finished, gave the Turf Club, Cairo, as his permanent address where letters would always reach him sooner or later, waved his hat to the assembled group upon the platform, and was gone. The last detail of him visible was the hand that held the waving hat. It looked bigger, darker, thought Tom, than ever. It was almost disfiguring. It stirred a hint of dislike in him. He turned his eyes away.

But Tom Kelverdon remembered that last night in the hotel for another reason too. In the small hours of the morning he woke up, hearing a sound close beside him in the room. He listened a moment, then turned on the light above the bed. The sound, of an unusual and peculiar character, continued faintly. But it was not actually in the room as he first supposed. It was outside.

More than ten years had passed since he had heard that sound. He had expected it that day on the mountains when the wavy feeling and the

Whiff had come to him. Sooner or later he felt positive he would hear it. He heard it now. It had merely been delayed, postponed. Something gathering slowly and steadily behind his life was drawing nearer—had come already very close. He heard the dry, rattling Sound that was associated with the Wave and with the Whiff. In it, too, was a vague familiarity.

And then he realised that the wind was rising. A frozen pine-branch, stiff with little icicles, was rattling and scraping faintly outside the wooden framework of the double windows. It was the icy branch that made the dry, rattling sound. He listened intently; the sound was repeated at certain intervals, then ceased as the wind died down. And he turned over and fell asleep again, aware that what he had heard was an imitation only, but an imitation strangely accurate—of a reality. Similarly, the wave of snow was but an imitation of a reality to come. This reality lay waiting still beyond him. One day—one day soon—he would know it face to face. The Wave, he felt, was rising behind his life, and his life was rising with it towards a climax. On the little level platform where the years had landed him for a temporary pause, he began to shuffle with his feet in dream. And something deeper than his mind—looked back....

The instinct, or by whatever name he called that positive, interior affirmation, proved curiously right. Life rose with the sweep and power of a wave, bearing him with it towards various climaxes. His powers, such as they were, seemed all in the ascendant. He passed from that level platform as with an upward rush, all his enterprises, all his energies, all that he wanted and tried to do, surging forward towards the crest of successful accomplishment.

And a dozen times at least he caught himself asking mentally for his cousin Tony; wishing he had confided in him more, revealed more of this curious business to him, exchanged sympathies with him about it all. A kind of yearning rose in him for his vanished friend. Almost he had missed an opportunity. Tony would have understood and helped to clear things up; to no other man of his acquaintance could he have felt similarly. But Tony was now out of reach in Egypt, chasing his birds among the temples of the haunted Nile, already, doubtless, the centre of a circle of new friends and acquaintances who found him as attractive and fascinating as the little Zakopané group had found him. Tony must keep.

Tom Kelverdon meanwhile, his brief holiday over, returned to his work at Warsaw, and brought it to a successful conclusion with a rapidity no one had foreseen, and he himself had least of all expected. The power of the rising wave was in all he did. He could not fail. Out of the success grew other contracts highly profitable to his firm. Some energy that overcame all obstacles, some clarity of judgment that selected unerringly the best ways and means, some skill and wisdom in him that made all his powers work in unison till they became irresistible, declared themselves, yet naturally and without adventitious aid. He seemed to have found himself anew. He felt pleased and satisfied with himself: always self-confident, as a man of ability ought to be, he now felt proud; and, though conceit had never been his failing, this new-born assurance moved distinctly towards pride. In a moment of impulsive pleasure he wrote to Tony, at the Turf Club, Cairo, and told him of his success.... The senior partner, his father's old friend, wrote and asked his advice upon certain new proposals the firm had in view; it was a question of big docks to be constructed at Salonica, and something to do with a barrage on the Nile as well—there were several juicy contracts to choose between, it seemed,—and Sir William proposed a meeting in Switzerland, on his way out to the Near East; he would break the journey before crossing the Simplon for Milan and Trieste. The final telegram said Montreux, and Kelverdon hurried to Vienna and caught the night express to Lausanne by way of Bâle.

And at Montreux further evidence that the wave of life was rising then declared itself, when Sir William, having discussed the various propositions with him, listening with attention, even with deference, to Kelverdon's opinion, told him quietly that his brother's retirement left a vacancy in the firm which—he and his co-directors hoped confidently— Kelverdon might fill with benefit to all concerned. A senior partnership was offered to him before he was thirty-five! Sir William left the same night for his steamer, and Tom was to wait at Montreux, perhaps a month, perhaps six weeks, until a personal inspection of the several sites enabled the final decision to be made; he was then to follow and take charge of the work itself.

Tom was immensely pleased. He wrote to his married sister in her Surrey vicarage, told her the news with a modesty he did not really feel, and sent her a handsome cheque by way of atonement for his bursting pride.

For simple natures, devoid of a saving introspection and self-criticism, upon becoming unexpectedly successful easily develop an honest yet none the less corroding pride. Tom felt himself rather a desirable person suddenly; by no means negligible at any rate; pleased and satisfied with himself, if not yet overweeningly so. His native confidence took this exaggerated turn and twist. His star was in the ascendant, a man to be counted with....

The hidden weakness rose—as all else in him was rising—with the Wave. But he did not call it pride, because he did not recognise it. It was akin, perhaps, to that fatuous complacency of the bigoted religionist who, thinking he has discovered absolute truth, looks down from his narrow cell upon the rest of the world with a contemptuous pity that in itself is but the ignorance of crass self-delusion. Tom felt very sure of himself. For a rising wave drags up with it the mud and rubbish that have hitherto lain hidden out of sight in the ground below. Only with the fall do these undesirable elements return to their proper place again—where they belong and are of value. Sense of proportion is recovered only with perspective, and Tom Kelverdon, rising too rapidly, began to see himself in disproportionate relation to the rest of life. In his solid, perhaps stolid, way he considered himself a Personality—indispensable to no small portion of the world about him.

CHAPTER VIII

It was towards the end of March, and spring was flowing down almost visibly from the heights behind the town. April stood on tiptoe in the woods, finger on lip, ready to dance out between the sunshine and the rain.

Above four thousand feet the snows of winter still clung thickly, but the lower slopes were clear, men and women already working busily among the dull brown vineyards. The early mist cleared off by ten o'clock, letting through floods of sunshine that drenched the world, sparkled above the streets crowded with foreigners from many lands, and lay basking with an appearance of July upon the still, blue lake. The clear brilliance of the light had a quality of crystal. Sea-gulls fluttered along the shores, tame as ducks and eager to be fed. They lent to this inland lake an atmosphere of the sea, and Kelverdon found himself thinking of some southern port, Marseilles, Trieste, Toulon.

In the morning he watched the graceful fishing-boats set forth, and at night, when only the glitter of the lamps painted the gleaming water for a little distance, he saw the swans, their heads tucked back impossibly into the centre of their backs, scarcely moving on the unruffled surface as they slept into the night. The first sounds he heard soon after dawn through his wide-opened windows were the whanging strokes of their powerful wings flying low across the misty water; they flew in twos and threes, coming from their nests now building in the marshes beyond Villeneuve. This, and the screaming of the gulls, usually woke him. The summits of Savoy, on the southern shore, wore pink and gold upon their heavy snows; the sharp air nipped; far in the west a few stars peeped before they faded; and in the distance he heard the faint, drum-like mutter of a paddle-steamer, reminding him that he was in a tourist centre after all, and that this was busy, little, organised Switzerland.

But sometimes it was the beating strokes of the invisible paddle-steamer that woke him, for it seemed somehow a continuation of dreams he could never properly remember. That he had been dreaming busily every night of late he knew as surely as that he instantly forgot these dreams. That muffled, drum-like thud, coming nearer and nearer towards him out of the quiet distance, had some connection—undecipherable as yet—with the curious, dry, rattling sound belonging to the Wave. The two were so dissimilar, however, that he was unable to discover any theory that could harmonise them. Nor, for that matter, did he seek it. He merely registered a mental note, as it were, in passing. The beating and the rattling were associated.

He chose a small and quiet hotel, as his liking was, and made himself comfortable, for he might have six weeks to wait for Sir William's
telegram, or even longer, if, as seemed likely, the summons came by
post. And Montreux was a pleasant place in early spring, before the heat
and glare of summer scorched the people out of it towards the heights.
He took long walks towards the snow-line beyond Les Avants and Les
Pléiades, where presently the carpets of narcissus would smother the
fields with white as though winter had returned to fling, instead of crystal
flakes, a hundred showers of white feathers upon the ground. He discovered paths that led into the whispering woods of pine and chestnut. The
young larches wore feathery green upon their crests, primroses shone on
slopes where the grass was still pale and dead, snowdrops peeped out
beside the wooden fences, and here and there, shining out of the brown
decay of last year's leaves and thick ground-ivy, he found hepaticas. He
had never felt the spring so marvellous before; it rose in a wave of colour
out of the sweet brown earth.

Though outwardly nothing of moment seemed to fill his days, inwardly he was aware of big events—maturing. There was this sense of
approach, of preparation, of gathering. How insipid external events were
after all, compared to the mass, the importance of interior changes! A
change of heart, an altered point of view, a decision taken—these were
the big events of life.

Yet it was a pleasant thing to be a senior partner. Here by the quiet
lake, stroking himself complacently, he felt that life was very active,
very significant, as he wondered what the choice would be. He rather
hoped for Egypt, on the whole. He could look up Tony and the birds.
They could go after duck and snipe together along the Nile. He would,
moreover, be quite an important man out there. Pride and vanity rose in
him, but unobserved. For the Wave was in this too.

One afternoon, late, he returned from a long scramble among icy
rocks about the Dent de Jaman, changed his clothes, and sat with a cigarette beside the open window, watching the throng of people underneath.
In a steady stream they moved along the front of the lake, their voices
rising through the air, their feet producing a dull murmur as of water. The
lake was still as glass; gulls asleep on it in patches, and here and there
a swan, looking like a bundle of dry white paper, floated idly. Off-shore
lay several fishing-boats, becalmed; and far beyond them, a rowing-skiff
broke the surface into two lines of widening ripples. They seemed floating in mid-air against the evening glow. The Savoy Alps formed a deep
blue rampart, and the serrated battlements of the Dent du Midi, full in the
blaze of sunset, blocked the Rhone Valley far away with its formidable
barricade.

He watched the glow of approaching sunset with keen enjoyment; he sat back, listening to the people's voices, the gentle lap of the little waves; and the pleasant lassitude that follows upon hard physical exertion combined with the even pleasanter stimulus of the tea to produce a state of absolute contentment with the world....

Through the murmur of feet and voices, then, and from far across the water, stole out another sound that introduced into his peaceful mood an element of vague disquiet. He moved nearer to the window and looked out. The steamer, however, was invisible; the sea of shining haze towards Geneva hid it still; he could not see its outline. But he heard the echoless mutter of the paddle-wheels, and he knew that it was coming nearer. Yet at first it did not disturb him so much as that, for a moment, he heard no other sound: the voices, the tread of feet, the screaming of the gulls all died away, leaving this single, distant beating audible alone—as though the entire scenery combined to utter it. And, though no ordinary echo answered it, there seemed—or did he fancy it?—a faint, interior response within himself. The blood in his veins went pulsing in rhythmic unison with this remote hammering upon the water.

He leaned forward in his chair, watching the people, listening intently, almost as though he expected something to happen, when immediately below him chance left a temporary gap in the stream of pedestrians, and in this gap—for a second merely—a figure stood sharply defined, cut off from the throng, set by itself, alone. His eyes fixed instantly upon its appearance, movements, attitude. Before he could think or reason he heard himself exclaim aloud:

'Why—it's——'

He stopped. The rest of the sentence remained unspoken. The words rushed down again. He swallowed, and with a gulp he ended—as though the other pedestrians all were men—'——a woman!'

The next thing he knew was that the cigarette was burning his fingers—had been burning them for several seconds. The figure melted back into the crowd. The throng closed round her. His eyes searched uselessly; no space, no gap was visible; the stream of people was continuous once more. Almost, it seemed, he had not really seen her—had merely thought her—up against the background of his mind.

For ten minutes, longer perhaps, he sat by that open window with eyes fastened on the moving crowd. His heart was beating oddly; his breath came rapidly. 'She'll pass by presently again,' he thought; 'she'll come back!' He looked alternately to the right and to the left, until, finally, the sinking sun blazed too directly in his eyes for him to see at all. The glare blurred everybody into a smudged line of golden colour, and the faces became a series of artificial suns that mocked him.

He did, then, an unusual thing—out of rhythm with his normal self,—he acted on impulse. Kicking his slippers off, he quickly put on a pair of boots, took his hat and stick, and went downstairs. There was no reflection in him; he did not pause and ask himself a single question; he ran to join the throng of people, moved up and down with them, in and out, passing and re-passing the same groups over and over again, but seeing no sign of the particular figure he sought so eagerly. She was dressed in black, he knew, with a black fur boa round her neck; she was slim and rather tall; more than that he could not say. But the poise and attitude, the way the head sat on the shoulders, the tilt upwards of the chin—he was as positive of recognising these as if he had seen her close instead of a hundred yards away.

The sun was down behind the Jura Mountains before he gave up the search. Sunset slipped insensibly into dusk. The throng thinned out quickly at the first sign of chill. A dozen times he experienced the thrill—his heart suddenly arrested—of seeing her, but on each occasion it proved to be some one else. Every second woman seemed to be dressed in black that afternoon, a loose black boa round the neck. His eyes ached with the strain, the change of focus, the question that burned behind and in them, the joy—the strange rich pain.

But half, at least, of these dull people, he renumbered, were birds of passage only; to-morrow or the next day they would take the train. He said to himself a dozen times, 'Once more to the end and back again!' For she, too, might be a bird of passage, leaving to-morrow or the next day, leaving that very night, perhaps. The thought afflicted, goaded him. And on getting back to the hotel he searched the Liste des Étrangers as eagerly as he had searched the crowded front—and as uselessly, since he did not even know what name he hoped to find.

But later that evening a change came over him. He surprised some sense of humour: catching it in the act, he also surprised himself a little—smiling at himself. The laughter, however, was significant. For it was just that restless interval after dinner when he knew not what to do with the hours until bedtime: whether to sit in his room and think and read, or to visit the principal hotels in the hope of chance discovery. He was even considering this wild-goose chase to himself, when suddenly he realised that his course of procedure was entirely the wrong one.

This thing was going to happen anyhow, it was inevitable; but—it would happen in its own time and way, and nothing he might do could hurry it. To hunt in this violent manner was to delay its coming. To behave as usual was the proper way. It was then he smiled.

He crossed the hall instead, and put his head in at the door of the little Lounge. Some Polish people, with whom he had a bowing acquaintance, were in there smoking. He had seen them enter, and the Lounge was so small that he could hardly sit in their presence without some effort at conversation. And, feeling in no mood for this, he put his head past the edge of the glass door, glanced round carelessly as though looking for some one—then drew sharply back. For his heart stopped dead an instant, then beat furiously, like a piston suddenly released. On the sofa, talking calmly to the Polish people, was—the figure. He recognised her instantly.

Her back was turned; he did not see her face. There was a vast excitement in him that seemed beyond control. He seemed unable to make up his mind. He walked round and round the little hall examining intently the notices upon the walls. The excitement grew into tumult, as though the meeting involved something of immense importance to his inmost self—his soul. It was difficult to account for. Then a voice behind him said, 'There is a concert to-night. Radwan is playing Chopin. There are tickets in the Bureau still—if Monsieur cares to go.' He thanked the speaker without turning to show his face: while another voice said passionately within him, 'I was wrong; she is slim, but she is not so tall as I thought.' And a minute later, without remembering how he got there, he was in his room upstairs, the door shut safely after him, standing before the mirror and staring into his own eyes. Apparently the instinct to see what he looked like operated automatically. For he now remembered—realised— another thing. Facing the door of the Lounge was a mirror, and their eyes had met. He had gazed for an instant straight into the kind and beautiful Eyes he had first seen twenty years ago—in the Wave.

His behaviour then became more normal. He did the little, obvious things that any man would do. He took a clothes-brush and brushed his coat; he pulled his waistcoat down, straightened his black tie, and smoothed his hair, poked his hanging watch-chain back into its pocket. Then, drawing a deep breath and compressing his lips, he opened the door and went downstairs. He even remembered to turn off the electric light according to hotel instructions. 'It's perfectly all right,' he thought, as he reached the top of the stairs. 'Why shouldn't I? There's nothing unusual about it.' He did not take the lift, he preferred action. Reaching the salon floor, he heard voices in the hall below. She was already leaving therefore, the brief visit over. He quickened his pace. There was not the slightest notion in him what he meant to say. It merely struck him that—idiotically—he had stayed longer in his bedroom than he realised; too long; he might have missed his chance. The thought urged him forward more rapidly again.

In the hall—he seemed to be there without any interval of time—he saw her going out; the swinging doors were closing just behind her. The

Polish friends, having said good-bye, were already rising past him in the lift. A minute later he was in the street. He realised that, because he felt the cool night air upon his cheeks. He was beside her—looking down into her face.

'May I see you back—home—to your hotel?' he heard himself saying. And then the queer voice—it must have been his own—added abruptly, as though it was all he really had to say: 'You haven't forgotten me really. I'm Tommy—Tom Kelverdon.'

Her reply, her gesture, what she did and showed of herself in a word, was as queer as in a dream, yet so natural that it simply could not have been otherwise: 'Tom Kelverdon! So it is! Fancy—you being here!' Then: 'Thank you very much. And suppose we walk; it's only a few minutes—and quite dry.'

How trivial and commonplace, yet how wonderful!

He remembers that she said something to a coachman who immediately drove off, that she moved beside him on this Montreux pavement, that they went up-hill a little, and that, very soon, a brilliant door of glass blazed in front of them, that she had said, 'How strange that we should meet again like this. Do come and see me—any day—just telephone. I'm staying some weeks probably,'—and he found himself standing in the middle of the road, then walking wildly at a rapid pace downhill, he knew not whither, that he was hot and breathless, that stars were shining, and swans, like bundles of white newspaper, were asleep on the lake, and—that he had found her.

He had walked and talked with Lettice. He bumped into more than one irate pedestrian before he realised it; they knew it better than he did, apparently. 'It was Lettice Aylmer, Lettice…' he kept saying to himself. 'I've found her. She shook hands with me. That was her voice, her touch, her perfume. She's here—here in little Montreux—for several weeks. After all these years! Can it be true—really true at last? She said I might telephone—might go and see her. She's glad to see me— again.'

How often he paced the entire length of the deserted front beside the lake he did not count: it must have been many times, for the hotel door, which closed at midnight, was locked and the night-porter let him in. He went to bed—if there was rose in the eastern sky and upon the summits of the Dent du Midi, he did not notice it. He dropped into a half-sleep in which thought continued but not wearily. The excitement of his nerves relaxed, soothed and mothered by something far greater than his senses, stronger than his rushing blood. This greater Rhythm took charge of him most comfortably. He fell back into the mighty arms of something that was rising irresistibly—something inevitable and—half-familiar. It had long been gathering; there was no need to ask a thousand questions, no need to fight it anywhere. From the moment when he glanced idly into the Lounge he had been aware of it. It had driven him downstairs without reflection, as it had driven him also uphill till the blazing door was reached. He smelt it, heard it, saw it, touched it. It was the Wave.

Time certainly proved its unreality that night; the hours seemed both endless and absurdly brief. His mind flew round and round in a circle, lingering over every detail of the short interview with a tumultuous pleasure that hid pain very thinly. He felt afraid, felt himself on the brink of plunging headlong into a gigantic whirlpool. Yet he wanted to plunge.... He would.... He had to.... It was irresistible.

He reviewed the scene, holding each detail forcibly still, until the last delight had been sucked out of it. At first he remembered next to nothing—a blur, a haze, the houses flying past him, no feeling of pavement under his feet, but only her voice saying nothing in particular, her touch, as he sometimes drew involuntarily against her arm, her eyes shining up at him. For her eyes remained the chief impression perhaps—so kind, so true, so very sweet and frank—soft Irish eyes with something mysterious and semi-eastern in them. The conversation seemed to have entirely escaped recovery.

Then, one by one, he remembered things that she had said. Sentences offered themselves of their own accord. He flung himself upon them, trying to keep tight hold of their first meaning—before he filled them with significance of his own. It was a desperate business altogether; emotion distorted her simple words so quickly. 'I was thinking of you only to-day. I had the feeling you were here. Curious, wasn't it?' He distinctly remembered her saying this. And then another sentence: 'I should have known you anywhere; though, of course, you've changed a lot. But I knew your eyes. Eyes don't change much, do they?' The meanings he read into these simple phrases filled an hour at least; he lost entirely their simple first significance. But this last remark brought up another in its train. As the tram went past them she had raised her voice a little and looked up into his face—it was just then they had cannonaded. People who like one another always cannonade, he reflected. And her remark— 'Ah, it comes back to me. You're so very like your sister Mary. I've seen her several times since the days in Cavendish Square. There's a strong family likeness.'

He disliked the last part of the sentence. Mary, besides, had mentioned nothing; her rare letters made no reference to it. The schooldays' friendship had evaporated perhaps. This sent his thoughts back upon the early trail of those distant months when Lettice was at a Finishing School in France and he had kept that tragic Calendar....

Another sentence interrupted them: 'I had, oddly enough, been think-ing of you this very afternoon. I knew you the moment you put your head in at the door, but, for the life of me, I couldn't get the name. All I got was 'Tommy'!' And only his sense of humour prevented the obvious rejoinder, 'I wish you would always call me that.' It struck him sharply. Such talk could have no part in a meeting of this kind; the idea of flirta-tion was impossible, not even thought of. Yet twice she had said, 'I was thinking of you only to-day!'

But other things came back as well. It was strange how much they had really said to each other in those few brief minutes. Next day he retraced the way and discovered that, even walking quickly, it took him a good half hour; yet they had walked slowly, even leisurely. But, try as he would, he was unable to force deeper meanings into these other remarks that he recalled. She was evidently pleased to see him, that at least was certain, for she had asked him to come and see her, and she meant it. He remembered his reply, 'I'll come to-morrow—may I?' and then abruptly realised for the first time that the plunge was taken. He felt himself com-mitted, sink or swim. The Wave already had lifted him off his feet.

And it was on this his whirling thoughts came down to rest at last, and sleep crept over him—just as dawn was breaking. He felt himself in the 'sea' with Lettice, there was nothing he could do, no course to choose, no decision to be made. Though married, she was somehow free—he felt it in her attitude. That sense of fatalism known in boyhood took charge of him. The Wave was rising towards the moment when it must invariably break and fall, and every impulse in him rising in it without a shade of denial or resistance. It would hurt—the fall and break would cause atro-cious pain. But it was somewhere necessary to him. No atom of him held back or hesitated. For there was joy beyond it somehow—an intense and lasting joy, like the joy that belongs to growth and development after accepted suffering.

Vaguely—not put into definite words—it was this he felt, when at length sleep took him. Yet just before he slept he remembered two other little details, and smiled to himself as they rose before his sleepy mind, yet not understanding exactly why he smiled: for he did not yet know her name—and there was, of course, a husband.

CHAPTER IX

This resumption of a childhood's acquaintance that, by one at least, had been imaginatively coaxed into a relationship of ideal character, at once took on a standing of its own. It started as from a new beginning.

Tom Kelverdon did not forget the childhood part, but he neglected it at first. It was as if he met now for the first time—a woman who charmed him beyond anything known before; he longed for her; that he had longed for her subconsciously these twenty years slipped somehow or other out of memory. With it slipped also those strange corroborative details that imagination had clung to so tenaciously during the interval. The Whiff, the Sound, the other pair of Eyes, the shuffling feet, the joy that cloaked the singular prophecy of pain—all these, if not entirely forgotten, ceased to intrude themselves. Even when looking into her clear, dark eyes, he no longer quite realised them as the 'eastern eyes' of his dim, dim dream; they belonged to a woman, and a married woman, whom he desired with body, heart and soul. Calm introspection was impossible, he could only feel, and feel intensely. He could not fuse this girl and woman into one continuous picture: each was a fragment of some much older, larger picture. But this larger canvas he could never visualise successfully. It was coloured, radiant, gorgeous; it blazed as with gold, a gold of sun and stars. But the strain of effort caused rupture instantly. The vaster memory escaped him. He was conscious of reserve.

The comedy of telephoning to a name he did not know was obviated next morning by the arrival of a note: 'Dear Tom Kelverdon,' it began, and was signed 'Yours, Lettice Jaretzka.' It invited him to come up for déjeuner in her hotel. He went. The luncheon led naturally to a walk together afterwards, and then to other luncheons and other walks, to evening rows upon the lake, and to excursions into the surrounding country.... They had tea together in the lower mountain inns, picked flowers, photographed one another, laughed, talked and sat side by side at concerts or in the little Montreux cinema theatre. It was all as easy and natural as any innocent companionship well could be—because it was so deep. The foundations were of such solid strength that nothing on the surface trembled.... Madame de Jaretzka was well known in the hotel— she came annually, it seemed, about this time and made a lengthy stay,— but no breath of anything untoward could ever be connected with her. He, too, was accepted by one and all, no glances came their way. He was her friend: that was apparently enough. And though he desired her, body, heart and soul, he was quick to realise that the first named in the trio had no rôle to play. Something in her, something of attitude and atmosphere, rendered it inconceivable. The reserve he was conscious of lay very deep in him; it lay in her too. There was a fence, a barrier he must not, could not pass—both recognised it. Being a man, romance for him drew some tendril doubtless from the creative physical, but the shade of passing disappointment, if it existed, was renounced as instantly as recognised. Yet he was not aware at first of any incompleteness in her. He felt only a bigger thing. There seemed something in this simple woman that bore him to the stars.

For simple she undoubtedly was, not in the way of shallowness, but because her nature seemed at harmony with itself: uncomplex, natural, frank and open, and with an unconventional carelessness that did no evil for the reason that she thought and meant none. She could do things that must have made an ordinary worldly woman the centre of incessant talk and scandal. There was, indeed, an extraordinary innocence about her that perturbed the judgment, somewhat baffling it. Whereas with many women it might have roused the suspicion of being a pose, an affectation, with her, Tom felt, it was a genuine innocence, beyond words delightful and refreshing. And it arose, he soon discovered, from the fact that, being good and true herself, she thought everybody else was also good and true. This he realised before two days' intercourse had made it seem as if they had been together always and were made for one another. Something bigger and higher than he had ever felt before stirred in him for this woman, whom he thought of now invariably as Madame de Jaretzka, rather than as Lettice of his younger dream. If she woke something nobler in him that had slept, he did not label it as such: nor, if a portion of his younger dream was fulfilling itself before his eyes, in a finer set of terms, did he think it out and set it down in definite words. There was this intense and intimate familiarity between them both, but somehow he did not call it by these names. He just thought her wonderful—and longed for her. The reserve began to trouble him....

'It's sweet,' she said, 'when real people come together—find each other.'

'Again,' he added. 'You left that out. For I've never forgotten—all these years.'

She laughed. 'Well, I'll tell you the truth,' she confessed frankly. 'I hadn't forgotten either; I often thought of you and wondered——'

'What I was like now?'

'What you were doing, where you were,' she said. 'I always knew what you were like. But I often wondered how far on you had got.'

'You had no news of me?'

'None. But I always believed you'd do something big in the world.'

Something in her voice or manner made it wholly natural for him to tell her of his boyhood love. He mentioned the Wave and wavy feeling, the nightmare too, but when he tried to go beyond that, something checked him; he felt a sudden shyness. It 'sounds so silly,' was his thought. 'But I always know a real person,' he said aloud, 'anybody who's going to be real in my life; they always arrive on a wave, as it were. My wavy feeling announces them.' And the interest with which she responded prevented his regretting having made his confession.

'It's an instinct, I think,' she agreed, 'and instincts are meant to be listened to. I've had something similar, though with me it's not a wave.' Her voice grew slower, she made a pause; when he looked up—her eyes were gazing across the lake as though in a moment of sudden absent-mindedness. . . . 'And what's yours?' he asked, wondering why his heart was beating as though something painful was to be disclosed.

'I see a stream,' she went on slowly, still gazing away from him across the expanse of shining water, 'a flowing stream—with faces on it. They float down with the current. And when I see one I know it's somebody real—real to me. The unreal faces are always on the bank. I pass them by.'

'You've seen mine?' he asked, unable to hide the eagerness. 'My face?'

'Often, yes,' she told him simply. 'I dream it usually, I think: but it's quite vivid.'

'And is that all? You just see the faces floating down with the current?'

'There's one other thing,' she answered, 'if you'll promise not to laugh.'

'Oh, I won't laugh,' he assured her. 'I'm awfully interested. It's no funnier than my Wave, anyhow.'

'They're faces I have to save,' she said. 'Somehow I'm meant to rescue them.' In what way she did not know. 'Just keep them above water, I suppose!' And the smile in her face gave place to a graver look. The stream of faces was real to her in the way his Wave was real. There was meaning in it. 'Only three weeks ago,' she added, 'I saw you like that.' He asked where it was, and she told him Warsaw. They compared notes; they had been in the town together, it turned out. Their outer paths had been converging for some time, then.

'Why—did you leave?' he asked suddenly. He wanted to ask why she was there at all, but something stopped him.

'I usually come here,' she said quietly, 'about this time. It's restful. There's peace in these quiet hills above the town, and the lake is soothing. I get strength and courage here.'

He glanced at her with astonishment a moment. Behind the simple language another meaning flashed. There was a look in the eyes, a hint in the voice that betrayed her.... He waited, but she said no more. Not that she wished to conceal, but that she did not wish to speak of something. Warsaw meant pain for her, she came here to rest, to recuperate after a time of stress and struggle, he felt. And looking at the face he recognised for the first time that behind its quiet strength there lay deep pain and sadness, yet accepted pain and sadness conquered, a suffering she had turned to sweetness. Without a particle of proof, he yet felt sure of this. And an immense respect woke in him. He saw her saving, rescuing others, regardless of herself: he felt the floating faces real; the stream was life—her life.... And, side by side with the deep respect, the bigger, higher impulse stirred in him again. Name it he could not: it just came: it stole into him like some rare and exquisite new fragrance, and it came from her.... He saw her far above him, stooping down from a higher level to reach him with her little hand.... He knew a yearning to climb up to her—a sudden and searching yearning in his soul. 'She's come back to fetch me,' ran across his mind before he realised it; and suddenly his heart became so light that he thought he had never felt such happiness before. Then, before he realised it, he heard himself saying aloud—from his heart:

'You do me an awful lot of good—really you do. I feel better and happier when I'm with you. I feel—' He broke off, aware that he was talking rather foolishly. Yet the boyish utterance was honest; she did not think it foolish apparently. For she replied at once, and without a sign of lightness:

'Do I? Then I mustn't leave you, Tom!'

'Never!' he exclaimed impetuously.

'Until I've saved you.' And this time she did not laugh.

She was still looking away from him across the water, and the tone was quiet and unaccented. But the words rang like a clarion in his mind. He turned; she turned too: their eyes met in a brief but penetrating gaze. And for an instant he caught an expression that frightened him, though he could not understand its meaning. Her beauty struck him like a sheet of fire—all over. He saw gold about her like the soft fire of the southern stars. With any other woman, at any other time, he would—but the thought utterly denied itself before it was half completed even. It sank back as though ashamed. There was something in her that made it ugly, out of rhythm, undesirable, and undesired. She would not respond—she would not understand.

In its place another blazed up with that strange, big yearning at the back of it, and though he gazed at her as a man gazes at a woman he needs and asks for, her quiet eyes did not lower or turn aside. The cheaper feeling 'I'm not worthy of you,' took in his case a stronger form: 'I'll be better, bigger, for you.' And then, so gently it might have been a mother's action, she put her hand on his with firm pressure, and left it lying there a moment before she withdrew it again. Her long white glove, still fastened about the wrist, was flung back so that it left the palm and fingers bare, and the touch of the soft skin upon his own was marvellous; yet he did not attempt to seize it, he made no movement in return. He kept control of himself in a way he did not understand. He just sat and looked into her face. There was an entire absence of response from her—in one sense. Something poured from her eyes into his very soul, but something beautiful, uplifting. This new yearning emotion rose through him like a wave, bearing him upwards.... At the same time he was vaguely aware of a lack as well... of something incomplete and unawakened....

'Thank you—for saying that,' he was murmuring; 'I shall never forget it,'; and though the suppressed passion changed the tone and made it tremble even, he held himself as rigid as a statue. It was she who moved. She leaned nearer to him. Like a flower the wind bends on its graceful stalk, her face floated very softly against his own. She kissed him. It was all very swift and sudden. But, though exquisite, it was not a woman's kiss.... The same instant she was sitting straight again, gazing across the blue lake below her.

'You're still a boy,' she said, with a little innocent laugh, 'still a wonderful, big boy.'

'Your boy,' he returned. 'I always have been.'

There was deep, deep joy in his heart, it lifted him above the world—with her. Yet with the joy there was this faint touch of disappointment too.

'But, I say—isn't it awfully strange?' he went on, words failing him absurdly. 'It's very wonderful, this friendship. It's so natural.' Then he began to flush and stammer.

In an even tone of voice she answered: 'It's wonderful, Tom, but it's not strange.' And again he was vaguely aware that something which might have made her words yet more convincing was not there.

'But I've got that curious feeling—I could swear it's all happened before.' He moved closer as he spoke; her dress was actually against his coat, but he could not touch her. Something made it impossible, wrong, a false, even a petty thing. It would have taken away the kiss. 'Have you?' he asked abruptly, with an intensity that seemed to startle her, 'have you got that feeling of familiarity too?'

And for a moment in the middle of their talk they both, for some reason, grew very thoughtful....

'It had to be—perhaps,' she answered simply a little later. 'We are both real, so I suppose—yes, it has to be.'

There was the definite feeling that both spoke of a bigger thing that neither quite understood. Their eyes searched, but their hearts searched too. There was a gap in her that somehow must be filled, Tom felt…. They stared long at one another. He was close upon the missing thing— when suddenly she withdrew her eyes. And with that, as though a wave had swept them together and passed on, the conversation abruptly changed its key. They fell to talking of other things. The man in him was again aware of disappointment.

The change was quite natural, nothing forced or awkward about it. The significance had gone its way, but the results remained. They were in the 'sea' together. It 'had to be.' As from the beginning of the world they belonged to one another, each for the other—real. There was nothing about it of a text-book 'love affair,' absolutely nothing. Deeper far than a passional relationship, guiltless of any fruit of mere propinquity, the foundations of the sudden intimacy were as ancient as immovable. The inevitable touch lay in it. And Tom knew this partly confirmed, at any rate, by the emotion in him when she said 'my boy,' for the term woke no annoyance, conveyed no lightness. Yet there was a flavour of disappointment in it somewhere—something of necessary value that he missed in her…. To a man in love it must have sounded superior, contemptuous: whereas to him it sounded merely true. He was her boy. This mother-touch was in her. To care, to cherish, somehow even to rescue, she had come to find him out—again. She had come back…. It was thus, at first, he felt it. From somewhere above, beyond the place where he now stood in life, she had 'come back, come down, to fetch him.' She was further on than he was. He longed to stand beside her. Until he did so… this gap in her must prevent absolute union. On both sides it was not entirely natural as yet…. Thought grew confused in him.

And, though he could not understand, he accepted it as inevitable. The joy, moreover, was so urgent and uprising, that it smothered a delicate whisper that yet came with it—that the process involved also— pain. Though aware, from time to time, of this vague uneasiness, he easily brushed it aside. It was the merest gossamer-thread of warning that with each recurrent appearance became more tenuous, until finally it ceased to make its presence felt at all….

In the entire affair of this sudden intercourse he felt the Wave, yet the Wave, though steadily rising, ceased to make its presence too consciously known; the Whiff, the Sound, the Eyes seemed equally forgotten: that is, he did not realise them. He was living now, and introspection was a waste of time, living too intensely to reflect or analyse. He felt swept onwards upon a tide that was greater than he could manage, for instead of swimming consciously, he was borne and carried with it. There was certainly no attempt to stem. Life was rising. It rushed him forwards too deliciously to think....

He began asking himself the old eternal question: 'Do I love? Am I in love—at last, then?'... Some time passed, however, before he realised that he loved, and it was in a sudden, curious way that this realisation came. Two little words conveyed the truth—some days later, as they were at tea on the verandah of her hotel, watching the sunset behind the blue line of the Jura Mountains. He had been talking about himself, his engineering prospects—rather proudly—his partnership and the letter he expected daily from Sir William. 'I hope it will be Assouan,' he said, 'I've never been in Egypt. I'm awfully keen to see it.' She said she hoped so too. She knew Egypt well: it enchanted, even enthralled her: 'familiar as though I'd lived there all my life. A change comes over me, I become a different person—and a much older one; not physically,' she explained with a curious shy gaze at him, 'but in the sense that I feel a longer pedigree behind me.' She gave the little laugh that so often accompanied her significant remarks. 'I always think of the Nile as the 'stream' where I see the floating faces.'

They went on chatting for some minutes about it. Tom asked if she had met his cousin out there; yes, she remembered vaguely a Mr. Winslowe coming to tea on her dahabieh once, but it was only when he described Tony more closely that she recalled him positively. 'He interested me,' she said then: 'he talked wildly, but rather picturesquely, about what he called the 'spiral movement of life,' or something.' 'He goes after birds,' Tom mentioned. 'Of course,' she replied, 'I remember distinctly now. It was something about the flight of birds that introduced the spiral part of it. He had a good deal in him, that man,' she added, 'but he hid it behind a lot of nonsense—almost purposely, I felt.'

'That's Tony all over,' Tom assented, 'but he's a rare good sort and I'm awfully fond of him. He's 'real' in our sense too, I think.'

She said then very slowly, as though her thoughts were far away in Egypt at the moment: 'Yes, I think he is. I've seen his face too.'

'Floating down, you mean—or on the bank?'

'Floating,' she answered. 'I'm sure I have.'

Tom laughed happily. 'Then you've got him to rescue too,' he said. 'But, remember, if we're both drowning, I come first.'

She looked into his face and smiled her answer, touching his fingers with her hand. And again it was not a woman's touch.

'He was in Warsaw, too, a few weeks ago,' Tom went on, 'so we were all three there together. Rather odd, you know. He was ski-ing with me in the Carpathians,'; and he described their meeting at Zakopané after the long interval since boyhood. 'He told me about you in Egypt, too, now

I come to think of it. He mentioned the dahabieh, but called you a Russian—yes, I remember now,—and a Russian Princess into the bargain. Evidently you made less impression on Tony than——'

It was then he stopped as though he had been struck. The idle conversation changed. He heard her interrupting words from a curious distance. They fell like particles of ice upon his heart.

'Polish, of course, not Russian,' she mentioned casually, 'but the rest is right, though I never use the title. My husband, in his own country, is a Prince, you see.'

Something reeled in him, then instantly righted itself. For a moment he felt as though the freedom of their intercourse had received a shock that blighted it. The words, 'my husband,' struck chill and ominous into his heart. The recovery, however,—almost simultaneous—showed him that both the freedom and the intercourse were right and unashamed. She gave him nothing that belonged to any other: she was loyal and true to that other as she was loyal and true to himself. Their relationship was high above mere passional intrigue; it could exist—in the way she knew it, felt it— side by side with that other one, before that other one's very eyes, if need be.... He saw it true: he saw it innocent as daylight.... For what he felt was somehow this: the woman in her was not his, but more than that—it was not any one's. It still lay dormant....

If there was a momentary confusion in his own mind, there was none, he felt positive, in hers. The two words that struck him such a blow, she uttered as lightly, innocently, as the rest of the talk between them. Indeed, had that other—even in thought Tom preferred the paraphrase—been present, she would have introduced them to each other then and there. He heard her saying the little phrases even: 'My husband,' and, 'This is Tom Kelverdon whom I've loved since childhood.'

Nothing brought more home to him the high innocence, the purity and sweetness of this woman than the reflections that flung after one another in his mind as he realised that his hope of her being a widow was not justified, and at the same moment that he desired exclusive possession of her—that he was definitely in love.

That she was unaware of any discovery, even if she divined the storm in him at all, was clear from the way she went on speaking. For, while all this flashed through his mind, she added quietly: 'He is in Warsaw now. He—lives there. I go to him for part of every year.' To which Tom heard his voice reply something as natural and commonplace as 'Yes—I see.'

Of the hundred pregnant questions that presented themselves, he did not ask a single one: not that he lacked the courage so much as that he felt the right was—not yet—his. Moreover, behind her quiet words he divined a tragedy. The suffering that had become sweetness in her face was half explained, but the full revelation of it belonged to 'that other' and to herself alone. It had been their secret, he remembered, for at least fifteen years.

CHAPTER X

Yet, knowing himself in love, he was able to set his house in order. Confusion disappeared. With the method and thoroughness of his character he looked things in the face and put them where they belonged. Even to wake up to an untidy room was an affliction. He might arrive in a hotel at midnight, but he could not sleep until his trunks were empty and everything in its place. In such outer details the intensity of his nature showed itself: it was the intensity, indeed, that compelled the orderliness.

And the morning after this conversation, he woke up to an ordered mind— thoughts and emotions in their proper places where he could see and lay his hand upon them. The strength and weakness of his temperament betrayed themselves plainly here, for the security that pedantic order brought precluded the perspective of a larger vision. This careful labelling enclosed him within somewhat rigid fences. To insist upon this precise ticketing had its perilous corollary; the entire view—perspective, proportion, vision—was lost sight of.

'I'm in love: she's beautiful, body, mind and soul. She's high above me, but I'll climb up to where she is.' This was his morning thought, and the thought that accompanied him all day long and every day until the moment came to separate again.... 'She's a married woman, but her husband has no claim on her.' Somehow he was positive of that; the husband had forfeited all claim to her; details he did not know; but she was free; she did no wrong.

In imagination he furnished plausible details from sensational experiences life had shown him. These may have been right or wrong; possibly the husband had ill-treated, then deserted her; they were separated possibly, though—she had told him this—there were no children to complicate the situation. He made his guesses.... There was a duty, however, that she would not, did not neglect: in fulfilment of its claim she went to Warsaw every year. What it was, of course, he did not know; but this thought and the emotions caused by it, he put away into their proper places; he asked no questions of her; the matter did not concern him really. The shock experienced the day before was the shock of realising that—he loved. Those two significant words had suddenly shown it to him. The order of his life was changed. 'She is essential to me; I am essential to her.' But 'She's all the world to me,' involved equally 'I'm all the world to her.' The sense of his own importance was enormously increased. The Wave surged upwards with a sudden leap....

There was one thing lacking in this love, perhaps, though he hardly noticed it—the element of surprise. Ever since childhood he had suspected this would happen. The love was predestined, and in so far seemed a deliberate affair, pedestrian, almost calm. This sense of the inevitable robbed it of that amazing unearthly glamour which steals upon those who love for the first time, taking them deliciously by surprise. He saw her beautiful, and probably she was, but her beauty was familiar to him. He had come up with the childhood dream, and in coming up with it he recognised it. It seemed thus somewhat.... But her mind and soul were beautiful too, only these were more beautiful than he had dreamed. In that lay surprise and wonder too. There was genuine magic here, discovery and exhilarating novelty. He had not caught up with that. The love as a whole, however, was expected, natural. It was inevitable. The familiarity alone remained strange, a flavour of the uncanny about it almost—yet certainly real.

And these things also he tried to face and label, though with less success. To bring order into them was beyond his powers. She had outstripped him somehow in her soul, but had come back to fetch him—also to get something for herself she lacked. The rest was oddly familiar: it had happened before. It was about to happen now again, but on a higher level; only before it could happen completely he must overtake her. The spiral idea lay in it somewhere. But the Wave contained and drove it.... His mind was not supple; analogy, that spiritual solvent, did not help him. Yet the fact remained that he somehow visualised the thing in picture form; a rising wave bore them charging up the spiral curve to a point whence they both looked down upon a passage they had made before. She was always a little in front of him, beyond him. But when the Wave finally broke they would rush together—become one... there would be pain, but joy would follow.

And during all their subsequent happy days of companionship this one thing alone marred his supreme contentment—this sense of elusiveness, that while he held her she yet slipped between his fingers and escaped. He loved; but whereas to most men love brings a feeling of finality and rest, as of a search divinely ended, to Tom came the feeling that his search was merely resumed, or, indeed, had only just begun. He had not come into full possession of this woman: he had only found her.... She was deep; her deceptive simplicity hid surprises from him; much—and it was the greater part—he could not understand. Only when he came up with that would possession be complete. Not that she said or did a single thing that suggested this; she was not elusive of set purpose; she was entirely guiltless of any desire to hold back a fraction of herself, and to conceal was as foreign to her nature as to play with him; but that some part of her hung high above his reach, and that he, knowing this, admitted a subtle pain behind the joy. 'I can't get at her—quite,' he put it to himself. 'Some part of her is not mine yet—doesn't belong to me.'

He thought chiefly, that is, of his own possible disabilities rather than of hers.

'I often wonder why we've come together like this,' he said once, as they lay in the shade of a larch wood above Corvaux and looked towards the snowy summits of Savoy. 'What brought us together, I mean? There's something mysterious about it to me——'

'God,' she said quietly. 'You needed me. You've been lonely. But you'll never be lonely again.'

Her introduction of the Deity into a conversation did not displease. Fate, or any similar word, could have taken its place; she merely conveyed her sense that their coming together was right and inevitable. Moreover, now that she said it, he recognised the fact of loneliness—that he always had been lonely, but that it was no longer possible. He felt like a boy and spoke like a boy. She had come to look after, care for him. She asked nothing for herself. The thought gave him a sharp and sudden pang.

'But my love means a lot to you, doesn't it?' he asked tenderly. 'I mean, you need me too?'

'Everything, Tom,' she told him softly. He was conscious of the mother in her, as though the mother overshadowed the woman. But while he loved it, the tinge of resentment still remained.

'You couldn't do without me, could you?' He took the hand she placed upon his knee and looked up into her quiet eyes. 'You'd be lonely too if—I went?'

For a moment she gazed down at him and did not answer; he was aware of both the pain and sweetness in her face; an interval of thoughtfulness again descended on them both: then a great tenderness came welling up into her eyes as she answered slowly: 'You couldn't go, Tom. You couldn't leave me ever.'

Her hand was on his shoulder, almost about his neck as she said it, and he came in closer, and before he knew what he was doing his face was buried in her lap. Her hand stroked his hair. Twenty-five years dropped from him—he was a child again, a little boy, and she, in some divine, half-impersonal sense he could not understand, was mothering him. No foolish feeling of shame came with it; the mood was too sudden for analysis, it passed away swiftly too; but he knew, for a brief second, all the sensations of a restless and dissatisfied boy who needed above all else—comfort: the comfort that only an inexhaustible mother-love could give.... And this love poured from her in a flood. Till now he had never known it, nor known the need of it. And because it had been curiously lacking he suddenly wondered how he had done without it. A strange sense of tears rose in his heart. He felt pain and tragedy somewhere. For there was another thing he wanted from her too…. Through the sparkle of his joy peeped out that familiar, strange, rich pain, but so swiftly he hardly recognised it. It withdrew again. It vanished.

'But you couldn't leave me either, could you?' he asked, sitting erect again. He made a movement as though to draw her head down upon his shoulder in the protective way of a man who loves, but—he could not do it. It was curious. She did nothing to prevent, only somehow the position would be a false one. She did not need him in that way. He was not yet big enough to protect. It was she who protected him. And when she answered the same second, the familiar sentence flashed across his mind again: 'She has come back to fetch me.'

'I shall never, never leave you, Tom. We're together for always. I know it absolutely.' The girl of seventeen, the unawakened woman who was desired, the mother who thought not of herself,—all three spoke in those quiet words; but with them, too, he was aware of this elusive other thing he could not name. Perhaps her eyes conveyed it, perhaps the pain and sweetness in the little face so close above his own. She was bending over him. He looked up. And over his heart rushed again that intolerable yearning—the yearning to stand where she stood, far, far beyond him, yet with it the certainty that pain must attend the effort. Until that pain, that effort were accomplished, she could not entirely belong to him. He had to win her yet. Yet also he had to teach her something…. Meanwhile, in the act of protecting, mothering him she must use pain, as to a learning child. Their love would gain completeness only thus.

Yet in words he could not approach it; he knew not how to.

'It's a strange relationship,' he stammered, concealing, as he thought, the deep emotions that perplexed him. 'The world would misunderstand it utterly.' She smiled, nodding her head. 'I wish——' he added, 'I mean it comes to me sometimes—that you don't need me quite as I need you. You're my whole life, you know—now.'

'You're growing imaginative, Tom,' she teased him smilingly. Then, catching the earnest expression in his face, she added: 'My life has been very full, you see, and I've always had to stand alone. There's been so much for me to do that I've had no time to feel loneliness perhaps.'

'Rescuing the other floating faces!'

A slight tinge of a new emotion slipped through his mind, something he had never felt before, yet so faint he could not even recapture it, much less wonder whether it were jealousy or envy. It rose from the depths; it vanished into him again…. Besides, he saw that she was smiling; the teasing mood that so often baffled him was upon her; he heard her give that passing laugh that almost 'kept him guessing,' as the Americans say, whether she was in play or earnest.

'It's worth doing, anyhow—rescuing the floating faces,' she said: 'worth living for.' And she half closed her eyes so that he saw her as a girl again. He saw her as she had been even before he knew her, as he used to see her in his dream. It was the dream-eyes that peered at him through long, thick lashes. They looked down at him. He felt caught away to some remote, strange place and time. He was aware of gold, of colour, of a hotter blood, a fiercer sunlight....

And the sense of familiarity became suddenly very real; he knew what she was going to say, how he would answer, why they had come together. It all flashed near, yet still just beyond his reach. He almost understood. They had been side by side like this before, not in this actual place, but somewhere—somewhere that he knew intimately. Her eyes had looked down into his own precisely so, long, long ago, yet at the same time strangely near. There was a perfume, a little ghostly perfume—it was the Whiff. It was gone instantly, but he had tasted it.... A veil drew up.... He saw, he knew, he remembered—almost.... Another second and he would capture the meaning of it all. Another moment and it would reveal itself—then, suddenly, the whole sensation vanished. He had missed it by the minutest fraction in the world, yet missed it utterly. It left him confused and baffled.

The veil was down again, and he was talking with Madame Jaretzka, the Lettice Aylmer of his boyhood days. Such moments of the déjà-vu leave bewilderment behind them, like the effect of sudden change of focus in the eye; and with the bewilderment a sense of insecurity as well.

'Yes,' he said half dreamily, 'and you've rescued a lot already, haven't you?' as though he still followed in speech the direction of the vanished emotion.

'You know that, Tom?' she enquired, raising her eyelids, thus finally restoring the normal.

He stammered rather: 'I have the feeling—that you're always doing good to some one somewhere. There's something,'—he searched for a word— 'impersonal about you—almost.' And he knew the word was nearly right, though found by chance. It included 'un-physical,' the word he did not like to use. He did not want an angel's love; the spiritual, to him, rose from the physical, and was not apart from it. He was not in heaven yet, and had no wish to be. He was on earth; and everything of value—love, above all—must spring from earth, or else remain incomplete, insecure, ineffective even.

And again a tiny dart of pain shot through him. Yet he was glad he said it, for it was true. He liked to face what hurt him. To face it was to get it over....

But she was laughing again gently to herself, though certainly not at him. 'What were you thinking about so long?' she asked. 'You've been silent for several minutes and your thoughts were far away.' And as he did not reply immediately, she went on: 'If you go to Assouan you mustn't fall into reveries like that or you'll leave holes in the dam, or whatever your engineering work is—Tom!'

She spoke the name with a sudden emphasis that startled him. It was a call.

'Yes,' he said, looking up at her. He was emerging from a dream.

'Come back to me. I don't like your going away in that strange way—forgetting me.'

'Ah, I like that. Say it again,' he returned, a deeper note in his voice.

'You were away—weren't you?'

'Perhaps,' he said slowly. 'I can't say quite. I was thinking of you, wherever I was.' He went on, holding her eyes with a steady gaze: 'A curious feeling came over me like—like heat and light. You seemed so familiar to me all of a sudden that I felt I had known you ages and ages. I was trying to make out where—it was——'

She dropped her eyelids again and peered at him, but no longer smiling. There was a sterner expression in her face. The lips curved a moment in a new strange way. The air seemed to waver an instant between them. She peered down at him as through a mist....

'There—like that!' he exclaimed passionately. 'Only I wish you wouldn't. There's something I don't like about it. It hurts,'—and the same minute felt ashamed, as though he had said a foolish thing. It had come out in spite of himself.

'Then I won't, Tom—if you'll promise not to go away again. I was thinking of Egypt for a second—I don't know why.'

But he did not laugh with her; his face kept the graver expression still.

'It changes you—rather oddly,' he said quietly, 'that lowering of the eyelids. I can't say why exactly, but it makes you look——Eastern.' Again he had said a foolish thing. A kind of spell seemed over him.

'Irish eyes!' he heard her saying. 'They sometimes look like that, I'm told. But you promise, don't you?'

'Of course I promise,' he answered bluntly enough, because he meant it. 'I can never go away from you because,'—he turned and looked very hard at her a moment—'because there's something in you I need in my very soul,' he went on earnestly, 'yet that always escapes me. I can't get hold of— all of you.'

And though she refused his very earnest mood, she answered with obvious sincerity at once. 'That's as it should be, Tom. A man tires of a woman the moment he gets to the end of her.' She gave her little laugh and touched his hand. 'Perhaps that's what I'm meant to teach you. When you know all of me——'

'I shall never know all of you,' said Tom.

'You never will,' she replied with meaning, 'for I don't even know it all myself.' And as she said it, he thought he had never seen anything so beautiful in all the world before, for the breeze caught her long gauzy veil of blue and tossed it across her face so that the eyes seemed gazing at him from a distance, but a distance that had height in it. He felt her above him, beyond him, on this height, a height he must climb before he could know complete possession.

'By Jove!' he thought, 'isn't it rising just!' For the Wave was under them tremendously.

* * * *

April meanwhile had slipped into May, and their daily companionship had become the most natural thing in the world, when the telegram arrived that threatened to interrupt the delightful intercourse. But it was not the telegram Tom expected. Neither Greece nor Egypt claimed his talents yet, for the contracts both at Assouan and Salonica were postponed until the autumn, and the routine of a senior partner's life in London was to be his immediate fate. He brought her the news at once: they discussed it together in all its details and as intimately as though it affected their joint lives similarly. His first thought was to run and talk it over with her; hers, how the change might influence their intercourse, their present and their future. Their relationship was now established in this solid, natural way. He told her everything as a son might tell his mother: she asked questions, counselled, made suggestions as a woman whose loving care considered his welfare and his happiness before all else.

However, it brought no threatened interruption after all—involved, indeed, less of separation than if he had been called away as they expected: for though he must go to London that same week, she would shortly follow him. 'And if you go to Egypt in the autumn, Tom,'—she smiled at the way they influenced the future nearer to the heart's desire—'I may go with you. I could make my arrangements accordingly— take my holiday out there earlier instead of here as usual in the spring.'

The days passed quickly. Her first duty was to return to Warsaw; she would then follow him to London and help him with his flat. No man could choose furniture and carpets and curtains properly. They discussed the details with the enthusiasm of children: she would come up several times a week from her bungalow in Kent and make sure that his wallpapers did not clash with the general scheme. Brown was his colour, he told her, and always had been. It was the dominant shade of her eyes as well. He made her promise to stand in the rooms with her eyes opened very wide so that there could be no mistake, and they laughed over the picture happily.

She came to the train, and although he declared vehemently that he disliked 'being seen off,' he was secretly delighted. 'One says such silly things merely because one feels one must say something. And those silly things remain in the memory out of all proportion to their value.' But she insisted. 'Good-byes are always serious to me, Tom. One never knows. I want to see you to the very last minute.' She had this way of making him feel little things significant with Fate. But another little thing also was in store for him. As the train moved slowly out he noticed some letters in her hand; and one of them was addressed to Warsaw. The name leaped up and stung him—Jaretzka. A spasm of pain shot through him. She was leaving in the morning, he knew....

'Write to me from Warsaw,' he said. 'Take care! We're moving!'

'I'll write every day, my dearest Tom, my boy. You won't forget me. I shall see you in a fortnight.'

He let go the little hand he held till the last possible minute. The bells drowned her final words. She stood there waving her hand with the unposted letters in them, till the station pillars intervened and hid her from him.

And this time no 'silly last things' had been said that could 'stay in the memory out of all proportion to their value.' It was something he had noticed on the envelope that stayed—not the husband's name, but a word in the address, a peculiar Polish word he happened to know:— 'Tworki'—the name of the principal maison de santé that stood just outside the city of Warsaw....

Half an hour, perhaps an hour, he sat smoking in his narrow sleeping compartment, thinking with a kind of intense confusion out of which no order came.... At Pontarlier he had to get out for the Customs formalities. It was midnight. The stars were bright. The keen spring air from the wooded Jura Mountains had a curious effect, for he returned to his carriage feeling sleepy, the throng of pictures drowned into calmness by one master-thought that reduced their confusion into order. He looked back over the past weeks and realised their intensity. He had lived. There was a change in him, the change of growth, development. He loved. There was now a woman who was his entire world, essential to him. He was essential to her too. And the importance of this ousted all lesser things, even the senior partnership. This was the master-thought—that he now lived for her. He was 'real' even as she was 'real,' each to the other real. The Wave had lifted him to a level never reached before. And it was rising still....

He fell asleep on this, to dream of a mighty stream that swept them together irresistibly towards some climax that he never could quite see. She floated near to save him. She floated down. Her little hands were stretched. It was a gorgeous and stupendous dream—a dream of rising life itself—rising till it would curve and break and fall, and the inevitable thing would happen that would bring her finally into his hungry arms, complete, mother and woman, a spiritual love securely founded on the sweet and wholesome earth....

CHAPTER XI

During the brief separation of a fortnight Tom was too busy in London to allow himself much reflection. Absence, once the first keen sense of loss is over, is apt to bring reaction. The self makes an automatic effort to regain the normal life it led before the new emotion dislocated the long-accustomed routine. It tries to run back again along the line of least resistance that habit has made smooth and easy. If the reaction continues to assert its claim, the new emotion is proved thereby a delusion. The test lies there.

In Tom's case, however, the reaction was a feeble reminder merely that he had once lived—without her. It took the form of regret for all the best years of his life he had endured—how, he could not think—without this tender, loving woman at his side. That is, he recognised that his love was real and had changed his outlook fundamentally. He could never do without her from this moment onwards. She equally needed him. He would never leave her.... Further than that, for the present, he did not allow himself to think. Having divined something of her tragedy, he accepted the definite limitations. Speculations concerning another he looked on as beside the point. As far as possible he denied himself the indulgence in them. But another thing he felt as well—the right to claim her, whether he exercised that right or not.

Concerning his relationship with her, however, he did not deny speculation, though somehow this time the perspective was too vast for him to manage quite. There was a strange distance in it: he lost himself in remoteness. In either direction it ran into mists that were interminable, as though veils and curtains lifted endlessly, melting into shadowy reaches beyond that baffled all enquiry. The horizons of his life had grown so huge. This woman had introduced him to a scale of living that he could only gaze at with wondering amazement and delight, too large as yet to conform to the order that his nature sought. He could not properly find himself.

'It feels almost as if I've loved her before like this—yet somehow not enough. That's what I've got to learn,' was the kind of thought that came to him, at odd moments only. The situation seemed so curiously familiar, yet only half familiar. They were certainly made for one another, and the tie between them had this deep touch of the inevitable about it that refused to go. That notion of the soul's advance in a spiral cropped up in his mind again. He saw her both coming nearer and retreating—as a moving figure against high light leaves the spectator uncertain whether it is advancing or retiring. He would have liked to talk to Tony all about it, for Tony would be sympathetic. He wanted a confidant and turned instinctively to his cousin…. She already understood more than he did, though perhaps not consciously, and therein lay the secret of her odd elusiveness. Yet, in another sense, his possession was incomplete because a part of her still lay unawakened. 'I must love her more and more and more,' he told himself. But, at the same time, he took it for granted that he was indispensable to her, as she was to him.

These flashes of perception, deeper than anything he had experienced in life hitherto, came occasionally while he waited in London for her return; and though puzzled—his straightforward nature disliked all mystery—he noted them with uncommon interest. Nothing, however, could prevent the rise upwards of the Wave that bore the situation on its breast. The affair swept him onwards; it was not to be checked or hindered. He resigned direction to its elemental tide.

The faint uneasiness, also, recurred from time to time, especially now that he was alone again. He attributed it to the unsatisfied desire in his heart, the knowledge that as yet he had no exclusive possession, and did not really own her; the sense of insecurity unsettled him, the feeling that she was open to capture by any one—'who understands and appreciates her better than I do,' was the way he phrased it sometimes. He was troubled and uneasy because so much of her lay unresponsive to his touch— not needing him. While he was climbing up to reach her, another, with a stronger claim, might step in—step back—and seize her.

It made him smile a little even while he thought of it, for her truth and constancy were beyond all question. And then, suddenly, he traced the uneasiness to its source. There was 'another' who had first claim upon her—who had it once, at any rate. Though at present some cloud obscured and negatived that claim, the cloud might lift, the situation change, the claim become paramount again, as once it surely had been paramount. And, disquieting though the possibility was, Tom was pleased with himself—he was so naïve and simple towards life—for having discerned it clearly. He recognised the risk and thus felt half prepared in advance…. In another way it satisfied him too. With this dream-like suggestion that it all had happened before, he had always felt that a further detail was lacking to complete the scene he half remembered. Something, as yet, was wanting. And this item needed to make the strange repetition of the scene fulfil itself seemed, precisely, the presence of 'another.'

Their intercourse, meanwhile, proved beyond words delightful during the following weeks, when, after her return from Warsaw, she kept her word and helped him in the prosaic business of furnishing his flat and settling down, as in a hundred other details of his daily life as well. All that they did and said together confirmed their dear relationship and established it beyond reproach. There was no question of anything false, illicit, requiring concealment: nothing to hide and no one to evade. In their own minds their innocence was so sure, indeed, that it was not once alluded to between them. It was impossible to look at her and doubt: nor could the most cynical suspect Tom Kelverdon of an undesirable intrigue with the wife of another man. His acquaintance, moreover, were not of the kind that harboured the usual 'worldly' thoughts; he went little into society, whereas the comparatively few Londoners she knew were almost entirely—he discovered it by degrees—people whose welfare in one way or another she had earnestly at heart. It was a marvel to him, indeed, how she never wearied of helping ungrateful folk, for the wish to be of service seemed ingrained in her. Her first thought on making new acquaintances was always what she could do for them, not with money necessarily, but by 'seeing' them in their proper milieu and planning to bring about the conditions they needed in order to realise themselves fully. Failure, discontent, unhappiness were due to wrong conditions more than to radical fault in the people themselves; once they 'found themselves,' the rest would follow. It amounted to a genius in her.

It seemed the artist instinct that sought this unselfish end rather than any religious tendency. She felt it ugly to see people at issue with their surroundings. Her religion was humanity, and had no dogmas. Even Tony Winslowe, now in England again, came in for his share of this sweet fashioning energy in her; much to his own bewilderment and to Tom's amusement....

The summer passed towards early autumn and London emptied, but it made no difference to them. Tom had urgent work to do and was absorbed in it, never forgetting for a moment that he was now a Partner in the Firm. He spent frequent week-ends at Madame Jaretzka's Kentish bungalow, where she had for companion at the moment an Irish cousin who, as Tom easily guessed, was also a dependant. This cousin had been invited with her child, Molly, for the summer holidays, and these summer holidays had run on into three months at least.

A tall, thin, angular woman, of uncertain manners and capricious temperament, Mrs. Haughstone had perhaps lived so long upon another's bounty that she had come to take her good fortune for granted, and permitted herself freely two cardinal indulgences—grumbling and jealousy. Having married unwisely, in order to better herself rather than because she loved, her shiftless husband had disgraced himself with an adventuress governess, leaving her with three children and something below £150 a year. Madame Jaretzka had stepped in to bring them together again: she provided schooling abroad, holidays, doctors, clothes, and all she could devise by way of helping them 'find themselves' again, and so turning their broken lives to good account. With the husband, sly, lazy, devoid of both pride and honesty, she could do little, and she was quite aware that he and his wife put their heads together to increase the flow of 'necessaries' she generously supplied.

It was a sordid, commonplace story, sordidly treated by the soured and vindictive wife, whose eventual aims upon her saviour's purse were too obvious to be mistaken. Even Tom perceived the fact without delay. He also perceived, behind the flattering tongue, an acid and suspicious jealousy that regarded new friends with ill-disguised alarm. Mrs. Haughstone thought of herself and her children before all else. She mistook the impersonal attitude of her benefactress for credulous weakness. A new friend was hostile to her shameless ambitions and disliked accordingly.... Tom scented an enemy the first time he met her. To him she expressed her disapproval of Tony, and vice versa, while to her hostess she professed she liked them both—'but': the 'but' implying that men were selfish and ambitious creatures who thought only of their own advantage.

His country visits, therefore, were not made happier by the presence in the cottage of this woman and her child, but the manner in which the benefactress met the situation justified the respect he had felt first months before. It increased his love and admiration. Madame Jaretzka behaved unusually. That she grasped the position there could be no doubt, but her manner of dealing with it was unique. For when Mrs. Haughstone grumbled, Madame Jaretzka gave her more, and when Mrs. Haughstone yielded to jealousy, Madame Jaretzka smiled and said no word. She won her victories with further generosity.

'Another face that has to be rescued?' Tom permitted himself to say once, after an unfortunate scene in which his hostess had been subtly accused of favouritism to another child in the house. He could hardly suppress the annoyance and impatience that he felt.

'Oh, I never thought about it in that way,' she answered with her little laugh, quite unruffled by what had happened. 'The best way is to help them to—see themselves. Then they try to cure themselves.' She laughed again, as though she had said a childish thing instead of something distinctly wise. 'I can't cure them,' she added. 'I can only help.'

Tom looked at her. 'Help others to see themselves—as they are,' he repeated slowly. 'So that's how you do it, is it?' He reflected a moment. 'That's being impersonal. You rouse no opposition that way. It's good.'

'Is it?' she replied, as though guiltless of any conscious plan. 'It seems the natural thing to do.' Then, as he was evidently preparing for discussion in his honest and laborious way, she stopped him with a look, smiling, sighing, and holding up her little finger warningly. He understood. Analysis and argument she avoided always; they obscured the essential thing; here was the intuitive method of grasping the solution the instant the problem was stated. Detailed examination exhausted her merely. And Tom obeyed that look, that threatening finger. In little things he invariably yielded, while in big things he remained firm, even obstinate, though without realising it.

Her head inclined gracefully, acknowledging her victory. 'That's one reason I love you, Tom,' she told him as reward; 'you're a boy on the surface and a man inside.'

Tom saw beauty flash about her as she said it; emotion rose through him in a sudden tumult; he would have seized her, kissed her, crumpled her little self against his heart and held her there, but for the tantalising truth that the thing he wanted would have escaped him in the very act. The loveliness he yearned for, craved, was not open to physical attack; it was a loveliness of the spirit, a bird, a star, a wild flower on some high pinnacle near the snow: to obtain it he must climb to where it soared above the earth—rise up to her.

He laughed and took her little finger in both hands. He felt awkward, big and clumsy, a giant trying to catch an elusive butterfly. 'You turn us all round that!' he declared. 'You turn her,' nodding towards the door, 'and me,' kissing the tip quickly, 'and Tony too. Only she and Tony don't know you twiddle them—and I do.'

She let him kiss her hand, but when he drew nearer, trying to set his lips upon the arm her summer dress left bare, she put up her face instead and kissed him lightly on the cheek. Her free hand made a caressing gesture across his neck and shoulder, as she stood on tiptoe to reach him. The mother in her, not the woman, caressed him dearly. It was wonderful; but the surge of mingled emotions clouded something in his brain, and a string of words came tumbling out in a fire of joy and pain. 'You're a queen and a conqueror,' he said, longing to seize her, yet holding himself back strongly. 'Somewhere I'm your helpless slave, but somewhere I'm your master.' The protective sense came up in him. 'It's too delicious! I'm in a dream! Lettice,' he whispered, 'it's my Wave! The Wave is behind it! It's behind us both!'

For an instant she half closed her eyelids in the way she knew both pleased and frightened him. Invariably this gave her the advantage. He felt her above him when she looked like this, he kneeling with hands outstretched, yearning to be raised to where she stood. 'You're a baby, a poet, and a man rolled into a dear big boy,' she said quickly, moving towards the door away from him. 'And now I must go and get my garden hat, for it's time to meet Tony and Moyra at the train, and as you have so much surplus energy to-day we'll walk through the woods instead of going in the motor.' She waved her hand and vanished behind the door. He heard the patter of her feet as she ran upstairs.

He went to the open window, lit his pipe, leaned out with his head among the climbing roses, and thought of many things. Great joy was in him, but behind it, far down where he could not reach it quite, hid a gnawing pain that was obscure uneasiness. Pictures came floating across his mind, rising and falling, sometimes rushing hurriedly; he saw things and faces mixed, his own and hers chief among them. Her little finger pointed to a star. He sighed, he wondered, he half prayed. Would he ever understand, rise to her level, possess her for his very own? She seemed so far beyond him. It was only part of her he touched.

The faces fluttered and looked into his own, one among them an imagined face—the husband's. It was a face with light blue eyes, moreover. He saw Tony's too, frank, laughing, irresponsible, and the face of the Irish girl who was Tony's latest passion. Tony could settle down to no one for long. Tom remembered suddenly his remark at Zakopané months ago, that the bee never sipped the last drop of honey from the flower.... His thoughts tumbled and flew in many directions, yet all at once. Life seemed very full and marvellous; it had never seemed so intense before; it bore him onwards, upwards, forwards, with a rush beyond all possible control and guidance. He acknowledged a rather delicious sense of helplessness. The Wave was everywhere behind and under him. It was sweeping him along.

Then thought returned to Tony and the Irish girl who were coming down for the Sunday, and he smiled to himself as he recalled his cousin's ardent admiration at a theatre party a few nights ago in town. Tony had something that naturally attracted women, dominating them too easily. Was he heartless a little in the business? Would he never, like Tom, settle down with one? His thought passed to the latest capture: there were signs, indeed, that here Tony was caught at last.

For Tom, Tony, and Madame Jaretzka formed an understanding trio, and there were few expeditions, town or country, of which the lively bird-enthusiast did not form an active member. Tony took it all very lightly, unaware of any serious intention behind the pleasant invitations. Tom was amused by it. He looked forward to his cousin's visit now. He was feeling the need of a confidant, and Tony might so admirably fill the rôle. It was curious, a little: Tom often felt that he wanted to confide in Tony, yet somehow or other the confidences were never actually made. There was something in Tony that invited that free, purging confidence which is a need of every human being. It was so easy to tell things, difficult things, to this careless, sympathetic being; yet Tom never passed the frontier into definite revelation. At the last moment he invariably held back.

Thought passed to his hostess, already manœuvring to help Tony 'find himself.' It amused Tom, even while he gave his willing assistance; for Tony was of evasive, slippery material, like a fluid that, pressed in one given direction, resists and runs away into several others. 'He scatters himself too much,' she remarked, 'and it's a pity; there's waste.' Tom laughed, thinking of his episodic love affairs. 'I didn't mean that,' she added, smiling with him; 'I meant generally. He's full of talent and knowledge. His power over women is natural, but it comes of mere brilliance. If all that were concentrated instead, he would do something real; he might be extraordinarily effective in life. Yes, Tom, I mean it.' But Tom, though he smiled, agreed with her, feeling rather flattered that she liked his cousin.

'But he breaks too many hearts,' he said lightly, thinking of his last conquest, and then added, hardly knowing why he said it, 'By the by, did you ever notice his hands?'

The way she quickly looked up at him proved that she divined his meaning. But the glance had a flash of something that escaped him.

'You're very observant, Tommy,' she said evasively. It seemed impossible for her to say a disparaging thing of anybody. She invariably picked out and emphasised the best. 'You don't admire them?'

'Do you, Lettice?'

She paused for an imperceptible second, then smiled. 'I rather like big rough hands in a man—perhaps,' she said without any particular interest, 'though—in a way—they frighten me sometimes. Tony's are ugly, but there's power in them.' And she placed her own small gloved hand upon his arm. 'He's rather irresponsible, I know,' she added gently, 'but he'll grow out of that in time. He's beginning to improve already.'

'You see, he's got no mother,' Tom observed.

'No wife either—yet,' she added with a laugh.

'Or work,' put in Tom, with a touch of self-praise, and thinking of his own position in the world. Her interest in Tony had the effect of making himself seem worthier, more important. This fine woman, who judged people from so high a standpoint, had picked out—himself! He had an absurd yet delightful feeling as though Tony was their child, and the perfectly natural way she took him under her mothering wing stirred an admiring pity in him.

Then as they walked together through the fragrant pine-woods to the station, an incident at a recent theatre party rose before his memory. Tony and his Amanda had been with them. The incident in question had left a singular impression on his mind, though why it emerged now, as they wandered through the quiet wood, he could not tell. It had occurred a week or two ago. He now saw it again—in a tenth of the time it takes to tell.

* * * *

The scene was laid in ancient Egypt, and while the play was commonplace, the elaborate production—scenery, dresses, atmosphere—was good. But Tom, unable to feel interest in the trivial and badly acted story, had felt interest in another thing he could not name. There was a subtle charm, a delicate glamour about it as of immensely old romance, but some lost romance of very far away. Yet, whether this charm was due to the stage effects or to themselves, sitting there in the stalls together, escaped him. For in some singular way the party, his hostess certainly, seemed to interpenetrate the play itself. She, above all, and Tony vaguely, seemed inseparable from what he gazed at, heard, and felt.

Continually he caught himself thinking how delightful it was to know himself next to Madame Jaretzka, so close that he shared her atmosphere, her perfume, touched her even; that their minds were engaged intimately together watching the same scene; and also, that on her other side, sat Tony, affectionate, whimsical, fascinating Tony, whom they were trying to help 'find himself'; and that he, again, was next to a girl he liked. The harmonious feeling of the four was pleasurable to Tom. He felt himself, moreover, an important and indispensable item in its composition. It was vague; he did not attempt to analyse it as self-flattery, as vanity, as pride—he was aware, merely, that he felt very pleased with himself and so with everybody else. It was gratifying to sit at the head of the group; everybody could see how beautiful she was; the dream of exclusive ownership stole over him more definitely than ever before. 'She's chosen me! She needs me—a woman like that!'

The audience, the lights, the colour, the music influenced him. It seemed he caught something from the crude human passion that was being ranted on the stage and transferred it unconsciously into his relations with the party he belonged to, but, above all, into his relationship with her—and with another. But he refused to let his mind dwell upon that other. He found himself thinking instead of the divine tenderness that was in her, yet at the same time of her elusiveness and the curious pain it caused him. Whence came, he wondered, the sweet and cruel flavour? It seemed like a memory of something suffered long ago, the sweetness in it true and exquisite, the cruelty an error on his own part somehow. The old hint of uneasiness, the strange, rich pain he had known in boyhood, stole faintly over him; its first and immediate effect heightening the sense of dim, old-world romance already present....

And he had turned cautiously to look at her. She was leaning forward a little as though the play absorbed her, and the attitude startled him. It caused him almost a definite shock. The face had pain in it.

She was not aware that he stared; her attention was fastened upon the stage; but the eyes were fixed, the little mouth was fixed as well, the lips compressed; and all her features wore this expression of curious pain. There was sternness in them, something almost hard. He watched her for some minutes, surprised and fascinated. It came over him that he almost knew what that was in her mind. Another moment and he would discover it—when, past her profile, he caught his cousin's eyes peering across at him. Tony had felt the direction of his glance and had looked round: and Tony—mischievously—winked!

The spell was broken. In that instant, however, through the heated air of the crowded stalls already weighted with sickly artificial perfumes, there reached him faintly, as from very far away, another and a subtler perfume, something of elusive fragrance in it. It was very poignant, instinct as with forgotten associations. It was the Whiff. It came, it went; but it was unmistakable. And he connected it, as by some instantaneous certitude, with the play—with Egypt.

'What do you think of it, Lettice?' he had whispered, nodding towards the stage.

She turned with a start. She came back. The expression of pain flashed instantly away. She had evidently not been thinking of the performance. 'It's not much, Tom, is it? But I like the scenery. It makes me feel strange somewhere—the change that comes over me in Egypt. We'll be there together—some day.' She leaned over with her lips against his ear.

And there was significance in the commonplace words, he thought—a significance her whisper did not realise, and certainly did not intend.

'All three of us,' he rejoined before he knew what he meant exactly.

And she nodded hurriedly. Either she agreed, or else she had not heard him. He did not insist, he did not repeat, he sat there wondering why on earth he said the thing. A touch of pain pricked him like an insect's sting, but a pain he could not account for. His blood, at the same time, leaped as she bent her face so near to his own. He felt his heart swell as he looked into her eyes. Her beauty astonished him; in this twilight of the theatre it glowed and burned like a veiled star. He fancied—it was the trick of the half-light, of course—she had grown darker and that a dusky flush lay on her cheeks.

'What were you thinking about?' he whispered lower again, changing the sentence slightly. And, as he asked it, he saw Tony still watching him, two seats away. It annoyed him; he drew his head back a little so that her face concealed him.

'I don't know,' she whispered back; 'nothing in particular.' She put her gloved hand stealthily towards him and touched his knee. The gesture, he felt, was intended to supplement the words. For the first time in his life he did not quite believe her. The thought was odious, but not to be denied. It merely flashed across him, however. He forgot it instantly.

'Seems oddly familiar somehow,' he said, 'doesn't it?'

Again she nodded, smiling, as she gazed for a moment first into one eye, then into the other, then turned away to watch the stage. And abruptly, as she did so, the entire feeling vanished, the mood evaporated, her expression was normal once more, and he fixed his attention on the stupid play.

He turned his interest into other channels; he would take his party on to supper. He did so. Yet an impression remained—the impression that the Wave had come nearer, higher, that it was rising and gaining impetus, accumulating mass, momentum, power. The gay supper could not dissipate that, nor could the happy ten minutes in a taxi, when he drove her to her door, decrease or weaken it. She was very tired. They spoke little, he remembered; she gave him a gentle touch as the cab drew up, and the few things she said had entirely to do with his comfort in his flat. He felt in that touch and in those tender questions the mother only. The woman, it suddenly occurred to him, had gone elsewhere. He had never had it, never even claimed it. A deep sense of loneliness touched him for a moment. His heart beat rapidly. He dreamed....

* * * *

Why the scene came back to him now as they walked slowly through the summery pine-wood he knew not. He caught himself thinking vividly of Egypt suddenly, of being in Egypt with her—and with another. But on that other he refused to let thought linger. Of set purpose he chose Tony in that other's place. He saw it in a picture: he and she together helping Tony, she and Tony equally helping him. It passed before him merely, a glowing coloured picture set in high light against the heavy background of these English fir-woods and the Kentish sky. Whether it came towards him or retreated, he could not say. It was very brief, instantaneous almost. The memory of the play, with its numerous attendant correlations, rose up, then vanished.

'Give me your arm, Tom, you mighty giant: these pine-needles are so slippery.' He felt her hand creep in and rest upon his muscles, and a glow of boyish pride came with it. In her summer dress of white, her big garden hat and flowing violet veil, she looked adorable. He liked the long white gauntlet gloves. The shadows of the trees became her well: against the thick dark trunks she seemed slim and dainty as a flower that the breeze bent over towards him. 'You're so horribly big and strong,' she said, and her eyes, full of expression, glanced up at him. He watched her little feet in the neat white shoes peep out in turn as they walked along; her fingers pressed his arm. He tried to take her parasol, but she prevented him, saying it was her only weapon of defence against a giant, 'and there is a giant in this forest, though only a baby one perhaps!' He felt the mother in her pour over him in a flood of tenderness that blessed and soothed and comforted. It was as if a divine and healing power streamed from her into him.

'And what were you thinking about, Tom?' she enquired teasingly. 'You haven't said a word for a whole five minutes!'

'I was thinking of Egypt,' he answered with truth.

She looked up quickly.

'I'm to go out in December,' he went on. 'I told you. It was decided at our last Board Meeting.'

She said she remembered. 'But it's funny,' she added, 'because I was thinking of Egypt too just then—thinking of the Nile, my river with the floating faces.'

* * * *

The week-end visit was typical of many others; Mrs. Haughstone, seeing safety in numbers possibly, was pleasant on the surface, Molly deflecting most of her poisoned darts towards herself; while Tom and Tony shared the society of their unconventional hostess with boyish enjoyment. Tom modified the air of ownership he indulged when alone with her, and no one need have noticed that there was anything more between them than a hearty, understanding friendship. Tony, for instance, may have guessed the true situation, or, again, he may not; for he said no word, nor showed the smallest hint by word, by gesture, or by silence—most significant betrayal of all—that he was aware of any special tie. Though a keen observer, he gave no sign. 'She's an interesting woman, Tom,' he remarked lightly yet with enthusiasm once, 'and a rare good hostess—a woman in a thousand, I declare. We make a famous trio. As you've got that Assouan job we'll have some fun next winter in Egypt, eh?'

And Tom, pleased and secretly flattered by the admiration, tried to make his confidences. Unless Tony had liked her this would have been impossible. But they formed such a natural, happy trio together, giving the lie to the hoary proverb, that Tom felt it was permissible to speak of her to his sympathetic cousin. Already they had laughingly discussed the half-forgotten acquaintanceship begun in the dahabieh on the Nile, Tony making a neat apology by declaring to her, 'Beautiful women blind me so, Madame Jaretzka, that I invariably forget all lesser details. And that's why I told Tom you were a Russian.'

On this particular occasion, too, it was made easier because Tony had asked his cousin's opinion about the Irish girl, invited for his special benefit. 'I was never so disappointed in my life,' he said in his convincing yet airy way. 'She looked so wonderful the other night. It was the evening dress, I suppose. You should always see a girl first in the daytime; the daylight self is the real self.' And Tom, amused by the irresponsible attitude towards the sex, replied that the right woman looked herself in any dress because it was as much a part of her as her own skin. 'Yes,' said Tony, 'it's the thing inside the skin that counts, of course; you're right; the rest is only a passing glamour. But friendship with a woman is the best of all, for friendship grows insensibly into the best kind of love. It's a delightful feeling,' he added sympathetically, 'that kind of friendship. Independent of what they wear!'

He enjoyed his pun and laughed. 'I say, Tom,' he went on suddenly with a certain inconsequence, 'have you ever met the Prince—Madame Jaretzka's husband—by the way? I wonder what he's like.' He looked up carelessly and raised his eyebrows.

'No,' replied Tom in a quiet tone, 'but I—exp—hope to some day.'

'I think he ran away and left her, or something,' continued the other. 'He's dead, anyhow, to all intents and purposes. But I've been wondering lately. I'll be bound there was ill-treatment. She looks so sad sometimes. The other night at the theatre I was watching her——'

'That Egyptian play?' broke in Tom.

'Yes; it was bad enough to make any one look sad, wasn't it? But it was curious all the same——'

'I didn't mean the badness.'

'Nor did I. It was odd. There was atmosphere in spite of everything.'

'I thought you were too occupied to notice the performance,' Tom hinted.

Tony laughed good-naturedly. 'I was a bit taken up, I admit,' he said. 'But there was something curious all the same. I kept seeing you and our hostess on the stage——'

'In Egypt!'

'In a way, yes.' He hesitated.

'Odd,' said his cousin briefly.

'Very. It seemed—there was some one else who ought to have been there as well as you two. Only he never came on.'

Tom made no comment. Was this thought-transference, he wondered?

The natural sympathy between them furnished the requisite conditions certainly.

'He never came on,' continued Tony, 'and I had the queer feeling that he was being kept off on purpose, that he was busy with something else, but that the moment he came on the play would get good and interesting—real. Something would happen. And it was then I noticed Madame Jaretzka——'

'And me, too, I suppose,' Tom put in, half amused, half serious. There was an excited yet uneasy feeling in him.

'Chiefly her, I think. And she looked so sad,—it struck me suddenly. D'you know, Tom,' he went on more earnestly, 'it was really quite curious. I got the feeling that we three were watching that play together from above it somewhere, looking down on it—sort of from a height above——'

'Above,' exclaimed his cousin. There was surprise in him—surprise at himself. That faint uneasiness increased. He realised that to confide in Tony was impossible. But why?

'H'm,' Tony went on in a reflective way as if half to himself. 'I may have seen it before and forgotten it.' Then he looked up at his cousin. 'And what's more—that we three, as we watched it, knew the same thing together—knew that we were waiting for another chap to come on, and that when he came the silly piece would turn suddenly interesting, dramatic in a true sense, only tragedy instead of comedy. Did you, Tom?' he asked abruptly, screwing up his eyes and looking quite serious a moment.

Tom had no answer ready, but his cousin left no time for answering.

'And the fact is,' he continued, lowering his voice, 'I had the feeling the other chap we were waiting for was him.'

Tom was too interested to smile at the grammar. 'You mean—her husband?' he said quietly. He did not like the turn the talk had taken; it pleased him to talk of her, but he disliked to bring the absent husband in. There was trouble in him as he listened.

'Possibly it was,' he added a trifle stiffly. Then, ashamed of his feeling towards his imaginative cousin, he changed his manner quickly. He went up and stood behind him by the open window. 'Tony, old boy, we're together somehow in this thing,' he began impulsively; 'I'm sure of it.' Then the words stuck. 'If ever I want your help——'

'Rather, Tom,' said the other with enthusiasm, yet puzzled, turning with an earnest expression in his frank blue eyes. In another moment, like two boys swearing eternal friendship, they would have shaken hands. Tom again felt the impulse to make the confidences that desire for sympathy prompted, and again realised that it was difficult, yet that he would accomplish it. Indeed, he was on the point of doing so, relieving his mind of the childhood story, the accumulated details of Wave and Whiff and Sound and Eyes, the singular Montreux meeting, the strange medley of joy and uneasiness as well, all in fact without reserve—when a voice from the lawn came floating into the room and broke the spell. It lifted him sharply to another plane. He felt glad suddenly that he had not spoken— afterwards, he felt very glad. It was not right in regard to her, he realised.

'You're never ready, you boys,' their hostess was saying, 'and Miss Monnigan declares that men always wait to be fetched. The lunch-baskets are all in, and the motor's waiting.'

'We didn't want to be in the way,' cried Tony gaily, ever ready with an answer first. 'We're both so big and clumsy. But we'll make the fire in the woods and do the work that requires mere strength without skill all right.' He leaped out of the window to join them, while Tom went by the door to fetch his cap and overcoat. Turning an instant he saw the three figures on the lawn standing in the sunlight, Madame Jaretzka with a loose, rough motor-coat over her white dress, a rose at her throat and the long blue veil he loved wound round her hair and face. He saw her eyes look up at Tony and heard her chiding him. 'You've been talking mischief in there together,' she was saying laughingly, giving him a searching glance in play, though the tone had meaning in it. 'We were talking of you,' swore Tony, 'and you,' he added, turning by way of polite after-thought to the girl. And one of his big hands he laid for a moment upon Madame Jaretzka's arm.

Tom turned sharply and hurried on into the hall. The first thought in his mind was how tender and gentle Madame Jaretzka looked standing in the sunshine, her eyes turned up at Tony. His second thought was vaguer: he felt glad that Tony admired and liked her so. The third was vaguer still: Tony didn't really care for the girl a bit and was only amusing himself with her, but Madame Jaretzka would protect her and see that no harm came of it. She could protect the whole world. That was her genius.

In a moment these three thoughts flashed through him, but while the last two vanished as quickly as they came, the first lingered like sunlight in him. It remained and grew and filled his heart, and all that day it kept close by him—her love, her comfort, her mothering compassion.

And Tom felt glad for some reason that his confidences to Tony after all had been interrupted and prevented. They remained thus interrupted and prevented until the end, even when the 'other' came upon the scene, and above all while that 'other' stayed. It all seemed curiously inevitable.

CHAPTER XII

The last few weeks of September they were much alone together, for Mrs. Haughstone had gone back to her husband's tiny house at Kew, Molly to the Dresden school, and Tony somewhere into space—northern Russia, he said, to watch the birds beginning to leave.

Meanwhile, with deepening of friendship, and experiences whose ordinariness was raised into significance because this woman shared them with him, Tom saw the summer fade in England and usher in the longer evenings. Light and heat waned from the sighing year; winds, charged with the memory of roses, took the paling skies; the swallows whispered together of the southern tour. New stars swam into their autumnal places, and the Milky Way came majestically to its own. He watched the curve of it on moonless nights, pouring its grand river across the heavens. And in the heart of its soft brilliance he saw Cygnus, cruciform and shining, immersed in the white foam of the arching wave.

He noticed these things now, as once long ago in early boyhood, because a time of separation was at hand. His yearning now was akin to his yearning then—it left a chasm in his soul that beauty alone could help to fill. At fifteen he was thirty-five, as now at thirty-five he was fifteen again.

Lettice was not, indeed, at a Finishing School across the Channel, but she was shortly going to Warsaw to spend October with her husband, and in November she was to sail for Egypt from Trieste. Tom was to follow in December, so a separation of three months was close at hand. 'But a necessary separation,' she said one evening as they motored home beneath the stars, 'is always bearable and strengthening; we shall both be occupied with things that must—I mean, things we ought to do. It's the needless separations that are hard to bear.' He replied that it would be wonderful meeting again and pretending they were strangers. He tried to share her mood, her point of view with honesty. 'Yes,' she answered, 'only that wouldn't be quite true, because you and I can never be separated—really. The curve of the earth may hide us from each other's sight like that,'—and she pointed to the sinking moon—'but we feel the pull just the same.'

They leaned back among the cushions, sharing the mysterious beauty of the night-sky in their hearts. They lowered their voices as though the hush upon the world demanded it. The little things they said seemed suddenly to possess a significance they could not account for quite and yet admitted.

He told her that the Milky Way was at its best these coming months, and that Cygnus would be always visible on clear nights. 'We'll look at that and remember,' he said half playfully. 'The astronomers say the Milky Way is the very ground-plan of the Universe. So we all come out of it. And you're Cygnus.' She called him sentimental, and he admitted that perhaps he was. 'I don't like this separation,' he said bluntly. In his mind he was thinking that the Milky Way had his wave in it, and that its wondrous arch, like his life and hers, rose out of the 'sea' below the world. In that sea no separation was possible.

'But it's not that that makes you suddenly poetic, Tom. It's something else.'

'Is it?' he answered. A whisper of pain went past him across the night. He felt something coming; he was convinced she felt it too. But he could not name it.

'The Milky Way is a stream as well as a wave. You say it rises in the autumn———?' She leaned nearer to him a little.

'But it's seen at its best a little later—in the winter, I believe.'

'We shall be in Egypt then,' she mentioned. He could have sworn she would say those very words.

'Egypt,' he repeated slowly. 'Yes—in Egypt.'

And a little shiver came over him, so slight, so quickly gone again, that he hoped it was imperceptible. Yet she had noticed it.

'Why, Tom, don't you like the idea?'

'I wonder—' he began, then changed the sentence—'I wonder what it will be like. I have a curious desire to see it—I know that.'

He heard her laugh under her breath a little. What came over them both in that moment he couldn't say. There was a sense of tumult in him somewhere, a hint of pain, of menace too. Her laughter, slight as it was, jarred upon him. She was not feeling quite what he felt—this flashed, then vanished.

'You don't sound enthusiastic,' she said calmly.

'I am, though. Only—I had a feeling———' He broke off. The truth was he couldn't describe that feeling even to himself.

'Tom, dear, my dear one—' she began, then stopped. She also stopped an impulsive movement towards him. She drew back her sentence and her arms. And Tom, aware of a rising passion in him he might be unable to control, turned his face away a moment. Something clutched at his heart as with cruel pincers. A chill followed close upon the shiver. He felt a moment of keen shame, yet knew not exactly why he felt it.

'I am a sentimental ass!' he exclaimed abruptly with a natural laugh. His voice was tender. He turned again to her. 'I believe I've never properly grown up.' And before he could restrain himself he drew her towards him, seized her hand and kissed it like a boy. It was that kiss, combined with her blocked sentence and uncompleted gesture, rather than any more passionate expression of their love for one another, that he remembered throughout the empty months to follow.

But there was another reason, too, why he remembered it. For she wore a silk dress, and the arm against his ear produced a momentary rustling that brought back the noise in the Zakopané bedroom when the frozen branch had scraped the outside wall. And with the Sound, absent now so long, the old strange uneasiness revived acutely. For that caressing gesture, that kiss, that phrase of love that blocked its own final utterance brought back the strange rich pain.

In the act of giving them, even while he felt her touch and held her within his arms—she evaded him and went far away into another place where he could not follow her. And he knew for the first time a singular emotion that seemed like a faint, distant jealousy that stirred in him, yet a spiritual jealousy… as of some one he had never even seen.

They lingered a moment in the garden to enjoy the quiet stars and see the moon go down below the pine-wood. The tense mood of half an hour ago in the motor-car had evaporated of its own accord apparently.

A conversation that followed emphasised this elusive emotion in him, because it somehow increased the remoteness of the part of her he could not claim. She mentioned that she was taking Mrs. Haughstone with her to Egypt in November; it again exasperated him; such unselfishness he could not understand. The invitation came, moreover, upon what Tom felt was a climax of shameless behaviour. For Madame Jaretzka had helped the family with money that, to save their pride, was to be considered lent. The husband had written gushing letters of thanks and promises that—Tom had seen these letters—could hardly have deceived a schoolgirl. Yet a recent legacy, which rendered a part repayment possible, had been purposely concealed, with the result that yet more money had been 'lent' to tide them over non-existent or invented difficulties.

And now, on the top of this, Madame Jaretzka not only refused to divulge that the legacy was known to her, but even proposed an expensive two months' holiday to the woman who was tricking her.

Tom objected strongly for two reasons; he thought it foolish kindness, and he did not want her.

'You're too good to the woman, far too good,' he said. But his annoyance was only increased by the firmness of the attitude that met him. 'No, Tom; you're wrong. They'll find out in time that I know, and see themselves as they are.'

'You forgive everything to everybody,' he observed critically. 'It's too much.'

She turned round upon him. Her attitude was a rebuke, and feeling rebuked he did not like it. For though she did not quote 'until seventy times seven,' she lived it.

'When she sees herself sly and treacherous like that, she'll understand,' came the answer, 'she'll get her own forgiveness.'

'Her own forgiveness!'

'The only real kind. If I forgive, it doesn't alter her. But if she understands and feels shame and makes up her mind not to repeat—that's forgiving herself. She really changes then.'

Tom gasped inwardly. This was a level of behaviour where he found the air somewhat rarified. He saw the truth of it, but had no answer ready.

'Remorse and regret,' she went on, 'only make one ineffective in the present. It's looking backwards, instead of looking forwards.'

He felt something very big in her as she said it, holding his eyes firmly with her own. To have the love of such a woman was, indeed, a joy and wonder. It was a keen happiness to feel that he, Tom Kelverdon, had obtained it. His admiration for himself, and his deep, admiring love for her rose side by side. He did not recognise the flattery of self in this attitude. The simplicity in her baffled him.

'I could forgive you anything, Lettice!' he cried.

'Could you?' she said gently. 'If so, you really love me.'

It was not the doubt in her voice that overwhelmed him then; she never indulged in hints. It was a doubt in himself, not that he loved her, but that his love was not yet big enough, unselfish enough, sufficiently large and deep to be worthy of this exquisite soul beside him. Perhaps it was realising he could not yet possess her spirit that made him seize the precious little body that contained it. Nothing could stop him. He took her in his arms and held her till she became breathless. The passionate moment expressed real spiritual yearning. And she knew it. She did not struggle, yet neither did she respond. They stood upon different levels somehow.

'There'll be nothing left to love,' she gasped, 'if you do that often!' She released herself quietly, tidying her hair and putting her hat straight while she smiled at him. Her dark veil had caught in his tie-pin. She disentangled it, her hands touching his mouth as she did so. He kissed them gently, bending his head down with an air of repentance.

'My God, Lettice—you're precious to me!' he stammered.

But even as he said it, even while he still felt her soft cheeks against his lips, her frail unresisting figure within his arms, there came this pang of sudden pain that was so acute it frightened him. There was something impersonal in her attitude that alarmed him. What was it? He was helpless to understand it. The excitement in his blood obscured inner perception…. Such tempestuous moments were rare enough between them, and when they came he felt that she endured them rather than responded. He was aware of a touch of shame in himself. But this pain——? Even while he held her it seemed again that she escaped him because of the heights she lived on, yet partly, too, because of the innocence which had not yet eaten of the tree of knowledge…. Was that, then, the lack in her? Had she yet to learn that the spiritual dare not be divorced wholly from the physical and that the divine blending of the two in purity of heart alone brings safety?

She slipped from his encircling arms and—rose. He struggled after her. But that air he could not breathe. She was too far above him. She had to stoop to meet the passionate man in him that sought to seize and hold her. She had—the earlier phrase returned—come back to fetch him. He did not really love yet as he ought to love. He loved himself—in her; selfishly somehow, somewhere. But this thought he did not capture wholly. It cast a shadow merely and was gone.

Somewhere, too, there was jealous resentment in him. He could not feel himself indispensable to a woman who occupied a pinnacle.

His cocksureness wavered a little before the sharp attack. Pang after pang stung him shrewdly, stung his pride, his confidence, his vanity, shaking the platform on which he stood till each separate plank trembled and the sense of security grew less.

But the confusion in his heart and mind bewildered him. It was all so strange and incomprehensible; he could not understand it. He knew she was true and loyal, her purity beyond reproach, her elusiveness not calculated or intended, yet that somewhere, somehow she could do without him, and that if he left her she—almost—would have neither remorse nor regret. She would just accept it and—forgive….

And he thought suddenly with an intense bitterness that amazed him—of the husband. The thought of that 'other' who had yet to come afflicted him desperately. When he met those light-blue eyes of the Wave he would surely know them…! He felt again the desire to seek counsel and advice from another, some one of his own sex, a sympathetic and understanding soul like Tony.

The turmoil in him was beyond elucidation: thoughts and emotions of nameless kind combined to produce a fluid state of insecurity he could not explain. As usual, however, there emerged finally the solid fact which seemed now the keynote of his character; at least, he invariably fell back upon it for support against these occasional storms: 'She has singled me out; she can't really do without me; we're necessary to each other; I'm safe.' The rest he dismissed as half realised only and therefore not quite real. His position with her was unique, of course, something the world could not possibly understand, and, while resenting what he called the 'impersonal' attitude in her, he yet knew that it was precisely this impersonal attitude that justified their love. Their love, in fine, was proved spiritual thereby. They were in the 'sea' together. Invariably in the end he blamed himself.

The rising Wave, it seemed, was bringing up from day to day new, unexpected qualities from the depths within him, just as it brings up mud and gravel from the ground-bed of the shore. He felt it driving him forward with increasing speed and power. With an irresistible momentum that left him helpless, it was hurrying him along towards the moment when it would lower its crest again towards the earth—and break.

He knew now where the smothering crash would come, where he would finally meet the singular details of his boyhood's premonition face to face,—the Sound, the Whiff, the other pair of Eyes. They awaited him—in Egypt. In Egypt, at last, he would find the entire series, recognise each item. He would also discover the nature of the wave that was neither of water nor of snow....

Yet, strange to say, when he actually met the pair of light-blue eyes, he did not recognise them. He encountered the face to which they belonged, but was not warned. While fulfilling its prophecy, the premonition failed, of course, to operate.

For premonitions are a delicate matter, losing their power in the act of justifying themselves. To prevent their fulfilment were to stultify their existence. Between a spiritual warning and its material consummation there is but a friable and gossamer alliance. Had he recognised, he might possibly have prevented; whereas the deeper part of him unconsciously invited and said, Come.

And so, not recognising the arrival of the other pair of eyes, Tom, when he met them, knew himself attracted instead of repelled. Far from being warned, he knew himself drawn towards their owner by natural sympathy, as towards some one whose deep intrusion into his inner life was necessary to its fuller realisation—the tumultuous breaking of the rapidly accumulating Wave.

CHAPTER XIII

The weeks that followed seemed both brief and long to Tom. The separation he felt keenly, though as a breathing spell the interval was even welcome in a measure. Since the days at Montreux he had been living intensely, swept along by a movement he could not control: now he could pause and think a moment. He tried to get the bird's-eye view in which alone details are seen in their accurate relations and proportions. There was much that perplexed his plain, straightforward nature. But the more he thought, the more puzzled he became, and in the end he resigned himself happily to the great flow of life that was sweeping him along. He was distinctly conscious of being 'swept along.' What was going to happen would happen. He wondered, watched and waited. The idea of Egypt, meanwhile, thrilled him with a curious anticipation each time he thought of it. And he thought of it a good deal.

He received letters from Warsaw, but they told nothing of her life there: she referred vaguely to duties whose afflicting nature he half guessed now; and the rest was filled with loving solicitude for his welfare. Even through the post she mothered him absurdly. He felt his life now based upon her. Her love was indispensable to him.

The last letters—from Vienna and Trieste—were full of a tenderness most comforting, and he felt relief that she had 'finished with Warsaw,' as he put it. His own last letter was timed to catch her steamer. 'You have all my love,' he wrote, 'but you can give what you can spare to Tony, as he's in Egypt by now, and tell him I shall be out a month from to-day. Everything goes well here. I'm to have full charge of the work at Assouan. The Firm has put everything in my hands, but there won't be much to do at first, and I shall be with you at Luxor a great deal. I'm looking forward to Egypt too—immensely. I believe all sorts of wonderful things are going to happen to us there.'

He was very pleased with himself, and very pleased with her, and very pleased with everything. The wave of his life was rising still triumphantly.

He kept her Warsaw letters and reread them frequently. She wrote admirably. Mrs. Haughstone, it seemed, complained about everything, from the cabin and hotel room 'which, she declares, are never so good as my own,' to her position as an invited guest, 'which she accepts as though she favoured me by coming, thinking herself both chaperone and indispensable companion. How little some people realise that no one is ever really indispensable!' And the first letter from Egypt told him to come out quickly and 'help me keep her in her place, as only a man can do. Tony wonders why you're so long about it.' It pleased him very much, and as the time approached for leaving, his spirits rose; indeed, he reached Marseilles much in the mood of a happy, confident boy who has passed all exams, and is off upon a holiday most thoroughly deserved.

There had been time for three or four letters from Luxor, and he read them in the train as he hurried along from Geneva towards the south, leaving the snowy Jura hills behind him. 'Those are the blue mountains we watched from Montreux together in the spring,' he said to himself, looking out of the window. 'Soon, in Egypt, we shall watch the Desert and the Nile instead.' And, remembering that dream-like, happy time of their earliest acquaintance, his heart beat in delighted anticipation. He could think of nothing else but her. Those Montreux days seemed years ago instead of a brief six months. What a lot he had to tell her, how much they would have to talk about. Life, indeed, was rich and full. He was a lucky man; yet—he deserved it all. Belief and confidence in himself increased. He gazed out of the window, thinking happily as the scenery rushed by.... Then he came back to the letters and read them over yet once again; he almost knew them now by heart; he opened his bag and read the Warsaw letters too. Then, putting them all away, he lay back in his corner and tried to sleep. The express train seemed so slow, but the steamer would seem slower still.... Thoughts and memories passed idly through his brain, grew mingled and confused; his eyes were closed; he fell into a doze: he almost slept—when something rose into his drowsy mind and made him suddenly wakeful.

What was it? He didn't know. It had vanished as soon as it appeared. But the drowsy mood had passed, the desire to sleep was gone. There was impatience in him, the keen wish to be in Egypt—immediately. He cursed the slow means of travel, longed to be out there, on the spot, with her and Tony. Her last letters had been full of descriptions of the place and people, of Tony and his numerous friends, his kindness in introducing her to the most interesting among them, their picnics together on the Nile and in the Desert, visits to the famous sites of tomb and temple, in particular of an all-night bivouac somewhere and the sunrise over the Theban hills.... Tom, as he read it all, felt this keen impatience to be sharing it with them; he was out of it; oh, how he would enjoy it all when he got there! The words 'Theban hills' called up a vivid and stimulating picture in particular.

But it was not this that chased the drowsy mood and made him wakeful. It was the letters themselves, something he had not noticed hitherto, something that had escaped him as he first read them one by one. Indefinable, it hid between the lines. Only on reading the series as a whole was it noticeable at all. He wondered. He asked himself vague questions.

Opening his bag again, he went through the letters in the order of their arrival; then put them back inside the elastic ring with a sensation of relief and a happy sigh. He had discovered the faint, elusive impression that had made him wakeful, but in discovering it had satisfied himself that it was imagination—caused by the increasing impatience of his impetuous heart. For it had seemed to him that he was aware of a change, though so slight as to be scarcely perceptible, and certainly not traceable to actual words or sentences. It struck him that the Warsaw letters felt the separation more keenly, more poignantly, than the Egyptian letters. This seemed due rather to omissions in the latter than to anything else that he could name, for while the Warsaw letters spoke frequently of the separation, of her longing to see him close, those from Luxor omitted all such phrases. There were pleas in plenty for his health, his comfort, his welfare and success—the Mother found full scope—but no direct expression of her need for him. This, briefly, was the notion he had caught faintly from 'between the lines.'

But, having run it to earth, he easily explained it too. At Warsaw she was unhappy; whereas now, in Egypt, their reunion was almost within sight: she felt happier, too, her unpleasant duties over. It was all natural enough. 'What a sentimental donkey a man is when he's in love!' he exclaimed with a self-indulgent smile of pleased forgiveness; 'but the fact is—when she's not by me to explain—I could imagine anything!' And he fell at length into the doze his excited fancy had postponed.

After leaving Marseilles his impatience grew with the slowness of the steamer. The voyage of four days seemed interminable. The sea and sky took on a deeper blue, the air turned softer, the sweetness of the south became more marked. His exhilaration increased with every hour, the desire to reach his destination increasing with it. There was an intensity about his feelings he could not entirely account for. The longing to see Egypt merged with the longing to see Lettice. But the two were separate. The latter was impatient happiness, while the former struck a slower note—respect and wonder that contained a hint of awe.

Somewhere in this anticipatory excitement, too, hid drama. And his first glimpse of the marvellous old land did prove dramatic in a sense. For when a passenger drew his attention to the white Alexandrian harbour floating on the shining blue, he caught his breath a moment and his heart gave a sudden unexpected leap. He saw the low-lying coast, a palm, a mosque, a minaret; he saw the sandy lip of—Africa.

That shimmering line of blue and gold was Egypt.... He had known it would look exactly thus, as he now saw it. The same instant his heart contracted a little.... He leaned motionless upon the rail and watched the coast-line coming nearer, ever nearer. It rose out of the burning haze of blue and gold that hung motionless between the water and the air. Bathed in the drenching sunlight, the fringe of the great thirsty Desert seemed to drink the sea....

His entry was accompanied by mingled emotions and sensations. That Lettice stood waiting for him somewhere behind the blaze of light contributed much; yet the thrill owned a more complex origin, it seemed. To any one not entirely callous to the stab of strange romance and stranger beauty, the first sight of Egypt must always be an event, and Tom, by no means thus insensitive, felt it vividly. He was aware of something not wholly unfamiliar. The invitation was so strong, it seemed to entice as with an attraction that was almost summons. As the ship drew nearer, and thoughts of landing filled his mind, he felt no opposition, no resistance, no difficulty, as with other countries. There was no hint of friction anywhere. He seemed instantly at home. Egypt not merely enticed—she pulled him in.

'Here I am at last!' whispered a voice, as he watched the noisy throng of Arabs, Nubians, Soudanese upon the crowded wharf. He delighted in the colour, the gleaming eyes, bronze skins, the white caftans with their red and yellow sashes. The phantasmal amber light that filled the huge, still heavens lit something similar in his mind and thoughts. Only the train, with its luxurious restaurant car, its shutters to keep out the dust and heat, appeared incongruous. He lost the power to think this or that. He could only feel, and feel intensely. His feet touched Egypt, and a deep glow of inner happiness possessed him. He was not disappointed anywhere, though as yet he had seen nothing but a steamer quay. Then he sent a telegram to Lettice: 'Arrived safely. Reach Luxor eight o'clock tomorrow morning.'; and, having slid through the Delta country with the flaming sunset, he had his first glimpse of the lordly Pyramids as the train drew into Cairo. Dim and immense he saw them across the swift-falling dusk, shadowy as forgotten centuries that cannot die. Though too distant to feel their menace, he yet knew them towering over him, mysterious, colossal, unintelligible, the sentinels of a gateway he had passed.

Such was the first touch of Egypt on his soul. It was as big and magical as he had known it would be. The magnificence and the glamour both were there. Europe already lay forgotten far behind him, non-existent. Some one tapped him on the shoulder, whispered a password, he was—in....

He dined in Cairo and took the night train on to Luxor, the white, luxurious wagon lit again striking an incongruous note. For he had stepped from a platform into space, a space that floated suns and constellations. About him was that sense of the illimitable which broods everywhere in Egypt, in sand and sky, in sun and stars; it absorbed him easily, small human speck in a toy train with electric lights and modern comforts! An emotion difficult to seize gripped his heart, as he slid deeper and deeper into the land towards Lettice…. For Lettice also was involved in this. With happiness, yet somehow, too, with tears, he thought of her waiting for him now, expecting him, perhaps reading his telegram for the twentieth time. Through a mist of blue and gold she seemed to beckon to him across the shimmer of the endless yellow sands. He saw the little finger he had kissed. The dear face smiled. But there was a change upon it somewhere, though a change too subtle to be precisely named. The eyelids were half closed, and in the smile was power; the beckoning finger conveyed a gesture that was new—command. It seemed to point; it had a motion downwards; about her aspect was some flavour of authority almost royal, borrowed, doubtless, from the regal gold and purple of the sky's magnificence.

Oddly, again, his heart contracted as this changed aspect of her, due to heightened imagination, rose before the inner eye. A sensation of uncertainty and question slipped in with it, though whence he knew not. A hint of insecurity assailed his soul—almost a sense of inferiority in himself. It even flashed across him that he was under orders. It was inexplicable…. A restlessness in his blood prevented sleep…. He drew the blind up and looked out.

There was no moon. The night was drowned in stars. The train rushed south towards Thebes along the green thread of the Nile; the Lybian desert keeping pace with it, immense and desolate, death gnawing eternally at the narrow strip of life…. And again he knew the feeling that he had stepped from a platform into space. Egypt lay spread below him. He fell towards it, plunging, and as he fell, looked down—upon something vaguely familiar and half known…. An underlying sadness, inexplicable but significant, crept in upon his thoughts.

They rushed past Bedrashein, a straggling Arab village where once great Memphis owned eighteen miles of frontage on the stately river; he saw the low mud huts, the groves of date-palms that now marked the vanished splendour. They slid by in their hundreds, the spectral desert gleaming like snow between the openings. The huge pyramids of Sakkhâra loomed against the faint western afterglow. He saw the shaft of strange green light they call zodiacal.

And the sadness in him deepened inexplicably—that strange Egyptian sadness which ever underlies the brilliance…. The watchful stars looked down with sixty listening centuries between them and a forgotten glory that dreamed now among a thousand sandy tombs. For the silent landscape flying past him like a dream woke emotions both sweet and painful that he could not understand—sweet to poignancy, exquisitely painful.

Perhaps it was natural enough, natural, too, that he should transfer these in some dim measure to the woman now waiting for him among the ruins of many-gated Thebes. The ancient city, dreaming still beside the storied river, assumed an appearance half fabulous in his thoughts. Egypt had wakened imagination in his soul. The change he fancied in Lettice was due, doubtless, to the transforming magic that mingled an actual present with a haunted past. Possibly this was some portion of the truth.... And yet, while the mood possessed him, some joy, some inner sheath, as it were, of anticipated happiness slipped off him into the encroaching yellow sand—as though he surrendered, not so much the actual happiness, as his right to it. A second's helplessness crept over him; another Self that was inferior peeped up and sighed and whispered.... He was aware of hidden touches that stabbed him into uneasiness, disquiet, almost pain.... Some outer tissue was stripped from his normal being, leaving him naked to the tang of extremely delicate shafts, buried so long that interpretation failed him.

The curious sensation, luckily, did not last; but this hint of a familiarity that seemed both sweet and dangerous, made it astonishingly convincing at the time. Some aspect of vanity, of confidence in himself distinctly weakened....

It passed with the spectral palm trees as the train sped farther south. He finally dismissed it as the result of fatigue, excitement and anticipation too prolonged.... Yes, he dismissed it. At any rate it passed. It sank out of sight and was forgotten. It had become, perhaps, an integral portion of his being. Possibly, it had always been so, and had been merely waiting to emerge....

But such intangible and elusive emotions were so new to him that he could not pretend to deal with them. There is a stimulus as of ether about the Egyptian climate that gets into the mind, it is said, and stirs unwonted dreams and fantasies. The climate becomes mental. His stolid temperament was, perhaps, pricked thus half unintelligibly. He could not understand it. He drew the blind down. But before turning out the light, he read over once again the note of welcome Lettice had sent to meet him at the steamer. It was brief, but infinitely precious. The thought of her love sponged all lesser feelings completely from his mind, and he fell asleep thinking only of their approaching meeting, and of his marvellous deep joy.

CHAPTER XIV

On reaching Luxor at eight o'clock in the morning, to his keen delight an Arab servant met him with an unexpected invitation. He had meant to go first to his hotel, but Lettice willed otherwise, everything thought out beforehand in her loving way. He drove accordingly to her house on the outskirts of the town towards Karnak, changed and bathed in a room where he recognised with supreme joy a hundred familiar touches that seemed transplanted from the Brown Flat at home—and found her at nine o'clock waiting for him on the verandah. Breakfast was laid in the shady garden just beyond.

It was ideal as a dream. She stood there dressed in white, wearing a big sun-hat with little roses, sparkling, radiant, a graceful fairy figure from the heart of spring. 'Here's the inevitable fly-whisk, Tom,' was the first thing she said, and as naturally as though they had parted a few hours before, 'it's to keep the flies away, and to keep you at your distance too!' And his first remark, escaping him impulsively in place of a hundred other things he had meant to say, was, 'You look different; you've changed. Lettice, you're far more lovely than I knew. I've never seen you look like that before!' He felt his entire being go out to her in a consuming flame. 'You look perfectly divine.' Sheer admiration took his breath away. 'I believe you're Isis herself,' he laughed in his delight, 'come back into her own!'

'Then you must be Osiris, Tom!' her happy voice responded, 'new risen from his sandy tomb!'

There was no time for private conversation, for Mrs. Haughstone appeared just then and enquired politely after his health and journey. 'The flies are awful,' she mentioned, 'but Lettice always insists on having breakfast out of doors. I hope you'll be able to stand it.' And she continued to flutter her horse-hair whisk as though she would have liked to sweep Egypt itself from the face of the map. 'No wonder the Israelites were glad to leave. There's sand in everything you eat and flies on everything you see.' Yet she said it with what passed in her case for good nature; she, too, was evidently enjoying herself in Egypt.

Tom said that flies and sand would not trouble him with such gorgeous sunlight to compensate, and that anyhow they were better than soot and fogs in London.

'You'll be tired of the sun before a week is over,' she replied, 'and long to see a cloud or feel a drop of rain.' She followed his eyes which seemed unable to leave the face and figure of his hostess. 'But it all agrees wonderfully with my cousin. Don't you find her looking well? She's quite changed into another person, I think,' the tone suggesting that it was not altogether a change that she herself approved of. 'We're all different here, a little. Even Mr. Winslowe's improved enormously. He's steadier and wiser than he used to be.' And Tom, laughing, said he hoped he would improve, too, himself.

The comforting hot coffee, the delicious rolls, the cool iced fruit, and, above all, Lettice beside him at last in the pleasant shade, gave Tom such high spirits that the woman's disagreeable personality produced no effect. Through the gate in the stone wall at the end of the garden, beneath masses of drooping bougainvillæa, the Nile dreamed past in a sheet of golden haze; the Theban hills, dipped in the crystal azure of the sky, rose stern and desolate upon the horizon; the air, at this early hour, was fresh and keen. He felt himself in some enchanted garden of the ancient world with a radiant goddess for companion.... There was a sound of singing from the river below—the song of the Nile boatman that has not changed these thousand years; a quaint piping melody floated in from the street outside; from the farther shore came the dull beating of a native tom-tom; and the still, burning atmosphere held the mystery of wonder in suspension. Her beauty, at last, had found its perfect setting.

'I never saw your eyes so wonderful—so soft and brilliant,' he whispered as soon as they were alone. 'You're very happy.' He paused, looking at her. 'That's me, isn't it? Lettice, say it is at once.' He was very playful in his joy; but he longed eagerly to hear her admit that his coming meant as much to her as it meant to him.

'I suppose it must be,' she replied, 'but it's the climate too. This keen dry air and the sunshine bring all one's power out. There's something magical in it. You forget the years and feel young—against the background of this old land a lifetime seems like an afternoon, merely. And the nights—oh, Tom, the stars are too, too marvellous.' She spoke with a kind of exuberance that seemed new in her.

'They must be,' he rejoined, as he gazed exultantly, 'for they're all in you, sun, air, and stars. You're a perfect revelation to me of what a woman——'

'Am I?' she interrupted, fluttering her whisk between her chair and his. 'But now, dear Tom, my headstrong boy, tell me how you are and all about yourself, your plans, and everything else in the world besides.' He told her what he could, answered all her questions, declared he and she were going to have the time of their lives, and behaved generally, as she told him, like a boy out of school. He admitted it. 'But I'm hungry, Lettice, awfully hungry.' He kept reminding her that he had been starving for two long months; surely she was starving too. He longed to hear her confess it with a sigh of happy relief. 'My arms and lips are hungry,' he went on incorrigibly, 'but I'm tired, too, from travelling. I feel like putting my head on your breast and going sound asleep.' 'My boy,' she said tenderly, 'you shall.' She responded instantly to that. 'You always were a baby and I'm here to take care of you.' He seized her hand and kissed it before she could draw it away. 'You must be careful, Tom. Everything has eyes in Egypt; the Arabs move like ghosts.' She glanced towards the windows. 'And the gossip is unbelievable.' She was quiet again now, and very gentle; it struck him how calm and sweet she was towards him, yet that there was a delightful happy excitement underneath that she only just controlled. He was aware of something wild in her just out of sight—a kind of mental effervescence, almost intoxication she deliberately suppressed.

'And so are you—unbelievable,' he exclaimed impetuously; 'unbelievably beautiful. This is your country with a vengeance, Lettice. You're like an Egyptian queen—a princess of the sun!'

He gazed critically at her till she lowered her eyes. He realised that, actually, they were not visible from the house and that the garden trees were thick about them; but he also received a faint impression that she did not want, did not intend, to allow quite the same intimacy as before. It just flashed across him with a hint of disappointment, then was gone. His boyish admiration, perhaps, annoyed her. He had felt for a second that her excuse of the windows and the gossip was not the entire truth. The merest shadow of a thought it was. He noticed her eyes fixed intently upon him. The same minute, then, she rose quietly and rustled over to his chair, kissed him on the cheek quickly, and sat down again. 'There!' she said playfully as though she had guessed his thoughts, 'I've done the awful thing; now you'll be reasonable, perhaps!' And whether or not she had divined his mood, she instantly dispelled it—for the moment....

They talked about a hundred things, moving their chairs as the blazing sunshine found them out, till finally they sat with cushions on the steps of stone that led down to the river beneath the flaming bougainvillæa. He felt the strange touch of Egypt all about them, that touch of eternity that floats in the very air, a hint of something deathless and sublime that whispers in the sunshine. Already he was aware of the long fading stretch of years behind. He thought of Egypt as two vast hands that held him, one of tawny gold and one of turquoise blue—the desert and the sky. In the hollow of those great hands, he lay with Lettice—two tiny atoms of sand....

He watched her every movement, every gesture, noted the slightest inflection of her voice, was aware that five years at least had dropped from her, that her complexion had grown softer, a shade darker, too, from the sun; but, above all, that there was a new expression, a new light certainly, soft and brilliant, in her eyes. It seemed, briefly put, that she had blossomed somehow into a fuller expression of herself. An overflowing vitality, masked behind her calmness, betrayed itself in every word and glance and gesture. There was an exuberance he called joy, but it was, somehow, a new, an unexpected joy.

She was, of course, aware of his untiring scrutiny; and presently, in a lull, keeping her eyes on the river below them, she spoke of it. 'You find me a little changed, Tom, don't you? I warned you that Egypt had a certain effect on me. It enflames the heart and———'

'But a very wonderful effect,' he broke in with admiration. 'You're different in a way—yes—but you haven't changed—not towards me, I mean.' He wanted to say a great deal more, but could not find the words; he divined that something had happened to her, in Warsaw probably, and he longed to question her about the 'other' who was her husband, but he could not, of course, allow himself to do so. An intuitive feeling came to him that the claim upon her of this other was more remote than formerly. His dread had certainly lessened. The claims upon her of this 'other' seemed no longer—dangerous.... He wondered.... There was a certain confusion in his mind.

'You got my letter at Alexandria?' she interrupted his reflections. He thanked her with enthusiasm, trying to remember what it said—but without success. It struck him suddenly that there was very little in it after all, and he mentioned this with a reproachful smile. 'That's my restraint,' she replied. 'You always liked restraint. Besides, I wasn't sure it would reach you.' She laughed and blew a kiss towards him. She made a curious gesture he had never seen her make before. It seemed unlike her. More and more he registered a difference in her, as if side by side with the increase of spontaneous vitality there ran another mood, another aspect, almost another point of view. It was not towards him, yet it affected him. There seemed a certain new lightness, even irresponsibility in her; she was more worldly, more human, not more ordinary by any means, but less 'impersonal.' He remembered her singular words: 'It enflames the heart.' He wondered—a little uneasily. There seemed a new touch of wonder about her that made him aware of something commonplace, almost inferior, in himself....

At the same time he felt another thing—a breath of coldness touched him somewhere, though he could not trace its origin to anything she did or said. Was it perhaps in what she left unsaid, undone? He longed to hear her confess how she had missed him, how thrilled she was that he had come: but she did not say these passionately desired things, and when he teased her about it, she showed a slight impatience almost: 'Tom, you know I never talk like that. Anything sentimental I abhor. But I live it.

Can't you see?' His ungenerous fancies vanished then at once; at a word, a smile, a glance of the expressive eyes, he instantly forgot all else.

'But I am different in Egypt,' she warned him playfully again, half closing her eyelids as she said it. 'I wonder if you'll like me—quite as well.'

'More,' he replied ardently, 'a thousand times more. I feel it already. There's mischief in you,' he went on watching the half-closed eyes, 'a touch of magic too, but very human magic. I love it.' And then he whispered, 'I think you're more within my reach.'

'Am I?' She looked bewitching, a being of light and air.

'Everybody will fall in love with you at sight.' He laughed happily, aware of an enchantment that fascinated him more and more, but when he suddenly went over to her chair, she stopped him with decision. 'Don't, Tom, please don't. Tony'll be here any minute now. It would be unpleasant if he saw you behaving wildly like this! He wouldn't understand.'

He drew back. 'Oh, Tony's coming—then I must be careful!' He laughed, but he was disappointed and he showed it: it was their first day together, and eager though he was to see his cousin, he felt it might well have been postponed a little. He said so.

'One must be natural, Tom,' she told him in reply; 'it's always the best way. This isn't London or Montreux, you see, and——'

'Lettice, I understand,' he interrupted, a trifle ashamed of himself. 'You're quite right.' He tried to look pleased and satisfied, but the truth was he felt suddenly—stupid. 'And we've got lots of time—three months or more ahead of us, haven't we?' She gave him an expressive, tender look with which he had to be contented for the moment.

'And by the by, how is old Tony, and who is his latest?' he enquired carelessly.

'Very excited at your coming, Tom. You'll think him improved, I hope. I believe I'm his latest,' she added, tilting her chin with a delicious pretence at mischief. And the gesture again surprised him. It was new. He thought it foreign to her. There seemed a flavour of impatience, of audacity, almost of challenge in it.

'Finding himself at last. That's good. Then you've been fishing to some purpose.'

'Fishing?'

'Rescuing floating faces.'

She pouted at him. 'I'm not a saint, Tom. You know I never was. Saints are very inspiring to read about, but you couldn't live with one— or love one. Could you, now?'

He gave an inward start she did not notice. The same instant he was aware that it was her happy excitement that made her talk in this exaggerated way. That was why it sounded so unnatural. He forgot it instantly.

They laughed and chatted as happily as two children—Tom felt a boy again—until Mrs. Haughstone appeared, marching down the river bank with an enormous white umbrella over her head, and the talk became general. Tom said he would go to his hotel and return for lunch; he wanted to telephone to Assouan. He asked where Tony was staying. 'But he knew I was at the Winter Palace,' he exclaimed when she mentioned the Savoy. 'He found some people there he wanted to avoid,' she explained, 'so moved down to the Savoy.'

Tom said he would do the same; it was much nearer to her house, for one thing: 'You'll keep him for lunch, won't you?' he said as he went off. 'I'll try,' she promised, 'but he's so busy with his numerous friends as usual that I can't be sure of him. He has more engagements here than in London,'—whereupon Mrs. Haughstone added, 'Oh, he'll stay, Mr. Kelverdon. I'm sure he'll stay. We lunch at one o'clock, remember.'

And in his room at the hotel Tom found a dozen signs of tenderness and care that increased his happiness; there were touches everywhere of her loving thought for his comfort and well-being—flowers, his favourite soap, some cigarettes, one of her own deck-chairs, books, and even a big box of crystallised dates as though he was a baby or a little boy. It all touched him deeply; no other woman in the world could possibly have thought out such dear reminders, much less have carried them into effect. There was even a writing-pad and a penholder with the special nib he liked. He laughed. But her care for him in such trivial things was exquisite because it showed she claimed the right to do them.

His heart brimmed over as he saw them. It was impossible to give up any room, even a hotel room, into which she had put her sweet and mothering personality. He could do without Tony's presence and companionship, rather than resign a room she had thus prepared for him. He engaged it permanently therefore. Then, telephoning to Assouan, he decided to take the night train and see what had to be done there. It all sounded most satisfactory; he foresaw much free time ahead of him; occasional trips to the work would meet the case at present....

Happier than ever, he returned to a lunch in the open air with her and Tony, and it was the gayest, merriest meal he had ever known. Mrs. Haughstone retired to sleep through the hotter hours of the afternoon, leaving the trio to amuse themselves in freedom. And though they never left the shady garden by the Nile, they amused themselves so well that tea was over and it was time for Tom to get ready for his train before he realised it. Tony and Madame Jaretzka drove him to his hotel, and afterwards to the station, sitting in the compartment with him until the train was actually moving. He watched them standing on the platform together, waving their hands. He waved his own. 'I'll be back to-morrow or the next day,' he cried. Emotions and sensations were somewhat tangled in him, but happiness certainly was uppermost.

'Don't forget,' he heard Tony shout.... And her eyes were on his own until the trees on the platform hid her from his sight behind their long deep shadows.

CHAPTER XV

The first excitement of arrival over, he drew breath, as it were, and looked about him. Egypt delighted and amazed him, surpassing his expectations. Its effect upon him was instantaneous and profound. The decisive note sounded at Alexandria continued in his ears. Egypt drew him in with golden, powerful arms. In every detail it was strange, yet with the strangeness of a predetermined welcome. It was not strange to him. The thrill of welcome made him feel at home. He had come back....

Here, at Assouan, he was aware of Africa, mystic, half-monstrous continent, lying with its heat and wonder just beyond the horizon. He saw the Southern Cross, pitched low above the sandy rim.... Yet Africa had no call for him. It left him without a thrill, an uninviting, undesirable land. It was Egypt that made the intimate and personal appeal, as of a deeply loved and half-familiar place. It seemed to gather him in against its mighty heart. He lay in some niche of comforting warm sand against the ancient mass that claimed him, tucked in by the wonder and the mystery, protected, even mothered. It was an oddly stimulated imagination that supplied the picture—and made him smile. He snuggled down deeper and deeper into this figurative warm bed of sand the ages had pre-ordained. He felt secure and sheltered—as though the wonder and the mystery veiled something that menaced joy in him, something that concealed a notion of attack. Almost there seemed a whisper in the wind, a watchful and unclosing eye behind the dazzling sunshine: 'Surrender yourself to me, and I will care for you. I will protect you against... yourself.... Beware!'

This peculiar excitement in his blood was somehow precisely what he had expected; the wonder and the thrill were natural and right. He had known that Egypt would mesmerise his soul exactly in this way. He had, it seemed, anticipated both the exhilaration and the terror. He thought much about it all, and each time Egypt looked him in the face, he saw Lettice too. They were inseparably connected, as it were. He saw her brilliant eyes peering through the great tawny visage. Together they bade him pause and listen.... The wind brought up its faint, elusive whisper: 'Wait.... We have not done with you.... Wait and listen! Watch...!'

Before his mind's eye the mighty land lay like a map, a blazing garden of intenser life that the desolation ill concealed. Europe seemed infinitely remote, the life he had been accustomed to unreal, of tepid interest, while the intimate appeal that Egypt made grew more insistent every hour of the day. It was Luxor, however, that called him peremptorily—Luxor where all that was dearest to him in life now awaited his return. He yearned for Luxor; Thebes drew him like a living magnet. Lettice was in Thebes, and Thebes also seemed the heart of ancient Egypt, its centre and its climax. 'Come back to us,' whispered the sweet desert wind; 'we are waiting....' In Thebes seemed the focus of the strange Egyptian spell.

At all hours of the day and night, here in Assouan, it caught him, asking forever the great unanswerable questions. In the pauses of his strenuous work, in the watches of the night, when he heard the little owls and the weird barking of the prowling jackals; in the noontide heat, and in the cold glimmer of the quiet stars, he was never unconscious of its haunting presence, he was never beyond its influence. He was never quite alone....

What did it mean? And why did this hint of danger, of pain, of loneliness lurk behind the exhilaration and the peace? Wherein lay the essence of the enchantment this singular Egyptian glamour laid upon his very soul?

In his laborious way, Tom worked at the disentanglement, but without much success. One curious thought, however, persisted with a strange enough significance. It rose, in a sense, unbidden. It was not his brain that discovered it. It just 'came.'

For he was thinking of other wonderful countries he had known. He remembered Japan and India, both surpassing Egypt in colour, sunshine, gorgeous pageantry, and certainly equalling it in historical association and the rest. Yet, for him, these old lands had no spell, no glamour comparable to what he now experienced. The mind contains them, understands them easily. They are continuous with their past. The traveller drops in and sees them as they always have been. They are still, so to speak, going on comfortably as before. There is no shock of dislocation. They have not died.

Whereas Egypt has left the world; Egypt is dead; there is no link with present things. Both heart and mind are aware of this deep vacuum they vainly strive to fill. That ancient civilisation, both marvellous and somewhere monstrous, breaking with beauty, burning with aspiration, mysterious and vital—all has vanished as completely as though it had not been. The prodigious ruins hint, but cannot utter. No reconstruction from tomb or temple can recall a great dream the world has lost. It is forgotten, swept away, there is no clue. Egypt has left the world....

Yet, as he thought about it in his uninspired way, it seemed that some part of him still beat in sympathy with the pulse of the forgotten dream. Egypt indeed was dead, yet sometimes—she came back.... She came to revisit her soft stars and moon, her great temples and her mighty tombs. She stole back into the sunshine and the sand; her broken, ruined heart at Thebes received her. He saw her as a spirit, a persistent, living presence, a stupendous Ghost.... And the idea, having offered itself, remained.

Both he and Lettice somehow were associated with it, and with this elusive notion of return. They, too, were entangled in the glamour and the spell. They, too, had stolen back as from some immemorial lost dream to revisit the scenes of an intenser yet forgotten life. And Thebes was its centre; the secretive and forbidding Theban Hills, with their desolate myriad sepulchres, its focus and its climax....

* * * *

Assouan detained him only a couple of days. He had capable lieutenants; there was delay, moreover, in the arrival of certain material; he could always be summoned quickly by telephone. He sent home his report and took the express train back to Luxor and to—her.

He had been too occupied, too tired at night, to do more than write a fond, short letter, then go to sleep; the heat was considerable; he realised that he was in Africa; the scenery fascinated him, the enormous tawny desert, the cataracts of golden yellow sand, the magical old river. The wonder of Philae, with its Osirian shrine and island sanctuary, caught him as it has caught most other humans. After the sheer bulk of the pyramids and temples, Philae bursts into the heart with almost lyrical sweetness. But his heart was fast in Thebes, and not all the enchantment of this desert paradise could seduce him. Moreover, one detail he disliked: the ubiquitous earthenware tom-tom that sounded day and night... he heard its sullen beating in his dreams.

Yet of one thing he was ever chiefly conscious—that he was impatient to be with Lettice, that his heart hungered without ceasing, that she meant more to him than ever. Her new beauty astonished him, there was a subtle charm in her presence he had not felt in London, her fresh spontaneous gaiety filled him with keen delight. And all this was his. His arrival gave her such joy that she could not even speak of it; yet he was the cause of it. It made him feel almost shy.

He received one characteristic letter from her. 'Come back as quickly as you can,' she wrote. 'Tony has gone down the river after his birds, and I feel lonely. Telegraph, and come to dinner or breakfast according to your train. I'll meet you if possible. You must come here for all your meals, as I'm sure the hotel food is poor and the drinking water unsafe. This is open house, remember, for you both.' And there was a delicious P.S. 'Mind you only drink filtered water, and avoid the hotel salads because the water hasn't been boiled.' He kissed the letter. He laughed. Her tender thought for him almost brought the tears into his eyes. It was the tenderness of his own mother who was dead.

He reached Luxor in the evening, and to his delight she was on the platform; long before the train stopped he recognised her figure, the wide sun-hat with the little roses, the white serge skirt and jacket of knitted yellow silk to keep the evening chill away. They drove straight to her house; the sun was down behind the rocky hills and the Nile lay in a dream of burnished gold; the little owls were calling; there was singing among the native boatmen on the water; they saw the fields of brilliant green with the sands beyond, and the keen air from the desert wafted down the street of what once was great hundred-gated Thebes. A strangely delicate perfume hung about the ancient city. Tom turned to look at the woman beside him in the narrow-seated carriage, and felt as if he were driving through a dream.

'I can stay a week or ten days at least,' he said at last. 'Is old Tony back?'

Yes, he had just arrived and telephoned to ask if he might come to dinner. 'And look, Tom, you can just see the heads of the Colossi rising out of the haze,'—she pointed quickly—'I thought we would go and show them you to-morrow. We might all take our tea and eat it in the clover. You've seen nothing of Egypt yet.' She spoke rapidly, eagerly, full of her little plan.

'All?' he repeated doubtfully.

'Yes, wouldn't you like it?'

'Oh, rather,' he said, wondering why he did not say another thing that rose for a moment in his mind.

'You must see everything,' she went on spontaneously, 'and a dragoman's a bore. Tony's a far better guide. He knows old Egypt as well as he knows his old birds.' She laughed. 'It's too ridiculous—his enthusiasm; he's been dying to explain it all to you as he did to me, and he does it exactly like a museum guide who is a scholar and a poet too. And he is a poet, you know. I'd never noticed it before.'

'Splendid,' said Tom. He was thinking several things at once, among them that the perfumed air reminded him of something he could not quite recall. It seemed far away and yet familiar. 'I'm a rare listener too,' he added.

'The King's Valley you really must do alone together,' she went on; 'I can't face it a second time—the heat, the gloom of it—it oppressed and frightened me a little. Those terrible grim hills—they're full of death, those Theban hills.'

'Tony took you?' he asked.

She nodded. 'We did the whole thing,' she added, 'every single Tomb. I was exhausted. I think we all were—except Tony.' The eager look in her face had gone. Her voice betrayed a certain effort. A darkness floated over it, like the shadow of a passing cloud.

'All of you!' he exclaimed, as though it were important. 'No bird-man ever feels tired.' He seemed to think a moment. There was a tiny pause. The carriage was close to the house now, driving up with a flourish, and Tony and Mrs. Haughstone, an incongruous couple, were visible standing against the luminous orange sky beside the river. Tom pointed to them with a chuckle. 'All right,' he exclaimed, with a gesture as though he came to a decision suddenly, 'it shall be the Colossi to-morrow. There are two of them, aren't there—only two?'

'Two, yes, the Twin Colossi they call them,' she replied, joining in his chuckle at the silhouetted figures in the sunset.

'Two,' he repeated with emphasis, 'not three.' But either she did not notice or else she did not hear. She was leaning forward waving her hand to her other guests upon the bank.

* * * *

There followed then the happiest week that Tom had ever known, for there was no incident to mar it, nor a single word or act that cast the slightest shadow. His dread of the 'other' who was to come apparently had left him, the faint uneasiness he had felt so often seemed gone. He even forgot to think about it. Lettice he had never seen so gay, so full of enterprise, so radiant. She sparkled as though she had recovered her girlhood suddenly. With Tony in particular she had incessant battles, and Tom listened to their conversations with amusement, for on no single subject were they able to agree, yet neither seemed to get the best of it. Tom felt unable to keep pace with their more nimble minds....

Tony was certainly improved in many ways, more serious than he had showed himself before, and extraordinarily full of entertaining knowledge into the bargain. Birds and the lore of ancient Egypt, it appeared, were merely two of his pet hobbies; and he talked in such amusing fashion that he kept Tom in roars of laughter, while stimulating Madame Jaretzka to vehement contradictions. They were much alone, and profited by it. The numerous engagements Lettice had mentioned gave no sign. Tony certainly was a brilliant companion as well as an instructive cicerone. There was more in him than Tom had divined before. His clever humour was a great asset in the longer expeditions. 'Tony, I'm tired and hot; please come and talk to me: I want refreshing,' was never addressed to Tom, for instance, whose good nature could not take the place of wit. Each of the three, as it were, supplied what the other lacked; it was not surprising they got on well together. Tom, however, though always happy provided Lettice was of the party, envied his cousin's fluid temperament and facile gifts—even in the smallest things. Tony, for instance, would mimic Mrs. Haughstone's attitude of having done her hostess a kindness in coming out to Egypt: 'I couldn't do it again, dear Lettice, even for you'—the way Tony said and acted it had a touch of inspiration.

Mrs. Haughstone herself, meanwhile, within the limits of her angular personality, Tom found also considerably improved. Egypt had changed her too. He forgave her much because she was afraid of the sun, so left them often alone. She showed unselfishness, too, even kindness, on more than one occasion. Tom was aware of a nicer side in her; in spite of her jealousy and criticism, she was genuinely careful of her hostess's reputation amid the scandal-loving atmosphere of Egyptian hotel life. It amused him to see how she arrogated to herself the place of chaperone, yet Tom saw true solicitude in it, the attitude of a woman who knew the world towards one who was too trustful. He figured her always holding up a warning finger, and Lettice always laughingly disregarding her advice.

Her warnings to Lettice to be more circumspect were, at any rate, by no means always wrong. Though not particularly observant as a rule, he caught more than once the tail-end of conversations between them in which advice, evidently, had been proffered and laughed aside. But, since it did not concern him, he paid little attention, merely aware that there existed this difference of view. One such occasion, however, Tom had good cause to remember, because it gave him a piece of knowledge he had long desired to possess, yet had never felt within his rights to ask for. It merely gave details, however, of something he already knew.

He entered the room, coming straight from a morning's work at his own hotel, and found them engaged hammer and tongs upon some dispute regarding 'conduct.' Tony, who had been rowing Madame Jaretzka down the river, had made his escape. Madame Jaretzka effected hers as Tom came in, throwing him a look of comical relief across her shoulder. He was alone with the Irish cousin. 'After all, she is a married woman,' remarked Mrs. Haughstone, still somewhat indignant from the little battle.

She addressed the words to him as he was the only person within earshot. It seemed natural enough, he thought.

'Yes,' said Tom politely. 'I suppose she is.'

And it was then, quite unexpectedly, that the woman spoke to him as though he knew as much as she did. He ought, perhaps, to have stopped her, but the temptation was too great. He learned the facts concerning Warsaw and the—husband. That the Prince had ill-treated her consistently during the first five years of their married life could certainly not justify her freedom, but that he had lost his reason incurably, no longer even recognised her, that her presence was discouraged by the doctors since it increased the violence of his attacks, and that his malady was hopeless and could end only in his death—all this, while adding to the wonder of her faithful pilgrimages, did assuredly at the same time set her free.... The effect upon his mind may be imagined; it deepened his love, increased his admiration, for it explained the suffering in the face she had turned to sweetness, while also justifying her conduct towards himself. With a single blow, moreover, it killed the dread Tom had been haunted by so long—that this was that 'other' who must one day take her from him, obedient to a bigger claim.

This knowledge, as though surreptitiously obtained, Tom locked within his breast until the day when she herself should choose to share it with him.

He remembered another little conversation too when, similarly, he disturbed them in discussion: this time it was Mrs. Haughstone who was called away.

'Behaving badly, Lettice, is she? Scolding you again?'

'Not at all. Only she sees the bad in every one and I see the good. She disapproves of Tony rather.'

'Then she will be less often deceived than you,' he replied laughingly. The reference to Tony had escaped him; his slow mind was on the general proposition.

'Perhaps. But you can only make people better by believing that they are better,' she went on with conviction—when Mrs. Haughstone joined them and took up her parable again:

'My cousin behaves like a child,' she said with amusing severity. 'She doesn't understand the world. But the world is hard upon grown-ups who behave like children. Lettice thinks everybody good. Her innocence gets her misjudged. And it's a pity.'

'I'll keep an eye on her,' Tom said solemnly, 'and we'll begin this very afternoon.'

'Do, Mr. Kelverdon, I'm glad to hear it.' And as she said it, he noticed another expression on her face as she glanced down the drive where Tony, dressed in grey flannels and singing to himself, was seen sauntering towards them. She wore an enigmatic smile by no means pleasant. It gave him a moment's twinge. He turned from her to Lettice by way of relief. She was waving her white-gloved hand, her eyes were shining, her little face was radiant—and Tom's happiness came back upon him in a rising flood again as he watched her beauty.... He thought that Egypt was the most marvellous place he had ever known. Even Tony looked enchanted—almost handsome. But Lettice looked divine. He felt more and more that the woman in her blossomed into life before his very eyes. His content was absolute.

CHAPTER XVI

With Tony as guide they took their fill of wonder. The principal expeditions were made alone, introducing Tom to the marvels of ancient Egypt which they already knew. On the sturdiest donkey Thebes could furnish, he raced his cousin across the burning sands, Madame Jaretzka following in a sand-cart, her blue veil streaming in the cool north wind. They played like children, defying the tide of mystery that this haunted land pours against the modern human soul, while yet the wonder and the mystery added to their enjoyment, deepening their happiness by contrast.

They ate their al fresco luncheons gaily, seated by hoary tombs that opened into the desolate hills; kings, priests, princesses, dead six thousand years, listening in caverns underground to their careless talk. Yet their gaiety had a hush in it, a significance behind the sentences; for even their lightest moments touched ever upon the borders of an awfulness that was sublime, and all that they said or did gained this hint of deeper value—that it was set against a background of the infinite, the deathless.

It was impossible to forget that this was Egypt, the deposit of immemorial secrets, the store-house of stupendous vanished dreams.

'There was a majesty, after all, about their strange old gods,' said Tony one afternoon as they emerged from the stifling darkness of a forgotten kingly tomb into the sunlight. 'They seem to thunder still—below the ground—subconsciously.' He was ever ready with the latest modern catchword. He flung himself down upon the sand, shaded from the glare by a recumbent column of granite exquisitely carved, then abandoned of the ages. 'They touch something in one even to-day—something superb. Human worship hasn't changed so fundamentally after all.'

'A sort of ghostly deathlessness,' agreed Lettice, making a bed of sand beside him. 'I think that's what one feels.'

Tony looked up. He glanced alertly at her. A question flashed a moment in his eyes, then passed unspoken.

'Perhaps,' Tony went on in a more flippant tone, 'even the dullest has to acknowledge the sublime in their conceptions. Isis! Why, the very name is a poem in a single word. Anubis, Nepthys, Horus— there's poetry in them all. They seem to sing themselves into the heart, as Petrie might have said—but didn't.'

'The names are rather splendid,' Tom put in, as he unpacked the kettle and spirit-lamp for tea. 'One can't forget them either.'

There was a moment's silence, then Tony spoke again. He had lost his flippant tone. He addressed his remark to Lettice. Tom was aware that she was somehow waiting for it.

'Their deathlessness! Yes, you're right.' He turned an instant to look at the colossal structure behind them, whence the imposing figures of a broken Pharaoh and his Queen stared to the east cross the shoulder of some granite Deity that had refused to crumble for three thousand years. 'Their deathlessness,' he repeated, lowering his voice, 'it's really startling.'

He looked about him. It was amazing how his little words, his gesture, his very atmosphere created a spontaneous expectancy—as though Thoth might stride sublimely up across the sand, or even Ra himself come blazing with extended wings and awful disk of fire.

Tom felt the touch of the unearthly as he watched and listened. Lettice—he was certain of it—shivered. He moved nearer and spread a rug across her feet.

'Don't, Tom, please! I'm hot enough already.' Her tone had a childish exasperation in it—as though he interrupted some mood that gave her pleasure. She turned her eyes to Tony, but Tony was busily opening sandwich packets with hands that—Tom thought—shared one quality at least of the stone effigies they had been discussing— size. And he laughed. The spell was broken. They fell hungrily upon their desert meal....

Yet, it was odd how Tony had expressed precisely what Tom had himself been vaguely feeling, though unable to find the language for his fancy—odd, too, that apparently all three of them had felt the same dim thing. No one among them was 'religious,' nor, strictly speaking, imaginative; poetical least of all in the regenerative, creative sense. Not one of the trio, that is, could have seized imaginatively the conception of an alien deity and made it live. Yet Tony's idle mood or idler words had done this very thing—and all three acknowledged it in their various ways. The flavour of a remote familiarity was manifest in each one of them—collectively as well.

Another time they sat by night in ruined Karnak, watching the silver moonlight bring out another world among the mighty pylons. It painted the empty and enormous aisles with crowding processions of lost ages. Speaking in whispers, they saw the stars peep down between the soaring forest of old stone; the cold desert wind brought with it a sadness, a mournful retrospect too vast to realise, the tragedy that such splendour left but a lifeless skeleton behind, a gigantic, soulless ruin. That such great prophecies remained unfulfilled was somewhere both terrible and melancholy. The immortal strength of these Egyptian stones conveyed a grandeur almost sinister. The huge dumb beauty seemed menacing, even ominous; they sat closer; they felt dwarfed uncomfortably, their selves reduced to insignificance, almost threatened. Even Tony sobered as they talked in lowered voices, seated in the shadow of the towering columns, their feet resting on the sand.

'I'm sure we've sat here before just like this, the three of us,' he said in a lowered voice; 'it all seems like a dream to me.'

Madame Jaretzka, who was between them, made no answer, and Tom, leaning forward, caught his cousin's eye beyond her.... The scene in the London theatre flashed across his mind. He felt very happy, very close to them both, extraordinarily at one with them, the woman he loved best in all the world, the man who was his greatest friend. He felt truth, not foolishness, in Tony's otherwise commonplace remarks that followed: 'I could swear I'd known you both before—here in Egypt.'

Madame Jaretzka moved a little, shuffling farther back so that she could lean against the great curved pillar. It brought them closer together still. She said no word, however.

'There's certainly a curious sympathy between the three of us,' murmured Tom, who usually felt out of his depth in similar talks, leaving his companions to carry it further while he listened merely. 'It's hard to believe that we meet for the first time now.'

He sat close to her, fingering her gauzy veil that brushed his face. There was a pause, and then Madame Jaretzka said, turning to Tony: 'We met here first anyhow, didn't we? Two winters ago, before I met Tom——'

But Tony said he meant something far older than that, much longer ago. 'You and Tom knew each other as children, you told me once. Tom and I were boys together too... but...'

His voice died away in Tom's ears; her answers also were inaudible as she kept her head turned towards Tony: his thoughts, besides, were caught away a moment to the days in Montreux and in London.... He fell into a reverie that lasted possibly a minute, possibly several minutes. The conversation between them left him somehow out of it; he had little to contribute; they had an understanding, as it were, on certain subjects that neglected him. His mind accordingly left them. He followed his own thoughts dreamily... far away ... past the deep black shadows and out into the soft blaze of moonlight that showered upon the distant Theban hills.... He remembered the curious emotions that had marked his entry into Egypt. He thought of a change in Lettice, at present still undefined. He wondered what it was about her now that lent to her gentle spirit a touch of authority, of worldly authority almost, that he dared not fail to recognise—as though she had the right to it. The flavour of uneasiness stole back. It occurred to him suddenly that he felt no longer quite at home with her alone as of old. Some one watched him: some one watched them both....

It was as though for the first time he realised distance—a new distance creeping in upon their relationship somewhere....

A slight shiver brought him back. The wind came moaning down the monstrous, yawning aisles against them. The overpowering effect of so much grandeur had become intolerable. 'Ugh! I'm cold,' he exclaimed abruptly. 'I vote we move a bit. I think—I'll move anyhow.'

Madame Jaretzka turned to him with a definite start; she straightened herself against the huge sandstone column. The moonlight touched her; it clothed her in gold and silver, the gold of the sand, the silver of the moon. She looked ethereal, ghostly, a figure of air and distance. She seemed to belong to her surroundings—another person somehow—faintly Egyptian almost.

'I thought you were asleep, Tom,' she said softly. She had been in the middle of an animated, though whispered, talk with Tony. She peered at him with a little smile that lifted her lip oddly.

'I was far away somewhere,' he returned, peering at her closely. 'I forgot all about you both. I thought, for a moment, I was quite— alone.'

He saw her start again. A significance he hardly intended had crept into his tone. Her face moved back into the shadow quickly beside Tony.

She teased Tom for his want of manners, then fell to caring for his comfort. 'It's icy,' she said, 'and you're in flannels. The sudden chill of these Egyptian nights is really treacherous,' and she took the rug from her lap and put it round his shoulders. As she did so, the strange appearance he had noted increased about her.

And Tom got up abruptly. 'No, Lettice dear, thank you; I think I'll move a bit.' He had said 'Lettice dear' without realising it, and before his cousin too. 'I'll take a turn and then come back for you. You stay here with Tony,' and he moved off somewhat briskly.

Then, instantly, the other two rose up like one person, following him to where the carriage waited....

'They're frightening rather, don't you think—these ancient places?' she said presently, as they drove along past palms and the flat-topped houses of the felaheen. 'There's something watching and listening all the time.'

Tom made no answer. He felt suddenly unsure of something—almost unsure of himself, it seemed.

'One feels a bit lost,' he said slowly after a bit, 'and lonely. It's the size, I think.'

'Perhaps,' she rejoined, peering at him with half-lowered eyelids, 'and the silence.' She broke off, then added, 'You can hear your thoughts too clearly.'

Tom was sitting back amid a bundle of rugs she had wrapped him in; Tony, beside her, on the front seat, seemed in a gentle doze. They drove the rest of the way in silence, dropping Tony first at the Savoy, then going on to Tom's hotel. She insisted, although her own house was in the opposite direction. 'And you're to take a hot whisky when you get into bed, remember, and don't get up to-morrow if you feel a chill.' She gave him orders for his health and comfort as though he were her son. Tom noticed it, told her she was divinely precious to him, and promised faithfully to obey.

'What do you think about Tony?' he asked suddenly, when they had driven alone for several minutes. 'I mean, what impression does he make on you? How do you feel him?'

'He's enjoying himself immensely with his numerous friends,' she replied at once. 'He grows on one rather. He's a dear, I think.' She looked at him, then turned away again. 'Don't you, Tom?'

'Oh, rather. I've always thought so. I told you first long ago, didn't I?' He made no reference to the exaggeration about the friends. 'And I think it's wonderful how well we—what a perfect trio we are.'

'Yes, isn't it?'

They both became thoughtful then. There fell a pause between them, when Tom broke in abruptly once again:

'But—what do you feel? Because I think he's half in love with you, if you want to know.' He leaned over and whispered in her ear. The words tumbled out as though they were in a hurry. 'It pleases me immensely, Lettice; it makes me feel so proud of you and happy. It'll do him a world of good, too, if he loves a woman like you. You'll teach him something.' She smiled shyly and said, 'I wonder, Tom. Do you really think so? He certainly seems fond of me, but I hadn't thought quite that. You think everybody must fall in love with me.' She pushed him away with a gentle yet impatient pressure of her arm, indicating the Arab coachman with a nod of her head. 'Take care of him, Lettice: he's a dear fellow; don't let him break his heart.'

Tom began to flirt outrageously; his arm crept round her, he leaned over and stole a kiss—and to his amazement she did not try to stop him. She did not seem to notice it. She sat very still—a stone statue in the moonlight.

Then, suddenly, he realised that she had not replied to his question. He promptly repeated it therefore. 'You put me off with what he feels, but I want to know what you feel,' he said with emphasis.

'But, Tom, I'm not putting you off, as you call it—with anything,' and there was a touch of annoyance in her tone and manner.

'Tell me, Lettice; it interests me. You're such a puzzle, d'you know, out here.' His tone unconsciously grew more earnest as he spoke.

Madame Jaretzka broke into a little laugh. 'You boy!' she exclaimed teasingly, 'you're trying to heighten his value so as to increase your own by contrast. The more people you can find in love with me, the more you'll be able to flatter yourself.'

Tom laughed with her, though he did not quite understand. He had never heard her say such a thing before. He accepted the cleverness she gave him credit for, however. 'Of course, and why shouldn't I?' And he was just going to put his original question in another form— had already begun it, in fact—when she interrupted him, putting her hand playfully over his mouth for a second: 'I do think Tony's a happy entertaining sort of man,' she told him, 'even fascinating in a certain kind of way. He's very stimulating to me. And I feel—don't you, Tom?'—a slight change—was it softness?—crept into her tone— 'a sort of beauty in him somewhere?'

'Yes, p'raps I do,' he assented briefly; 'but, I say, Lettice darling, you mischievous Egyptian princess.'

'Be quiet, Tom, and take your arm away. Here's the hotel in sight.' And yet, somehow, he fancied that she preferred his action to the talk.

'Tell me this first,' he went on, obeying her peremptory tone: 'do you think it's true that we three have been together before like that—as Tony said, I mean? It's a funny thing, but I swear it sounded true when he said it.' His tone was earnest again. 'It gave me the creeps a bit, and, d'you know, you looked so queer, so wonderful in the moonlight—you looked un-English, foreign—like one of those Egyptian figures come to life. That's what made me cold, I think.' His laughter died away. He was grave suddenly. He sighed a little and moved closer to her. 'That's— what made me get up and leave you,' he added abruptly.

'Oh, he's always saying that kind of thing,' she answered quickly, moving the rugs for him to get out as the carriage slowed up before the brilliantly lit hotel. She made no reference to his other words. 'There's a lot of poetry in Tony too—out here.'

'Said it before, has he?' exclaimed Tom with genuine astonishment. 'All three of us or—or just you and him? Am I in the business too?' He was now bubbling over with laughter again for some reason; it all seemed comical, almost. Yet it was a sudden, an emotional laughter. His emotion—his excitement surprised him even at the time.

'All three of us—I think,' she said, as he held her hand a moment, saying good-bye. 'Yes, all three of us, of course. Now good-night, you inquisitive and impertinent boy, and if you have to stay in bed to-morrow we'll come over and nurse you all day long.' He answered that he would certainly stay in bed in that case—and watched her waving her hand over the back of the carriage as she drove away into the moonlight like a fading dream of stars and mystery and beauty. Then he took his telegrams and letters from the Arab porter with the face of expressionless bronze, and went up to bed.

'What a strange and wonderful woman!' he thought as the lift rushed him up: 'out here she seems another being, and a thousand times more fascinating.' He felt almost that he would like to win her all over again from the beginning. 'She's different to what she was in England. Tony's different too. And so am I, I do believe!' he exclaimed in his bedroom, looking at his sunburned face in the glass a moment. 'We're all different!' He felt singularly happy, hilarious, stimulated—a deep and curious excitement was in him. Above all there was high pride that she belonged to him so absolutely. But the analysis he had indulged in England vanished here. He forgot it all.... He was in Egypt with her... now.

He read his letters and telegrams, only half realising at first that they called him back to Assouan. 'What a bore,' he thought; 'I simply shan't go. A week's delay won't matter. I can telephone.'

He laid them down upon the table beside him and walked out on to his balcony. Responsibility seemed less in him. He felt a little reckless. His position was quite secure. He was his own master. He meant to enjoy himself.... But another, deeper voice was sounding in him too. He heard it, but at first refused to recognise it. It whispered. One word it whispered: 'Stay...!'

* * * *

There was no sleep in him; with an overcoat thrown across his shoulders he watched the calm Egyptian night, the soft army of the stars, the river gleaming in a broad band of silver. Hitherto Lettice had monopolised his energies; he had neglected Egypt, whose indecipherable meaning now came floating in upon him with a strange insistence. Lettice came with it too. The two beauties were indistinguishable....

A flock of boats lay motionless, their black masts hanging in mid-air; all was still and silent, no voices, no footsteps, no movements anywhere. In the distance the desolate rocky hills rolled like a solid wave along the horizon. Gaunt and mysterious, they loomed upon the night. They were pierced by myriad tombs, those solemn hills; the stately dead lay there in hundreds—he imagined them looking forth a moment like himself across the peace and silence of the moonlit desert. They focussed upon Thebes, upon the white hotel, upon a modern world they could not recognise—upon his very windows. It seemed to him for a moment that their ancient eyes met his own across the sand, across the silvery river, and, as they met, a shadowy gleam of recognition passed between them and himself. At the same time he also saw the eyes he loved. They gazed through half-closed eyelids... the Eastern eyes of his early boyhood's dream. He remembered again the strange emotion of the day he first arrived in Egypt, weeks ago....

And then he suddenly thought of Tony, and of Tony's careless remark as they sat in ruined Karnak together: 'I feel as if we three had all been here before.'

Why it returned to him just now he did not know: for some reason unexplained the phrase revived in him. Perhaps he felt an instinctive sympathy towards the poet's idea that he and she were lovers of such long standing, of such ancient lineage. It flattered his pride, while at the same time it disturbed him. A sense of vague disquiet grew stronger in him. In any case, he did not dismiss it and forget—his natural way of treating fancies. 'Perhaps,' he murmured, 'the bodies she and I once occupied lie there now—lie under the very stars their eyes—our own— once looked upon.'

It was strange the fancy took such root in him.... He stood a long time gazing at the vast, lonely necropolis among the mountains. There was an extraordinary stillness over that western bank, where the dead lay in their ancient tombs. The silence was eloquent, but the whole sky whispered to his soul. And again he felt that Egypt welcomed him; he was curiously at home here. It moved the deeps in him, brought him out; it changed him; it brought out Lettice too— brought out a certain power in her. She was more of a woman here, a woman of the world. She was more wilful, and more human. Values had subtly altered. Tony himself was altered.... Egypt affected them all three....

The vague uneasiness persisted. His mood changed a little, the excitement gradually subsided; thought shifted to a minor key, subdued by the beauty of the southern night. The world lay in a mysterious glow, the hush was exquisite. Yet there was expectancy: that glow, that hush were ready to burst into flame and language. They covered secrets. Something was watching him. He was dimly aware of a thousand old forgotten things....

He no longer thought, but felt. The calm, the peace, the silence laid soothing fingers against the running of his blood; the turbulent condition settled down. Then, through the quieting surface of his reverie, stole up a yet deeper mood that seemed evoked partly by the mysterious glamour of the scene, yet partly by his will to let it come. It had been a long time in him; he now let it up to breathe. It came, moreover, with ease, and quickly.

For a gentle sadness rose upon him, a sadness deeply hidden that he suddenly laid bare as of set deliberation. The recent play and laughter, above all his own excitement, had purposely concealed it— from others possibly, but certainly from himself. The excitement had been a mask assumed by something deeper in him he had wished—and tried—to hide. Gently it came at first, this sadness, then with increasing authority and speed. It rose about him like a cloud that hid the stars and dimmed the sinking moon. It spread a veil between him and the rocky cemetery on those mournful hills beyond the Nile. In a sense it seemed, indeed, to issue thence. It emanated from their silence and their ancient tombs. It sank into him. It was penetrating—it was familiar—it was deathless.

But it was no mood of common sadness; there lay no physical tinge in it, but rather a deep, unfathomable sadness of the spirit: an inner loneliness. From his inmost soul it issued outwards, meeting half-way some sense of similar loneliness that breathed towards him from these tragic Theban hills....

And Tom, not understanding it, tried to shake himself free again; he called up cheerful things to balance it; he thought of his firm position in the world, of his proud partnership, of his security with her he loved, of his zest in life, of the happy prospect immediately in front of him. But, in spite of all, the mood crept upwards like a rising wave, swamping his best resistance, drowning all appeal to joy and confidence. He recognised an unwelcome revival of that earlier nightmare dread connected with his boyhood, things he had decided to forget, and had forgotten as he thought. The mood took him gravely, with the deepest melancholy he had ever known. It had begun so delicately; it became in a little while so determined, it threatened to overmaster him. He turned then and faced it, so to speak. He looked hard at it and asked of himself its meaning. Thought and emotion in him shuffled with their shadowy feet.

And then he realised that, in germ at any rate, the mood had lain actually a long time in him, deeply concealed—the surface excitement merely froth. He had hidden it from himself. It had been accumulating, gaining strength and impetus, pausing upon direction only. All the hours just spent at Karnak it had been there, drawing nearer to the surface; this very night, but a little while ago, during the drive home as well; before that even—during all the talks and out-door meals and expeditions; he traced its existence suddenly, and with tiny darts of piercing, unintelligible pain, as far back as Alexandria and the day of his arrival. It seemed to justify the vivid emotions that had marked his entry into Egypt. It became sharply clear now—this had been in him subconsciously since the moment when he read the little letter of welcome Lettice sent to meet him at the steamer, a letter he discovered afterwards was curiously empty. This disappointment, this underlying sadness he had kept hidden from himself: he now laid it bare and recognised it. He faced it. With a further flash he traced it finally to the journey in the Geneva train when he had read over the Warsaw and the Egyptian letters.

And he felt startled: something at the roots of his life was trembling. He tried to think. But Tom was slow; he could feel, but he could not dissect and analyse. Introspection with him invariably darkened vision, led to distortion and bewilderment. The effort to examine closely confused him. Instead of dissipating the emotion he intensified it. The sense of loneliness grew inexplicably—a great, deep loneliness, a loneliness of the spirit, a loneliness, moreover, that it seemed to him he had experienced before, though when, under what conditions, he could not anywhere remember.

His former happiness was gone, the false excitement with it. This freezing loneliness stole in and took their places. Its explanation lay hopelessly beyond him, though he felt sure it had to do with this haunted and mysterious land where he now found himself, and in a measure with her, even with Tony too....

The hint Egypt dropped into him upon his arrival was a true one— he had slipped over an edge, slipped into something underneath, below him—something past. But slipped with her. She had come back to fetch him. They had come back to fetch—each other... through pain....

And a shadow from those sombre Theban mountains crept, as it were, upon his life. He knew a sinking of the heart, a solemn, dark presentiment that murmured in his blood the syllables of 'tragedy.' To his complete amazement—at first he refused to believe it indeed— there came a lump into his throat, as though tears must follow to relieve the strain; and a moment later there was moisture, a perceptible moisture, in his eyes. The sadness had so swiftly passed into foreboding, with a sense of menacing tragedy that oppressed him without cause or explanation. Joy and confidence collapsed before it like a paper platform beneath the pressure of a wind. His feet and hands were cold. He shivered....

Then gradually, as he stood there watching the calm procession of the stars, he felt the ominous emotion draw down again, retreat. Deep down inside him whence it came, it retired into a kind of interior remoteness that lay beyond his reach. It was incredible and strange. The intensity had made it seem so real.... For, while it lasted, he had felt himself bereft, lonely beyond all telling, outcast, lost, forgotten, wrapped in a cold and desolate misery that frightened him past all belief. The hand that lit his pipe still trembled. But the mood had passed as mysteriously as it came. It left him curiously shaken in his heart. 'Perhaps this too,'— thought murmured from some depth in him he could neither control nor understand—'perhaps this too is—Egypt.'

He went to bed, emotion all smoothed out again, yet wondering a good deal at himself. For the odd upheaval was a new experience. Such an attack had never come to him before; he laughed at it, called it hysteria, and decided that its cause was physical; he persuaded himself that it had a very banal cause—a chill, even a violent chill, incipient fever and over-fatigue at the back of it. He smiled at himself, while obeying the loving orders he had received, and brewing the comforting hot mixture with his spirit-lamp.

Then drinking it, he looked round the room with satisfaction at the various evidences of precious motherly care. This mother-love restored his happiness by degrees. His more normal, stolid, unimaginative self climbed back into its place again—yet with a touch of awkwardness and difficulty. Something in him was changed, or changing; he had surprised it in the act.

The nature of the change escaped him, however. It seemed, perhaps— this was the nearest he could get to it—that something in him had weakened, some sense of security, of confidence, of self-complacency given way a little. Only it was not his certainty of the mother-love in her: that remained safe from all possible attack. A tinge of uneasiness still lay like a shadow on his mind—until the fiery spirit chased it away, and a heavy sleep came over him that lasted without a break until he woke two hours after sunrise.

CHAPTER XVII

He sprang from his bed, went to the open window and thrust his head out into the crystal atmosphere. It was impossible to credit the afflicting nightmare of a few hours ago. Gold lay upon the world, and the face of Egypt wore her great Osirian look.

In the air was that tang of mountain-tops that stimulated like wine. Everything sparkled, the river blazed, the desert was a sheet of burnished bronze. Light, heat, and radiance pervaded the whole glad morning, bathing even his bare feet on the warm, soft carpet. It was good to be alive. How could he not feel happy and unafraid?

The change, perhaps, was sudden; it certainly was complete…. These vivid alternations seemed characteristic of his whole Egyptian winter. Another self thrust up, sank out of sight, then rose again. The confusion seemed almost due to a pair of competing selves, each gaining the upper hand in turn—sometimes he lived both at once…. The uneasy mood, at any rate, had vanished with the darkness, for nothing sad or heavy-footed could endure amid this dancing exhilaration of the morning. Born of the brooding night and mournful hills, his recent pain was forgotten.

He dressed in flannels, and went his way to the house upon the Nile soon after nine o'clock; he certainly had no chill, there was only singing in his heart. The curious change in Lettice, it seemed, no longer troubled him. And, finding Tony already in the garden, they sat in the shade and smoked together while waiting for their hostess. Light-hearted as himself, Tony outlined various projects, to which the other readily assented. He persuaded himself easily, if recklessly; the work could wait. 'We simply must see it all together,' Tony urged. 'You can go back to Assouan next week. You'll find everything all right. Why hurry off?' … How his cousin had improved, Tom was thinking; his tact was perfect; he asked no awkward questions, showed no inquisitiveness. He just assumed that his companions had a right to be fond of each other, while taking his own inclusion in the collective friendship for granted as natural too.

And when Lettice came out to join them, radiant in white, with her broad sun-hat and long blue veil and pretty gauntlet gloves, Tony explained with enthusiasm at the beauty of the picture: 'She's come into her own out here with a vengeance,' he declared. 'She ought to live in Egypt always. It suits her down to the ground.' Whereupon Tom, pleased by the spontaneous admiration, whispered proudly to himself, 'And she is mine— all mine!' Tony's praise seemed to double her value in his eyes at once. So Tony, too, was aware that she had changed; had noted the subtle alteration, the enhancement of her beauty, the soft Egyptian transformation!

'You'd hardly take her for European, I swear—at a distance—now, would you?'

'N-no,' Tom agreed, 'perhaps you wouldn't——' at which moment precisely the subject of their remarks came up and threw her long blue veil across them both with the command that it was time to start.

The following days were one long dream of happiness and wonder spent between the sunlight and the stars. They were never weary of the beauty, the marvel, and the mystery of all they saw. The appeal of temple, tomb, and desert was so intimate—it seemed instinctive. The burning sun, the scented winds, great sunsets and great dawns, these with the palms, the river, and the sand seemed a perfect frame about a perfect picture. They knew a kind of secret pleasure that was satisfying. Egypt harmonised all three of them. And if Tom did not notice the change increasing upon one of them, it was doubtless because he was too much involved in the general happiness to see it separate.

There came a temporary interruption, however, in due course—his conscience pricked him. 'I really must take a run up to Assouan,' he decided. 'I've been rather neglecting things perhaps. A week at most will do it—and then for another ten days' holiday again!'

The rhythm broke, as it were, with a certain suddenness. A rift came in the collective dream. He saw details again—saw them separate. And the day before he left a trifling thing occurred that forced him to notice the growth of the change in Lettice. He focussed it. It startled him a little.

The others had not sought to change his judgment. But they planned an all-night bivouac in the desert for his return; they would sleep with blankets on the sand, cook their supper upon an open fire, and see the dawn. 'It's an exquisite experience,' said Tony. 'The stars fade quickly, there's a puff of warmer wind, and the sun comes up with a rush. It's marvellous. I'll get de Lorne and his sister to join us; he can tell stories round the fire, and perhaps she will get inspiration at last for her awful pictures.' Madame Jaretzka laughed. 'Then we must have Lady Sybil too,' she added; 'de Lorne may find courage to propose to her fortune at last.' Tom looked up at her with a momentary surprise. 'I declare, Lettice, you've grown quite worldly; that's a very cynical remark and point of view.'

He said it teasingly, but it was this innocent remark that served to focus the change in her he had been aware of vaguely for a long time. She was more worldly here, the ordinary 'woman' in her was more in evidence: and while he rather liked it—it brought her more within his reach, as it were, yet without lowering her—he felt also puzzled. Several times of late he had surprised this wholesome sign of sex in things she said and did, as though the woman-side, as he called it, was touched into activity at last. It added to her charm; at the same time it increased his burning desire to possess her absolutely for himself. What he felt as the impersonal—almost spiritually elusive—aspect of her he had first known, was certainly less in evidence. Another part of her was rising into view, if not already in the ascendant. The burning sun, the sensuous colour and beauty of the Egyptian climate, he had heard, could have this physiological effect. He wondered.

'Sybil has been waiting for him to ask her ever since I came out,' he heard her saying with a gesture almost of impatience. 'Only he thinks he oughtn't to speak because he's poor. The result is she's getting bolder in proportion as he gets more shy.'

They all laughingly agreed to help matters to a climax when Tom, looking up suddenly, saw Madame Jaretzka smiling at his cousin with her eyelids half closed in the way he once disliked but now adored. He wondered suddenly how much Tony liked her; the improvement in him was assuredly due to her, he felt; Tony had less and less time now for his other friends. It occurred to him for a second that the change in her was greater than he quite knew, perhaps. He watched them together for some moments. It gave him a proud sense of pleasure to feel that her influence was making a man out of the medley of talent and irresponsibility that was Tony. Tony was learning at last to 'find himself.' It must be quite a new experience for him to know and like a woman of her sort, almost a discovery. But with a flash—too swift and fleeting to be a definite thought—Tom was conscious of another thing as well—and for the first time: 'How she would put him in his place if he attempted any liberties with her!'

The same second he was ashamed that such a notion could ever have occurred to him: it was mean towards Tony, ungenerous towards her; and yet—he was aware of a distinct emotion, a touch of personal triumph in it somewhere....

His thoughts were interrupted by a sudden tumult. There was a scurry; Tony flung a stone; Madame Jaretzka leaped upon a boulder, gathering her skirts together hurriedly, with a little scream. 'Kill it, Tony! Quick!' he heard her cry. And he saw then a very large and hairy spider crawling swiftly across the white paper that had wrapped their fruit and sandwiches, an ugly and distressing sight. 'It's a tarantula,' she screamed, half laughing, half alarmed, showing neat ankles as she balanced precariously upon her boulder, 'and it's coming at me. Quick, Tony, another stone,' as he missed it for the second time, 'it's making for me! Oh, kill it, kill it!' Tony, still aiming badly, assured her it was not a tarantula, nor poisonous even; he knew the species well. 'It's quite harmless,' he cried, 'there's no need to kill it. It's not in a house———' And he flung another useless stone at it.

What followed happened very quickly, in a second or two at most. Tom saw it with sharp surprise, a curious distaste, almost with a shudder. It certainly astonished him, and in another sense it shocked him. He had done nothing himself because Lettice, he thought, was half in fun, making a diversion out of nothing. Only much later did it occur to him that she had turned instinctively to Tony for protection, rather than to himself. What caused him the unpleasant sensation, however, was that she deliberately stepped down from her perch of safety and kicked at the advancing horror. Probably her intention was merely to drive it away— she was certainly excited—but the result was that she set her foot upon the creature and crushed its life out with an instant's pressure of her dainty boot. 'There!' she cried. 'Oh, but I didn't mean to kill it! How frightful of me!'

He heard Tony say, 'Bravo, you are a brave woman! Such creatures have no right to live!' as he hid the disfigured piece of paper beneath some stones... and, after a few minutes' chatter, the donkey-boys had packed up the luncheon things and they were all on their way towards the next object of their expedition, as though nothing had happened. The entire incident had occupied a moment and a half at most. Madame Jaretzka was laughing and talking as before, gay as a child and pretty as a dream.

In Tom's mind, however, it went on happening—over and over again. He could not at once clean his mind of a disagreeable impression that remained. Another woman, any woman for that matter, might have done what she did without leaving a trace in him of anything but a certain admiration. It was a perfectly natural thing. The creature probably was poisonous as well as hideous; Tony merely said the contrary to calm her; moreover, he gave no help, and the insect was certainly making hurriedly towards her—she had to save and protect herself. There was nothing in the incident beyond an ugliness, a passing second of distress; and yet— this was what remained with him—it was not a natural thing for 'Lettice' to have done. Her intention, no doubt, was otherwise; there was miscalculation as well. She had only meant to frighten the scurrying creature. Yet at the same time the instinctive act issued, he felt, from another aspect, another part of her, a part that in London, in Montreux, lay unexpressed and unawakened. And it issued deliberately too. The exquisite tenderness that could not have put a fly to death was less in her. Egypt had changed her oddly. He was aware of something that made him shrink, though he did not use the phrase even to himself in thought;

of something hard and almost cruel, though both adjectives lay far from clothing the faint sensation in his mind with definite words.

Tom watched her instinctively from that moment, unconsciously, that is; less with his eyes than with a little pair of glasses in his heart. There was certainly a change in her that he could not quite account for; the notion came to him once or twice that some influence was upon her, some power that was outside herself, modifying the sharp outlines of her first peculiar tenderness. These dear outlines blurred a trifle in the fierce sunlight of this desert air. He knew not how to express it even to himself, for it was too tenuous to seize in actual words.

He arrived at this partial conclusion anyhow: that he was aware of what he called the 'woman' in her, but a very human woman—a certain wilfulness that was half wildness in it. There was a hint of the earthly, too, as opposed to spiritual, though in a sense that was wholesome, good, entirely right. Yet it was rather, perhaps, primitive than earthly in any vulgar meaning.... It had been absent or dormant hitherto. She needed it; something—was it Egypt? was it sex?—had stirred it into life. And its first expression—surprising herself as much as it surprised him—had an aspect of exaggeration almost.

The way she raced their donkeys in her sand-cart on the way home, by no means sparing the whip, was extremely human, but unless he had witnessed it he could never have pictured it as possible—so utterly un-like the gentle, gracious, almost fastidious being he had known first. There was a hint of a darker, stronger colour in the pattern of her being now, partly of careless and abundant spirits, partly of this new primi-tive savagery. He noticed it more and more, it was both repellant and curiously attractive; yet, while he adored it in her, he also shrank. He detected a touch even of barbaric vanity, and this singular touch of the barbaric veiled the tenderness. He almost felt in her the power to inflict pain without flinching—upon another....

The following day their time of gaiety was to end, awaiting only his return later from Assouan. Tony was going down to Cairo with some other friends. Tom would be away at least a week, and tried hard to per-suade his cousin to come with him instead; but Tony had given his word, and could not change. Moreover, he was dining with his friends that very night, and must hurry off at once. He said his good-byes and went.

'We're very rarely alone now, are we, Lettice?' Tom began abruptly the instant they were together. At the back of his mind rose something he did not understand that forced more significance into his tone than he intended. He felt very full—an accumulation that must have expression. He blurted it out without reflection. 'Hardly once since I arrived two weeks ago, now I come to think of it.' He looked at her half playfully, half reproachfully. 'We're always three,' he added with the frank pathos of a boy. And while one part of him felt ashamed, another part urged him onward and was glad.

But the way she answered startled him.

'Tom dear, don't scold me now. I am so tired.' It was the tone that took his breath away. For the first time in their acquaintance he noticed something like exasperation. 'I've been doing too much,' she went on more gently, smiling up into his face: 'I feel it. And that dreadful thing—that insect,'—she shuddered a little—'I never meant to hurt it. It's upset me. All this daily excitement, and the sun, and the jolting of that rickety sand-cart—There, Tom, come and sit beside me a moment and let's talk before you go. I'm really too done up to drive you to the station to-night. You'll understand and forgive me, won't you?' Her voice was very soft. She was excited, too, talking at random rather. Her being seemed confused.

He took his place on a sturdy cushion at her feet, full of an exaggerated remorse. She looked pale, though her eyes were very sparkling. His heart condemned him. He said nothing about the 'dreadful incident.'

'Lettice, dearest girl, I didn't mean anything. You have been doing far too much, and it's my fault; you've done it all for me—to give me pleasure. It's been too wonderful.' He took her hand, while her other stroked his head. 'You must rest while I'm away.'

'Yes,' she murmured, 'so as to be quite fresh when you come back. You won't be very long, will you?' He said he would risk his whole career to get back within the week. 'But, you know, I have neglected things rather—up there.' He smiled fondly as he said 'up there.' She looked down tenderly into his eyes. 'And I have neglected you—down here,' she said. 'That's what you mean, boy, isn't it?' And for the first time he did not like the old mode of address he once thought perfect. There seemed a flavour of pity in it. 'It would be nice to be alone sometimes, wouldn't it, Lettice? Quite alone, I mean,' he said with meaning.

'We shall be, we will be—later, Tom,' she whispered; 'quite alone together.' She paused, then added louder: 'The truth is, Egypt—the air and climate—stimulates me too much; it makes me restless. It excites me in a way I can't quite understand. I can't sit still and talk and be idle as one does in sleepy, solemn England.'

He was explaining with laborious logic that it was the dryness of the air that exhausted the nerves a bit, when she straightened herself up and took her hand away. 'Oh yes, Tom, I know, I know. That's perfectly true, and everybody says that—I mean, everybody feels it, don't they?' She said it quickly, almost impatiently.

The old uneasiness flashed through him at that moment: it occurred to him, 'I'm dull, I'm boring her.' She was over-tired, he remembered then, her nerves on edge a trifle; it was natural enough; he would just kiss her and leave her to rest quietly. Yet a tiny sense of resentment, even of chill, crept over him. This impatience in her was new to him. He wondered an instant, then crushed back the words that tried to rise. He said goodbye, taking her in his arms for a moment with an overmastering impulse he could not check. Deep love and tenderness were in his heart and eyes. He yearned to protect and guide her—keep her safe from harm. He felt his older years, his steadier strength; he was a man, she but a little gentle woman. And the elemental powers of life were very strong. With a sudden impulsive gesture, then, that surprised him, she returned the embrace with a kind of vehemence, pressing him closely to her heart and kissing him repeatedly on the cheeks and eyes.

Tom had expected her to resist and chide him. He was bewildered and delighted; he was also puzzled—for the first second only. 'You darling woman,' he cried, forgetting utterly the suspicion, the uneasiness, the passing cold of a moment before. He marvelled that his heart could have let such fancies come to birth. Surely he had changed for such a thing to be possible at all!... Various impulses and emotions that clamoured in him he kept back with an effort. He was aware of clashing contradictions. Confidence was less in him. He felt curiously unsure of himself—also, in a cruel, subtle way—of her. There was a new thing in her—rising. Was it against himself somewhere? The tangle in his heart and mind seemed inextricable: he wanted to seize her and carry her away, struggling but captured, and at the same time—singular contradiction—to entreat her humbly, though passionately, to love him more, and to show more that she loved him. Surely there were two selves in him.

He moved over to the door. 'Cataract Hotel, remember, finds me.' He stood still, looking back at her.

She smiled, repeating the words after him. 'And Lettice, you will write?' She blew a kiss to him by way of answer. Then, charged to the brim with a thousand things he ached to say, yet would not, almost dared not say, he added playfully—a child must have noticed that his voice was too deep for banter and his breath came oddly:

'And mind you don't let Tony lose his head too much. He's pretty far gone, you know, already.'

The same instant he could have bitten his tongue off to recall the words. Somewhere he had been untrue to himself, almost betrayed himself.

She rose suddenly from her sofa and came quickly towards him across the floor; he felt his heart sink a moment, then start hammering irregularly against his ribs. Something frightened him. For he caught in her face an expression he could not understand—the struggle of many strong emotions—anxiety and passion, fear and love; the eyes were shining, though the lids remained half closed; she made a curious gesture: she moved swiftly. He braced himself as against attack. He shrank. Her power over him was greater than he knew.

For he saw her in that instant as another person, another woman, foreign— almost Eastern; the barbaric primitive thing flamed out of her, but with something regal, queenly, added to it; she looked Egyptian; the Princess, as he called her sometimes, had come to life. And the same moment in himself this curious sense of helplessness appeared—he raged against it inwardly—as though he were in her power somehow, as though her little foot could crush him—too—into the yellow sand....

A spasm of acute and aching pain shot through him; he winced; he wanted to turn and fly, yet was held rooted to the floor. He could not escape. It had to be. For oddly, mysteriously, he felt pain in her quick approach: she was coming to do him injury and hurt. The incident of the afternoon flashed again upon his mind—with the idea of cruelty in it somewhere, but a deep surge of strange emotion that flung wild sentences into his mind at the same instant. He tightly shut his lips, lest a hundred thoughts that had lain in him of late might burst into words he would later regret intensely. He must not avoid, delay, an inevitable thing. To resist was somehow to be untrue to the deepest in him—to something painful he deserved, and, paradoxically, desired too. What could it all mean?... He shivered as he waited—watching her come nearer.

She reached his side and her arms were stretched towards him. To his amazement she folded him in closely against her breast and held him as though she never could let him go again. He stood there helpless; the revulsion of feeling took his strength away. He heard her breathless, yearning whisper as she kissed him: 'My Tom, my precious boy, I couldn't see a hair of your dear head injured—I couldn't see you hurt! Take care of yourself and come back quickly—do, do take care of yourself. I shall count the days——' she broke off, held his face between her hands, gazed into his astonished eyes, and kissed him with the utmost tenderness again, the tenderness of a mother who is forced to be separated from the boy she loves better than herself.

Tom stood there trembling before her, and no speech came to help him. The thing passed like a dream; the dread, the emotion left him; the nightmare touch was gone. Her self-betrayal his simple nature did not at once discern. He felt only her divine tenderness pour over him. A spring of joy rose bubbling in him that no words could tell. Also he felt afraid.

But the fear was no longer for himself. In some perplexing, singular way, he felt afraid for her.

Then, as a sentence came struggling to his lips, a step was heard upon the landing. There was time to resume conventional attitudes of good-bye when Mrs. Haughstone appeared on the staircase leading to the hall. Tom said his farewells hurriedly to both of them, making his escape as naturally as possible. 'I've just time to pack and catch the train,' he shouted, and was gone.

And what remained with him afterwards of the curious little scene was the absolute joy and confidence those last tender embraces had restored to him, side by side with another thing that he was equally sure about, yet refused to dwell upon because he dared not—yet. For, as she came across the floor of the sunny room towards him, he realised two things in her, two persons almost. Another influence, he was convinced, worked in her strangely—some older, long-buried presentment of her interpenetrating, even piercing through, the modern self. She was divided against herself in some extraordinary fashion, one half struggling fiercely, yet struggling bravely, honestly, against the other. And the relationship between himself and her, though the evidence was so negligibly slight as yet, he knew had definitely changed....

It came to him as the Mother and the Woman in her. The Mother belonged unchangeably to him: the Woman, he felt, was troubled, tempted, and afraid.

CHAPTER XVIII

Afterwards, months, years afterwards, looking back upon these strange weeks of his brief Egyptian winter, Tom marvelled at himself; he looked back, as it were, upon the thoughts and emotions of another man he could not recognise. This illusion involved his two companions also, Madame Jaretzka supremely, Tony slightly less, all three, however, together affected, all three changed.

As regards himself, however, there was always a part, it seemed, that remained unaffected. It looked on, it compared, it judged. He called it the Onlooker....

Explanation lay beyond his reach; he termed it enchantment: and there he left it. Insight seemed only to operate with regard to himself: of their feelings, thoughts, or point of view he was uninformed. They offered no explanations, and he sought none.... The man honest with himself is more rare than a January swallow. He alone is honest who can state a case without that bias of exaggeration favourable to himself which is almost lying. Try as he may, his statement leans one way or the other. The spirit-level of absolute honesty is hard to find, and, of course, Tom was no exception.... Occasionally he recalled the 'spiral theory,' which once, at least, had been in the minds of all three—the notion that their three souls lived over a former episode together, but from a higher point, and with the bird's-eye view which brought in understanding. But if this offered a hint of that winter's inner spiritual structure, Tom certainly did not claim it as a true solution. The whole thing began so stealthily, and progressed so slowly yet so surely....

He could only marvel at himself: he was so singularly changed—imagination so active, judgment alternately so positive and so faltering, every emotion so amazingly intensified. All the weakest and least admirable in him, the very dregs, seemed dragged up side by side with what was noblest, highest, and flung together in the rush and smother of the breaking Wave.

Events, in the dramatic meaning of the word, and outwardly, there were few perhaps, and those few meagre and unsensational. No one was shot or drowned, no one was hanged and quartered; the police were not called in; to outsiders there seemed no air or attitude of drama anywhere; but in three human hearts, thrown together as by chance currents of normal life, there came to pass changes of a spiritual kind, conflict between essential, primitive forces of the soul, battlings, temptings, aspirations, sacrifice, that are the truest drama always, because the inmost being, whether glorified or degraded, is thereby—changed.

In this fierce intensification of his own being, and in the events experienced, Tom recognised the rising of his childhood Wave towards the breaking point. The early premonition that had seemed causeless to his learned father, that stirred in his mother the deep instinct to protect, and that ever, more or less, hung poised above the horizon of his passing years, had its origin in the bed-rock of his nature. It was associated with memory and instinct; the native tendencies and forces of his being had dramatised their inevitable fulfilment in a dream. He recognised intuitively what was coming—and he welcomed it. The body shrank from pain; the soul held out her hands to it....

Thus, looking back, he saw it mapped below him from a higher curve in life's ascending spiral. In the glare of a drenching sunshine that seemed hauntingly familiar, in the stupendous blaze of Egypt that knew and favoured it, the action lay spread out: but in darkness, too, an oppressive, suffocating darkness as of the grave, as of the bottom of the sea. The map was streaked with this alternate light and gloom of elemental kind. It passed swiftly, he went swiftly with it. A few short crowded weeks of the intensest pain and happiness he had ever known,—and the Wave, its crest reflected in its origin, fell with a drowning crash. He merged into his background, yet he did not drown: in due course he again—emerged.

The sense of rushing that accompanied it all was in himself apparently: heightened by the contrast of the divine stillness which is Egypt— the golden, hanging days, the nights of cool, soft moonlight, the sighing winds with perfume in their breath, the mournful palms that fringed the peaceful river, the calm of multitudinous stars. The grim Theban hills looked on; the ruined Temples watched and knew; there were listening ears within a thousand tombs.... And there was the Desert—the endless emptiness where everything had already happened, the place where, therefore, everything could happen again without affronting time and space—the Desert seemed the infinite background whence the Wave tossed up three little specks of passionate human action and reaction. It was the 'sea,' a sea of dust. Yet out of the dust wild roses blossomed eventually with a sweetness of beauty unknown to any cultivated gardens....

And while he and his two companions made their moves upon this ancient chessboard of half-forgotten, half-remembered life, all natural things as well seemed raised to their most significant expression, sharing the joy and sadness, the beauty and the terror of his own experience. For the very scenery borrowed of his intensity, the familiar details urged a fraction beyond the normal, as though any moment they must break down into their elemental and essential nakedness. The pungent odour of the universal sand, the dust, the minute golden particles suspended in the flaming air, the marvellous dawns and sunsets, the mighty, awful pylons, and the heat—all these contributed their quota of wonder and mystery to what happened. Egypt inspired it, and was satisfied.

The sediment of his nature was drawn up, the rubbish floated before his eyes, he saw himself through the curtains of suspended dust—until the flood, retiring, left him high upon the shore, no longer shuffling with his earthly, physical feet.

* * * *

In the train to Assouan, Tom still felt the clinging arms about his neck, still heard the loving voice, eager with tenderness for his welfare and his quick return. She needed him: he was everything to her. He knew it, oh he was sure of it. He thought of his work, and knew some slight anxiety that he had neglected it. He would devote all his energies to the interests of his firm: there should be no shirking anywhere; his ten days' holiday was over. His mind fixed itself deliberately, though not too easily, on this alone.

He knew his own capacity, however, and that by concentration he could accomplish in a short time what other men might ask weeks to complete. Provided all was going well, he saw no reason why he could not be free again in a week at most. He knew quite well his value to the firm, but he knew also that he must continue to justify it. He was complacent, but, he hoped, not carelessly complacent. Tom felt very sure of himself again.

To his great relief he found things running smoothly. He examined every detail, interviewed all and sundry, supervised, decided, gave instructions. There was a letter from the London office conveying the formal satisfaction of the Board with results so far, praising especially certain reductions in cost he had judiciously effected; another private letter from the older partner referred confidently to greater profits than they had dared to anticipate; also there was a brief note from Sir William, the Chairman, now at Salonica, saying he might run over a little later and see for himself how the work was getting along.

Tom was supremely happy with it all. There was really very little for him to do; his engineers were highly competent; they could summon him at a day's notice from Luxor if anything went wrong. 'But there's no sign of difficulty, sir,' was their verdict; 'everything's going like clockwork; the men working splendidly; it's only a matter of time.'

It was the evening of the second day that Tom decided to go back to Luxor. He was eager for the promised bivouac they had arranged together. He had written once to say that all was well, but no word had yet come from her; she was resting, he was glad to think: Tony was away at

Cairo with his friends; there might be a letter for him in the morning, but that could be sent after him. Joy and impatience urged him. He chuckled happily over his boyish plan; he would not announce himself; he would surprise her. He caught a train that would get him in for dinner.

And during his journey of six hours he rehearsed this pleasure of surprising her. She was lonely without him. He visualised her delight and happiness. He would creep up to the window, to the edge of the verandah where she sat reading, Mrs. Haughstone knitting in a chair opposite. He would call her name 'Lettice....' Her eyes would lighten, her manner change. That new spontaneous joy would show itself....

* * * *

The sun was setting when the train got in, but by the time he had changed into flannels at his hotel the short dusk was falling. The entire western sky was gold and crimson, the air was sharp, the light dry desert wind blew shrewdly down the street. Behind the eastern hills rose a huge full moon, still pale with daylight, peering wisely over the enormous spread of luminous desert.... He drove to her house, leaving the arabyieh at the gates. He walked quickly up the drive. The heavy foliage covered him with shadows, and he easily reached the verandah unobserved; no one seemed about; there was no sound of voices; the thick creepers up the wooden pillars screened him admirably. There was a movement of a chair, his heart began to thump, he climbed up softly, and at the other end of the verandah saw—Mrs. Haughstone knitting. But there was no sign of Lettice—and the blood rushed from his heart.

He had not been noticed, but his game was spoilt. He came round to the front steps and wished her politely a good-evening. Her surprise once over and explanations made, she asked him, cordially enough, to stay to dinner. 'Lettice, I know, would like it. You must be tired out. She did not expect you back so soon; but she would never forgive me if I let you go after them.'

Tom heard the words as in a dream, and answered also in a dream—a dream of astonishment, vexation, disappointment, none of them concealed. His uneasiness returned in an acute, intensified form. For he learned that they were bivouacking on the Nile to see the sunrise. Tony had, after all, not gone to Cairo; de Lorne and Lady Sybil accompanied them. It was the picnic they had planned together against his return. 'Lettice wrote,' Mrs. Haughstone mentioned, 'but the letter must have missed you. I warned her you'd be disappointed—if you knew.'

'So Tony didn't go to Cairo after all?' Tom asked again. His voice sounded thin, less volume in it than usual. That 'if you knew' dropped something of sudden anguish in his heart.

'His friends put him off at the last moment—illness, he said, or something.' Mrs. Haughstone repeated the invitation to dine and make himself at home. 'I'm positive my cousin would like you to,' she added with a certain emphasis.

Tom thanked her. He had the impression there was something on her mind. 'I think I'll go after them,' he repeated, 'if you'll tell me exactly where they've gone.' He stammered a little. 'It would be rather a lark, I thought, to surprise them.' What foolish, what inadequate words!

'Just as you like, of course. But I'm sure she's quite safe,' was the bland reply. 'Mr. Winslowe will look after her.'

'Oh, rather,' replied Tom; 'but it would be good fun—rather a joke, you know—to creep upon them unawares,'—and then was surprised and sorry that he said it. 'Have they gone very far?' he asked, fumbling for his cigarettes.

He learned that they had left after luncheon, taking with them all necessary paraphernalia for the night. There were feelings in him that he could not understand quite as he heard it. But only one thing was clear to him—he wished to be quickly, instantly, where Lettice was. It was comprehensible. Mrs. Haughstone understood and helped him. 'I'll send Mohammed to get you a boatman, as you seem quite determined,' she said, ringing the bell: 'you can get there in an hour's ride. I couldn't go,' she added, 'I really felt too tired. Mr. Winslowe was here for lunch, and he exhausted us all with laughing so that I felt I'd had enough. Besides, the sun——'

'They all lunched here too?' asked Tom.

'Mr. Winslowe only,' she mentioned, 'but he was a host in himself. It quite exhausted me——'

'Tony can be frightfully amusing, can't he, when he likes?' said Tom. Her repetition of 'exhausted' annoyed him furiously for some reason.

He saw her hesitate then: she began to speak, but stopped herself; there was a curious expression in her face, almost of anxiety, he fancied. He felt the kindness in her. She was distressed. And an impulse, whence he knew not, rose in him to make her talk, but before he could find a suitable way of beginning, she said with a kind of relief in her tone and manner: 'I'm glad you're back again, Mr. Kelverdon.' She looked significantly at him. 'Your influence is so steadying, if you don't mind my saying so.' She gave an awkward little laugh, half of apology, half of shyness, or of what passed with her for shyness. 'This climate—upsets some of us. It does something to the blood, I'm sure——'

'You feel anxious about—anything in particular?' Tom asked, with a sinking heart. At any other time he would have laughed.

Mrs. Haughstone shrugged her shoulders and sighed. She spoke with an effort apparently, as though doubtful how much she ought to say. 'My cousin, after all, is—in a sense, at least—a married woman,' was the reply, while Tom remembered that she had said the same thing once before. 'And all men are not as careful for her reputation, perhaps, as you are.' She mentioned the names of various people in Luxor, and left the impression that there was considerable gossip in the air. Tom disliked exceedingly the things she said and the way she said them, but felt unable to prevent her. He was angry with himself for listening, yet felt it beyond him to change the conversation. He both longed to hear every word, and at the same time dreaded it unspeakably. If only the boat would give him quickly an excuse.... He therefore heard her to the end concerning the unwisdom of Madame Jaretzka in her careless refusal to be more circumspect, even—Mrs. Haughstone feared—to the point of compromising herself. With whom? Why, with Mr. Winslowe, of course. Hadn't he noticed it? No! Well, of course there was no harm in it, but it was a mistake, she felt, to be seen about always with the same man. He called, too, at such unusual hours....

And each word she uttered seemed to Tom exactly what he had expected her to utter, entering his mind as a keenly poisoned shaft. Something already prepared in him leaped swiftly to understanding; only too well he grasped her meaning. The excitement in him passed into a feverishness that was painful.

For a long time he merely stood and listened, gazing across the river but seeing nothing. He said no word. His impatience was difficult to conceal, yet he concealed it.

'Couldn't you give her a hint perhaps?' continued the other, as they waited on the steps together, watching the preparations for the boat below. She spoke with an assumed carelessness that was really a disguised emphasis. 'She would take it from you, I'm sure. She means no harm; there is no harm. We all know that. She told me herself it was only a boy and girl affair. Still——'

'She said that?' asked Tom. His tone was calm, even to indifference, but his eyes, had she looked round, must certainly have betrayed him. Luckily she kept her gaze upon the moon-lit river. She drew her knitted shawl more closely round her. The cold air from the desert touched them both. Tom shivered.

'Oh, before you came out, that was,' she mentioned; and each word was a separate stab in the centre of his heart. After a pause she went on: 'So you might say a little word to be more careful, if you saw your way. Mr. Winslowe, you see, is a poor guide just now: he has so completely lost his head. He's very impressionable—and very selfish—I think.'

Tom was aware that he braced himself. Various emotions clashed within him. He knew a dozen different pains, all equally piercing. It angered him, besides, to hear Lettice spoken of in this slighting manner, for the inference was unavoidable. But there hid below his anger a deep, dull bitterness that tried angrily to raise its head. Something very ugly, very fierce moved with it. He crushed it back.... A feeling of hot shame flamed to his cheeks.

'I should feel it an impertinence, Mrs. Haughstone,' he stammered at length, yet confident that he concealed his inner turmoil. 'Your cousin— I mean, all that she does is quite beyond reproach.'

Her answer staggered him like a blow between the eyes.

'Mr. Kelverdon—on the contrary. My cousin doesn't realise quite, I'm sure—that she may cause him suffering. She won't listen to me, but you could do it. You touch the mother in her.'

It was a merciless, keen shaft—these last six words. The sudden truth of them turned him into ice. He touched only the mother in her: the woman— but the thought plunged out of sight, smothered instantly as by a granite slab he set upon it. The actual thought was smothered, yes, but the feeling struggled horribly for breath; and another inference, more deadly than the first, stole with a freezing touch upon his soul.

He turned round quietly and looked at his companion. 'By Jove,' he said, with a laugh he believed was admirably natural, 'I believe you're right. I'll give her a little hint—for Tony's sake.' He moved down the steps. 'Tony is so—I mean he so easily loses his head. It's quite absurd.'

But Mrs. Haughstone did not laugh. 'Think it over,' she rejoined. 'You have excellent judgment. You may prevent a little disaster.' She smiled and shook a warning finger. And Tom, feigning amusement as best he might, murmured something in agreement and raised his helmet with a playful flourish.

Mohammed, soft of voice and moving like a shadow, called that the boat was ready, and Tom prepared to go. Mrs. Haughstone accompanied him half-way down the steps.

'You won't startle them, will you, Mr. Kelverdon?' she said. 'Lettice, you know, is rather easily frightened.' And she laughed a little. 'It's Egypt—the dry air—one's nerves——'

Tom was already in the boat, where the Arab stood waiting in the moonlight like a ghost.

'Of course not,' he called up to her through the still air. But, none the less, he meant to surprise her if he could. Only in his thought the pronoun insisted, somehow, on the plural form.

CHAPTER XIX

The boat swung out into mid-stream. Behind him the figure of Mrs. Haughstone faded away against the bougainvillæa on the wall; in front, Mohammed's head and shoulders merged with the opposite bank; beyond, the spectral palms and the shadowy fields of clover slipped into the great body of the moon-fed desert. The desert itself sank down into a hollow that seemed to fling those dark Theban hills upwards—towards the stars.

Everything, as it were, went into its background. Everything, animate and inanimate, rose out of a common ultimate—the Sea. Yet for a moment only. There was this sense of preliminary withdrawal backwards, as for a leap that was to come....

He, too, felt merged with his own background. In his soul he knew the trouble and tumult of the Wave—gathering for a surging rise to follow....

For some minutes the sense of his own identity passed from him, and he wondered who he was. 'Who am I?' would have been a quite natural question. 'Let me see; I'm Kelverdon, Tom Kelverdon.' Of course! Yet he felt that he was another person too. He lost his grip upon his normal modern self a moment, lost hold of the steady, confident personality that was familiar.... The voice of Mohammed broke the singular spell. 'Shi-cago, vair' good donkey. Yis, bes' donkey in Luxor—' and Tom remembered that he had a ride of an hour or so before he could reach the Temple of Deir El-Bahri where his friends were bivouacking. He tipped Mohammed as he landed, mounted 'Chicago,' and started off impatiently, then ran against little Mohammed coming back for a forgotten—kettle! He laughed. Every third Arab seemed called Mohammed. But he learned exactly where the party was. He sent his own donkey-boy home, and rode on alone across the moon-lit plain.

The wonder of the exquisite night took hold of him, searching his heart beyond all power of language—the strange Egyptian beauty. The ancient wilderness, so calm beneath the stars; the mournful hills that leaped to touch the smoking moon; the perfumed air, the deep old river—each, and all together, exhaled their innermost, essential magic. Over every separate boulder spilt the flood of silver. There were troops of shadows. Among these shadows, beyond the boulders, Isis herself, it seemed, went by with audible footfall on the sand, secretly guiding his advance; Horus, dignified and solemn, with hawk-wings hovering, and fierce, deathless eyes—Horus, too, watched him lest he stumble....

On all sides he seemed aware of the powerful Egyptian gods, their protective help, their familiar guidance. The deeps within him opened. He had done this thing before.... Even the little details brought the same lost message back to him, as the hoofs of his donkey shuffled through the sand or struck a loose stone aside with metallic clatter. He heard the lizards whistling....

There were other vaster emblems too, quite close. To the south, a little, the shoulders of the Colossi domed awfully above the flat expanse, and soon he passed the Ramesseum, the moon just entering the stupendous aisles. He saw the silvery shafts beneath the huge square pylons. On all sides lay the welter of prodigious ruins, steeped in a power and beauty that seemed borrowed from the scale of the immeasurable heavens. Egypt laid a great hand upon him, her cold wind brushed his cheeks. He was aware of awfulness, of splendour, of all the immensities. He was in Eternity; life was continuous throughout the ages; there was no death....

He felt huge wings, and a hawk, disturbed by his passing, flapped silently away to another broken pillar just beyond. He seemed swept forward, the plaything of greater forces than he knew. There was no question of direction, of resistance: the Wave rushed on and he rushed with it. His normal simplicity disappeared in a complexity that bewildered him. Very clear, however, was one thing—courage; that courage due to abandonment of self. He would face whatever came. He needed it. It was inevitable. Yes—this time he would face it without shuffling or disaster.... For he recognised disaster—and was aware of blood....

Questions asked themselves in long, long whispers, but found no answers. They emerged from that mothering background and returned into it again.... Sometimes he rode alone, but sometimes Lettice rode beside him: Tony joined them.... He felt them driven forward, all three together, obedient to the lift of the same rising wave, urged onwards towards a climax that was lost to sight, and yet familiar. He knew both joy and shrinking, a delicious welcome that it was going to happen, yet a dread of searing pain involved. A great fact lay everywhere about him in the night, but a fact he could not seize completely. All his faculties settled on it, but in vain—they settled on a fragment, while the rest lay free, beyond his reach. Pain, which was a pain at nothing, filled his heart; joy, which was joy without a reason, sang in him. The Wave rose higher, higher... the breath came with difficulty... the wind was icy... there was choking in his throat....

He noticed the same high excitement in him he had experienced a few nights ago beneath the Karnak pylons—it ended later, he remembered, in the menace of an unutterable loneliness. This excitement was wild with an irresponsible hilarity that had no justification. He felt exalté. The wave, he swinging in the crest of it, was going to break, and he knew the awful thrill upon him before the dizzy, smothering plunge.

The complex of emotions made clear thought impossible. To put two and two together was beyond him. He felt the power that bore him along immensely greater than himself. And one of the smaller, self-asking questions issued from it: 'Was this what she felt? Was Tony also feeling this? Were all three of them being swept along towards an inevitable climax?' … This singular notion that none of them could help themselves passed into him.…

And then he realised from the slower pace of the animal beneath him that the path was going uphill. He collected his thoughts and looked about him. The forbidding cliffs that guard the grim Valley of the Kings, the haunted Theban hills, stood up pale yellow against the stars. The big moon, no longer smoking in the earthbound haze, had risen into the clear dominion of the upper sky. And he saw the terraces and columns of the Deir El-Bahri Temple facing him at the level of his eyes.

* * * *

Nothing bore clearer testimony to the half-unconscious method by which the drama developed itself, to the deliberate yet uncalculated attitude of the actors towards some inevitable fulfilment, than the little scene which Tom's surprise arrival then discovered. According to the mood of the beholder it could mean much or little, everything or nothing. It was so nicely contrived between concealment and disclosure, and, like much else that happened, seemed balanced exquisitely, if painfully, between guilt and innocence. The point of view of the onlooker could alone decide. At the same time it provided a perfect frame for another picture that later took the stage. The stage seemed set for it exactly. The later picture broke in and used it too. That is to say, two separate pictures, distinct yet interfused, occupied the stage at once.

For Tom, dismounting, and leaving his animal with the donkey-boys some hundred yards away, approached stealthily over the sand and came upon the picnic group before he knew it. He watched them a moment before he announced himself. The scene was some feet below him. He looked down.

Two minutes sooner, he might conceivably have found the party quite differently grouped. Instead, however, his moment of arrival was exactly timed as though to witness a scene set cleverly by the invisible Stage Manager to frame two similar and yet different incidents.

Tom leaned against a broken column, staring.

Young de Lorne and Lady Sybil, he saw, were carefully admiring the moonlight on the yellow cliffs. Miss de Lorne stooped busily over rugs and basket packages. Her back was turned to Tony and Madame Jaretzka, who were intimately engaged, their faces very close together, in the half-prosaic, half-poetic act of blowing up a gipsy fire of scanty sticks and crumpled paper. The entire picture seemed arranged as though intended to convey a 'situation.' And to Tom a situation most certainly was conveyed successfully, though a situation of which the two chief actors— who shall say otherwise?—were possibly unconscious. For in that first moment as he leaned against the column, gazing fixedly, the smoking sticks between them burst into a flare of sudden flame, setting the two faces in a frame of bright red light, and Tom, gazing upon them from a distance of perhaps some twenty yards saw them clearly, yet somehow did not—recognise them. Another picture thrust itself between: he watched a scene that lay deep below him. Through the soft blaze of that Egyptian moonlight, across the silence of that pale Egyptian desert, beneath those old Egyptian stars, there stole upon him some magic which is deathless, though its outer covenants have vanished from the world.... Down, down he sank into the forgotten scenes whence it arose. Smothered in sand, it seemed, he heard the centuries roar past him....

He saw two other persons kneeling above that fire on the desert floor, two persons familiar to him, yet whom he could not wholly recognise. In that amazing second, while his heart stopped beating, it seemed as if thought in anguish cried aloud: 'So, there you are! I have the proof!' while yet all verification of the tragic 'you' remained just out of reach and undisclosed.

He did not recognise two persons whom he knew, while yet some portion of him keenly, fiercely searching, dived back into the limbo of unremembered time.... A thin blue smoke rose before his face, and to his nostrils stole a delicate perfume as of ambra. It was a picnic fire no longer. It was an Eastern woman he saw lean forward across the gleam of a golden brazier and yield a kiss to the lips of a man who claimed it passionately. He saw her small hands folded and clinging about his neck. The face of the man he could not see, the head and shoulders being turned away, but hers he saw clearly—the dark, lustrous eyes that shone between half-closed eyelids. They were highly placed in life, these two, for their aspect as their garments told it; the man, indeed, had gold about him somewhere and the woman, in her mien, wore royalty. Yet, though he but saw their hands and heads alone, he knew instinctively that, if not regal, they were semi-regal, and set beyond his reach in power natural to them both. They were high-born, the favoured of the world. Inferiority was his who watched them, the helpless inferiority of subordinate position. That, too, he knew... for a gasp of terror, though quickly smothered terror, rose vividly behind an anger that could gladly—kill.

There was a flash of fiery and intolerable pain within him....

The next second he saw merely—Lettice!—blowing the smoke from her face and eyes, with an impatient little gesture of both hands, while in front of her knelt Tony—fanning a reluctant fire of sticks and paper with his old felt hat.

He had been gazing at a coloured bubble, the bubble had burst into air and vanished, the entire mood and picture vanished with it—so swiftly, so instantaneously, moreover, that Tom was ready to deny the entire experience.

Indeed, he did deny it. He refused to credit it. It had been, surely, a feeling rather than a sight. But the feeling having utterly vanished, he discredited the sight as well. The fiery pain had vanished too. He found himself watching the semi-comical picture of de Lorne and Lady Sybil flirting in dumb action, and Tony and Lettice trying to make a fire without the instinct or ability to succeed. And, incontinently, he burst out laughing audibly.

Yet, apparently, his laughter was not heard; he had made no actual sound. There was, instead, a little scream, a sudden movement, a scurrying of feet among the sand and stones, and Lettice and Tony rose upon one single impulse, as once before he had seen them rise in Karnak weeks ago. They stood up like one person. They looked about them into the surrounding shadows, disturbed, afflicted, yet as though they were not certain they had heard... and then, abruptly, the figure of Tony went out... it disappeared. How, precisely, was not clear, but it was gone into the darkness....

And another picture—or another aspect of the first—dropped into place. There was an outline of a shadowy tent. The flap was stirring lightly, as though behind it some one hid—and watched. He could not tell. A deep confusion, as of two pictures interfused, was in him. For somehow he transferred his own self—was it physical desire? was it spiritual yearning? was it love?—projected his own self into the figure that had kissed her, taking her own passionate kiss in return. He actually experienced it. He did this thing. He had done it—once before! Knowing himself beside her, he both did it and saw himself doing it. He was both actor and onlooker....

There poured back upon him then, sweet and poignant, his love of an Egyptian woman, the fragrance of remembered tresses, the perfume of fair limbs that clung and of arms that lingered round his neck—yet that in the last moment slipped from his full possession. He was on his knees before her; he gazed up into her ardent eyes, set in a glowing face above his own; the face bent lower; he raised two slender hands, the fingers henna-stained, and pressed them to his lips. He felt their silken texture, the fragile pressure, her breath upon his face—yet all sharply withdrawn again before he captured them completely. There was the odour of long-forgotten unguents, sweet with a tang that sharpened them towards desire in days that knew a fiercer sunlight.... His brain went reeling. The effort to keep one picture separate from the other broke them both. He could not disentangle, could not distinguish. They intermingled. He was both the figure hidden behind the tent and the figure who held the woman in his arms. What his heart desired became, it seemed, that which happened....

And then the flap of the tent flung open, and out rushed a violent, leaping outline—the figure of a man. Another—it seemed himself—rushed to meet him. There was a gleam, a long deep cry.... A woman, with arms outstretched, knelt close beside the struggling figures on the sand. He saw two huge, dark, muscular hands about a bent and yielding neck, blood oozing thickly between the gripping fingers, staining them... then sudden darkness that blacked out the entire scene, and a choking effort to find breath.... But it was his own breath that failed, choked as by blood and fire that broke into his own throat.... Smothered in sand, the centuries roared past him, died away into the distance, sank back into the interminable desert.... He found his voice this time. He shouted.

He saw again—Lettice, blowing the smoke from her face and eyes with an impatient little gesture of both hands, while Tony knelt in front of her and fanned a reluctant fire with his old felt hat. The picture—the second picture—had been instantaneous. It had not lasted a fraction of a second even.

He shouted. And this time his voice was audible. Lettice and Tony stood up, as though a single person rose. Both turned in the direction of the sound. Then Tony moved off quickly. Tom's vision had interpenetrated this very action even while it was actually taking place—the first time.

'Why—I do declare—if it isn't—Tom!' he heard in a startled woman's voice.

He came down towards her slowly. Something of the 'pictures' still swam in between what was next said and done. It seemed in the atmosphere, pervading the three of them. But it was weakening, passing away quickly. For one moment, however, before it passed, it became overpowering again.

'But, Tom—is this a joke, or what? You frightened me,'—she gave a horrid gasp—'nearly to death! You've come back——!'

'It's a surprise,' he cried, trying to laugh, though his lips were dry and refused the effort. 'I have surprised you. I've come back!'

He heard the gasp prolonged. Breathing seemed difficult. Some deep distress was in her. Yet, in place of pity, exultation caught him oddly. The next instant he felt suddenly afraid. There was confusion in his soul. For it was he and she, it seemed, who had been 'surprised and caught.' And her voice called shrilly:

'Tony! Tony...!'

There was amazement in the sound of it—terror, relief, and passion too. The thin note of fear and anguish broke through the natural call. Then, as Tony came running up, a few sticks in his big hands—she screamed, yet with failing breath:

'Oh, oh...! Who are you...?'

For the man she summoned came, but came too swiftly. Moving with uncertain gait, he yet came rapidly—terribly, somehow, and with violence. Instantaneously, it seemed, he covered the intervening space. In the calm, sweet moonlight, beneath the blaze of the steady stars, he suddenly was—there, upon that patch of ancient desert sand. He looked half unearthly. The big hands he held outspread before him glistened a little in the shimmer of the moon. Yet they were dark, and they seemed menacing. They threatened—as with some power he meant to use, because it was his right. But the gleam upon them was not of swarthy skin alone. The gleam, the darkness, were of blood.... There was a cry again—a sound of anguish almost intolerable....

And the same instant Tom felt the clasp of his cousin's hand upon his own, and heard his jolly voice with easy, natural laughter in it: 'But, Tom, old chap, how ripping! You're really back! This is a grand surprise! It's splendid!'

* * * *

There was nothing that called upon either his courage or control. They were overjoyed to see him, the surprise he provided proved indeed the success of the evening.

'I thought at first you were Mohammed with the kettle,' exclaimed Madame Jaretzka, coming close to make quite sure, and murmuring quickly— nervously as well, he thought—'Oh, Tom, I am so glad,' beneath her breath. 'You're just in time—we all wanted you so.'

Explanations followed; Tony's friends had postponed the Cairo trip at the last moment; the picnic had been planned as a rehearsal for the real one that was to follow later. Tom's adroitness in finding them was praised; he became the unwilling hero of the piece, and as such had to make the fire a success and prove himself generally the clou of the party that hitherto was missing. He became at once the life and centre of the little group, gay and in the highest spirits, the emotion accumulated in him discharging itself in the entirely unexpected direction of hilarious fun and gaiety.

The sense of tragedy he had gathered on his journey, if it muttered at all, muttered out of sight. He looked back upon his feelings of an hour before with amazement, dismay, distress—then utterly forgot them. The picture itself—the vision—was as though it had not been at all. What, in the name of common sense, had possessed him that he could ever have admitted such preposterous uneasiness? He thought of Mrs. Haughstone's absurd warnings with a sharp contempt, and felt his spirits only rise higher than before. She was meanly suspicious about nothing. Of course he would give Lettice a hint: why not, indeed? He would give it then and there before them all and hear them laugh about it till they cried. And he would have done so, doubtless, but that he realised the woman's jealousy was a sordid topic to introduce into so gay a party.

'You arrived in the nick of time, Tom,' Lettice told him. 'We were beginning to feel the solemnity of these surroundings, the awful Tombs of the Kings and Priests and people. Those cliffs are too oppressive for a picnic.'

'A fact,' cried Tony. 'It feels like sacrilege. They resent us being here.' He glanced at Madame Jaretzka as he said it. 'If you hadn't come, Tom, I'm sure there'd have been a disaster somewhere. Anyhow, one must feel superstitious to enjoy a place like this. It's the proper atmosphere!'

Lettice looked up at Tom, and added, 'You've really saved us. The least we can do is to worship the sun the moment he gets up. We'll adore old Amon-Ra. It's obvious. We must!'

They made themselves merry over a rather sandy meal. She arranged a place for him close beside her, and her genuine pleasure at his unexpected return filled him with a joy that crowded out even the memory of other emotions. The mixture called Tom Kelverdon asserted itself: he felt ashamed; he heartily despised his moods, wondering whence they came so strangely. Tony himself was quiet and affectionate. If anything was lacking, Tom's high spirits carried him too boisterously to notice it. Otherwise he might possibly have thought that she spoke a little sharply once or twice to Tony, neglecting him in a way that was not quite her normal way, and that to himself, even before the others, she was unusually—almost too emphatically—dear and tender. Indeed, she seemed so pleased he had come that a cynical observer, cursed with an acute, experienced mind, might almost have thought she showed something not far from positive relief. But Tom, too happy to be sensitive to shades of feminine conduct, was aware chiefly, if not solely, of his own joy and welcome.

'You didn't get my letter, then, before you left?' she asked him once; and he replied, 'The answer, as in Parliament, is in the negative. But it will be forwarded all right.' He would get it the following night. 'Ah, but you mustn't read it now,' she said. 'You must tear it up unread,' and made him promise faithfully he would obey. 'I wrote to you too,' mentioned Tony, as though determined to be left out of nothing. 'You'll get it at the same time. But you mustn't tear mine up, remember. It's full of advice and wisdom you badly need.' And Tom promised that faithfully as well. The reply was in the affirmative.

The bivouac was a complete success; all looked back upon it as an unforgettable experience. They declared, of course, they had not slept a wink, yet all had snored quite audibly beneath the wheeling stars. They were fresh and lively enough, certainly, when the sun poured his delicious warmth across the cloudless sky, while Tom and Tony made the fire and set the coffee on for breakfast.

Of the marvellous beauty that preceded the actual sunrise no one spoke; it left them breathless rather; they watched the sky beyond the hills change colour; great shafts of gold transfixed the violet heavens; the Nile shone faintly; then, with a sudden drive, the stars rushed backwards in a shower, and the amazing sun came up as with a shout. Perfumes that have no name rose from the desert and the fields along the distant river banks. The silence deepened, for no birds sang. Light took the world—and it was morning.

And when the donkey-boys arrived at eight o'clock, the party were slow in starting: it was so pleasant to lie and bask in the sumptuous bath of heat and light that drenched them. The night had been chilly enough. They were a tired party. Once home again, all retired with one accord to sleep, remaining invisible until the sun was slanting over Persia and the Indian Ocean, gilding the horizon probably above the starry skies of far Cathay.

But as Tom dozed off behind the shuttered windows in the hotel towards eleven o'clock, having bathed and breakfasted a second time, he thought vaguely of what Mrs. Haughstone had said to him a few hours before. It seemed days ago already. He was too drowsy to hold the thought more than a moment in his mind, much less to reflect upon it. 'It may be just as well to give a hint,' occurred to him. 'Tony is a bit too fond of her—too fond for his happiness, perhaps.' Nothing had happened at the picnic to revive the notion; it just struck him as he fell asleep, then vanished; it was a moment's instinct. The vision—it had been an instantaneous flash after all and nothing more—had left his mind completely for the time.

But Tom looked back afterwards upon the all-night bivouac as an occasion marked specially in memory's calendar, yet for a reason that was unlike the reasons his companions knew. He remembered it with mingled joy and pain, also with a wonder that he could have been so blind—the last night of happiness in his brief Egyptian winter.

CHAPTER XX

He slept through the hot hours of the afternoon. In the cool of the evening, as he strolled along the river bank, he read the few lines Lettice had written to him at Assouan. For the porter had handed him half-a-dozen letters as he left the hotel. Tony's he put for the moment aside; the one from Lettice was all he cared about, quite forgetting he had promised to tear it up unread. It was short but tender—anxious about his comfort and well-being in a strange hotel 'when I am not there to take care of you.' It ended on a complaint that she was 'tired rather and spending my time at full length on a deck-chair in the garden.' She promised to write 'at greater length to-morrow.'

'Instead of which,' thought Tom with a boy's delight, 'I surprised her and we talked face to face.' But for the Arab touts who ran beside him, offering glass beads made in Birmingham, he could have kissed the letter there and then.

The resplendent gold on the river blinded him, he was glad to enter the darker street and shake off the children who pestered him for baksh-ish. Passing the Savoy Hotel, he hesitated a moment, then went on. 'No, I won't call in for Tony; I'll find her alone, and we'll have a cosy little talk together before the others come.' He quickened his pace, entered the shady garden, discovered her instantly, and threw himself down upon the cushions beside her deck-chair. 'Just what I hoped,' he said, with pleasure and admiration in his eyes, 'alone at last. That is good luck—isn't it, Lettice?'

'Of course,' she agreed, and smiled lazily, though some might have thought indifferently, as she watched him arranging the cushions. He flung himself back and gazed at her. She wore a dress of palest yellow, and the broad-brimmed hat with the little roses. She seemed part of the flaming sunset and the tawny desert.

'Well,' he grumbled playfully, 'it is true, isn't it? Our not being alone often, I mean?' He watched her without knowing that he did so.

'In a way—yes,' she said. 'But we can't have everything at once, can we, Tom?' Her voice was colourless perhaps. A tiny frown settled for an instant between her eyes, then vanished. Tom did not notice it. She sighed. 'You baby, Tom. I spoil you dreadfully, and you know I do.'

He liked her in this quiet, teasing mood; it was often the prelude to more delightful spoiling. He was in high spirits. 'You look as fresh as a girl of sixteen, Lettice,' he declared. 'I believe you're only this instant out of your bath and bed. D'you know, I slept like a baby too— the whole afternoon———'

He interrupted himself, for at that moment a cigarette-case on the sand beside him caught his eye. He picked it up—he recognised it. 'Yes—I wish you'd smoke,' she said the same instant, brushing a fly quickly from her cheek.

'Tony's,' he exclaimed, examining the case.

He noticed at the same time several burnt matches between his cushions and her chair.

'But he'd love you to smoke them: I'll take the responsibility.' She laughed quietly. 'I'm sure they're good—better than yours; he's wickedly extravagant.' She watched him as he took one out, examining the label critically, then lighting it slowly and inhaling the smoke to taste it. There was a faint perfume that clung to the case and its contents. 'Ambra,' said Lettice, a kind of watchful amusement in her eyes. 'You don't like it!'

Tom looked up sharply.

'Is that it? I didn't know.'

She nodded. 'It's Tony's smell; haven't you noticed it? He always has it about him. No, no,' she laughed, noticing his expression of disapproval, 'he doesn't use it. It's just in his atmosphere, I mean.'

'Oh, is it?' said Tom.

'I rather like it,' she went on idly, 'but I never can make out where it comes from. We call it ambra—the fragrance that hangs about the bazaars: I believe they used it for the mummies; but the desert perfume is in it too. It's rather wonderful—it suits him—don't you think? Penetrating, and so delicate.'

What a lot she had to say about it! He made no reply. He was looking down to see what caused him that sudden, inexplicable pain—and discovered that the lighted match had burned his fingers. The next minute he looked up again—straight into her eyes.

But, somehow, he did not say exactly what he meant to say. He said, in fact, something that occurred to him on the spur of the moment. His mind was simple, possibly, yet imps occasionally made use of it. An imp just then reminded him: 'Her letter made no mention of the picnic, of Tony's sudden change of plan, yet it was written yesterday morning when both were being arranged.'

So Tom did not refer to the ambra perfume, nor to the fact that Tony had spent the afternoon with her. He said quite another thing—said it rather bluntly too: 'I've just got your letter from Assouan, Lettice, and I clean forgot my promise that I wouldn't read it.' He paused a second. 'You said nothing about the picnic in it.'

'I thought you'd be disappointed if you knew,' she replied at once. 'That's why I didn't want you to read it.' And she fell to scolding him in the way he usually loved,—but at the moment found less stimulating for some reason. He smoked his stolen cigarette with energy for a measurable period.

'You're the spoilt child, not I,' he said at length, still looking at her. 'You said you were tired and meant to rest, and then you go for an exhausting expedition instead.'

The tiny frown reappeared between her eyes, lingered a trifle longer than before, and vanished. She made a quick gesture. 'You're in a very nagging mood, Tom; bivouacs don't agree with you.' She spoke lightly, easily, in excellent good temper really. 'It was Tony persuaded me, if you want to know the truth. He found himself free unexpectedly; he was so persistent; it's impossible to resist him when he's like that—the only thing is to give in and go.'

'Of course.' Tom's face was like a mask. He thought so, at least, as he laughed and agreed with her, saying Tony was an unscrupulous rascal at the best of times. Apparently there was a struggle in him; he seemed in two minds. 'Was he here this afternoon?' he asked. He learned that Tony had come at four o'clock and had tea with her alone. 'We didn't telephone because he said it would only spoil your sleep, and that a man who works as well as plays must sleep—longer than a younger man.' Then, as Tom said nothing, she added, 'Tony is such a boy, isn't he?'

There were several emotions in Tom just then. He hardly knew which was the true, or at least, the dominant one. He was thinking of several things at once too: of her letter, of that faint peculiar odour, of Tony's coming to tea, but chiefly, perhaps, of the fact that Lettice had not mentioned it,—but that he had found it out.... His heart sank. It struck him suddenly that the mother in her sought to protect him from the pain the woman gave.

'Is he—yes,' he said absent-mindedly. And she repeated quietly, 'Oh, I think so.'

The brief eastern twilight had meanwhile fallen, and the rapidly cooling air sighed through the foliage. It grew darker in their shady corner. The western sky was still a blaze of riotous colour, however, that filtered through the trees and shed a luminous glow upon their faces. It was a bewitching light—there was something bewitching about Lettice as she lay there. Tom himself felt a touch of that deep Egyptian enchantment. It stole in among his thoughts and feelings, colouring motives, lifting into view, as from far away, moods that he hardly understood and yet obeyed because they were familiar.

This evasive sense of familiarity, both welcome and unwelcome, swept in, dropped a fleeting whisper, and was gone again. He felt himself for an instant—some one else: one Tom felt and spoke, while another

Tom looked on and watched, a calm, outside spectator. And upon his heart came a touch of that strange, rich pain that was never very far away in Egypt.

'I say, Lettice,' he began suddenly, as though he came to an abrupt decision. 'This is an awful place for talk—these Luxor hotels——' He stuck. 'Isn't it? You know what I mean.' His laborious manner betrayed intensity, yet he meant to speak lightly, easily, and thought his voice was merely natural. He stared hard at the glowing tip of his cigarette.

Lettice looked across at him without speaking for a moment. Her eyelids were half closed. He felt her gaze and raised his own. He saw the smile steal down towards her lips.

'Tom, why are you glaring at me?'

He started. He tried to smile, but there was no smile in him.

'Was I, Lettice? Forgive me.' The talk that was coming would hurt him, yet somehow he desired it. He would give his little warning and take the consequences. 'I was devouring your beauty, as the Family Herald says.' He heard himself utter a dry and unconvincing laugh. Something was rising through him; it was beyond control; it had to come. He felt stupid, awkward, and was angry with himself for being so. For, somehow, at the same time he felt powerless too.

She came to the point with a directness that disconcerted him. 'Who has been talking about me?' she enquired, her voice hardening a little; 'and what does it matter if they have?'

Tom swallowed. There was something about her beauty in that moment that set him on fire from head to foot. He knew a fierce desire to seize her in his arms, hold her for ever and ever—lest she should escape him.

But he was unable to give expression in any way to what was in him. All he did was to shift his cushions slightly farther from her side.

'It's always wiser—safer—not to be seen about too much with the same man—alone,' he fumbled, recalling Mrs. Haughstone's words, 'in a place like this, I mean,' he qualified it. It sounded foolish, but he could evolve no cleverer way of phrasing it. He went on quicker, a touch of nervousness in his voice he tried to smother: 'No one can mistake our relationship, or think there's anything wrong in it.' He stopped a second, as she gazed at him in silence, waiting for him to finish. 'But Tony,' he concluded, with a gulp he prayed she did not notice, 'Tony is a little——'

'Well?' she helped him, 'a little what?'

'A little different, isn't he?'

Tom realised that he was producing the reverse of what he intended. Somehow the choice of words seemed forced upon him. He was aware of his own helplessness; he felt almost like a boy scolding his own wise, affectionate mother. The thought stung him into pain, and with the pain rose, too, a first distant hint of anger. The turmoil of feeling confused him. He was aware—by her silence chiefly—of the new distance between them, a distance the mention of Tony had emphasised. Instinctively he tried to hide both pain and anger—it could only increase this distance that was already there. At the same time he saw red.... Her answer, then, so gently given, baffled him absurdly. He felt out of his depth.

'I'll be more careful, Tom, dear—you wise, experienced chaperone.'

The words, the manner, stung him. Another emotion, wounded vanity, came into play. To laugh at himself was natural and right, but to be laughed at by a woman, a woman whom he loved, whom he regarded as exclusively his own, against whom, moreover, he had an accumulating grievance—it hurt him acutely, although he seemed powerless to prevent it. He felt his own stupidity increase.

'It's just as well, I think, Lettice.' It was the wrong, the hopeless thing to say, but the words seemed, in a sense, pushed quickly out of his mouth lest he should find better ones. He anticipated, too, her exasperation before her answer proved it: 'But, really, Tom, you know, I can look after myself rather well as a rule—don't you think?'

He interrupted her then, a mixture of several feelings in him—shame, the pain of frustrate yearning, perversity too. For, in spite of himself, he wanted to hear how she would speak of Tony. He meant to punish himself by hearing her praise him. He, too, meant to speak well of his cousin.

'He's a bit careless, though,' he blurted, 'irresponsible, in a way—where women are concerned. I'm sure he means no harm, of course, but——' He paused in confusion, he was no longer afraid that harm might come to Tony; he was afraid for her, but now also for himself as well.

'Tom, I do believe you're jealous!'

He laughed boisterously when he heard it. It was really comical, absurdly comical, of course. It sounded, too, the way she said it—ugly, mean, contemptible. The touch of shame came back.

'Lettice! But what an idea!' He gasped, turning round upon his other elbow, closer to her. But the sinking of his heart increased; he felt an inner cold. And a moment of deep silence followed the empty laughter. The rustle of the foliage alone was audible.

Lettice looked down sideways at him through half-closed eyelids; propped on his cushions beside her, this was natural: yet he felt it mental as well as physical. There was pity in her attitude, a concealed exasperation, almost contempt. At the same time he realised that she had never seemed so adorably lovely, so exquisite, so out of his reach. He had never felt her so seductively desirable. He made an impetuous gesture towards her before he knew it.

'Don't, Tom; you'll upset my papers and everything,' she said calmly, yet with the merest suspicion of annoyance in her tone. She was very gentle, she was also very cold—cold as ice, he felt her, while he was burning as with fire. He was aware of this unbridgeable distance between his passion and her indifference; and a dreadful thought leaped up in him with stabbing pain: 'Her answer to Tony would have been quite otherwise.'

'I'm sorry, Lettice—so sorry,' he said brusquely, to hide his mortification. 'I'm awfully clumsy.' She was putting her papers tidy again with calm fingers, while his own were almost cramped with the energy of suppressed desire. 'But, seriously,' he went on, refusing the rebuff by pretending it was play on his part, 'it isn't very wise to be seen about so much alone with Tony. Believe me, it isn't.' For the first time, he noticed, it was difficult to use the familiar and affectionate name. But for a sense of humour he could have said 'Anthony.'

'I do believe you, Tom. I'll be more careful.' Her eyes were very soft, her manner quiet, her gentle tone untinged with any emotion. Yet Tom detected, he felt sure, a certain eagerness behind the show of apparent indifference. She liked to talk—to go on talking—about Tony. 'Do you really think so, really mean it?' he heard her asking, and thus knew his thought confirmed. She invited more. And, with open eyes, with a curious welcome even to the pain involved, Tom deliberately stepped into the cruel little trap. But he almost felt that something pushed him in. He talked exactly like a boy: 'He—he's got a peculiar power with women,' he said. 'I can't make it out quite. He's not good-looking—exactly—is he?' It was impossible to conceal his eagerness to know exactly what she did feel.

'There's a touch of genius in him,' she answered. 'I don't think looks matter so much—I mean, with women.' She spoke with a certain restraint, not deliberately saying less than she thought, but yet keeping back the entire truth. He suddenly realised a relationship between her and Tony into which he was not admitted. The distance between them increased visibly before his very eyes.

And again, out of a hundred things he wanted to say, he said—as though compelled to—another thing.

'Rather!' he burst out honestly. 'I should hate it if—you hadn't liked him.' But a week ago he would have phrased this differently—'If he had not liked you.'

There were perceptible pauses between their sentences now, pauses that for him seemed breaking with a suspense that was painful, almost cruel. He knew worse was coming. He both longed for it yet dreaded it. He felt at her mercy, in her power somehow.

'It's odd,' she went on slowly, 'but in England I thought him stupid rather, whereas out here he's changed into another person.'

'I think we've all changed—somehow,' Tom filled the pause, and was going to say more when she interrupted.

She kept the conversation upon Tony. 'I shall never forget the day he walked in here first. It was the week I arrived. You'll laugh, Tom, when I tell you——' She hesitated—almost it seemed on purpose.

'How was it? How did he look?' The forced indifference of the tone betrayed his anxiety.

'Well, he's not impressive exactly—is he?—as a rule. That little stoop—and so on. But I saw his figure coming up the path before I recognised who it was, and I thought suddenly of an Egyptian, almost an old Pharaoh, walking.'

She broke off with that little significant laugh Tom knew so well. But, comical though the picture might have been—Tony walking like a king,—Tom did not laugh. It was not ludicrous, for it was somewhere true. He remembered the singular inner mental picture he had seen above the desert fire, and the pain within him seemed the forerunner of some tragedy that watched too close upon his life. But, for another and more obvious reason, he could not laugh; for he heard the admiration in her voice, and it was upon that his mind fastened instantly. His observation was so mercilessly sharp. He hated it. Where was his usual slowness gone? Why was his blood so quickly apprehensive?

She kept her eyes fixed steadily on his, saying what followed gently, calmly, yet as though another woman spoke the words. She stabbed him, noting the effect upon him with a detached interest that seemed indifferent to his pain. Something remote and ancient stirred in her, something that was not of herself To-day, something half primitive, half barbaric.

'It may have been the blazing light,' she went on, 'the half-savage effect of these amazing sunsets—I cannot say,—but I saw him in a sheet of gold. There was gold about him, I mean, as though he wore it—and when he came close there was that odd, faint perfume, half of the open desert and half of ambra, as we call it——' Again she broke off and hesitated, leaving the impression there was more to tell, but that she could not say it. She kept back much. Into the distance now established between them Tom felt a creeping sense of cold, as of the chill desert wind that follows hard upon the sunset. Her eyes still held him steadily. He seemed more and more aware of something merciless in her.

He sat and gazed at her—at a woman he loved, a woman who loved him, but a woman who now caused him pain deliberately because something beyond herself compelled. Her tenderness lay inactive, though surely not forgotten. She, too, felt the pain. Yet with her it was in some odd way—impersonal.... Tom, hopelessly out of his depth, swept onward by this mighty wave behind all three of them, sat still and watched her— fascinated, even terrified. Her eyelids were half closed again. Another look stole up into her face, driving away the modern beauty, replacing its softness, tenderness with another expression he could not fathom. Yet this new expression was somehow, too, half recognisable. It was difficult to describe—a little sterner, a little wilder, a faint emphasis of the barbaric peering through it. It was darker. She looked eastern. Almost, he saw her visibly change—here in the twilight of the little Luxor garden by his side. Distance increased remorselessly between them. She was far away, yet ever close at the same time. He could not tell whether she was going away from him or coming nearer. The shadow of tragedy fell on him from the empty sky....

In his bewilderment he tried to hold steady and watch, but the soul in him rushed backwards. He felt, but could not think. The wave surged under him. Various impulses urged him into a pouring flood of words; yet he gave expression to none of them. He laughed a little dry, short laugh. He heard himself saying lightly, though with apparent lack of interest: 'How curious, Lettice, how very odd! What made him look like that?'

But he knew her answer would mean pain. It came just as he expected:

'He is wonderful—out here—quite different——' Another minute and she would have added 'I'm different, too.' But Tom interrupted hurriedly:

'Do you always see him—like that—now? In a sheet of gold—with beauty?' His tongue was so hot and dry against his lips that he almost stammered.

She nodded, her eyelids still half closed. She lay very quiet, peering down at him. 'It lasts?' he insisted, turning the knife himself.

'You'll laugh when I tell you something more,' she went on, making a slight gesture of assent, 'but I felt such joy in myself—so wild and reckless—that when I got to my room that night I danced—danced alone with all my clothes off.'

'Lettice!'

'The spontaneous happiness was like a child's—a sort of freedom feeling. I had to shake my clothes off simply. I wanted to shake off the walls and ceiling too, and get out into the open desert. Tom—I felt out of myself in a way—as though I'd escaped—into—into quite different conditions——'

She gave details of the singular mood that had come upon her with the arrival of Tony, but Tom hardly heard her. Only too well he knew the explanation. The touch of ecstasy was no new thing, although its manifestation may have been peculiar. He had known it himself in his own lesser love affairs. But that she could calmly tell him about it, that she could deliberately describe this effect upon her of another man—! It baffled him beyond all thoughts or words.... Was the self-revelation an unconscious one? Did she realise the meaning of what she told him? The Lettice he had known could surely not say this thing. In her he felt again, more distinctly than before, another person—division, conflict. Her hesitations, her face, her gestures, her very language proved it. He shrank, as from some one who inflicted pain as a child, unwittingly, to see what the effect would be.... He remembered the incident of the insect in the sand....

'And I feel—even now—I could do it again,' her voice pierced in across his moment of hidden anguish. The knife she had thrust again into his breast was twisted then.

It was time that he said something, and a sentence offered itself in time to save him. The desire to hide his pain from her was too strong to be disobeyed. He wanted to know, yet not, somehow, to prevent. He seized upon the sentence, keeping his voice steady with an effort that cut his very flesh: 'There's nothing impersonal exactly in that, Lettice!' he exclaimed with an exaggerated lightness.

'Oh no,' she agreed. 'But it's only in England, perhaps, that I'm impersonal, as you call it. I suppose, out here, I've changed. The beauty, the mystery,—this fierce sunshine or something—stir——' She hesitated for a fraction of a second.

'The woman in you,' he put in, turning the knife this time with his own fingers deliberately. The words seemed driven out by their own impetus; he did not choose them. A faint ghastly hope was in him—that she would shake her head and contradict him.

She waited a moment, then turned her eyes aside. 'Perhaps, Tom. I wonder....!'

And as she said it, Tom knew suddenly another thing as well. It stood out clearly, as with big printed letters that violent advertisements use upon the hoardings. Her new joy and excitement, her gaiety and zest for life— all had been caused, not by himself, but by another. Heavens! how blind he had been! He understood at last, and a flood of freezing water drenched him. His heart stopped beating for a moment. He gasped. He could not get his breath. His accumulating doubts hitherto unexpressed, almost unacknowledged even, were now confirmed.

He got up stiffly, awkwardly, from his cushions, and moved a few steps towards the house, for there stole upon her altered face just then the very expression of excitement, of radiant and spontaneous joy, he had believed until this moment were caused by himself. Tony was coming up the darkened drive. He was exactly in her line of sight. And a severe, embittered struggle then took place in a heart that seemed strangely divided against itself. He felt as though a second Tom, yet still himself, battled against the first, exchanging thrusts of indescribable torture. The complexity of emotions in his heart was devastating beyond anything he had ever known in his thirty-five years of satisfied, self-centred life. Two voices spoke in clear, sharp sentences, one against the other:

'Your suspicions are unworthy, shameful. Trust her. She's as loyal and true and faithful as yourself!' cried the first.

And the second:

'Blind! Can't you see what's going on between them? It has happened to other men, why not to you? She is playing with you; she has outgrown your love.' It was the older voice that used the words.

'Impossible, ridiculous!' the first voice cried. 'There's something wrong with me that I can have such wretched thoughts. It's merely innocence and joy of life. No one can take my place.'

To which, again, the second Tom made bitter answer. 'You are too old for her, too dull, too ordinary! You hold the loving mother still, but a younger man has waked the woman in her. And you must let it come. You dare not blame. Nor have you the right to interfere.'

So acute, so violent was the perplexity in him that he knew not what to say or do at first. Unable to come to a decision, he stood there, waving his hand to Tony with a cry of welcome. His first vehement desire to be alone, to make an excuse, to get to his room and think, had passed: a second, a maturer attitude, conquered it: to take whatever came, to face it, in a word to know the worst.... And the extraordinary pain he hid by an exuberance of high spirits that surprised himself. It was, of course, the suppressed emotional energy finding another outlet. A similar state had occurred that 'Karnak night' of a long ten days ago, though he had not understood it then. Behind it lay the misery of loneliness that he knew in his very bones was coming.

'Tony! So it is. I was afraid he'd change his mind and leave us in the lurch.'

Tom heard the laugh of happiness as she said it; he heard the voice distinctly—the change of tone in it, the softness, the half-caressing tenderness that crept unconsciously in, the faint thrill of womanly passion. Unconsciously, yes! he was sure, at least, of that. She did not know quite yet, she did not realise what had happened. Honest to the core, he felt her. His love surged up tumultuously. He could face pain, loss, death—or, as he put it, 'almost anything,' if it meant happiness to her. The thought, at any rate, came to him thus.... And Tom believed it.

At the same moment he heard her voice, close behind him this time. She had left her chair, meaning to go indoors and prepare for supper before Tony actually arrived. 'Tom, dear boy,' her hand upon his shoulder a moment as she passed, 'you're tired or something. I can see it. I believe you're worrying. There's something you haven't told me—isn't there now?' She gave him a loving glance that was of purest gold. 'You shall tell me all about it when we're alone. You must tell me everything.'

The pain and joy in him were equal then. He was a boy of eighteen, aching over his first love affair; and she was divinely mothering him. It was extraordinary; it was past belief; another minute, had they been alone, he could almost have laid his head upon her breast, complaining in anguish to the mother in her that the woman he loved was gone: 'I feel you're slipping from me! I'm losing you…!'

Instead he stammered some commonplace unreality about his work at Assouan and heard her agree with him that he certainly must not neglect it—and she was gone into the house. The swinging curtains of dried grasses hid her a few feet beyond, but between them, he felt, stretched five thousand years and half a dozen continents as well.

* * * *

'Tom, old chap, did you get my letter? You promised to read it. Is it all right, I mean? I wouldn't for all the world let anything——'

Tom stopped him abruptly. He wished to read the letter for himself without foreknowledge of its contents.

'Eh? No—that is, I got it,' he said confusedly, 'but I haven't read it yet. I slept all the afternoon.'

An expression of anxiety in Tony's face came and vanished. 'You can tell me to-morrow—frank as you like, mind,' he replied, to which Tom said quite eagerly, 'Rather, Tony: of course. I'll read your old letter the moment I get back to-night.' And Tony, merry as a sandboy, changed the subject, declaring that he had only one desire in life just then, and that was—food.

CHAPTER XXI

The conflict in Tom's puzzled heart sharpened that evening into dreadful edges that cut him mercilessly whichever way he turned. One minute he felt sure of Lettice, the next the opposite was clear. Between these two certainties he balanced in secret torture, one factor alone constant—that his sense of security was shaken to the foundations.

Belief in his own value had never been thus assailed before; that he was indispensable had been an ultimate assurance. His vanity and self-esteem now toppled ominously. A sense of inferiority crept over him, as on the first day of his arrival at Alexandria. There seemed the flavour of some strange authority in her that baffled all approach to the former intimacy. He hardly recognised himself, for, the foundations being shaken, all that was built upon them trembled too.

The insecurity showed in the smallest trifles—he expressed himself hesitatingly; he felt awkward, clumsy, ineffective; his conversation became stupid for all the false high spirits that inflated it, his very manners gauche; he said and did the wrong things; he was boring. Being ill at ease and out of harmony with himself, he found it impossible to play his part in the trio as of old; the trio, indeed, had now divided itself—one against two.

That is, keenly, and in spite of himself, he watched the other two; he watched them as a detective does, for evidence. He became uncannily observant. And since Tony was especially amusing that evening, Lettice, moreover, apparently absorbed in his stimulating talk, Tom's alternate gaucheries and silence passed unnoticed, certainly uncommented. In schoolboy phraseology, Tom felt out of it. His presence was tolerated—as by favour. The two enjoyed a mutual understanding from which he was excluded, a private intimacy that was spiritual, mental,— physical.

He even found it in him for the first time to marvel that Lettice had ever cared for him at all. Beside Tony's brilliance he felt himself cheaper, almost insignificant. He felt old.... His pain, moreover, was twofold: his own selfish sense of personal loss produced one kind of anguish, but the possibility that she was playing false produced another. The first was manageable: the second beyond words appalling.

Against this background of emotional disturbance he watched the evening pass. It developed as the hours moved. Tony, he noticed, though so full of life, betrayed a certain malaise towards himself and avoided that direct meeting of the eye that was his characteristic. More and more, especially when Mrs. Haughstone had betaken herself to bed, and the trio sat in the cooler garden alone, Tom became aware of a subtle intimacy between his companions that resented all his efforts to include him too.

It was, moreover—his heart warned him now,—an affectionate, a natural intimacy, built upon many an hour of intercourse while he was yet in England, and, worst of all, that it was secret. But more—he realised that the missing part of her was now astir, touched into life by another, and a younger, man. It was ardent and untamed. It had awakened from its slumber. He even fancied that something of challenge flashed from her, though without definite words or gesture.

With a degree of acute perception wholly new to him, he watched the evidence of inner proximity, yet watched it automatically and certainly not meanly nor with slyness. The evidence that was sheer anguish thrust itself upon him. His eyes had opened; he could not help himself.

But he watched himself as well. Only at moments was he aware of this—a kind of higher Self, detached from shifting moods, looked on calmly and took note. This Self, placed high above the stage, looked down. It was a Self that never acted, never wept or suffered, never changed. It was secure, superb, it was divine. Its very existence in him hitherto had been unknown. He was now vividly aware of it. It was the Onlooker.

The explanation of his mysterious earlier moods offered itself with a clarity that was ghastly. Watching the happiness of these two, he recalled a hundred subconscious hints he had disregarded: the empty letter at Alexandria, her dislike of being alone with him, the increasing admiration for his cousin, a thousand things she had left unsaid, above all, the exuberance and radiant joy that Tony's presence woke in her. The gradual but significant change, the singular vision in the desert, his own foretaste of misery as he watched the Theban Hills from the balcony of his bedroom—all, all returned upon him, arranged in a phalanx of neglected proofs that the new Tom offered cruelly to the old. But it was her slight exasperation, her evasion when he questioned her, that capped the damning list. And her silence was the culminating proof.

Then, inexplicably, he shifted to the other side that the old, the normal Tom presented generously to the new. While this reaction lasted he laughed away the evidence, and honestly believed he was exaggerating trifles. The new zest that Egypt woke in her—God bless her sweetness and simplicity!—was only natural; if Tony stimulated the intellectual side of her, he could feel only pleasure that her happiness was thus increased. She was innocent. He could not possibly doubt or question, and shame flooded him till he felt himself the meanest man alive. Suspicion was no normal part of him. He crushed it out of sight, scotched as he thought to death. To lose belief in her would mean to lose belief in everybody. It was inconceivable. Every instinct in him repelled the vile suggestion. And while this reaction lasted his security returned.

Only it did not last; it merged invariably into its opposite again; and the alternating confidence and doubt produced a state of confused emotion that contained the nightmare touch in its most essential form. The Wave hung, poised above him—but would not fall—quite yet.

* * * *

It was later in the evening that the singular intensity introduced itself into all they said and did, hanging above them like a cloud. It came curiously, was suddenly there—without hint or warning. Tom had the feeling that they moved amid invisible dangers, almost as though explosives lay hidden near them, ready any moment to bring destruction with a sudden crash—final destruction of the happy pre-existing conditions. The menace of a thunder-cloud approached as in his childhood's dream; disaster lurked behind the quiet outer show. The Wave was rising almost audibly.

For upon their earlier mood of lighter kind that had preceded Mrs. Haughstone's exit, and then upon the more serious talk that followed in the garden, there descended abruptly this uncanny quiet that one and all obeyed. The contrast was most marked. Tom remembered how their voices hushed upon a given moment, how they looked about them during the brief silence following, peering into the luminous darkness as though some one watched them—and how Madame Jaretzka, remarking on the chilly air, then rose suddenly and led the way into the house. Both she and Tony, he remembered, had been restless for some little time. 'It's chilly. We shall be cosier indoors,' she said lightly, and moved away, followed by his cousin.

Tom lingered a few minutes, watching them pass along the verandah to the room beyond. He did not like the change. In the open air, the intimacy he dreaded was less suggested than in the friendly familiarity of a room, her room; out of doors it was more diffused; he preferred the remoteness that the garden lent. At the same time he was glad of a moment by himself—though a moment only. He wanted to collect his thoughts and face things as they were. There should be no 'shuffling' if he possibly could prevent it.

He lingered with his cigarette behind the others. A red moon hung above the mournful hills, and the stars shone in their myriads. Both lay reflected in the quiet river. The night was very peaceful. No wind stirred.... And he strove to force the exquisite Egyptian silence upon the turmoil that was in his soul—to gain that inner silence through which the voice of truth might whisper clearly to him. The poise he craved lay all about him in the solemn stillness, in stars and moon and desert; the temple columns had it, the steadfast, huge Colossi waiting for the sun, the bleak stone hills, the very Nile herself. Something of their immemorial resolution and resistance he might even borrow for his little tortured self… before he followed his companions. For it came to him that within the four walls of her room all that he dreaded must reveal itself in such concentrated, visible form that he no longer would be able to deny it: the established intimacy, the sweetness, the desire, and—the love.

He made this effort, be it recorded in his favour, and made it bravely; while every minute that he left his companions undisturbed was a long-drawn torment in his heart. For he plainly recognised now a danger he knew not how he might adequately meet. Here was the strangeness of it: that he did not distrust Lettice, nor felt resentment against Tony. Why this was so, or what the meaning was, he could not fathom. He felt vaguely that Lettice, like himself, was the plaything of greater forces than she knew, and that her perplexing conduct was based upon disharmony in herself beyond her possible control. Some part of her, long hidden, had emerged in Egypt, brought out by the deep mystery and passion of the climate, by its burning, sensuous splendour: its magic drove her along unconsciously. There were two persons in her.

It may have been absurd to divide the woman and the mother as he did; probably it was false psychology as well; where love is, mother and woman blend divinely into one. He did not know: it seemed, as yet, they had not blended. He was positive only that while part of her was going from him, if not already gone, the rest, and the major part, was true and loyal, loving and marvellously tender. The conflict of these certainties left hopeless disorder in every corner of his being.…

Tossing away his cigarette, he moved slowly up the verandah steps. The Wave was never more sensibly behind, beneath him, than in that moment. He rose upon it, it was under him, he felt its lift and irresistible momentum; almost it bore him up the steps. For he meant to face what-ever came; deliberately he welcomed the hurt; it had to come; beyond the suffering beckoned some marvellous joy, pure as the dawn beyond the cruel desert. There was in him that rich, sweet pain he knew of old. It beckoned and allured him even while he shrank. Alone the supreme Self in him looked calmly on, seeming to lessen the part that trembled and knew fear.

Then, as he neared the room, a sound of music floated out to meet him— Tony was singing to his own accompaniment. Lettice, upon a sofa in the corner, looked up and placed a finger on her lips, then closed her eyes again, listening to the song. And Tom was glad she closed her eyes, glad also that Tony's back was towards him, for as he crossed the threshold a singular impulse took possession of his legs and he was only just able to stop a ridiculous movement of shuffling with his feet upon the matting. Quickly he gained a sofa by the window and dropped down upon it, watching, listening. Tony was singing softly, yet with deep expression half suppressed:

> *We were young, we were merry, we were very very wise,*
> *And the door stood open at our feast,*
> *When there passed us a woman with the West in her eyes,*
> *And a man with his back to the East.*
> *O, still grew the hearts that were beating so fast,*
> *The loudest voice was still.*
> *The jest died away on our lips as they passed,*
> *And the rays of July struck chill.*

He sang the words with an odd, emphatic slowness, turning to look at Lettice between the phrases. He was not yet aware that Tom had entered. The tune held all the pathos and tragedy of the world in it. 'Both going the same way together,' he said in a suggestive undertone, his hands playing a soft running chord; 'the man and the woman.' He again leaned in her direction. 'It's a pregnant opening, don't you think? The music I found in the very depths of me somewhere. Lettice, I believe you're asleep!' he whispered tenderly after a second's pause.

She opened her eyes then and looked meaningly at him. Tom made no sound, no movement. He saw only her eyes fixed steadily on Tony, whose last sentence, using the Christian name so softly, rang on inside him like the clanging of a prison bell.

'Sing another verse first,' said Madame Jaretzka quietly, 'and we'll pass judgment afterwards. But I wasn't asleep, was I, Tom?' And, following the direction of her eyes, Tony started, and turned round. 'I shut my eyes to listen better,' she added, almost impatiently. 'Now, please go on; we want to hear the rest.'

'Of course,' said Tom, in as natural a tone as possible. 'Of course we do. What is it?' he asked.

'Mary Coleridge—the words,' replied Tony, turning to the piano again. 'In a moment of aberration I thought I could write the music for it——' The softness and passion had left his voice completely.

'Oh, the tune is yours?'

His cousin nodded. There was a little frown between the watching eyes upon the sofa. 'Tom, you mustn't interrupt; it spoils the mood—the rhythm,' and she again asked Tony to go on. The difference in the two tones she used was too obvious to be missed by any man who heard them—the veiled exasperation and—the tenderness.

Tony obeyed at once. Striking a preliminary chord as the stool swung round, he said for Tom's benefit, 'To me there's tragedy in the words, real tragedy, so I tried to make the music fit it. Madame Jaretzka doesn't agree.' He glanced towards her; her eyes were closed again; her face, Tom thought, was like a mask. Tony did not this time use the little name.

The next verse began, then suddenly broke off. The voice seemed to fail the singer. 'I don't like this one,' he exclaimed, a suspicion of trembling in his tone. 'It's rather too awful. Death comes in, the bread at the feast turns black, the hound falls down—and so on. There's general disaster. It's too tragic, rather. I'll sing the last verse instead.'

'I want to hear it, Tony. I insist,' came the command from the sofa. 'I want the tragic part.'

To Tom it seemed precisely as though the voice had said, 'I want to see Tom suffer. He knows the meaning of it. It's right, it's good, it's necessary for him.'

Tony obeyed. He sang both verses:

> *The cups of red wine turned pale on the board,*
> *The white bread black as soot.*
> *The hound forgot the hand of his lord,*
> *She fell down at his foot.*
> *Low let me lie, where the dead dog lies,*
> *Ere I sit me down again at a feast,*
> *When there passes a woman with the West in her eyes,*
> *And a man with his back to the East.*

The song stopped abruptly, the music died away, there was an interval of silence no one broke. Tom had listened spellbound, haunted. He was no judge of poetry or music; he did not understand the meaning of the words exactly; he knew only that both words and music expressed the shadow of tragedy in the air as though they focussed it into a tangible presence. A woman and a man were going in the same direction; there was an onlooker.... A spontaneous quality in the words, moreover, proved that they came burning from the writer's heart, and in Tony's music, whether good or bad, there was this same proof of genuine feeling. Judge or no judge, Tom was positive of that. He felt himself the looker-on, an intruder, almost a trespasser.

This sense of exclusion grew upon him as he listened; it passed without warning into the consciousness of a mournful, freezing isolation. These two, sitting in the room, and separated from him by a few feet of coloured Persian rug, were actually separated from him by unbridgeable distance, wrapped in an intimacy that kept him inexorably outside—because he did not understand. He almost knew an objective hallucination—that the sofa and the piano drew slightly nearer to one another, whereas his own chair remained fixed to the floor, immovable—outside.

The intensity of his sensations seemed inexplicable, unless some reality, some truth, lay behind them. The bread at the feast turned black before his very eyes. But another line rang on with a sound of ominous and poignant defeat in his heart, now lonely and bereft: 'Low let me lie, where the dead dog lies...' To the onlooker the passing of the pair meant death....

Then, through his confusion, flashed clearly this bitter certitude: Tom suddenly realised that after all he knew nothing of her real, her inner life; he knew her only through himself and in himself—knew himself in her. Tony, less self-centred, less rigidly contained, had penetrated her by an understanding sympathy greater than his own. She was unintelligible to him, but not to Tony. Tony had the key.... He had touched in her what hitherto had slept.

As the music wailed its dying cadences into this fateful silence, Tom met her eyes across the room. They were strong, and dark with beauty. He met them with no outer quailing, though with a sense of drenching tears within. They seemed to him the eyes of the angel gazing through the gate. He was outside....

He was the first to break a silence that had grown unnatural, oppressive.

'What was it?' he asked again abruptly. 'Has it got a name, I mean?' His voice had the cry of a wounded creature in it.

Tony struck an idle chord from the piano as he turned on his stool, 'Oh, yes, it's got a name. It's called "Unwelcome." And Tom, aware that he winced, was also aware that something in his life congealed and stopped its normal flow.

'Tony, you are a genius,' broke in quickly the voice from the other side of the room; 'I always said so. Do you know, that's the most perfect accompaniment I ever heard.' She spoke with feeling, her tone full of admiration.

Tony made no reply. He strummed softly, swaying to the rhythm of what he played.

'I meant the setting,' explained Lettice, 'the music. It expresses the emotion of the words too, too exactly. It's wonderful!'

'I didn't know you composed,' put in Tom stupidly. He had to say something. He saw them exchange a glance. She smiled. 'When did you do it?'

'Oh, the other day in a sudden fit,' said Tony, without turning. 'While you were at Assouan, I think.'

'And the words, Tom; don't you think they're wonderful, too, and strange?' asked Lettice. 'I find them really haunting.'

'Y-es,' he agreed, without looking at her. He realised that the lyric, though new to him, was not new to them; they had discussed it together already; they felt the same emotion about it; it had moved and stirred them before, moved Tony so deeply that he had found the music for it in the depths of himself. It was an enigmatical poem, it now became symbolic. It embodied the present situation somehow for him. Tom did not understand its meaning as they did; to him it was a foreign language. But they knew the language easily. It betrayed their deep emotional intimacy.

'You didn't hear the first part?' said Tony.

'Not quite. You had just started—when I came in.' Tom easily read the meaning in the question. And in his heart the name of the poem repeated itself with significant insistence: Unwelcome! It had come like a blow in the face when Tony mentioned it, bruising him internally. He was bleeding.... He watched the big, dark hands upon the keys as they moved up and down. It suddenly seemed they moved towards himself. There was power, menace in them—there was death. He felt as if they seized—choked him.... They grew stained....

The voices of his companions came to him across great distance; there was a gulf between them, they on that side, he on this: he was aware of antagonism between himself and Tony, and between himself and Lettice. It was very dreadful; his feet and hands were cold; he shivered. But he gave no outer sign that he was suffering, and a desperate pride—though he knew it was but a sham, a temporary pride—came to his assistance. Yet at the same time—he saw red. He felt like a boy at school again.

In imagination, then, he visualised swiftly a definite scene:

'Tony,' he heard himself say, 'you're coming between us. It means all the world to me, to you it means only a passing game. If it means more, it's time for you to say so plainly—and let her decide.'

The situation seemed all cleared up; the clouds of tragedy dissipated, the dreadful accumulation of emotion, suspense, and hidden pain, too long suppressed, too intense to be borne another minute, discharged itself in an immense relief. Lettice at last spoke freely and explained: Tony expressed regret, laughing it all away with his accustomed brilliance and irresponsibility.

Then, horribly, he heard Tony give a different answer that was far more possible and likely:

'I knew you were great friends, but I did not guess there was anything more between you. You never told me. I'm afraid I—I am desperately fond of her, and she of me. We must leave it—yes, to her. There is no other way.'

He was lounging on his sofa by the window, his eyes closed, while these thoughts flashed through him. He had never known such insecurity before; he felt sure of nothing; the foundations of his being seemed sliding into space…. For it came to him suddenly that he was a slave and that she was set upon a throne far, far beyond his reach….

Across the room, lit only by a single lamp upon the piano, the voices of his companions floated to him, low pitched, a ceaseless murmuring stream. He had been listening even while busy with his own reflections, intently listening. They were still talking of the poem and the music, exchanging intimate thoughts in the language he could not understand. They had passed on to music and poetry at large—dangerous subjects by whose means innocent words, donning an easy mask, may reveal passionate states of mental and physical kind—and so to personal revelations and confessions the apparently innocent words interpreted. He heard and understood, yet could not wholly follow because the key was missing. He could not take part, much less object. It was all too subtle for his mind. He listened….

The moonlight fell upon his stretched-out figure, but left his face in shadow; opening his eyes, he could see the others clearly; the intent expression upon her face fascinated him as he watched. Yet before his eyes had opened, the feeling again came to him that they had changed their positions somehow, and the verification of this feeling was the first detail he then noticed. Tony's stool was nearer to the bass keys of the piano, while the sofa Lettice lay upon had certainly been drawn up towards him. And Tony leaned over as he talked, bringing their lips within whispering distance. It was all done with that open innocence which increased the cruelty of it. Tom saw and heard and felt all over his body. He lay very still. He half closed his eyes again.

'I do believe Tom's dropped asleep,' said Lettice presently. 'No, don't wake him,' as Tony half turned round, 'he's tired, poor boy!'

But Tom could not willingly listen to a private conversation.

'I'm not asleep,' he exclaimed, 'not a bit of it,' and noticed that they both were startled by the suddenness and volume of his voice. 'But I am tired rather,' and he got up, lit a cigarette, wandered about the room a minute, and then leaned out of the open window. 'I think I shall slip off to bed soon—if you'll forgive me, Lettice.'

He said it on impulse; he did not really mean to go; to leave them alone together was beyond his strength. She merely nodded. The woman he had felt so proudly would put Tony in his place—nodded consent!

'I must be going too in a moment,' Tony murmured. He meant it even less than Tom did. He shifted his stool towards the middle of the piano and began to strum again.

'Sing something more first, Tony; I love your ridiculous voice.'

Tom heard it behind his back; it was said half in banter, half in earnest; yet the tone pierced him. She used the private language she and Tony understood. The little sentence was a paraphrase that, being interpreted, said plainly: 'He'll go off presently; then we can talk again of the things we love together—the things he doesn't understand.'

With his face thrust into the cold night air Tom felt the blood go throbbing in his temples. He watched the moonlight on the sandy garden paths. The leaves were motionless, the river crept past without a murmur, the dark hills rose out of the distant desert like a wave. There was faint fragrance as of wild flowers, very tiny, very soft. But he kept his eyes upon the gliding river rather than on those dark hills crowded with their ancient dead. For he felt as if some one watched him from their dim recesses. It almost seemed that from those bleak, lonely uplands, silent amid the stream of hurrying life to-day, came his pain, his agony. He could not understand it; the strange, sinister mood he had known already once before stole out from the desolate Theban hills and mastered him again. Any moment, if he looked up, he would meet eyes—eyes that gazed with dim yet definite recognition into his own across the night. They would gaze up at him, for somehow he was placed above them.... He had known all this before, this very situation, these very actors—he now looked down upon it all, a scene mapped out below him. There were two pictures that yet were one.

'What shall it be?' the voice of Tony floated past him through the open window.

'The gold and ambra one—I like best of all,' her voice followed like a sigh across the air. 'But only once—it makes me cry.'

To Tom, as he heard it, came the shattering conviction that the words were not in English, and that it was neither Lettice nor his cousin who had used them. Reality melted; he felt himself—brain, heart, and body— dropping down through empty space as though towards the speakers. This was another language that they spoke together. He had forgotten it.... They were themselves, yet different. Amazement seized him. A familiarity, intense with breaking pain, came with it. Where, O where...?

He heard the music steal past him towards these Theban hills.

His heart was no longer beating; it was still. Life paused, as it were, to let the voice insert itself into another setting, out of due place, yet at the same time true and natural. An intolerable sweetness in the music swept him. But there was anguish too. The pain and pleasure were but one sensation.... All the melancholy blue and gold of Egypt's beauty passed in that singing before his soul, and something of transcendant value he had lost, something ancient it seemed as those mournful Theban hills, rose with it. It was offered to him again. He saw it rise within his reach—once more. Upon this tide of blue and of gold it floated to his hand, could he but seize it.... Emotion then blocked itself through sheer excess; the tide receded, the vision dimmed, the gold turned dull and faded, the music and the singing ceased. Yet an instant, above the pain, Tom had caught a flush of inexplicable happiness. Beyond the anguish he felt joy breaking upon him like the dawn....

'Joy cometh in the morning,' he remembered, with a feeling as of some modern self and sanity returning. He had been some one else; he now was Tom again. The pain belonged to that 'some one else.' It must be faced, for the final outcome would be joy.... He turned round into the room now filled with tense silence only.

'Tony,' he asked, 'what on earth was it?' His voice was low but did not tremble. The atmosphere seemed drawn taut before him as though it must any instant split open upon a sound of crying. He saw Lettice on her sofa, the lamplight in her wide-open eyes that shone with moisture. She looked at Tony, not at him. There was no decipherable expression on her face. That elusive Eastern touch hung mysteriously about her. It was all half fabulous.

Without turning Tony answered shortly: 'Oh, just a little native Egyptian song—very old—dug up somewhere, I believe,' and he strummed softly to himself as though he did not wish to talk more about it.

Lettice watched him for several minutes, then fixed her eyes on Tom; they stared at each other across the room; her expression was enigmatical, yet he read resolution into it, a desire and a purpose. He returned her gaze with a baffled yearning, thinking how mysteriously beautiful she looked, frail, elusive, infinitely desirable, yet hopelessly beyond his reach.... And then he saw the eyelids lower slightly, and a shadowy darkness like a veil fall over her. A smile stole down towards the lips. Terror and fascination caught him; he turned away lest she should reach his secret and communicate her own. She looked right through him. Words, too, were spoken, ordinary modern words, though he did not hear them properly: 'You're tired out... you know. There's no need to be formal where I'm concerned...' or something similar. He listened, but he did not hear; they were remote, unreal, not audible quite; they were far away in space. He was only aware that the voice was tender and the tone was very soft....

He made no answer. The pain in her leaped forth to clasp his own, it seemed. For in that instant he knew that the joy divined a little while before was her, but also that he must wade through intolerable pain to reach it.

* * * *

The spell was broken. The balance of the evening, a short half-hour at the most, was uninspired, even awkward. There was strain in the atmosphere, cross-purposes, these purposes unfulfilled, each word and action charged with emotion that was unable to express itself. A desultory talk between Tony and his hostess seemed to struggle through clipped sentences that hung in the air as though afraid to complete themselves. The unfinished phrases floated, but dared not come to earth; they gathered but remained undelivered. Tom had divined the deep, essential intimacy at last, and his companions knew it.

He lay silent on his sofa by the window, or nearly silent. The moonlight had left him, he lay in shadow. Occasionally he threw in words, asked a question, ventured upon a criticism; but Lettice either did not hear or did not feel sufficient interest to respond. She ignored his very presence, though readily, eagerly forthcoming to the smallest sign from Tony. She hid herself with Tony behind the shadowy screen of words and phrases.

Tony himself was different too, however. There was acute disharmony in the room, where a little time before there had been at least an outward show of harmony. A heaviness as of unguessed tragedy lay upon all three, not only upon Tom. Spontaneous gaiety was gone out of his cousin, whose attempts to be his normal self became forced and unsuccessful. He sought relief by hiding himself behind his music, and his choice, though natural enough, seemed half audacious and half challenging—the choice of a devious soul that shirked fair open fight and felt at home in subterfuge. From Grieg's Ich liebe Dich he passed to other tender, passionate fragments Tom did not recognise by name yet understood too well, realising that sense of ghastly comedy, and almost of the ludicrous, which ever mocks the tragic.

For Tony certainly acknowledged by his attitude the same threatening sense of doom that lay so heavy upon his cousin's heart. There was presentiment and menace in every minute of that brief half-hour. Never had Tom seen his gay and careless cousin in such guise: he was restless, silent, intense and inarticulate. 'He gives her what I cannot give,' Tom faced the situation. 'They understand one another.... It's not her fault.... I'm old, I'm dull. She's found a stronger interest.... The bigger claim at last has come!'

They brewed their cocoa on the spirit-lamp, they munched their biscuits, they said good-night at length, and Tom walked on a few paces ahead, impatient to be gone. He did not want to go home with Tony, while yet he could not leave him there. He longed to be alone and think. Tony's hotel was but a hundred yards away. He turned and called to him.

He saw them saying goodnight at the foot of the verandah steps. Lettice was looking up into his cousin's face....

They went off together. 'Night, night,' cried Tony, as he presently turned up the path to his own hotel. 'See you in the morning.'

And Tom walked down the silent street alone. On his skin he still felt her fingers he had clasped two minutes before. But his eyes saw only—her face and figure as she stood beside his cousin on the steps. For he saw her looking up into his eyes as once before on the lawn of her English bungalow four months ago. And Tony's two great hands were laid upon her arm.

'Lettice, poor child...!' he murmured strangely to himself. For he knew that her suffering and her deep perplexity were somewhere, some-how almost equal to his own.

CHAPTER XXII

He walked down the silent street alone.... How like a theatre scene it was! Supers dressed as Arabs passed him without a word or sign; the Nile was a painted back-cloth; the columns of the Luxor Temple hung on canvas. The memory of a London theatre flitted through his mind.... He was playing a part upon the stage, but for the second time, and this second performance was better than the first, different too, a finer interpretation as it were. He could not manage it quite, but he must play it out in order to know joy and triumph at the other end.

This sense of the theatre was over everything. How still and calm the night was, the very stars were painted on the sky, the lights were low, there lay a hush upon the audience. In his heart, like a weight of metal, there was sadness, deep misgiving, sense of loss. His life was fading visibly; it threatened to go out in darkness. Yet, like Ra, great deity of this ancient land, it would suffer only a temporary eclipse, then rise again triumphant and rejuvenated as Osiris....

He walked up the sweep of sandy drive to the hotel and went through the big glass doors. The huge brilliant building swallowed him. Crowds of people moved to and fro, chattering and laughing, the women gaily, fashionably dressed; the band played with that extravagant abandon hotels demanded. The contrast between the dark, quiet street and this busy modern scene made him feel it was early in the evening, instead of close on midnight.

He was whirled up to his lofty room above the world. He flung himself upon his bed; no definite thought was in him; he was utterly exhausted. There was a vicious aching in his nerves, his muscles were flaccid and unstrung; a numbness was in his brain as well. But in the heart there was vital energy. For his heart seemed alternately full and empty; all the life he had was centred there.

And, lying on his bed in the darkened room, he sighed, as though he struggled for breath. The recent strain had been even more tense than he had guessed—the suppressed emotion, the prolonged and difficult effort at self-control, the passionate yearning that was denied relief in words and action. His entire being now relaxed itself; and his physical system found relief in long, deep sighs.

For a long time he lay motionless, trying vainly not to feel. He would have welcomed instantaneous sleep—ten hours of refreshing, dreamless sleep. If only he could prevent himself thinking, he might drop into blissful unconsciousness. It was chiefly forgetfulness he craved. A few minutes, and he would perhaps have slipped across the border—when something startled him into sudden life again. He became acutely wakeful.

His nerves tingled, the blood rushed back into the brain. He remembered Tony's letter—returned from Assouan. A moment later he had turned the light on and was reading it. It was, of course, several days old already:—

Savoy Hotel, Luxor.

Dear old Tom—What I am going to say may annoy you, but I think it best that it should be said, and if I am all wrong you must tell me. I have seldom liked any one as much as I like you, and I want to preserve our affection to the end.

The trouble is this:—I can't help feeling—I felt it at the Bungalow, in London too, and even heard it said by some one—whom, possibly, you may guess—that you were very fond of her, and that she was of you. Various little things said, and various small signs, have strengthened this feeling. Now, instinctively, I have a feeling also that she and I have certain things in common, and I think it quite possible that I might have a bad effect on her.

I do not suppose for one moment that she would ever care for me, but, from one or two signs in her, I do see possibilities of a sort of playing with fire between us. One feels these things without apparent cause; and all I can say is that, absurd as it may sound, I scent danger. To put it quite frankly, I can imagine myself becoming sufficiently excited by her to lose my head a little, and to introduce an element of sex into our friend-ship which might have some slight effect on us both. I don't mean any-thing serious, but, given the circumstances, I can imagine myself playing the fool; and the only serious thing is that I can picture myself growing so fond of her that I would not think it playing the fool at the time.

Now, if I am right in thinking that you love her, it is obvious that I must put the matter before you, Tom, as I am here doing. I would rather have your friendship than her possible excitement—and I repeat that, absurd as it may seem, I do scent the danger of my getting worked up, and, to some extent, infecting her. You see, I know myself and know the wildness of my nature. I don't fool about with women at all, but I have had affairs in my life and can judge of the utter madness of which I am capable, madness which, to my mind, must affect and stimulate the person towards whom it is directed.

On my word of honour, Tom, I am not in love with her now at all, and it will not be a bit hard for me to clear out if you want me to. So tell me quite straight: shall I make an excuse, as, for example, that I want to avoid her for fear of growing too fond of her, and go? Or can we meet as friends? What I want you to do is to be with us if we are together, so that we may try to make a real trinity of our friendship. I enjoy talking to her; and I prefer you to be with me when I am with her—really, believe me, I do.

Words make things sound so absurd, but I am writing like this be-cause I feel the presence of clouds, almost of tragedy, and I can't for the life of me think why. I want her friendship and 'motherly' care badly. I want your affection and friendship exceedingly. But I feel as though I were unconsciously about to trouble your life and hers; and I can only suppose it is that hard-working subconsciousness of mine which sees the possibility of my suddenly becoming attracted to her, suddenly losing control, and suddenly being a false friend to you both.

Now, Tom, old chap, you must prevent that—either by asking me to keep away, or else by making yourself a definite part of my friendship with her.

I want you to say no word to her about this letter, and to keep it absolutely between ourselves; and I am very hopeful—I feel sure, in fact—that we shall make the jolliest trio in the world.—Yours ever, Tony.

Tom, having read it through without a single stop, laid it down upon his table and walked round the room. In doing so, he passed the door. He locked it, then paused for a moment, listening. 'Why did I lock it? What am I listening for?' he asked himself. He hesitated. 'Oh, I know,' he went on, 'I don't want to be disturbed. Tony knows I shall read this letter to-night. He might possibly come up—' He walked back to the table again slowly. 'I couldn't see him,' he realised; 'it would be impossible!' If any one knocked, he would pretend to be asleep. His face, had he seen it in the glass, was white and set, but there was a curious shining in his eyes, and a smile was on the lips, though a smile his stolid features had never known before. 'I knew it,' said the Smile, 'I knew it long ago.'

His hand stretched out and picked the letter up again. But at first he did not look at it; he looked round the room instead, as though he felt that he was being watched, as though somebody were hiding. And then he said aloud, but very quietly:

'Light-blue eyes, by God! The light-blue eyes!'

The sound startled him a little. He repeated the sentence in a whisper, varying the words. The voice sounded like a phonograph.

'Tony's got light-blue eyes!'

He sat down, then got up again.

'I never, never thought of it! I never noticed. God! I'm as blind as a bat!'

For some minutes he stood motionless, then turned and read the letter through a second time, lingering on certain phrases, and making curious unregulated gestures as he did so. He clenched his fists, he bit his lower lip. The feeling that he was acting on a stage had left him now. This was reality.

He walked over to the balcony and drew the cold night air into his lungs. He remembered standing once before on this very spot, that fore-boding of coming loneliness so strangely in his heart. 'It's come,' he said dully to himself. 'It's justified. I understand at last.' And then he repeated with a deep, deep sigh: 'God—how blind I've been! He's taken her from me! It's all confirmed. He's wakened the woman in her!'

It seemed, then, he sought a mitigation, an excuse—for the man who wrote it, his pal, his cousin, Tony. He wanted to exonerate, if it were possible. But the generous impulse remained frustrate. The plea escaped him—because it was not there. The falseness and insincerity were too obvious to admit of any explanation in the world but one. He dropped into a chair, shocked into temporary numbness.

Gradually, then, isolated phrases blazed into prominence in his mind, clearest of all—that what Tony pretended might happen in the future had already happened long ago. 'I can picture myself growing too fond of her,' meant 'I am already too fond of her.' That he might lose his head and 'introduce an element of sex' was conscience confessing that it had been already introduced. He 'scented danger... tragedy' because both were in the present—now.

Tony hedged like any other coward. He had already gone too far, he felt shamed and awkward, he had to put himself right, as far as might be, with his trusting, stupid cousin, so he warned him that what had already taken place in the past might take place—he was careful to mention that he had no self-control—in the future. He begged the man he had injured to assist him; and the method he proposed was that old, well-proved one of assuring the love of a hesitating woman—'I'll tell her I'm too fond of her, and go!'

The letter was a sham and a pretence. Its assurance, too, was un-mistakable: Tony felt certain of his own position. 'I'm sorry, old chap, but we love each other. Though I've sometimes wondered, you never definitely told me that you did.'

He read once again the cruellest phrase of all: 'From one or two signs in her, I do see possibilities of a sort of playing with fire between us.' It was cleverly put, yet also vilely; he laid half the burden of his treachery on her. The 'introduction of sex' was gently mentioned three lines lower down. Tony already had an understanding with her—which meant that she had encouraged him. The thought rubbed like a jagged file against his heart. Yet Tom neither thought this, nor definitely said it to himself. He felt it; but it was only later that he knew he felt it.

And his mind, so heavily bruised, limped badly. The same thoughts rose again and again. He had no notion what he meant to do. There was an odd, half-boyish astonishment in him that the accumulated warnings of these recent days had not shown him the truth before. How could he have known the Eyes of his Dream for months, have lived with them daily for three weeks—the light-blue eyes—yet have failed to recognise them? It passed understanding. Even the wavy feeling that had accompanied Tony's arrival in the Carpathians—the Sound heard in his bedroom the same night—had left him unseeing and unaware. It seemed as if the recognition had been hidden purposely; for, had he recognised it, he would have been prepared, he might even have prevented. It now dawned upon him slowly that the inevitable may not be prevented. And the cunning of it baffled him afresh: it was all planned consummately.

Tom sat for a long time before the open window in a state of half stupor, staring at the pictures his mind offered automatically. A deep, vicious aching gnawed without ceasing at his heart: each time a new picture rose a fiery pang rose with it, as though a nerve were bared....

He drew his chair closer into the comforting darkness of the night. All was silent as the grave. The stars wheeled overhead with their accustomed majesty; he could just distinguish the dim river in its ancient bed; the desert lay watchful for the sun, the air was sharp with perfume. Countless human emotions had these witnessed in the vanished ages, countless pains and innumerable aching terrors; the emotions had passed away, yet the witnesses remained, steadfast, unchanged, indifferent. Moreover, his particular emotion now seemed known to them—known to these very stars, this desert, this immemorial river; they witnessed now its singular repetition. He was to experience it unto the bitter end again—yet somehow otherwise. He must face it all. Only in this way could the joy at the end of it be reached.... He must somehow accept and understand.... This confused, unjustifiable assurance strengthened in him.

Yet this last feeling was so delicate that he scarcely recognised its intense vitality. The cruder sensations blinded him as with thick, bitter smoke. He was certain of one thing only—that the fire of jealousy burned him with its atrocious anguish... an anguish he had somewhere known before.

Then presently there was a change. This change had begun soon after he drew his chair to the balcony, but he had not noticed it. The effect upon him, nevertheless, had been gradually increasing.

The psychological effects of sound, it would seem, are singular. Even when heard unconsciously, the result continues; and Tom, hearing this sound unconsciously, did not realise at first that another mood was stealing over him. Then hearing became conscious hearing—listening. The sound rose to his ears from just below his balcony. He listened. He rose, leaned over the rail, and stared. The crests of three tall palms immediately below him waved slightly in the rising wind. But the fronds of a palm-tree in the wind produce a noise that is unlike the rustle of any other foliage in the world. It was a curious, sharp rattling that he heard. It was the Sound.

His entire being was at last involved—the Self that used the separate senses. His thoughts swooped in another direction—he suddenly fixed his attention upon Lettice. But it was an inner attention of a wholesale kind, not of the separate mind alone. And this entire Self included regions he did not understand. Mind was the least part of it. The 'whole' of him that now dealt with Lettice was far above all minor and partial means of knowing. For it did not judge, it only saw. It was, perhaps, the soul.

For it seemed the pain bore him upwards to an unaccustomed height. He stood for a moment upon that level where she dwelt, even as now he stood on this balcony looking down upon the dim Egyptian scene. She was beside him; he gazed into her eyes, even as now he gazed across to the dark necropolis among the Theban hills. But also, in some odd way, he stood outside himself. He swam with her upon the summit of the breaking Wave, lifted upon its crest, swept onward irresistibly…. No halt was possible… the inevitable crash must come. Yet she was with him. They were involved together…. The sea!…

The first bitterness passed a little, the sullen aching with it. He was aware of high excitement, of a new reckless courage; a touch of the impersonal came with it all, one Tom playing the part of a spectator to another Tom—an onlooker at his own discomfiture, at his own suffering, at his own defeat.

This new exalted state was very marvellous; for while it lasted he welcomed all that was to come. 'It's right and necessary for me,' he recognised; 'I need it, and I'll face it. If I refuse it I prove myself a failure—again. Besides… she needs it too!'

For the entire matter then turned over in his mind, so that he saw it from a new angle suddenly. He looked at it through a keyhole, as it were—the extent was large yet detailed, the picture distant yet very clearly focussed. It lay framed within his thoughts, isolated from the rest of life, isolated somehow even from the immediate present. There was perspective in it. This keyhole was, perhaps, his deep, unalterable love, but cleansed and purified….

It came to him that she, and even Tony, too, in lesser fashion, were, like himself, the playthings of great spiritual forces that made alone for good. The Wave swept all three along. The attitude of his youth returned; the pain was necessary, yet would bring inevitable joy as its result. There had been cruel misunderstanding on his part somewhere; that misunderstanding must be burned away. He saw Lettice and his cousin helping towards this exquisite deliverance somehow. It was like a moment of clear vision from a pinnacle. He looked down upon it….

Lettice smiled into his eyes through half-closed eyelids. Her smile was strangely distant, strangely precious: she was love and tenderness incarnate; her little hands held both of his…. Through these very eyes, this smile, these little hands, his pain would come; she would herself inflict it—because she could not help herself; she played her inevitable rôle as he did. Yet he kissed the eyes, the hands, with an absolute self-surrender he did not understand, willing and glad that they should do their worst. He had somewhere dreadfully misjudged her; he must, he would atone. This passion burned within him, a passion of sacrifice, of resignation, of free, big acceptance. He felt joy at the end of it all—the joy of perfect understanding… and forgiveness . . . on both sides….

And the moment of clear vision left its visible traces in him even after it had passed. If he felt contempt for his cousin, he felt for Lettice a deep and searching pity—she was divided against herself, she was playing a part she had to play. The usual human emotions were used, of course, to convey the situation, yet in some way he was unable to explain she was— being driven. In spite of herself she must inflict this pain…. It was a mystery he could not solve….

His exaltation, naturally, was of brief duration. The inevitable reaction followed it. He saw the situation again as an ordinary man of the world must see it…. The fires of jealousy were alight and spreading. Already they were eating away the foundations of every generous feeling he had ever known…. It was not, he argued, that he did not trust her. He did. But he feared the insidious power of infatuation, he feared the burning glamour of this land of passionate mirages, he feared the deluding forces of sex which his cousin had deliberately awakened in her blood—and other nameless things he feared as well, though he knew not exactly what they were. For it seemed to him that they were old as dreams, old as the river and the menace of these solemn hills…. From childhood up, his own trust in her truth and loyalty had remained unalterably fixed, ingrained in the very essence of his being. It was more than his relations with a woman he loved that were in danger: it was his belief and trust in Woman, focussed in her self symbolically, that were threatened…. It was his belief in Life.

With Lettice, however, he felt himself in some way powerless to deal; he could watch her, but he could not judge… least of all, did he dare prevent…. Her attitude he could not know nor understand….

There was a pink glow upon the desert before he realised that a reply to Tony's letter was necessary; and that pink was a burning gold when he knew his answer must be of such a kind that Tony felt free to pursue his course unchecked. Tom held to his strange belief to 'Let it all come,' he would not try to prevent; he would neither shirk nor dodge. He doubted whether it lay in his power now to hinder anything, but in any case he would not seek to do so. Rather than block coming events, he must encourage their swift development. It was the best, the only way; it was the right way too. He belonged to his destination. He went into his own background....

The sky was alight from zenith to horizon, the Nile aflame with sunrise, by the time the letter was written. He read it over, then hurriedly undressed and plunged into bed. A long, dreamless sleep took instant charge of him, for he was exhausted to a state of utter depletion.

Dear Tony—I have read your letter with the greatest sympathy—it was forwarded from Assouan. It cost you a good deal, I know, to say what you did, and I'm sure you mean it for the best. I feel it like that too—for the best.

But it is easier for you to write than for me to answer. Her position, of course, is an awfully delicate one; and I feel— no doubt you feel too—that her standard of conduct is higher than that of ordinary women, and that any issue between us—if there is an issue at all!—should be left to her to decide.

Nothing can touch my friendship with her; you needn't worry about that. But if you can bring any added happiness into her life, it can only be welcomed by all three of us. So go ahead, Tony, and make her as happy as you can. The important things are not in our hands to decide in any case; and, whatever happens, we both agree on one thing—that her happiness is the important thing.—Yours ever, Tom.

CHAPTER XXIII

He was wakened by the white-robed Arab housemaid with his break-fast. He felt hungry, but still tired; sleep had not rested him. On the tray an envelope caught his eye—sent by hand evidently, since it bore no stamp. The familiar writing made the blood race in his veins, and the instant the man was gone he tore it open. There was burning in his eyes as he read the pencilled words. He devoured it whole with a kind of visual gulp—a flash; the entire meaning first, then lines, then separate words.

> Come for lunch, or earlier. My cousin is invited out, and Tony has suddenly left for Cairo with his friends. I shall be lonely. How beautiful and precious you were last night. I long for you to comfort me. But don't efface yourself again—it gave me a horrid, strange presentiment—as if I were losing you—almost as if you no longer trusted me. And don't forget that I love you with all my heart and soul. I had such queer, long dreams last night—terrible rather. I must tell you. Do come.—Yours, L.
>
> P.S. Telephone if you can't.

Sweetness and pain rose in him, then numbness. For his mind flung itself with violence upon two sentences: he was 'beautiful and precious'; she longed for him to 'comfort' her. Why, he asked himself, was his conduct beautiful and precious? And why did she need his comfort? The words were like vitriol in the eyes.

Long before reason found the answer, instinct—swift, merciless interpreter—told him plainly. While the brain fumbled, the heart already understood. He was stabbed before he knew what stabbed him.

And hope sank extinguished. The last faint doubt was taken from him. It was not possible to deceive himself an instant longer, for the naked truth lay staring into his eyes.

He swallowed his breakfast without appetite... and went downstairs. He sighed, but something wept inaudibly. A wall blocked every step he took. The devastating commonplace was upon him—it was so ordinary. Other men... oh, how often he had heard the familiar tale! He tried to grip himself. 'Others... of course... but me!' It seemed impossible.

In a dream he crossed the crowded hall, avoiding various acquaintances with unconscious cunning. He found the letter-box and—posted his letter to Tony. 'That's gone, at any rate!' he realised. He told the porter to telephone that he would come to lunch. 'That's settled too!' Then, hardly knowing what blind instinct prompted, he ordered a carriage... and presently found himself driving down the hot, familiar road to—Karnak. For some faultless impulse guided him. He turned to the gigantic temple, with its towering, immense proportions—as though its grandeur might somehow protect and mother him.

In those dim aisles and mighty halls brooded a Presence that he knew could soothe and comfort. The immensities hung still about the fabulous ruin. He would lose his tortured self in something bigger—that beauty and majesty which are Karnak. Before he faced Lettice, he must forget a moment—forget his fears, his hopes, his ceaseless torment of belief and doubt. It was, in the last resort, religious—a cry for help, a prayer. But also it was an inarticulate yearning to find that state of safety where he and she dwelt secure from separation—in the 'sea.' For Karnak is a spiritual experience, or it is nothing. There, amid the deep silence of the listening centuries, he would find peace; forgetting himself a moment, he might find—strength.

Then reason parsed the sentences that instinct already understood complete. For Lettice—the tender woman of his first acquaintance— had obviously experienced a moment of reaction. She realised he was wounded at her hands. She felt shame and pity. She craved comfort and forgiveness—his comfort, his forgiveness. Conscience whispered. As against the pain she inflicted, he had been generous, long-suffering— therefore his conduct was 'beautiful and precious.' Tony, moreover, had hidden himself until his letter should be answered—and she was 'lonely.'

With difficulty Tom suppressed the rising bitterness of contempt and anger in him. His cousin's obliquity was a sordid touch. He forgot a moment the loftier point of view; but for a short time only. The contempt merged again in something infinitely greater. The anger disappeared. Her attitude occupied him exclusively. The two phrases rang on with insistent meaning in his heart, as with the clang of a fateful sentence of exile, execution—death:

'How beautiful you were last night, and precious... I long for you to comfort me....'

While the carriage crawled along the sun-baked sand, he watched the Arab children with their blue-black hair, who ran beside it, screaming for bakshish. The little faces shone like polished bronze; they held their hands out, their bare feet pattered in the sand. He tossed small coins among them. And their cries and movements fell into the rhythm of the song, whose haunting refrain pulsed ever in his blood: 'We were young, we were merry, we were very very wise....'

They were soon out-distanced, the palm-trees fell away, the soaring temple loomed against the blazing sky. He left the arabyieh at the western entrance and went on foot down the avenue of headless rams. The huge Khonsu gateway dropped its shadow over him. Passing through the Court with its graceful colonnades, and the Chapel, flanked by cool, dark

"Do you want to go to the hotel or do you want to move into the old Sumner House? The family gave up last year when the husband died of pneumonia. Randolph said it's open for the taking and we can live there unless you decide to turn around and go back to Boise."

"Hotel tonight. We have no idea what we are going to find at the old Sumner House."

———

Maggie raised her hand to shade her eyes. In the sun's glare, she hated the ugly little house. She felt weary walking on its steps. She didn't want to go inside; the mere passing over the threshold gave her goose bumps. This house had a sad history. She was tired of living in places of heartbreak. She passed through the door thinking that she hadn't been able to control Randolph at all.

She stood in the middle of the biggest room of two. The walls had been wallpapered with newspaper. It had two glass windows that were too dirty to see out. A rusted cast iron kettle still sat on a stove. They'd left the log benches but took the table.

"Come on, bring the soap," William said as he passed her with buckets of fresh water.

Maggie studied her surroundings. She was here. She could hare off to the next wild goose chase, or she could make this successful. She could stop, and...and be more like her mother. A woman of great measure. Maggie took in a deep breath.

All right, they were going to homestead together. William and Maggie. It was like Guy had planned it.

William handed her a brush to "scrub those floorboards."

He was better, more capable, more confident away from his father. She was going to have time to get to know him better. She made a sour face into a small mirror that hung on the wall.

By dusk, her arms itched under her sleeves, where harsh soap had repeatedly run and dried. Cobwebs stuck in her hair and the chambers, where the Sacred Boat floated on its tideless sea beyond the world, he moved on across the sandy waste of broken stone again, and reached in a few minutes the towering grey and reddish sandstone that was Amon's Temple.

This was the goal of his little pilgrimage. Sublimity closed round him. The gigantic pylon, its shoulders breaking the sky four-square far overhead, seemed the prodigious portal of another world. Slowly he passed within, crossed the Great Court where the figures of ancient Theban deities peered at him between the forest of broken monoliths and lovely Osiris pillars, then, moving softly beneath the second enormous pylon, found himself on the threshold of the Great Hypostyle Hall itself.

He caught his breath, he paused, then stepped within on tiptoe, and the hush of four thousand years closed after him. Awe stole upon him; he felt himself included in the great ideal of this older day. The stupendous aisles lent him their vast shelter; the fierce sunlight could not burn his flesh; the air was cool and sweet in these dim recesses of unremembered time. He passed his hand with reverence over the drum-shaped blocks that built up the majestic columns, as they reared towards the massive, threatening roof. The countless inscriptions and reliefs showered upon his sight bewilderingly.

And he forgot his lesser self in this crowded atmosphere of ancient divinities and old-world splendour. He was aware of kings and queens, of princes and princesses, of stately priests, of hosts and conquests; forgotten gods and goddesses trooped past his listening soul; his heart remembered olden wars, and the royalty of golden days came back to him. He steeped himself in the long, long silence in which an earlier day lay listening with ears of stone. There was colour; there was spendthrift grandeur, half savage, half divine. His imagination, wakened by Egypt, plunged backwards with a sense of strange familiarity. Tom easily found the mightier scale his aching heart so hungrily desired. It soothed his personal anguish with a sense of individual insignificance which was comfort....

The peace was marvellous, an unearthly peace; the strength unwearied, inexhaustible. The power that was Amon lingered still behind the tossed and fabulous ruin. Those soaring columns held up the very sky, and their foundations made the earth itself swing true. The silence, profound, unalterable, was the silence in the soul that lies behind all passion and distress. And these steadfast qualities Tom absorbed unconsciously through his very skin.... The Wave might fall indeed, but it would fall into the mothering sea where levels must be restored again, secure upon unshakable foundations.... And as he paced these solemn aisles, his soul drank in their peace and stillness, their strength of calm resistance.

Though built upon the sand, they still endured, and would continue to endure. They pointed to the stars.

And the effect produced upon him, though the adjective was not his, seemed spiritual. There was a power in the mighty ruin that lifted him to an unaccustomed level from which he looked down upon the inner drama being played. He reached a height; the bird's-eye view was his; he saw and realised, yet he did not judge. The vast structure, by its harmony, its power, its overmastering beauty, made him feel ashamed and mortified. A sense of humiliation crept into him, melting certain stubborn elements of self that, grown out of proportion, blocked his soul's clear vision. That he must stand aside had never occurred to him before with such stern authority; it occurred to him now. The idea of sacrifice stole over him with a sweetness that was deep and marvellous. It seemed that Isis touched him. He looked into the eyes of great Osiris,... and that part of him that ever watched—the great Onlooker—smiled.

His being, as a whole, remained inarticulate as usual; no words came to his assistance. It was rather that he attained—as once before, in another moment of deeper insight—that attitude towards himself which is best described as impersonal. Who was he, indeed, that he should claim the right to thwart another's happiness, hinder another's best self-realisation? By what right, in virtue of what exceptional personal value, could he, Tom Kelverdon, lay down the law to this other, and say, 'Me only shall you love... because I happen to love you...?'

And, as though to test what of strength and honesty might lie in this sudden exaltation of resolve, he recognised just then the very pylon against whose vast bulk they had rested together that moonlit night a few short weeks before... when he saw two rise up like one person... as he left them and stole away into the shadows.

'So I knew it even then—subconsciously,' he realised. 'The truth was in me even then, a few days after my arrival.... And they knew it too. She was already going from me, if not already gone...!'

He leaned against that same stone column, thinking, searching in his mind, feeling acutely. Reactions caught at him in quick succession. Doubt, suspicion, anger clouded vision; pain routed the impersonal conception. Loneliness came over him with the cool wind that stirred the sand between the columns; the patches of glaring sunshine took on a ghastly whiteness; he shivered.... But it was not that he lost belief in his moment of clear vision, nor that the impersonal attitude became untrue. It was another thing he realised: that the power of attainment was not yet in him... quite. He could renounce, but not with complete acceptance....

As he drove back along the sandy lanes of blazing heat a little later, it seemed to him that he had been through some strenuous battle that had taxed his final source of strength. If his position was somewhat vague, this was due to his inability to analyse such deep interior turmoil. He was sure, at least, of one thing—that, before he could know this final joy awaiting him, he must first find in himself the strength for what seemed just then an impossible, an ultimate sacrifice. He must forget himself—if such forgetfulness involved the happiness of another. He must slip out. The strength to do it would come presently. And his heart was full of this indeterminate, half-formed resolve as he entered the shady garden and saw Lettice lying in her deck-chair beneath the trees, awaiting him.

CHAPTER XXIV

Events, however slight, which involve the soul are drama; for once the soul takes a hand in them their effects are permanent and reproductive. Not alone the relationship between individuals are determined this way or that, but the relationships of these individuals towards the universe are changed upon a scale of geometrical progression. The results are of the eternal order. Since that which persists—the soul—is radically affected, they are of ultimate importance.

Had the strange tie between Tom and Lettice been due to physical causes only, to mental affinity, or to mere sympathetic admiration of each other's outward strength and beauty, a rupture between them could have been of a passing character merely. A pang, a bitterness that lasted for a day or for a year—and the gap would be filled again by some one else. They had idealised; they would get over it; they were not indispensable to one another; there were other fish in the sea, and so forth.

But with Tom, at any rate, there was something transcendental in their intimate union. Loss, where she was concerned, involved a permanent and irremediable bereavement—no substitute was conceivable. With him, this relationship seemed foreordained, almost prenatal—it had come to him at the very dawn of life; it had lasted through years of lonely waiting; no other woman had ever threatened its fixed security, and the sudden meeting in Switzerland had seemed to him reunion rather than discovery. Moreover, he had transferred his own sense of security to her; had always credited her with similar feelings; and the suspicion now that he had deceived himself in this made life tremble to the foundations. It was a terrible thought that robbed him of every atom of self-confidence. It affected his attitude to the entire universe.

The intensity of this drama, however, being interior, caused little outward disturbance that casual onlookers need have noticed. He waved his hat as he walked towards the corner where she lay, greeting her with a smile and careless word, as though no shadow stood between them. A barrier, nevertheless, was there he knew. He felt it almost sensibly. Also—it had grown higher. And at once he was aware that the Lettice who returned his smile with a colourless 'Good morning, Tom, I'm so glad you could come,' was not the Lettice who had known a moment's reaction a little while before. He told by her very attitude that now there was lassitude, even weariness in her. Her eyes betrayed none of the excitement and delight that another could wake in her. His own presence certainly no longer brought the thrill, the interest that once it did. She was both bored and lonely.

And, while an exquisite pain ran through him, he made a prodigious effort to draw upon the strength he had felt in Karnak a short half-hour ago. He struggled bravely to forget himself. 'So Tony's gone!' he said lightly, 'run off and left us without so much as a word of warning or good-bye. A rascally proceeding, I call it! Rather sudden, too, wasn't it?'

He sat down beside her and began to smoke. She need not answer unless she wanted to. She did answer, however, and at once. She did not look at him; her eyes were on the golden distance. It had to be said; she said it. 'He's only gone for two or three days. His friends suddenly changed their minds, and he couldn't get out of it. He said he didn't want to go—a bit.'

How did she know it, Tom wondered, glancing up over his cigarette? And how had she read his mind so easily?

'He just popped in to tell me,' she added, 'and to say good-bye. He asked me to tell you.' She spoke without a tremor, as if Tom had no right to disapprove.

'Pretty early, wasn't it?' It was not the first time either. 'He comes at such unusual hours'—he remembered Mrs. Haughstone's words.

'I was only just up. But there was time to give him coffee before the train.'

She offered no further comment; Tom made none; he sat smoking there beside her, outwardly calm and peaceful as though no feeling of any kind was in him. He felt numb perhaps. In his mind he saw the picture of the breakfast-table beneath the trees. The plan had been arranged, of course, beforehand.

'Miss de Lorne's coming to lunch,' she mentioned presently. 'She's to bring her pictures—the Deir-el-Bahri ones. You must help me criticise them.'

So they were not to be alone even, was Tom's instant thought. Aloud he said merely, 'I hope they're good.' She flicked the flies away with her horse-hair whisk, and sighed. He caught the sigh. The day felt empty, uninspired, the boredom of cruel disillusion in it somewhere. But it was the sigh that made him realise it. Avoiding the subject of Tony's abrupt departure, he asked what she would like to do that afternoon. He made various proposals; she listened without interest. 'D'you know, Tom, I don't feel inclined to do anything much, but just lie and rest.'

There was no energy in her, no zest for life; expeditions had lost their interest; she was listless, tired. He felt impatience in him, sharp disappointment too; but there was an alert receptiveness in his mind that noted trifles done or left undone. She made no reference, for instance, to the fact that they might be frequently alone together now. A faint hope that had been in him vanished quickly.... He wondered when she was going to speak of her letter, of his conduct the night before that was 'beautiful and precious,' of the 'comfort' she had needed, or even of the dreams that she had mentioned. But, though he waited, giving various openings, nothing was forthcoming. That side of her, once intimately precious and familiar, seemed buried, hidden away, perhaps forgotten. This was not Lettice—it was some one else.

'You had dreams that frightened you?' he enquired at length. 'You said you'd tell them to me.' He moved nearer so that he could watch her face.

She looked puzzled for a second. 'Did I?' she replied. She thought a moment. 'Oh yes, of course I did. But they weren't much really. I'd forgotten. It was about water or something. Ah, I remember now—we were drowning, and you saved us.' She gave a little unmeaning laugh as she said it.

'Who were drowning?'

'All of us—me and you, I think it was—and Tony——'

'Oh, of course.'

She looked up. 'Tom, why do you say "of course" like that?'

'It was your old idea of the river and the floating faces, I meant,' he answered. 'I had the feeling.'

'You said it so sharply.'

'Did I!' He shrugged his shoulders slightly. 'I didn't mean to.' He noticed the beauty of her ear, the delicate line of the nostrils, the long eyelashes. The graceful neck, with the firm, slim line of the breast below, were exquisite. The fairy curve of her ankle was just visible. He could have knelt and covered it with kisses. Her coolness, the touch of contempt in her voice made him wild.... But he understood his rôle; and—he remembered Karnak.

A little pause followed. Lettice made one of her curious gestures, half impatience, half weariness. She stretched; the other ankle appeared. Tom, as he saw it, felt something in him burst into flame. He came perilously near to saying impetuously a hundred things he had determined that he must not say. He felt the indifference in her, the coolness, almost the cruelty. Her negative attitude towards him goaded, tantalised. He was full of burning love, from head to foot, while she lay there within two feet of him, calm, listless, unresponsive, passionless. The bitter pain of promises unfulfilled assailed him acutely, poignantly. Yet in ordinary life the situation was so commonplace. The 'strong man' would face her with it, have it out plainly; he would be masterful, forcing a climax of one kind or another, behaving as men do in novels or on the stage.

Yet Tom remained tongue-tied and restrained; he seemed unable to take the lead; an inner voice cried sternly No to all such natural promptings. It would be a gross mistake. He must let things take their course. He must not force a premature disclosure. With a tremendous effort, he controlled himself and smothered the rising fires that struggled towards speech and action. He would not even ask a single question. Somehow, in any case, it was impossible.

The subject dropped; Lettice made no further reference to the letter.

'When you feel like going anywhere, or doing anything, you'll let me know,' he suggested presently. 'We've been too energetic lately. It's best for you to rest. You're tired.' The words hurt and stung him as though he were telling lies. He felt untrue to himself. The blood boiled in his veins.

She answered him with a touch of impatience again, almost of exasperation. He noticed the emphasis she used so needlessly.

'Tom, I'm not tired—not in the way you mean. It's just that I feel like being quiet for a bit. Really it's not so remarkable! Can't you understand?'

'Perfectly,' he rejoined calmly, lighting another cigarette. 'We'll have a programme ready for later—when Tony gets back.' The blood rushed from his heart as he said it.

Her face brightened instantly, as he had expected—dreaded; there was no attempt at concealment anywhere; she showed interest as frankly as a child. 'It was stupid of him to go, just when we were enjoying everything so,' she said again. 'I wonder how long he'll stay——'

'I'll write and tell him to hurry up,' suggested Tom. He twirled his fly-whisk energetically.

'Tell him we can't get on without our dragoman,' she added eagerly with her first attempt at gaiety; and then went on to mention other things he was to say, till her pleasure in talking about Tony was so obvious that Tom yielded to temptation suddenly. It was more than he could bear. 'I strongly suspect a pretty girl in the party somewhere,' he observed carelessly.

'There is,' came the puzzling reply, 'but he doesn't care for her a bit. He told me all about her. It's curious, isn't it, how he fascinates them all? There's something very remarkable about Tony—I can't quite make it out.'

Tom leaned forward, bringing his face in front of her own, and closer to it. He looked hard into her eyes a moment. In the depths of her steady gaze he saw shadows, far away, behind the open expression. There was trouble in her, but it was deep, deep down and out of sight. The eyes of some one else, it seemed, looked through her into his. An older world came whispering across the sunlight and the sand.

'Lettice,' he said quietly, 'there's something new come into your life these last few weeks—isn't there?' His voice grated—like machinery started with violent effort against resistance. 'Some new, big force, I mean? You seem so changed, so different.' He had not meant to speak like this. It was forced out. He expressed himself badly too. He raged inwardly.

She smiled, but only with her lips. The shadows from behind her eyes drew nearer to the surface. But the eyes themselves held steady. That other look peered out of them. He was aware of power, of something strangely bewitching, yet at the same time fierce, inflexible in her… and a kind of helplessness came over him, as though he was suddenly out of his depth, without sure footing. The Wave roared in his ears and blood.

'Egypt probably—old Egypt,' she said gently, making a slow gesture with one hand towards the river and the sky. 'It must be that.' The gesture, it seemed to him, had royalty in it somewhere. There was stateliness and dignity—an air of authority about her. It was magnificent. He felt worship in him. The slave that lies in worship stirred. He could yield his life, suffer torture for days to give her a moment's happiness.

'I meant something personal, rather,' he prevaricated.

'You meant Tony. I know it. Didn't you, Tom?'

His breath caught inwardly. In spite of himself, and in spite of his decision, she drew his secret out. Enchantment touched him deliciously, an actual torture in it.

'Yes,' he said honestly, 'perhaps I did.' He said it shamefacedly rather, to his keen vexation. 'For it has to do with Tony somehow.'

He got up abruptly, tossed his cigarette over the wall into the river, then sat down again. 'There's something about it—strange and big. I can't make it out a bit.' He faltered, stammered over the words. 'It's a long way off—then all at once it's close.' He had the feeling that he had put a match to something. 'I've done it now,' he said to himself like a boy, as though he expected that something dramatic must happen instantly.

But nothing happened. The river flowed on silently, the heat blazed down, the leaves hung motionless as before, and far away the lime-stone hills lay sweltering in the glare. But those hills had glided nearer. He was aware of them,—the Valley of the Kings,—the desolate Theban Hills with their myriad secrets and their deathless tombs.

Lettice gave her low, significant little laugh. 'It's odd you should say that, Tom—very odd. Because I've felt it too. It's awfully remote and quite near at the same time——'

'And Tony's brought it,' he interrupted eagerly, half passionately. 'It's got to do with him, I mean.'

It seemed to him that the barrier between them had lowered a little. The Lettice he knew first peered over it at him.

'No,' she corrected, 'I don't feel that he's brought it. He's in it some-how, I admit, but he has not brought it exactly.' She hesitated a moment. 'I think the truth is he can't help himself—any more than we— you or I—can.'

There was a caressing tenderness in her voice as she said it, but whether for himself or for another he could not tell. In his heart rose a frantic impulse just then to ask—to blurt it out: 'Do you love Tony? Has he taken you from me? Tell me the truth and I can bear it. Only, for heaven's sake, don't hide it!' But, instead of saying this absurd, theatrical thing, he looked at her through the drifting cigarette smoke a moment without speaking, trying to read the expression in her face. 'Last night, for instance,' he exclaimed abruptly; 'in the music room, I mean. Did you feel that?—the intensity—a kind of ominous feeling?'

Her expression was enigmatical; there were signs of struggle in it, he thought. It was as if two persons fought within her which should answer. Apparently the dear Lettice of his first acquaintance won—for the moment.

'You noticed it too!' she exclaimed with astonishment. 'I thought I was the only one.'

'We all—all three of us—felt it,' he said in a lower tone. 'Tony certainly did——'

Lettice raised herself suddenly on her elbow and looked down at him with earnestness. Something of the old eagerness was in her. The barrier between them lowered perceptibly again, and Tom felt a momentary return of the confidence he had lost. His heart beat quickly. He made a half-impetuous gesture towards her—'What is it? What does it all mean, Lettice?' he exclaimed. 'D'you feel what I feel in it—danger some-where—danger for us?' There was a yearning, almost a cry for mercy in his voice.

She drew back again. 'You amaze me, Tom,' she said, as she lay among her cushions. 'I had no idea you were so observant.' She paused, putting her hand across her eyes a moment. 'N-no—I don't feel danger exactly,' she went on in a lower tone, speaking half to herself and half to him; 'I feel—' She broke off with a little sigh; her hand still covered her eyes. 'I feel,' she went on slowly, with pauses between the words, 'a deep, deep something—from very far away—that comes over me at times— only at times, yes. It's remote, enormously remote—but it has to be. I've never given you all that I ought to give. We have to go through with it——'

'You and I?' he whispered. He was listening intently. The beats of his heart were most audible.

She sighed. 'All three of us—somehow,' she replied equally low, and speaking again more to herself than to him. 'Ah! Now my dream comes back a little. It was the river—my river with the floating faces. And the thing I feel comes—from its source, far, far away—its tiny source among the hills——' She sighed again, more deeply than before. Her breast heaved slightly. 'We must go through it—yes. It's necessary for us—necessary for you—and me——'

'Lettice, my precious, my wonderful!' Tom whispered as though the breath choked and strangled him. 'But we stay together through it? We stay together afterwards? You love me still?' He leaned across and took her other hand. It lay unresistingly in his. It was very cold—without a sign of response.

Her faint reply half staggered him: 'We are always, always together, you and I. Even if you married, I should still be yours. He will go out——'

Fear clashed with hope in his heart as he heard these words he could not understand. He groped and plunged after their meaning. He was bewildered by the reference to marriage—his marriage! Was she, then, already aware that she might lose him?... But there was confession in them too, the confession that she had been away from him. That he felt clearly. Now that the dividing influence was removed, she was coming back perhaps! If Tony stayed away she would come back entirely; only then the thing that had to happen would be prevented—which was not to be thought of for a moment.... 'Poor Lettice....' He felt pity, love, protection that he burned to give; he felt a savage pain and anger as well. In the depths of him love and murder sat side by side.

'Oh, Lettice, tell me everything. Do share with me—share it and we'll meet it together.' He drew her cold hand towards him, putting it inside his coat. 'Don't hide it from me. You're my whole world. My love can never change.... Only don't hide anything!' The words poured out of him with passionate entreaty. The barrier had melted, vanished. He had found her again, the Lettice of his childhood, of his dream, the true and faithful woman he had known first. His inexpressible love rose like a wave upon him. Regardless of where they were he bent over to take her in his arms—when she suddenly withdrew her hand from his. She removed the other from her eyes. He saw her face. And he realised in an instant that his words had been all wrong. He had said precisely again what he ought not to have said. The moment in her had passed.

The sudden change had a freezing effect upon him.

'Tom, I don't understand quite,' she said coldly, her eyes fixed on his almost with resentment in them. 'I'm not hiding anything from you. Why do you say such things? I'm true—true to myself.'

The barrier was up again in an instant, of granite this time, with jagged edges of cut glass upon it, so that he could not approach it even. It was not Lettice that spoke then:

'I don't know what's come over you out here,' she went on, each word she uttered increasing the distance between them; 'you misunderstand everything I say and criticise all I do. You suspect my tenderest instincts. Even a friendship that brings me happiness you object to and—and exaggerate.'

He listened till she ceased; it was as if he had received a blow in the face; he felt disconcerted, keenly aware of his own stupidity, helpless. Something froze in him. He had seen her for a second, then lost her utterly.

'No, no, Lettice,' he stammered, 'you read all that into me—really, you do. I only want your happiness.'

Her eyes softened a little. She sighed wearily and turned her face away.

'We were only talking of this curious, big feeling that's come——' he went on.

'You were speaking of Tony—that's what you really meant, Tom,' she interrupted. 'You know it perfectly well. It only makes it harder—for me?'

He felt suddenly she was masquerading, playing with him again, playing with his very heart and soul. The devil tempted him. All the things he had decided he would not say rose to the tip of his tongue. The worst of them—those that hurt him most—he managed to force down. But even the one he did suffer to escape gave him atrocious pain:

'Well, Lettice, to tell the truth, I do think Tony has a bad—a curious influence on you. I do feel he has come between us rather. And I do think that if you would only share with me——'

The sudden way she turned upon him, rising from her chair and standing over him, was so startling that he got up too. They faced each other, he in the blazing sunshine, she in the shade. She looked so different that he was utterly taken aback. She wore that singular Eastern appearance he now knew so well. Expression, attitude, gesture, all betrayed it. That inflexible, cruel thing shone in her eyes.

'Tom, dear,' she said, but with a touch of frigid exasperation that for a moment paralysed thought and utterance in him, 'whatever happens, you must realise this—that I am myself and that I can never allow my freedom to be taken from me. If you're determined to misjudge, the fault is yours, and if our love, our friendship, cannot understand that, there's something wrong with it.'

The word 'friendship' was like a sword thrust. It went right through him. 'I trust you,' he faltered, 'I trust you wholly. I know you're true.' But the words, it seemed, gave expression to an intense desire, a fading hope. He did not say it with conviction. She gazed at him for a moment through half-closed eyelids.

'Do you, Tom?' she whispered.

'Lettice…!'

'Then believe at least—' her voice wavered suddenly, there came a little break in it—'that I am true to you, Tom, as I am to myself. Believe in that… and—Oh! for the love of heaven—help me!'

Before he could respond, before he could act upon the hope and passion her last unexpected words set loose in him—she turned away to go into the house. Voices were audible behind them, and Miss de Lorne was coming up the sandy drive with Mrs. Haughstone. Tom watched her go. She moved with a certain gliding, swaying walk as she passed along the verandah and disappeared behind the curtains of dried grass. It almost seemed—though this must certainly have been a trick of light and shadow—that she was swathed from head to foot in a clinging garment not of modern kind, and that he caught the gleam of gold upon the flesh of dusky arms that were bare above the elbow. Two persons were visible in her very physical appearance, as two persons had just been audible in her words. Thence came the conflict and the contradictions.

CHAPTER XXV

A few minutes later Lettice was presiding over her luncheon table as though life were simple as the sunlight in the street outside, and no clouds could ever fleck the procession of the years. She was quiet and yet betrayed excitement. Tom, at the opposite end of the table, watched her girlish figure, her graceful gestures. Her eyes were very bright, no shadows in their depths; she returned his gaze with untroubled frankness. Yet the set of her little mouth had self-mastery in it somewhere; there was no wavering or uncertainty; her self-possession was complete. But above his head the sword of Damocles hung. He saw the thread, taut and gleaming in the glare of the Egyptian sunlight.... He waited upon his cousin's return as men once waited for the sign thumbs up, thumbs down....

'Molly has sent me her album,' mentioned Mrs. Haughstone when the four of them were lounging in the garden chairs; 'she wonders if you would write your name in it. It's her passion—to fill it with distinguished names.' And when the page was found, she pointed to the quotation against his birthday date with the remark, in a lowered voice: 'It's quite appropriate, isn't it? For a man, I mean,' she added, 'because when a man's unhappy he's more easily tempted to suspicion than a woman is.'

'What is the quotation?' asked Lettice, glancing up from her deck chair.

Tom was carefully inscribing his 'distinguished' name in the child's album, as Mrs. Haughstone read the words aloud over his shoulder:

'"Whatever the circumstances, there is no man so miserable that he need not be true." It's anonymous,' she added, 'but it's by some one very wise.'

'A woman, probably,' Miss de Lorne put in with a laugh.

They discussed it, while Tom laboriously wrote his name against it with a fountain pen. His writing was a little shaky, for his sight was blurred and ice was in his veins.

'There's no need for you to hurry, is there?' said Lettice presently. 'Won't you stay and read to me a bit? Or would you rather look in—after dinner—and smoke?' The two selves spoke in that. It was as if the earlier, loving Lettice tried to assert itself, but was instantly driven back again. How differently she would have said it a few months ago.... He made excuses, saying he would drop in after dinner if he might. She did not press him further.

'I am tired a little,' she said gently. 'I'll sleep and rest and write letters too, then.'

She was invariably tired now, Tom soon discovered—until Tony returned from Cairo....

And that evening he escaped the invitations to play bridge, and made his way back, as in a dream, to the little house upon the Nile. He found her bending over the table so that the lamp shone on her abundant coils of hair, and as he entered softly he saw the address on the envelope beside her writing pad, several pages of which were already covered with her small, fine writing. He read the name before he could turn his eyes away.

'I was writing to Tony,' she said, looking up with an untroubled smile, 'but I can finish later. And you've come just in time to take my part. Ettie's been scolding me severely again.'

She blotted the lines and put the paper on one side, then turned with a challenging expression at her cousin who was knitting by the open window. The little name sounded so incongruous; it did not suit the big gaunt woman who had almost a touch of the monstrous in her. Tom stared a moment without speaking. The playful challenge had reality in it. Lettice intended to define her position openly. She meant that Tom should support her too.

He smiled as he watched them. But no words came to him. Then, remembering all at once that he had not kept his promise, he said quietly: 'I must send a line as well. I quite forgot.'

'You can write it now,' suggested Lettice, 'and I'll enclose it in mine.' And she pointed to the envelopes and paper before him on the table.

There was a moment of acute and painful struggle in him; pride and love fought the old pitched battle, but on a field of her own bold choosing! Tom knew murder in his heart, but he knew also that strange rich pain of sacrifice. It was theatrical: he stood upon the stage, an audience watching him with intent expectancy, wondering upon his decision. Mrs. Haughstone, Lettice and another part of himself that was Onlooker were the audience; Mrs. Haughstone had ceased knitting, Lettice leaned back in her chair, a smile in the eyes, but the lips set very firmly together. The man in him, with scorn and anger, seemed to clench his fists, while that other self—as with a spirit's voice from very far away—whispered behind his pain: 'Obey. You must. It has to be, so why not help it forward!'

To play the game, but to play it better than before, flashed through him.... Half amazed at himself, yet half contented, he sat down mechanically and scribbled a few lines of urgent entreaty to his cousin to come back soon.... 'We want you here, it's dull, we can't get on without you...' knowing that he traced the sentences of his own death-warrant. He folded it and passed it across to Lettice, who slipped it unread into her envelope. 'That ought to bring him, you think?' she observed, a happy light in her eyes, yet with a faint sigh half suppressed, as though she did a thing which hurt her too.

'I hope so,' replied Tom. 'I think so.'

He knew not what she had written to Tony; but whatever it was, his own note would appear to endorse it. He had perhaps placed in her hand the weapon that should hasten his own defeat, stretch him bleeding on the sand. And yet he trusted her; she was loyal and true throughout. The quicker the climax came, the sooner would he know the marvellous joy that lay beyond the pain. In some way, moreover, she knew this too. Actually they were working together, hand in hand, to hasten its inevitable arrival. They merely used such instruments as fate offered, however trivial, however clumsy. They were being driven. They could neither choose nor resist. He found a germ of subtle comfort in the thought. The Wave was under them. Upon its tumultuous volume they swept forward, side by side... striking out wildly.

'And will you also post it for me when you go?' he heard. 'I'll just add a line to finish up with.' Tom watched her open the writing-block again and trace a hurried sentence or two; she did it openly; he saw the neat, small words flow from the nib; he saw the signature: 'Lettice.'

'Fasten it down for me, Tom, will you? It's such an ugly thing for a woman to do. It's absurd that science can't invent a better way of closing an envelope, isn't it?' He was oddly helpless; she forced him to obey out of some greater knowledge. And while he did the ungraceful act, their eyes met across the table. It was the other person in her—the remote, barbaric, eastern woman, set somehow in power over him—who watched him seal his own discomfiture, and smiled to know his obedience had to be. It was, indeed, as though she tortured him deliberately, yet for some reason undivined.

For a passing second Tom felt this—then the strange exaggeration vanished. They played a game together. All this had been before. They looked back upon it, looked down from a point above it.... Tom could not read her heart, but he could read his own.

In a few minutes at most all this happened. He put the letter in his pocket, and Lettice turned to her cousin, challenge in her manner, an air of victory as well. And Tom felt he shared that victory somehow too. It was a curious moment, charged with a subtle perplexity of emotions none of them quite understood. It held such singular contradictions.

'There, Ettie!' she exclaimed, as much as to say 'Now you can't scold me any more. You see how little Mr. Kelverdon minds!'

While she flitted into the next room to fetch a stamp, Mrs. Haughstone, her needles arrested in mid-air, looked steadily at Tom. Her face was white. She had watched the little scene intently.

'The only thing I cannot understand, Mr. Kelverdon,' she said in a low tone, her voice both indignant and sympathetic, 'is how my cousin can give pain to a man like you. It's the most heartless thing I've ever seen.'

'Me!' gasped Tom. 'But I don't understand you!'

'And for a creature like that!' she went on quickly, as Lettice was heard in the passage; 'a libertine,'—she almost hissed the word out—'who thinks every pretty woman is made for his amusement—and false into the bargain——'

Tom put the stamp on. A few minutes later he was again walking along the narrow little Luxor street, the sentences just heard still filling the silent air about him, emotions charging wildly, each detail of the familiar little journey associated already with present pain and with prophecies of pain to come. The bewilderment and confusion in him were beyond all quieting. One moment he saw the picture of a slender foot that deliberately crushed life into the dust, the next he gazed into gentle, loving eyes that would brim with tears if a single hair of his head were injured.

A cold and mournful wind blew down the street, ruffling the darkened river. The black line of hills he could not see. Mystery, enchantment hung in the very air. The long dry fingers of the palm trees rattled overhead, and looking up, he saw the divine light of the starry heavens.... Surely among those comforting stars he saw her radiant eyes as well....

A voice, asking in ridiculous English the direction to a certain house, broke his reverie, and, turning round, he saw the sheeted figure of an Arab boy, the bright eyes gleaming in the mischievous little face of bronze. He pointed out the gateway, and the boy slipped off into the darkness, his bare feet soundless and mysterious on the sand. He disappeared up the driveway to the house—her house. Tom knew quite well from whom the telegram came. Tony had telegraphed to let her know of his safe arrival. So even that was necessary! 'And to-morrow morning,' he thought, 'he'll get my letter too. He'll come posting back again the very next day.' He clenched his teeth a moment; he shuddered. Then he added: 'So much the better!' and walked on quickly up the street. He posted her letter at the corner.

He went up to his bedroom. His sleepless nights had begun now....

What was the use of thinking, he asked himself as the hours passed? What good did it do to put the same questions over and over again, to pass from doubt to certainty, only to be flung back again from certainty to doubt? Was there no discoverable centre where the pendulum ceased from swinging? How could she be at the same time both cruel and tender, both true and false, frank and secretive, spiritual and sensual? Each of these pairs, he realised, was really a single state of which the adjectives represented the extremes at either end. They were ripples. The central personality travelled in one or other direction according to circumstances, according to the pull or push of forces—the main momentum of the parent wave. But there was a point where the heart felt neither one nor other, neither cruel nor tender, false nor true. Where, on the thermometer, did heat begin and cold come to an end? Love and hate, similarly, were extremes of one and the same emotion. Love, he well knew, could turn to virulent hatred—if something checked and forced it back upon the line of natural advance. Could, then, her tenderness be thus reversed, turning into cruelty.... Or was this cruelty but the awakening in her of another thing?...

Possibly. Yet at the centre, that undiscovered centre at present beyond his reach, Lettice, he knew, remained unalterably steadfast. There he felt the absolute assurance she was his exclusively. His centre, moreover, coincided with her own. They were in the 'sea' together. But to get back into the sea, the Wave now rolling under them must first break and fall....

The sooner, then, the better! They would swing back with it together eventually.

He chose, that is—without knowing it—a higher way of moulding destiny. It was the spiritual way, whose method and secret lie in that subtle paradox: Yield to conquer.

CHAPTER XXVI

Yes, she was always 'tired' now, though the 'always' meant but three days at most. It was the starving sense of loneliness, the aching sense of loss, the yearning and the vain desire that made it seem so long. Lettice evaded him with laughter in her eyes, or with a tired smile. But the laughter was for another. It was merciless and terrible—so slightly, faintly indicated, yet so overwhelmingly convincing.

The talk between them rarely touched reality, as though a barrier deadened their very voices. Even her mothering became exasperating; it was so unforced and natural; it seemed still so right that she should show solicitude for his physical welfare. And therein lay the anguish and the poignancy. Yet, while he resented fiercely, knowing this was all she had to offer now, he struggled at the same time to accept. One moment he resisted, the next accepted. One hour he believed in her, the next he disbelieved. Hope and fear alternately made tragic sport of him.

Two personalities fought for possession of his soul, and he could not always keep back the lower of the two. They interpenetrated—as, at Dehr-el-Bahri, two scenes had interpenetrated, something very, very old projected upon a modern screen.

Lettice too—he was convinced of it—was undergoing a similar experience in herself. Only in her case just now it was the lower, the primitive, the physical aspect that was uppermost. She clung to Tony, yet struggled to keep Tom. She could not help herself. And he himself, knowing he must shortly go, still clung and hesitated, hoping against hope. More and more now, until the end, he was aware that he stood outside his present-day self, and above it. He looked back—looked down—upon former emotions and activities; and hence the confusing alternating of jealousy and forgiveness.

There were revealing little incidents from time to time. On the following afternoon he found her, for instance, radiant with that exuberant happiness he had learned now to distrust. And for a moment he half believed again that the menace had lifted and the happiness was for him. She held out both hands towards him, while she described a plan for going to Edfu and Abou Simbel. His heart beat wildly for a second.

'But Tony?' he asked, almost before he knew it. 'We can't leave him out!'

'Oh, but I've had a letter.' And as she said it his eye caught sight of a bulky envelope lying in the sand beside her chair.

'Good,' he said quietly, 'and when is he coming back? I haven't heard from him.' The solid ground moved beneath his feet. He shivered, even in the blazing heat.

'To-morrow. He sends you all sorts of messages and says that something you wrote made him very happy. I wonder what it was, Tom?'

Behind her voice he heard the north wind rattling in the palms; he heard the soft rustle of the acacia leaves as well; there was the crashing of little waves upon the river; but a deep, deep shadow fell upon the sky and blotted out the sunshine. The glory vanished from the day, leaving in its place a painful glare that hurt the eyes. The soul in him was darkened.

'Ah!' he exclaimed with assumed playfulness, 'but that's my secret!' Men do smile, he remembered, as they are led to execution.

She laughed excitedly. 'I shall find it out——'

'You will,' he burst out significantly, 'in the end.'

Then, as she passed him to go into the house, he lost control a moment. He whispered suddenly:

'Love has no secrets, Lettice, anywhere. We're in the Sea together. I shall never let you go.' The intensity in his manner betrayed him; he adored her; he could not hide it.

She turned an instant, standing two steps above him; the sidelong downward glance lent to her face a touch of royalty, half pitying, half imperious. Her exquisite, frail beauty held a strength that mocked the worship in his eyes and voice. Almost—she challenged him:

'Soothsayer!' she whispered back contemptuously. 'Do your worst!'—and was gone into the house.

Desire surged wildly in him at that moment; impatience, scorn, fury even, raised their heads; he felt a savage impulse to seize her with violence, force her to confess, to have it out and end it one way or the other. He loathed himself for submitting to her cruelty, for it was intentional cruelty—she made him writhe and suffer of set purpose. And something barbaric in his blood leaped up in answer to the savagery in her own... when at that instant he heard her calling very softly:

'Tom! Come indoors to me a moment; I want to show you something!'

But with it another sentence sprang across him and was gone. Like a meteor it streaked the screen of memory. Seize it he could not. It had to do with death—his death. There was a thought of blood. Outwardly what he heard, however, was the playful little sentence of to-day. 'Come, I want to show you something.'

At the sound of her voice so softly calling all violence was forgotten; love poured back in a flood upon him; he would go through fire and water to possess her in the end. In this strange drama she played her inevitable part, even as he did; there must be no loss of self-control that might frustrate the coming climax. There must be no thwarting. If he felt jealousy, he must hide it; anger, scorn, desire must veil their faces.

He crossed the passage and stood before her in the darkened room, afraid and humble, full of a burning love that the centuries had not lessened, and that no conceivable cruelty of pain could ever change. Almost he knelt before her. Even if terrible, she was utterly adorable.

For he believed she was about to make a disclosure that would lay him bleeding in the dust; singularly at her mercy he felt, his heart laid bare to receive the final thrust that should make him outcast. Her little foot would crush him....

The long green blinds kept out the glare of the sunshine; and at first he saw the room but dimly. Then, slowly, the white form emerged, the broad-brimmed hat, the hanging violet veil, the yellow jacket of soft, clinging silk, the long white gauntlet gloves. He saw her dear face peering through the dimness at him, the eyes burning like two dark precious stones. A table stood between them. There was a square white object on it. A moment's bewilderment stole over him. Why had she called him in? What was she going to say? Why did she choose this moment? Was it the threat of Tony's near arrival that made her confession—and his dismissal—at last inevitable?

Then, suddenly, that night in the London theatre flashed back across his mind—her strange absorption in the play, the look of pain in her face, the little conversation, the sense of familiarity that hung about it all. He remembered Tony's words later: that another actor was expected with whose entry the piece would turn more real—turn tragic.

He waited. The dimness of the room was like the dimness of that theatre. The lights were lowered. They played their little parts. The audience watched and listened.

'Tom, dear,' her voice came floating tenderly across the air. 'I didn't like to give it you before the others. They wouldn't understand—they'd laugh at us.'

He did not understand. Surely he had heard indistinctly. He waited, saying nothing. The tenderness in her voice amazed him. He had expected very different words. Yet this was surely Lettice speaking, the Lettice of his spring-time in the mountains beside the calm blue lake. He stared hard. For the voice was Lettice, but the eyes and figure were another's. He was again aware of two persons there—of perplexing and bewildering struggle. But Lettice, for the moment, dominated as it seemed.

'So I put it here,' she went on in a low gentle tone, 'here, Tommy, on the table for you. And all my love is in it—my first, deep, fond love—our childhood love.' She leaned down and forward, her face in her hands, her elbows on the dark cloth; she pushed the square, white packet across to him. 'God bless you,' floated to him with her breath.

The struggle in her seemed very patent then. Yet in spite of that other, older self within her, it was still the voice of Lettice....

There was a moment's silence while her whisper hung, as it were, upon the air. His entire body seemed a single heart. Exactly what he felt he hardly knew. There was a simultaneous collapse of several huge emotions in him.... But he trusted her.... He clung to that beloved voice. For she called him 'Tommy'; she was his mother; love, tenderness, and pity emanated from her like a cloud of perfume. He heard the faint rustle of her dress as she bent forward, but outside he heard the dry, harsh rattle of the palm trees in the northern wind. And in that—was terror.

'What—what is it, Lettice?' The voice sounded like a boy's. It was outrageous. He swallowed—with an effort.

'Tommy, you—don't mind? You will take it, won't you?' And it was as if he heard her saying 'Help me...' once again, 'Trust me as I trust you....'

Mechanically he put his hand out and drew the object towards him. He knew then what it was and what was in it. He was glad of the darkness, for there was a ridiculous moisture in his eyes now. A lump was in his throat!

'I've been neglecting you. You haven't had a thing for ages. You'll take it, Tommy, won't you—dear?'

The little foolish words, so sweetly commonplace, fell like balm upon an open wound. He already held the small white packet in his hand. He looked up at her. God alone knows the strain upon his will in that moment. Somehow he mastered himself. It seemed as if he swallowed blood. For behind the mothering words lurked, he knew, the other self that any minute would return.

'Thank you, Lettice, very much,' he said with a strange calmness, and his voice was firm. Whatever happened he must not prevent the delivery of what had to be. Above all, that was clear. The pain must come in full before the promised joy.

Was it, perhaps, this strength in him that drew her? Was it his moment of iron self-mastery that brought her with outstretched, clinging arms towards him? Was it the unshakable love in him that threatened the temporary ascendancy of that other in her who gladly tortured him that joy might come in a morning yet to break?

For she stood beside him, though he had not seen her move. She was close against his shoulder, nestling as of old. It was surely a stage effect. A trap-door had opened in the floor of his consciousness; his first, early love sheltered in his aching heart again. The entire structure of the drama they played together threatened to collapse.

'Tom... you love me less?'

He held her to him, but he did not kiss the face she turned up to his. Nor did he speak.

'You've changed somewhere?' she whispered. 'You, too, have changed?'

There was a pause before he found words that he could utter. He dared not yield. To do so would be vain in any case.

'N—no, Lettice. But I can't say what it is. There is pain.... It has turned some part of me numb... killed something, brought something else to life. You will come back to me... but not quite yet.'

In spite of the darkness, he saw her face clearly then. For a moment—it seemed so easy—he could have caught her in his arms, kissed her, known the end of his present agony of heart and mind. She would have come back to him, Tony's claim obliterated from her life. The driving power that forced an older self upon her had weakened before the steadfast love he bore her. She was ready to capitulate. The little, childish present in his hands was offered as of old.... Tears rose behind his eyes.

How he resisted he never understood. Some thoroughness in him triumphed. If he shirked the pain to-day, it would have to be faced to-morrow—that alone was clear in his breaking heart. To be worthy of the greater love, the completer joy to follow, they must accept the present pain and see it through—experience it—exhaust it once for all. To refuse it now was only to postpone it. She must go her way, while he went his....

Gently he pushed her from him, released his hold; the little face slipped from his shoulder as though it sank into the sea. He felt that she understood. He heard himself speaking, though how he chose the words he never knew. Out of new depths in himself the phrases rose—a regenerated Tom uprising, though not yet sure of himself:

'You are not wholly mine. I must first—oh, Lettice!—learn to do without you. It is you who say it.'

Her voice, as she answered, seemed already changed, a shade of something harder and less yielding in it:

'That which you can do without is added to you.'

'A new thing... beginning,' he whispered, feeling it both belief and prophecy. His whisper broke in spite of himself. He saw her across the room, the table between them again. Already she looked different, 'Lettice' fading from her eyes and mouth.

She said a marvellous, sweet thing before that other self usurped her then:

'One day, Tom, we shall find each other in a crowd....'

There was a yearning cry in him he did not utter. It seemed she faded from the atmosphere as the dimness closed about her. He saw a darker figure with burning eyes upon a darker face; there was a gleam of gold; a faint perfume as of ambra hung about the air, and outside the palm leaves rattled in the northern wind. He had heard awful words, it seemed, that sealed his fate. He was forsaken, lonely, outcast. It was a sentence of death, for she was set in power over him....

* * * *

A flood of dazzling sunshine poured into the room from a lifted blind, as the others looked in from the verandah to say that they were going and wanted to say good-bye. A moment later all were discussing plans in the garden, Tom as loudly and eagerly as any of them. He held his square white packet. But he did not open it till he reached his room a little later, and then arranged the different articles in a row upon his table: the favourite cigarettes, the soap, the pair of white tennis socks with his initial neatly sewn on, the tie in the shade of blue that suited him best... the writing-pad and the dates!

A letter from Tony next caught his eye and he opened it, slowly, calmly, almost without interest, knowing exactly what it would say:

'... I was delighted, old chap, to get your note,' he read. 'I felt sure it would be all right, for I felt somehow that I had exaggerated your feeling towards her. As you say, what one has to think of with a woman in so delicate a position is her happiness more than one's own. But I wouldn't do anything to offend you or cause you pain for worlds, and I'm awfully glad to know the way is clear. To tell you the truth, I went away on purpose, for I felt uneasy. I wanted to be quite sure first that I was not trespassing. She made me feel I was doing you no wrong, but I wanted your assurance too....'

There was a good deal more in similar vein—he laid the burden upon her—ending with a word to say he was coming back to Luxor immediately. He would arrive the following day.

As a matter of fact Tony was already then in the train that left Cairo that evening and reached Luxor at eight o'clock next morning. Tom, who had counted upon another twenty-four hours' respite, did not know this; nor did he know till later that another telegram had been carried by a ghostly little Arab boy, with the result that Tony and Lettice enjoyed their hot rolls and coffee alone together in the shady garden where the cool northern wind rattled among the palm trees. Mrs. Haughstone mentioned it in due course, however, having watched the tête-à-tête from her bedroom window, unobserved.

CHAPTER XXVII

And next day there was one more revealing incident that helped, yet also hindered him, as he moved along his via dolorosa. For every step he took away from her seemed also to bring him nearer. They followed opposing curves of a circle. They separated ever more widely, back to back, yet were approaching each other at the same time. They would meet face to face....

He found her at the piano, practising the song that now ran ever in his blood; the score, he noticed, was in Tony's writing.

'Unwelcome!' he exclaimed, reading out the title over her shoulder.

'Tom! How you startled me! I was trying to learn it.' She turned to him; her eyes were shining. He was aware of a singular impression—struggle, effort barely manageable. Her beauty seemed fresh made; he thought of a wild rose washed by the dew and sparkling in the sunlight.

'I thought you knew it already,' he observed.

She laughed significantly, looking up into his face so close he could have kissed her lips by merely bending his head a few inches. 'Not quite— yet,' she answered. 'Will you give me a lesson, Tom?'

'Unpaid?' he asked.

She looked reproachfully at him. 'The best services are unpaid always.'

'I'm afraid I have neither the patience nor the knowledge,' he replied.

Her next words stirred happiness in him for a moment; the divine trust he fought to keep stole from his heart into his eyes: 'But you would never, never give up, Tom, no matter how difficult and obstinate the pupil. You would always understand. That I know.'

He moved away. Such double-edged talk, even in play, was dangerous. A deep weariness was in him, weakening self-control. Sensitive to the slightest touch just then, he dared not let her torture him too much. He felt in her a strength far, far beyond his own; he was powerless before her. Had Tony been present he could not have played his part at all. Somehow he had a curious feeling, moreover, that his cousin was not very far away.

'Tony will be here later, I think,' she said, as she followed him outside. 'But, if not, he's sure to come to dinner.'

'Good,' he replied, thinking that the train arrived in time to dress, and in no way surprised that she divined his thoughts. 'We can decide our plans then.' He added that he might be obliged to go back to Assouan, but she made no comment. Speech died away between them, as they sat down in the old familiar corner above the Nile. Tom, for the life of him, could think of nothing to say. Lettice, on the other hand, wanted to say nothing. He felt that she had nothing to say. Behind, below the numbness in him, meanwhile, her silence stabbed him without ceasing. The intense yearning in his heart threatened any minute to burst forth in vehement speech, almost in action. It lay accumulating in him dangerously, ready to leap out at the least sign—the pin-prick of a look, a word, a gesture on her part, and he would smash the barrier down between them and—ruin all. The sight of Tony, for instance, just then must have been as a red rag to a bull.

He traced figures in the sand with his heel, he listened to the wind above them, he never ceased to watch her motionless, indifferent figure stretched above him on the long deck-chair. A book peeped out from behind the cushion where her head rested. Tom put his hand across and took it suddenly, partly for something to do, partly from curiosity as well. She made a quick, restraining gesture, then changed her mind. And again he was conscious of battle in her, as if two beings fought.

'The Mary Coleridge Poems,' she said carelessly. 'Tony gave it me. You'll find the song he put to music.'

Tom vigorously turned the leaves. He had already glanced at the title-page with the small inscription in one corner: 'To L. J., from A. W.' There was a pencil mark against a poem half-way through.

'He's going to write music for some of the others too,' she added, watching him; 'the ones he has marked.' Her voice, he fancied, wavered slightly.

Tom nodded his head. 'I see,' he murmured, noticing a cross in pencil. A sullen defiance rose in his blood, but he forced it out of sight. He read the words in a low voice to himself. It was astonishing how the powers behind the scenes forced a contribution from the commonest incidents:

> *The sum of loss I have not reckoned yet, I cannot tell.*
> *For ever it was morning when we met,*
> *Night when we bade farewell.*

Perhaps the words let loose the emotion, though of different kinds, pent up behind their silence. The strain, at any rate, between them tightened first, then seemed to split. He kept his eyes upon the page before him; Lettice, too, remained still as before; only her lips moved as she spoke:

'Tom....' The voice plunged into his heart like iron.

'Yes,' he said quietly, without looking up.

'Tom,' she repeated, 'what are you thinking about so hard?'

He found no answer.

'And all to yourself?'

The blood rushed to his face; her voice was so soft.

He met her eyes and smiled. 'The same as usual, I suppose,' he said.

For a moment she made no reply, then, glancing at the book lying in his hand, she said in a lower voice: 'That woman had suffered deeply. There's truth and passion in every word she writes; there's a marvellous restraint as well. Tom,' she added, gazing hard at him, 'you feel it, don't you? You understand her?' For an instant she knit her brows as if in perplexity or misgiving.

'The truth, yes,' he replied after a moment's hesitation; 'the restraint as well.'

'And the passion?'

He nodded curtly by way of agreement. He turned the pages over very rapidly. His fingers were as thick and clumsy as rigid bits of wood. He fumbled.

'Will you read it once again?' she asked. He did so... in a low voice. With difficulty he reached the end. There was a mist before his eyes and his voice seemed confused. He dared not look up.

'There's a deep spiritual beauty,' he went on slowly, making an enormous effort, 'that's what I feel strongest, I think. There's renunciation, sacrifice——'

He was going to say more, for he felt the words surge up in his throat. This talk, he knew, was a mere safety valve to both of them; they used words as people attacked by laughter out of due season seize upon anything, however far-fetched, that may furnish excuse for it. The flood of language and emotion, too long suppressed, again rose to his very lips—when a slight sound stopped his utterance. He turned. Amazement caught him. Her frozen immobility, her dead indifference, her boredom possibly—all these, passing suddenly, had melted in a flood of tears. Her face was covered by her hands. She lay there sobbing within a foot of his hungry arms, sobbing as though her heart must break. He saw the drops between her little fingers, trickling.

It was so sudden, so unexpected, that Tom felt unable to speak or act at first. Numbness seized him. His faculties were arrested. He watched her, saw the little body heave down its entire length, noted the small convulsive movements of it. He saw all this, yet he could not do the natural thing. It was very ghastly.... He could not move a muscle, he could not say a single word, he could not comfort her—because he knew those tears were the tears of pity only. It was for himself she sobbed. The tenderness in her—in 'Lettice'—broke down before his weight of pain, the weight of pain she herself laid upon him. Nothing that he might do or say could comfort her. Divining what the immediate future held in store for him, she wept these burning tears of pity. In that poignant moment of self-revelation Tom's cumbersome machinery of intuition did not fail him. He understood. It was a confession—the last perhaps. He saw ahead with vivid and merciless clarity of vision. Only another could comfort her.... Yet he could help. Yes—he could help—by going. There was no other way. He must slip out.

And, as if prophetically just then, she murmured between her tight-pressed fingers: 'Leave me, Tom, for a moment... please go away... I'm so mortified... this idiotic scene.... Leave me a little, then come back. I shall be myself again presently.... It's Egypt—this awful Egypt....'

Tom obeyed. He got up and left her, moving without feeling in his legs, as though he walked in his sleep, as though he dreamed, as though he were—dead. He did not notice the direction. He walked mechanically. It felt to him that he simply walked straight out of her life into a world of emptiness and ice and shadows....

The river lay below him in a flood of light. He saw the Theban Hills rolling their dark, menacing wave along the far horizon. In the blistering heat the desert lay sun-drenched, basking, silent. Its faint sweet perfume reached him in the northern wind, that pungent odour of the sand, which is the odour of this sun-baked land etherealised.

A fiery intensity of light lay over it, as though any moment it must burst into sheets of flame. So intense was the light that it seemed to let sight through to—to what? To a more distant vision, infinitely remote. It was not a mirror, but a transparency. The eyes slipped through it marvel-lously.

He stood on the steps of worn-out sandstone, listening, staring, feel-ing nothing... and then a little song came floating across the air towards him, sung by a boatman in mid-stream. It was a native melody, but it had the strange, monotonous lilt of Tony's old-Egyptian melody.... And feel-ing stole back upon him, alternately burning and freezing the currents of his blood. The childhood nightmare touch crept into him: he saw the wave-like outline of the gloomy hills, he heard the wind rattling in the leaves behind him, to his nostrils came the strange, penetrating perfume of the tawny desert that encircles ancient Thebes, and in the air before him hung two pairs of eyes, dark, faithful eyes, cruel and at the same time tender, true yet merciless, and the others—treacherous, false, light blue in colour.... He began to shuffle furiously with his feet.... The soul in him went under.... He turned to face the menace coming up behind... the falling Wave....

'Tom!' he heard—and turned back towards her. And when he reached her side, she had so entirely regained composure that he could hardly believe it was the same person. Fresh and radiant she looked once more, no sign of tears, no traces of her recent emotion anywhere. Perhaps the interval had been longer than he guessed, but, in any case, the change was swift and half unaccountable. In himself, equally, was a calmness that seemed unnatural. He heard himself speaking in an even tone about the view, the river, the gold of the coming sunset. He wished to spare her, he talked as though nothing had happened, he mentioned the deep purple colour of the hills—when she broke out with sudden vehemence.

'Oh, don't speak of those hills, those awful hills,' she cried. 'I dread the sight of them. Last night I dreamed again—they crushed me down into the sand. I felt buried beneath them, deep, deep down—buried.' She whispered the last word as though to herself. She hid her face.

The words amazed him. He caught the passing shiver in her voice.

'"Again"?' he asked. 'You've dreamed of them before?' He stood close, looking down at her. The sense of his own identity returned slowly, yet he still felt two persons in him.

'Often and often,' she said in a lowered tone, 'since Tony came. I dream that we all three lie buried somewhere in that forbidding valley. It terrifies me more and more each time.'

'Strange,' he said. 'For they draw me too. I feel them somehow known— familiar.' He paused. 'I believe Tony was right, you know, when he said that we three——'

How she stopped him he never quite understood. At first he thought the curious movement on her face portended tears again, but the next second he saw that instead of tears a slow strange smile was stealing upon her— upwards from the mouth. It lay upon her features for a second only, but long enough to alter them. A thin, diaphanous mask, transparent, swiftly fleeting, passed over her, and through it another woman, yet herself, peered up at him with a penetrating yet somehow distant gaze. A shudder ran down his spine; there was a sensation of inner cold against his heart; he trembled, but he could not look away.... He saw in that brief instant the face of the woman who tortured him. The same second, so swiftly was it gone again, he saw Lettice watching him through half-closed eyelids. He heard her saying something. She was completing the sentence that had interrupted him:

'We're too imaginative, Tom. Believe me, Egypt is no place to let imagination loose, and I don't like it.' She sighed: there was exhaustion in her. 'It's stimulating enough without our help. Besides—' she used a curious adjective—'it's dangerous too.'

Tom willingly let the subject drop; his own desire was to appear natural, to protect her, to save her pain. He thought no longer of himself. Drawing upon all his strength, forcing himself almost to breaking-point, he talked quietly of obvious things, while longing secretly to get away to his own room where he could be alone. He craved to hide himself; like a stricken animal his instinct was to withdraw from observation.

The arrival of the tea-tray helped him, and, while they drank, the sky let down the emblazoned curtain of a hundred colours lest Night should bring her diamonds unnoticed, unannounced. There is no dusk in Egypt; the sun draws on his opal hood; there is a rush of soft white stars: the desert cools, and the wind turns icy. Night, high on her spangled throne, watches the sun dip down behind the Libyan sands.

Tom felt this coming of Night as he sat there, so close to Lettice that he could touch her fingers, feel her breath, catch the lightest rustle of her thin white dress. He felt night creeping in upon his heart. Swiftly the shadows piled. His soul seemed draped in blackness, drained of its shining gold, hidden below the horizon of the years. It sank out of sight, cold, lost, forgotten. His day was past and over....

They had been sitting silent for some minutes when a voice became audible, singing in the distance. It came nearer. Tom recognised the tune—'We were young, we were merry, we were very, very wise,'; and Lettice sat up suddenly to listen. But Tom then thought of one thing only—that it was beyond his power just now to meet his cousin. He knew his control was not equal to the task; he would betray himself; the rôle was too exacting. He rose abruptly.

'That must be Tony coming,' Lettice said. 'His tea will be all cold!' Each word was a caress, each syllable alive with interest, sympathy, excited anticipation. She had become suddenly alive. Tom saw her eyes shining as she gazed past him down the darkening drive. He made his absurd excuse. 'I'm going home to rest a bit, Lettice. I played tennis too hard. The sun's given me a headache. We'll meet later. You'll keep Tony for dinner?' His mind had begun to work, too; the evening train from Cairo, he remembered, was not due for an hour or more yet. A hideous suspicion rushed like fire through him.

But he asked no question. He knew they wished to be alone together. Yet also he had a wild, secret hope that she would be disappointed. He was speedily undeceived.

'All right, Tom,' she answered, hardly looking at him. 'And mind you're not late. Eight o'clock sharp. I'll make Tony stay.'

He was gone. He chose the path along the river bank instead of going by the drive. He did not look back once. It was when he entered the road a little later that he met Mrs. Haughstone coming home from a visit to some friends in his hotel. It was then she told him....

'What a surprise you must have had,' Tom believes he said in reply. He said something, at any rate, that he hoped sounded natural and right.

'Oh, no,' Mrs. Haughstone explained. 'We were quite prepared. Lettice had a telegram, you see, to let her know.'

She told him other things as well....

CHAPTER XXVIII

Tony had come back. The Play turned very real.

The situation à trois thenceforward became, for Tom, an acutely afflicting one. He found no permanent resting-place for heart or mind. He analysed, asked himself questions without end, but a final decisive judgment evaded him. He wrote letters and tore them up again. He hid himself in Assouan with belief for a companion, he came back and found that companion had been but a masquerader—disbelief. Suspicion grew confirmed into conviction. Vanity persuaded him against the weight of evidence, then left him naked with his facts. He wanted to kill, first others, then himself. He laughed, but the same minute he could have cried. Such complicated tangles of emotion were beyond his solving—it amazed him; such prolonged and incessant torture, so delicately applied—he marvelled that a human heart could bear it without breaking. For the affection and sympathy he felt for his cousin refused to die, while his worship and passion towards an unresponsive woman increasingly consumed him.

He no longer recognised himself, his cousin, Lettice; all three, indeed, were singularly changed. Each duplicated into a double rôle. Towards their former selves he kept his former attitude—of affection, love, belief; towards the usurping selves he felt—he knew not what. Therefore he drifted…. Strange, mysterious, tender, unfathomable Woman! Vain, primitive, self-sufficing, confident Man! In him the masculine tried to reason and analyse to the very end; in her the feminine interpreted intuitively: the male and female attitudes, that is, held true throughout. The Wave swept him forward irresistibly, his very soul, it seemed, went shuffling to find solid ground….

Meanwhile, however, no one broke the rules—rules that apparently had made themselves: subtle and delicate, it took place mostly out of sight, as it were, inside the heart. Below the mask of ordinary surface-conduct all agreed to wear, the deeper, inevitable intercourse proceeded, a Play within a Play, a tragedy concealed thinly by general consent under the most commonplace comedy imaginable. All acted out their parts, rehearsed, it seemed, of long ago. For, more and more, it came to Tom that the one thing he must never lose, whatever happened, was his trust in her. He must cling to that though it cost him all—trust in her love and truth and constancy. This singular burden seemed laid upon his soul. If he lost that trust and that belief, the Wave could never break, she could never justify that trust and that belief.

This 'enchantment' that tortured him, straining his whole being, was somehow a test indeed of his final worthiness to win her. Somehow, somewhence, he owed her this…. He dared not fail. For if he failed the Wave that should sweep her back into the 'sea' with him would not break—he would merely go on shuffling with his feet to the end of life. Tony and Lettice conquered him till he lay bleeding in the sand; Tom played the rôle of loss—obediently almost; the feeling that they were set in power over him persisted strangely. It dominated, at any rate, the resistance he would otherwise have offered. He must learn to do without her in order that she might in the end be added to him. Thus, and thus alone, could he find himself, and reach the level where she lived. He took his fate from her gentle, merciless hands, well knowing that it had to be. In some marvellous, sweet way the sacrifice would bring her back again at last, but bring her back completed—and to a Tom worthy of her love. The self-centred, confident man in him that deemed itself indispensable must crumble. To find regeneration he must risk destruction.

Events—yet always inner events—moved with such rapidity then that he lost count of time. The barrier never lowered again. He played his ghastly part in silence—always inner silence. Out of sight, below the surface, the deep wordless Play continued. With Tony's return the drama hurried. The actor all had been waiting for came on, and took the centre of the stage, and stayed until the curtain fell—a few weeks, all told, of their short Egyptian winter.

In the crowded rush of action Tom felt the Wave—bend, break, and smash him. At its highest moment he saw the stars, at its lowest the crunch of shifting gravel filled his ears, the mud blinded sight, the rubbish choked his breath. Yet he had seen those distant stars…. Into the mothering sea, as he sank back, the memory of the light went with him. It was a kind of incredible performance, half on earth and half in the air: it rushed with such impetuous momentum.

Amid the intensity of his human emotions, meanwhile, he lost sight of any subtler hints, if indeed they offered: he saw no veiled eastern visions any more, divined no psychic warnings. His agony of blinding pain, alternating with briefest intervals of shining hope when he recovered belief in her and called himself the worst names he could think of—this seething warfare of cruder feelings left no part of him sensitive to the delicate promptings of finer forces, least of all to the tracery of fancied memories. He only gasped for breath—sufficient to keep himself afloat and cry, as he had promised he would cry, even to the bitter end: 'I'll face it… I'll stick it out… I'll trust….!'

The setting of the Play was perfect; in Egypt alone was its production possible. The brilliant lighting, the fathomless, soft shadows, deep covering of blue by day, clear stars by night, the solemn hills, and the slow, eternal river—all these, against the huge background of the Desert, silent, golden, lonely, formed the adequate and true environment. In no other country, in England least of all, could the presentation have been real. Tony, himself, and Lettice belonged, one and all, it seemed, to Egypt—yet, somehow, not wholly to the Egypt of the tourist hordes and dragoman, and big hotels. The Onlooker in him, who stood aloof and held a watching brief, looked down upon an ancient land unvexed by railways, graciously clothed and coloured gorgeously, mapped burningly mid fiercer passions, eager for life, contemptuous of death. He did not understand, but that it was thus, not otherwise, he knew....

Her beauty, too, both physical and spiritual, became for him strangely heightened. He shifted between moods of worship that were alternately physical and spiritual. In the former he pictured her with darker colouring, half barbaric, eastern, her slender figure flitting through a grove of palms beyond a river too wide for him to cross; gold bands gleamed upon her arms, bare to the shoulder; he could not reach her; she was with another—it was torturing; she and that other disappeared into the covering shadows.... In the latter, however, there was no unworthy thought, no faintest desire of the blood; he saw her high among the little stars, gazing with tender, pitying eyes upon him, calling softly, praying for him, loving him, yet remote in some spiritual isolation where she must wait until he soared to join her.

Both physically and spiritually, that is, he idealised her—saw her divinely naked. She did not move. She hung there like a star, waiting for him, while he was carried past her, swept along helplessly by a tide, a flood, a wave, though a wave that was somehow rising up to where she dwelt above him....

It was a marvellous experience. In the physical moods he felt the fires of jealousy burn his flesh away to the bare nerves—resentment, rage, a bitterness that could kill; in the alternate state he felt the uplifting joy and comfort of ultimate sacrifice, sweet as heaven, the bliss of complete renunciation—for her happiness. If she loved another who could give her greater joy, he had no right to interfere.

It was this last that gradually increased in strength, the first that slowly, surely died. Unsatisfied yearnings hunted his soul across the empty desert that now seemed life. The self he had been so pleased with, had admired so proudly with calm complacence, thinking it indispensable— this was tortured, stabbed and mercilessly starved to death by slow degrees, while something else appeared shyly, gently, as yet unaware of itself, but already clearer and stronger. In the depths of his being, below an immense horizon, shone joy, luring him onward and brightening as it did so.

Love, he realised, was independent of the will—no one can will to love: she was not anywhere to blame, a stronger claim had come into life and changed her. She could not live untruth, pretending otherwise. He, rather, was to blame if he sought to hold her to a smaller love she had outgrown. She had the inalienable right to obey the bigger claim, if such it proved to be. Personal freedom was the basis of their contract. It would have been easier for him if she could have told him frankly, shared it with him; but, since that seemed beyond her, then it was for him to slip away. He must subtract himself from an inharmonious three, leaving a perfect two. He must make it easier for her.

* * * *

The days of golden sunshine passed along their appointed way as before, leaving him still without a final decision. Outwardly the little party a trois seemed harmonious, a coherent unit, while inwardly the accumulation of suppressed emotion crept nearer and nearer to the final breaking point. They lived upon a crater, playing their comedy within sight and hearing of destruction: even Mrs. Haughstone, ever waiting in the wings for her cue, came on effectively and filled her rôle, insignificant yet necessary. Its meanness was its truth.

'Mr. Winslowe excites my cousin too much; I'm sure it isn't good for her— in England, yes, but not out here in this strong, dangerous climate.'

Tom understood, but invariably opposed her:

'If it makes her happy for a little while, I see no harm in it; life has not been too kind to her, remember.'

Sometimes, however, the hint was barbed as well: 'Your cousin is a delightful being, but he can talk nonsense when he wants to. He's actually been trying to persuade me that you're jealous of him. He said you were only waiting a suitable moment to catch him alone in the Desert and shoot him!'

Tom countered her with an assumption of portentous gravity: 'Sound travels too easily in this still air,' he reminded her; 'the Nile would be the simplest way.' After which, confused by ridicule, she renounced the hint direct, indulging instead in facial expression, glances, and innuendo conveyed by gesture.

That there was some truth, however, behind this betrayal of her hostess and her fellow-guest, Tom felt certain; it lied more by exaggeration than by sheer invention: he listened while he hated it; ashamed of himself, he yet invited the ever-ready warnings, though he invariably defended the object of them—and himself.

Alternating thus, he knew no minute of happiness; a single day, a single hour contained both moods, trust ousted suspicion, and suspicion turned out trust. Lettice led him on, then abruptly turned to ice. In the morning he was first and Tony nowhere, the same afternoon this was reversed precisely—yet the balance growing steadily in his cousin's favour, the evidence accumulating against himself. It was not purposely contrived, it was in automatic obedience to deeper impulses than she knew. Tom never lost sight of this amazing duality in her, the struggle of one self against another older self to which cruelty was no stranger—or, as he put it, the newly awakened Woman against the Mother in her.

He could not fail to note the different effects he and his cousin produced in her—the ghastly difference. With himself she was captious, easily exasperated; her relations with Tony, above all, a sensitive spot on which she could bear no slightest pressure without annoyance; while behind this attitude, hid always the faithful motherly care that could not see him in distress. That touch of comedy lay in it dreadfully:—wet feet, cold, hungry, tired, and she flew to his consoling! Towards Tony this side of her remained unresponsive; he might drink unfiltered water for all she cared, tire himself to death, or sit in a draught for hours. It could have been comic almost but for its significance: that from Tony she received, instead of gave. The woman in her asked, claimed even—of the man in him. The pain for Tom lay there.

His cousin amused, stimulated her beyond anything Tom could offer; she sought protection from him, leant upon him. In his presence she blossomed out, her eyes shone the moment he arrived, her voice altered, her spirits became exuberant. The wholesome physical was awakened by him. He could not hope to equal Tony's address, his fascination. He never forgot that she once danced for happiness.... Helplessness grew upon him—he had no right to feel angry even, he could not justly blame herself or his cousin. The woman in her was open to capture by another; so far it had never belonged to him. In vain he argued that the mother was the larger part; it was the woman that he wanted with it. Having separated the two aspects of her in this way, the division, once made, remained.

And every day that passed this difference in her towards himself and Tony grew more mercilessly marked. The woman in her responded to another touch than his. Though neither lust nor passion, he knew, dwelt in her pure being anywhere, there were yet a thousand delicate unconscious ways by which a woman betrayed her attraction to a being of the opposite sex; they could not be challenged, but equally they could not be misinterpreted. Like the colour and perfume of a rose, they emanated from her inmost being.... In this sense, she was sexually indifferent to Tom, and while passion consumed his soul, he felt her, dearly mothering, yet cold as ice. The soft winds of Egypt bent the full-blossomed rose into another's hand, towards another's lips.... Tony had entered the garden of her secret life.

CHAPTER XXIX

And so the fires of jealousy burned him. He struggled hard, smothering all outward expression of his pain, with the sole result that the suppression increased the fury of the heat within. For every day the tiniest details fed its fierceness. It was inextinguishable. He lost his appetite, his sleep, he lost all sense of what is called proportion. There was no rest in him, day and night he lived in the consuming flame.

His cousin's irresponsibility now assumed a sinister form that shocked him. He recognised the libertine in his careless play with members of the other sex who had pleased him for moments, then been tossed aside. He became aware of grossness in his eyes and lips and bearing. He understood, above all, his—hands.

Against the fiery screen of his emotions jealousy threw violent pictures which he mistook for thought…, and there burst through this screen, then, scattering all lesser feelings, the flame of a vindictive anger that he believed was the protective righteous anger of an outraged man. 'If Tony did her wrong,' he told himself, 'I would kill him.'

Always, at this extravagant moment, however, he reached a climax, then calmed down again. A sense of humour rose incongruously to check loss of self-restraint. The memory of her daily tenderness swept over him; and shame sent a blush into his cheeks. He felt mortified, ungenerous, a foolish figure even. While the reaction lasted he forgave, felt her above reproach, cursed his wretched thoughts that had tried to soil her, and lost the violent vindictiveness that had betrayed him. His affection for his cousin, always real, and the sympathy between them, always genuine, returned to complete his own discomfiture. His mood swayed back to the first, happy days when the three of them had laughed and played together.

And to punish himself while this reaction lasted, he would seek her out and see that she inflicted the punishment itself. He would hear from her own lips how fond she was of Tony, fighting to convince himself, while he listened, that she was above suspicion, and that his pain was due solely to unworthy jealousy. He would be specially nice to Tony, making things easier for him, even urging him, as it were, into her very arms.

These moments of generous reaction, however, seemed to puzzle her. The exalted state of emotion was confined, perhaps, to himself. At any rate, he produced results the very reverse of what he intended; Tony became more cautious, Lettice looked at himself with half-questioning eyes.… There was falseness in his attitude, something unnatural. It was not the part he was cast for in the Play. He could not keep it up. He fell back once more to watching, listening, playing his proper rôle of a slave who was forced to observe the happiness of others set somehow over him, while suffering in silence. The inner fires were fed anew thereby. He knew himself flung back, bruised and bleeding, upon his original fear and jealousy, convinced more than ever before that this cruelty and torture had to be, and that his pain was justified. To resist was only to delay the perfect dawn.

> *The sum of loss I have not reckoned yet,*
> *I cannot tell*
> *For ever it was morning when we met,*
> *Night when we bade farewell.*

He changed the pronouns in the last two lines, for always it was morning when they met, night when they bade farewell.

Mrs. Haughstone, meanwhile, neglected no opportunity of dotting the vowel for his benefit; she crossed each t that the writing of the stars dropped fluttering across her path. 'Mr. Winslowe has emotions,' she mentioned once, 'but he has no heart. If he ever marries and settles down, his wife will find it out.'

'My cousin is not the kind to marry,' Tom replied. 'He's too change-able, and he knows it.'

'He's young,' she said, 'he hasn't found the right woman yet. He will improve—a woman older than himself with the mother strong in her might hold him. He needs the mother too. Most men do, I think; they're all children really.'

Tom laughed. 'Tony as father of a family—I can't imagine it.'

'Once he had children of his own,' she suggested, 'he would steady wonderfully. Those men often make the best husbands—don't you think?'

'Perhaps,' Tom replied briefly. 'Provided there's real heart beneath.'

'In the woman, yes,' returned the other quietly. 'Too much heart in the man can so easily cloy. A real man is always half a savage; that's why the woman likes him. It's the woman who guards the family.'

Tom, knowing that her words veiled other meanings, pretended not to notice. He no longer rose to the bait she offered. He detected the non-sense, the insincerity as well, but he could not argue successfully, and generalisations were equally beyond him. Too polite to strike back, he always waited till she had talked herself out; besides he often acquired information thus, information he both longed for yet disliked intensely. Such information rarely failed: it was, indeed, the desire to impart it with an air of naturalness that caused the conversation almost invariably. It appeared now. It was pregnant information, too. She conveyed it in a lowered tone: there was news from Warsaw. The end, it seemed, was expected by the doctors; a few months at most. Lettice had been warned, however, that her appearance could do no good; the sufferer mistook her for a relative who came to persecute him. Her presence would only hasten the end. She had cabled, none the less, to say that she would come. This was a week ago; the answer was expected in a day or two.

And Tom had not been informed of this.

'Mr. Winslowe thinks she ought to go at once. I'm sure his advice is wise. Even if her presence can do no good, it might be an unceasing regret if she was not there....'

'Your cousin alone can judge,' he interrupted coldly. 'I'd rather not discuss it, if you don't mind,' he added, noticing her eagerness to continue the conversation.

'Oh, certainly, Mr. Kelverdon—just as you feel. But in case she asks your advice as well—I only thought you'd like to know—to be prepared, I mean.'

Only long afterwards did it occur to him that Tony's informant was possibly this jealous parasite herself, who now deliberately put the matter in another light, hoping to sow discord to her own eventual benefit. All he realised at the moment was the intolerable pain that Lettice should tell him nothing. She looked to Tony for help, advice, possibly for consolation too.

There were moments of another kind, however, when it seemed quite easy to talk plainly. His position was absurd, undignified, unmanly. It was for him to state his case and abide by the result. Hearts rarely break in two, for all that poets and women might protest.

These moments, however, he did not use. It was not that he shrank from hearing his sentence plainly spoken, nor that he decided he must not prevent something that had to be. The reason lay deeper still:—it was impossible. In her presence he became tongue-tied, helpless. His own stupidity overwhelmed him. Silence took him. He felt at a hopeless disadvantage, ashamed even. No words of his could reach her through the distance, across the barrier, that lay between them now. He made no single attempt. His aching heart, filled with an immeasurable love, remained without the relief of utterance. He had lost her. But he loved now something in her place beyond the possibility of loss—an indestructible ideal.

Words, therefore, were not only impossible, they were vain. And when the final moment came they were still more useless. He could go, but he could not tell her he was going. Before that moment came, however, another searching experience was his: he saw Tony jealous—jealous of himself! He actually came to feel sympathy with his cousin who was his rival! It was his faithful love that made that possible too.

He realised this suddenly one day at Assouan.

He had been thinking about the long conversations Tony and Lettice enjoyed together, wondering what they found to discuss at such interminable length. From that his mind slipped easily into another question—how she could be so insensible to the pain she caused him?—when, all in a flash, he realised the distance she had travelled from him on the road of love towards Tony. The moment of perspective made it abruptly clear. She now talked with Tony as once, at Montreux and elsewhere, she had talked with himself. He saw his former place completely occupied. As an accomplished fact he saw it.

The belief that Tony's influence would weaken deserted him from that instant. It had been but a false hope created by desire and yearning.

There was a crash. He reached the bottom of despair. That same evening, on returning to his hotel from the Works, he found a telegram. It had been arranged that Lettice, Tony, Miss de Lorne and her brother should join him in Assouan. The telegram stated briefly that it was not possible after all:—she sent an excuse.

The sleepless night was no new thing to him, but the acuteness of new suffering was a revelation. Jealousy unmasked her amazing powers of poisonous and devastating energy.… He visualised in detail. He saw Lettice and his cousin together in the very situations he had hitherto reserved imaginatively for himself, both sweets hoped for and delights experienced, but raised now a hundredfold in actuality. Like pictures of flame they rose before his inner eye; they seared and scorched him; his blood turned acid; the dregs of agony were his to drink. The happiness he had planned for himself, down to the smallest minutiæ of each precious incident, he now saw transferred in this appalling way—to another. Not deliberately summoned, not morbidly evoked—the pictures rose of their own accord against the background of his mind, yet so instinct with actuality, that it seemed he had surely lived them, too, himself with her, somewhere, somehow… before. There was that same haunting touch of familiarity about them.

In the long hours of this particular night he reached, perhaps, the acme of his pain; imagination, whipped by jealousy, stoked the furnace to a heat he had not known as yet. He had been clinging to a visionary hope. 'I've lost her… lost her… lost her,' he repeated to himself, as though with each repetition the meaning of the phrase grew clearer. Numbness followed upon misery; there were long intervals when he felt nothing at all, periods when he thought he hated her, when pride and anger whispered he could do without her.… A state of negative insensibility followed.... On the heels of it came a red and violent vindictiveness; next—resignation, complete acceptance, almost peace. Then acute sensitiveness returned again—he felt the whole series of emotions over and over without one omission. This numbness and sensitiveness alternated with a kind of rhythmic succession.... He reviewed the entire episode from beginning to end, recalled every word she had uttered, traced the gradual influence of Tony on her, from its first faint origin to its present climax. He saw her struggles and her tears... the mysterious duality working to possess her soul. It was all plain as daylight. No justification for any further hope was left to him. He must go.... It was the thunder, surely, of the falling Wave.

For Tony, he realised at last, had not merely usurped his own place, but had discovered a new Lettice to herself, and setting her thus in a new, a larger world, had taught her a new relationship. He had achieved—perhaps innocently enough so far as his conscience was concerned?—a new result, and a bigger one than Tom, with his lesser powers, could possibly have effected.

There was no falseness, no duplicity in her. 'She still loves me as before, the mother still gives me what she always gave,' Tom put it to himself, 'but Tony has ploughed deeper—reached the woman in her. He loves a Lettice I have never realised. It is this new Lettice that loves him in return.... What right have I, with my smaller claim, to stand in her way a single moment?... I must slip out.'

He had lost the dream that Tony but tended a blossom, the fruit of which would come sweetly to his plucking afterwards. The intense suffering concealed all prophecy, as the jealousy killed all hope. He spent that final night of awful pain on his balcony, remembering how weeks before in Luxor the first menacing presentiment had come to him. He stared out into the Egyptian wonder of outer darkness. The stillness held a final menace as of death. He recalled a Polish proverb: 'In the still marshes there are devils.' The world spread dark and empty like his life; the Theban Hills seemed to have crept after him, here to Assouan; the stars, incredibly distant, had no warmth or comfort in them; the river roared with a dull and lonely sound; he heard the palm trees rattling in the wind. The pain in him was almost physical....

* * * *

Dawn found him in the same position—yet with a change. Perhaps the prolonged agony had killed the ache of ceaseless personal craving, or perhaps the fierceness of the fire had burned it out. Tom could not say; nor did he ask the questions. A change was there, and that was all he knew. He had come at last to a decision, made a final choice. He had somehow fought his battle out with a courage he did not know was courage. Here at Assouan, he turned upon the Wave and faced it. He saw her happiness only, fixed all his hope and energy on that. A new and loftier strength woke in him. There was no shuffling now.

He would give her up. In his heart she would always remain his dream and his ideal—but outwardly he would no longer need her. He would do without her. He forgave—if there was anything to forgive—forgave them both....

Something in him had broken.

He could not explain it, though he felt it. Yet it was not her that he had given up—it was himself.

The first effect of this, however, was to think that life lay in ruins round him, that, literally, the life in him was smothered by the breaking wave....

* * * *

And yet he did not break—he did not drown.

For, as though to show that his decision was the right, inevitable one, small outward details came to his assistance. Fate evidently approved. For Fate just then furnished relief by providing another outlet for his energies: the Works went seriously wrong: Tom could think of nothing else but how he could put things right again. Reflection, introspection, brooding over mental and spiritual pain became impossible.

The lieutenants he trusted had played him false; sub-contracts of an outrageous kind, flavoured by bribery, had been entered into; the cost of certain necessaries had been raised absurdly, with the result that the profits of the entire undertaking to the Firm must be lowered correspondingly. And the blame, the responsibility was his own; he had unwisely delegated his powers to underlings whose ambitions for money exceeded their sense of honour. But Tom's honour was involved as well. He had delegated his powers in writing. He now had to pay the price of his prolonged neglect of duty.

The position was irremediable; Tom's neglect and inefficiency were established beyond question. He had failed in a position of high trust. And to make the situation still less pleasant, Sir William, the Chairman of the Company—Tom's chief, the man to whom he owed his partnership and post of trust—telegraphed that he was on the way at last from Salonika. One way alone offered—to break the disastrous contracts by payments made down without delay. Tom made these payments out of his own pocket; they were large; his private resources disappeared in a single day.... But, even so, the delay and bungling at the Works were not to be concealed. Sir William, shrewd, experienced man of business, stern of heart as well as hard of head, could not be deceived. Within half an hour of his arrival, Tom Kelverdon's glaring incompetency—worse, his unreliability, to use no harsher word—were all laid bare. His position in the Firm, even his partnership, perhaps, became untenable. Resignation stared him in the face.

He saw his life go down in ruins before his very eyes; the roof had fallen long ago. The pillars now collapsed. The Wave, indeed, had turned him upside down; its smothering crash left no corner of his being above water; heart, mind, and character were flung in a broken tangle against the cruel bottom as it fell to earth.

But, at any rate, the new outlet for his immediate energies was offered. He seized it vigorously. He gave up his room at Luxor, and sent a man down to bring his luggage up. He did not write to Lettice. He faced the practical situation with a courage and thoroughness which, though too late, were admirable. Moreover, he found a curious relief in the new disaster, a certain comfort even. There was compensation in it somewhere. Everything was going to smash—the sooner, then, the better! This recklessness was in him. He had lost Lettice, so what else mattered? His attitude was somewhat devil-may-care, his grip on life itself seemed slipping.

This mood could not last, however, with a character like his. It seized him, but retained no hold. It was the last cry of despair when he touched bottom, the moment when weaker temperaments think of the emergency exit, realise their final worthlessness—proving themselves worthless, indeed, thereby.

Tom met the blow in other fashion. He saw himself unworthy, but by no means worthless. Suicide, whether of death or of final collapse, did not enter his mind even. He faced the Wave, he did not shuffle now. He sent a telegram to Lettice to say he was detained; he wrote to Tony that he had given up his room in the Luxor hotel, an affectionate, generous note, telling him to take good care of Lettice. It was only right and fair that Tony should think the path for himself was clear. Since he had decided to 'slip out' this attitude towards his cousin was necessarily involved. It must not appear that he had retired, beaten and unhappy. He must do no single thing that might offer resistance to the inevitable fate, least of all leave Tony with the sense of having injured him. True sacrifice forbade; renunciation, if real, was also silent—the smiling face, the cheerful, natural manner!

Tom, therefore, fixed his heart more firmly than ever upon one single point: her happiness. He fought to think of that alone. If he knew her happy, he could live. He found life in her joy. He lived in that. By 'slipping out,' no word of reproach, complaint, or censure uttered, he would actually contribute to her happiness. Thus, vicariously, he almost helped to cause it. In this faint, self-excluding bliss, he could live— even live on—until the end. That seemed true forgiveness.

Meanwhile, not easily nor immediately, did he defy the anguish that, day and night, kept gnawing at his heart. His one desire was to hide it, and—if the huge achievement might lie within his powers— to change it sweetly into a source of strength that should redeem him. The 'sum of loss,' indeed, he had not 'reckoned yet,' but he was beginning to add the figures up. Full measurement lay in the long, long awful years ahead. He had this strange comfort, however—that he now loved something he could never lose because it could not change. He loved an ideal. In that sense, he and Lettice were in the 'sea' together. His belief and trust in her were not lost, but heightened. And a hint of mothering contentment stole sweetly over him behind this shadowy yet genuine consolation.

The childhood nightmare was both presentiment and memory. The crest of the falling Wave was reflected in its base.

CHAPTER XXX

Tom took his passage home; he also told Sir William that his resignation, whether the Board accepted it or not, was final. His reputation, so far as the Firm was concerned, he knew was lost. His own self-respect had dwindled dangerously too. He had the feeling that he wanted to begin all over again from the very bottom. It seemed the only way. The prospect, at his age, was daunting. He faced it.

At the very moment in life when he had fancied himself most secure, most satisfied mentally, spiritually, materially—the entire structure on which self-confidence rested had given way. Even the means of material support had vanished too. The crash was absolute. This brief Egyptian winter had, indeed, proved the winter of his loss. The Wave had fallen at last.

During the interval at Assouan—ten days that seemed a month!—he heard occasionally from Lettice. 'To-day I miss you,' one letter opened. Another said: 'We wonder when you will return. We all miss you very much: it's not the same here without you, Tom.' And all were signed 'Your ever loving Lettice.' But if hope for some strange reason refused to die completely, he did not allow himself to be deceived. His task—no easy one—was to transmute emotion into the higher, self-less, ideal love that was now—oh, he knew it well enough—his only hope and safety. In the desolate emptiness of desert that yawned ahead, he saw this single tree that blossomed, and offered shade. Beauty and comfort both were there. He believed in her truth and somehow in her faithfulness as well.

* * * *

Tom sent his heavy luggage to Port Said, and took the train to Luxor. He had decided to keep his sailing secret. He could mention honestly that he was going to Cairo. He would write a line from there or, better still, from the steamer itself.

And the instinct that led to this decision was sound and wise. The act was not as boyish as it seemed. For he feared a reaction on her part that yet could be momentary only. His leaving so suddenly would be a shock, it might summon the earlier Lettice to the surface, there might be a painful scene for both of them. She would realise, to some extent at any rate, the immediate sense of loss; for she would surely divine that he was going, not to England merely, but out of her life. And she would suffer; she might even try to keep him—the only result being a revival of pain already almost conquered, and of distress for her.

For such reaction, he divined, could not be permanent. The Play was over; it must not, could not be prolonged. He must go out. There must be no lingering when the curtain fell. A curtain that halts in its descent upon the actors endangers the effect of the entire Play.

He wired to Cairo for a room. He wired to her too: 'Arrive to-morrow, en route Cairo. Leave same night.' He braced himself. The strain would be cruelly exacting, but the worst had been lived out already; the jealousy was dead; the new love was established beyond all reach of change. These last few hours should be natural, careless, gay, no hint betraying him, flying no signals of distress. He could just hold out. The strength was in him. And there was time before he caught the evening train for a reply to come: 'All delighted; expect you breakfast. Arranging picnic expedition.—Lettice.'

And that one word 'all' helped him unexpectedly to greater steadiness. It eliminated the personal touch even in a telegram.

In the train he slept but little; the heat was suffocating; there was a Khamsîn blowing and the fine sand crept in everywhere. At Luxor, however, the wind remained so high up that the lower regions of the sky were calm and still. The sand hung in fog-like clouds shrouding the sun, dimming the usual brilliance. But the heat was intense, and the occasional stray puffs of air that touched the creeping Nile or passed along the sweltering street, seemed to issue from the mouth of some vast furnace in the heavens. They dropped, then ceased abruptly; there was no relief in them. The natives sat listlessly in their doorways, the tourists kept their rooms or idled complainingly in the hotel halls and corridors. The ominous touch was everywhere. He felt it in his heart as well—the heart he thought broken beyond repair.

Tom bathed and changed his clothes, then drove down to the shady garden beside the river as of old. He felt the gritty sand between his teeth, it was in his mouth and eyes, it was on his tongue.... He met Lettice without a tremor, astonished at his own coolness and self-control; he watched her beauty as the beauty of a picture, something that was no longer his, yet watched it without envy and, in an odd sense, almost without pain. He loved the fairness of it for itself, for her, and for another who was not himself. Almost he loved their happiness to come—for her sake. Her eyes, too, followed him, he fancied, like a picture's eyes. She looked young and fresh, yet something mysterious in the following eyes. The usual excited happiness was less obvious, he thought, than usual, the mercurial gaiety wholly absent. He fancied a cloud upon her spirit somewhere. He imagined tiny, uncertain signs of questioning distress. He wondered.... This torture of a last uncertainty was also his.

Yet, obviously, she was glad to see him; her welcome was genuine; she came down the drive to meet him, both hands extended. Apparently, too, she was alone, Mrs. Haughstone still asleep, and Tony not yet arrived. It was still early morning.

'Well, and how did you get on without me—all of you?' he asked, adding the last three words with emphasis.

'I thought you were never coming back, Tom; I had the feeling you were bored here at Luxor and meant to leave us.' She looked him up and down with a curious look—of admiration almost, an admiration he believed he had now learned to do without. 'How lean and brown and well you look!' she went on, 'but thin, Tom. You've grown thinner.' She shook her finger at him. Her voice was perilously soft and kind, a sweet tenderness in her manner, too. 'You've been over-working and not eating enough. You've not had me to look after you.'

He flushed. 'I'm awfully fit,' he said, smiling a little shyly. 'I may be thinner. That's the heat, I suppose. Assouan's a blazing place—you feel you're in Africa.' He said the banal thing as usual.

'But was there no one there to look after you?' She gave him a quick glance. 'No one at all?'

Tom noticed the repeated question, wondering a little. But there was no play in him; in place of it was something stern, unyielding as iron, though not tested yet.

'The Chairman of my Company, nine hundred noisy tourists, and about a thousand Arabs at the Works,' he told her. 'There was hardly a soul I knew besides.'

She said no more; she gave a scarcely audible sigh; she seemed unsatisfied somewhere. To his surprise, then, he noticed that the familiar little table was only laid for two.

'Where's Tony?' he asked. 'And, by the by, how is he?'

He thought she hesitated a moment. 'Tony's not coming till later,' she told him. 'He guessed we should have a lot to talk about together, so he stayed away. Nice of him, wasn't it?'

Behind the commonplace sentences, the hidden wordless Play also drew on towards its Curtain.

'Well, it is my turn rather for a chat, perhaps,' he returned presently with a laugh, taking his cup of steaming coffee from her hand. 'I can see him later in the day. You've arranged something, I'm sure. Your wire spoke of a picnic, but perhaps this heat—this beastly Khamsîn——'

'It's passing,' she mentioned. 'They say it blows for three days, for six days, or for nine, but as a matter of fact, it does nothing of the sort. It's going to clear. I thought we might take our tea into the Desert.'

She went on talking rapidly, almost nervously, it seemed to Tom. Her mind was upon something else. Thoughts of another kind lay unexpressed behind her speech. His own mind was busy too—Tony, Warsaw, the long long interval he had been away, what had happened during his absence, and so forth? Had no cable come? What would she feel this time to-morrow when she knew?—these and a hundred others seethed below his quiet manner and careless talk. He noticed then that she was exquisitely dressed; she wore, in fact, the very things he most admired—and wore them purposely: the orange-coloured jacket, the violet veil, the hat with the little roses on the brim. It was his turn to look her up and down.

She caught his eye. Uncannily, she caught his thought as well. Tom steeled himself.

'I put these on especially for you, you truant boy,' she said deliciously across the table at him. 'I hope you're sensible of the honour done you.'

'Rather, Lettice! I should think I am, indeed!'

'I got up half an hour earlier on purpose too. Think what that means to a woman like me.' She handed him a grape-fruit she had opened and prepared herself.

'My favourite hat, and my favourite fruit! I wish I were worthy of them!' He stammered slightly as he said the stupid thing: the blood rushed up to his very forehead, but she gave no sign of noticing either words or blush. The strong sunburn hid the latter doubtless. There was a desperate shyness in him that he could not manage quite. He wished to heaven the talk would shift into another key. He could not keep this up for long; it was too dangerous. Her attitude, it seemed, had gone back to that of weeks ago; there was more than the mother in it, he felt: it was almost the earlier Lettice—and yet not quite. Something was added, but something too was missing. He wondered more and more... he asked himself odd questions.... It seemed to him suddenly that her mood was assumed, not wholly natural. The flash came to him that disappointment lay behind it, yet that the disappointment was not with—himself.

'You're wearing a new tie, Tom,' her voice broke in upon his moment's reverie. 'That's not the one I gave you.'

It was so unexpected, so absurd. It startled him. He laughed with genuine amusement, explaining that he had bought it in Assouan in a moment of extravagance—'the nearest shade I could find to the blue you gave me. How observant you are!' Lettice laughed with him. 'I always notice little things like that,' she said. 'It's what you call the mother in me, I suppose.' She examined the tie across the table, while they smoked their cigarettes. He looked aside. 'I hope it was admired. It suits you.' She fingered it. Her hand touched his chin.

'Does it? It's your taste, you know.'

'But was it admired?' she insisted almost sharply.

'That's really more than I can say, Lettice. You see, I didn't ask Sir William what he thought, and the natives are poor judges because they don't wear ties.' He was about to say more, talking the first nonsense that came into his head, when she did a thing that took his breath away, and made him tremble where he sat. Regardless of lurking Arab servants, careless of Mrs. Haughstone's windows not far behind them, she rose suddenly, tripped round the little table, kissed him on his cheek—and was back again in her chair, smoking innocently as before. It was a repetition of an earlier act, yet with a difference somewhere.

The world seemed unreal just then; things like this did not happen in real life, at least not quite like this; nor did two persons in their respective positions talk exactly thus, using such banal language, such insignificant phrases half of banter, half of surface foolishness. The kiss amazed him—for a moment. Tom felt in a dream. And yet this very sense of dream, this idle exchange of trivial conversation cloaked something that was a cruel, an indubitable reality. It was not a dream shot through with reality, it was a reality shot through with dream. But the dream itself, though old as the desert, dim as those grim Theban Hills now draped with flying sand, was also true and actual.

The hidden Play had broken through, merging for an instant with the upper surface-life. He was almost persuaded that this last, strange action had not happened, that Lettice had never really left her chair. So still and silent she sat there now. She had not stirred from her place. It was the burning wind that touched his cheek, a waft of heated atmosphere, lightly moving, that left the disquieting trail of perfume in the air. The glowing heavens, luminous athwart the clouds of fine, suspended sand, laid this ominous hint of dream upon the entire day.... The recent act became a mere picture in the mind.

Yet some little cell of innermost memory, stirring out of sleep, had surely given up its dead.... For a second it seemed to him this heavy, darkened air was in the recesses of the earth, beneath the burden of massive cliffs the centuries had piled. It was underground. In some cavern of those mournful Theban Hills, some one—had kissed him! For over his head shone painted stars against a painted blue, and in his nostrils hung a faint sweetness as of ambra....

He recovered his balance quickly. They resumed their curious masquerade, the screen of idle talk between significance and emptiness, like sounds of reality between dream and waking.

And the rest of that long day of stifling heat was similarly a dream shot through with incongruous touches of reality, yet also a reality shot through with the glamour of some incredibly ancient dream. Not till he stood later upon the steamer deck, the sea-wind in his face and the salt spray on his lips, did he awake fully and distinguish the dream from the reality—or the reality from the dream. Nor even then was the deep, strange confusion wholly dissipated. To the end of life, indeed, it remained an unsolved mystery, labelled a Premonition Fulfilled, without adequate explanation....

* * * *

The time passed listlessly enough, to the accompaniment of similar idle talk, careless, it seemed to Tom, with the ghastly sense of the final minutes slipping remorselessly away, so swiftly, so poignantly unused. For each moment was gigantic, brimmed full with the distilled essence, as it were, of intensest value, value that yet was not his to seize. He never lost the point of view that he watched a picture that belonged to some one else. His own position was clear; he had already leaped from a height; he counted, as he fell, the blades of grass, the pebbles far below; slipping over Niagara's awful edge, he noted the bubbles in the whirlpools underneath. They talked of the weather....!

'It's clearing,' said Lettice. 'There'll be sand in our tea and thin bread and butter. But anything's better than sitting and stifling here.'

Tom readily agreed. 'You and I and Tony, then?'

'I thought so. We don't want too many, do we?'

'Not for our la—not for a day like this.' He corrected himself just in time. 'Tony will be here for lunch?' he asked.

She nodded. 'He said so, at any rate, only one never quite knows with Tony.' And though Tom plainly heard, he made no comment. He was puzzled.

Most of the morning they remained alone together. Tom had never felt so close to her before; it seemed to him their spirits touched; there was no barrier now. But there was distance. He could not explain the paradox. A vague sweet feeling was in him that the distance was not of height, as formerly. He had risen somehow; he felt higher than before; he saw over the barrier that had been there. Pain and sacrifice, perhaps, had lifted him, raised him to the level where she dwelt; and in that way he was closer. A new strength was in him. At the same time, behind her outer quietness and her calm, he divined struggle still. In her atmosphere was a hint of strain, disharmony. He was positive of this. From time to time he caught trouble in her eyes. Could she, perhaps, discern—foreknow—the shadow of the dropping Curtain? He wondered.... He detected something in her that was new.

If any weakening of resolve were in himself, it disappeared long before Tony's arrival on the scene. A few private words from Mrs. Haughstone later banished it effectually. 'Your telegram, Mr. Kelverdon, came as a great surprise. We had planned a three-day trip to the Sphinx and Pyramids. Mr. Winslowe had written to you; he hoped to persuade you to join us. Again you left Assouan before the letter arrived. It's a habit with you!'

'Apparently.'

The poison no longer fevered him; he was immune.

'Mr. Winslowe—I had better warn you before he comes—was disappointed.'

'I'm sorry I spoilt the trip. It was most inconsiderate of me. But you can make it later when I'm gone—to Cairo, can't you?'

Mrs. Haughstone watched him somewhat keenly. Did she discover anything, he wondered? Was she aware that he was no longer within reach of her little shafts?

'It's all for the best, I think,' she went on in a casual tone. 'Lettice was too easily persuaded—she didn't really want to go without you. She said so. And Mr. Winslowe soon gets over his sulks——'

Tom interrupted her, turning sharply round. 'Oh,' he laughed, 'was that why he wouldn't come to breakfast, then?' And whether it was pain or pleasure that he felt, he did not know. The moment's anguish—he verily believed it—was for Lettice. And for Tony? Something akin to sympathy perhaps! If Tony should ever suffer pain like his—even temporarily....!

The other shrugged her angular shoulders a little. 'It's all passed now,' she observed; 'he's forgotten it, I'm sure. You needn't notice anything, by the way,' she added, 'if—if he seems ungracious.'

'Not for worlds,' replied Tom, throwing stones into the sullen river below. 'I'm far too tactful.'

Mrs. Haughstone looked away. There was a moment's expression of admiration on her face. 'You're big, Mr. Kelverdon, very big. I wish all men were as generous.' She spoke hurriedly below her breath. 'I saw this coming before you arrived. I wish I could have saved you. You've got the hero in you.'

Tom changed the subject, and presently moved away: it was time for lunch for one thing, and for another he wanted to hide his face from her too peering eyes. He was not quite sure of himself just then; his lips trembled a little; he could not altogether control his facial muscles. Tony jealous! Lettice piqued! Was this the explanation of her new sweetness towards himself! The position tried him sorely, testing his new strength from such amazing and unexpected angles. It was all beyond him somehow, the reversal of rôles so afflicting, tears and laughter so oddly mingled. Yet the sheet-anchor—his self-less love—held fast and true. There was no dragging, no shuffling where he stood.

Nor was there any weakening of resolution in him, any dimming of the new dawn within his heart. He felt sure of something that he did not understand, aware of a radiant promise some one whispered marvellously in his ear. He was alone, yet not alone, outcast yet companioned sweetly, bereft of all the world holds valuable, yet possessor of riches that the world passed by. He felt a conqueror. The pain was somehow turning into joy. He seemed above the earth. Only one thing mattered— that his ideal love should have no stain upon it.

The lunch he dreaded passed smoothly and without alarm. Tony was gay, light-hearted as usual, belying Mrs. Haughstone's ominous prediction. They smoked together afterwards, walking up and down the garden arm-in-arm, Tony eagerly discussing expeditions, picnics, birds, anything and everything that offered, with keen interest as of old; he even once suggested coming back to Assouan with his cousin—alone... Tom made no comment on the adverb. Nor was his sympathy mere acting; he genuinely felt it; the affection for Tony somehow was not dead.... The joy in him grew, meanwhile, brighter, clearer, higher. It was alive. Some courage of the sun was in him. There seemed a great understanding with it, and a greater forgiveness.

Of one thing only did he feel uncertain. He caught himself sharply wondering more than once. For he had the impression—the conviction almost—that something had happened during his absence at Assouan— that there was a change in her attitude to Tony. It was a subtle change; it was beginning merely; but it was there. Her behaviour at breakfast was not due to pique, not solely due to pique, at any rate. It had a deeper origin. Almost he detected signs of friction between herself and Tony. Very slight they were indeed, if not imagined altogether. His perception was still exceptionally alert, its acuteness left over, apparently, from the earlier days of pain and jealousy. Yet the result upon him was confusing chiefly.

In very trivial ways the change betrayed itself. The talk between the three of them remained incongruously upon the surface always. The play and chatter went on independently of the Play beneath, almost ignoring it. In that Wordless Play, however, the change was registered.

'Tom, you've got the straightest back of any man I ever saw,' Lettice exclaimed once, eyeing them critically with an amused smile as they came back towards her chair. 'I've just been watching you both.'

They laughed, while Tony turned it wittily into fun. 'It's always safer to look a person in the face,' he observed. If he felt the comparison was made to his disadvantage he did not show it. Tom, wondering what she meant and why she said it, felt that the remark annoyed him. For there was disparagement of Tony in it.

'I can read your soul from your back alone,' she added.

'And mine!' cried Tony, laughing: 'what about my back too? Or have I got no soul misplaced between my shoulder-blades?'

Tom laid his hand between those slightly-rounded shoulders then—and rather suddenly.

'It's bent from too much creeping after birds,' he exclaimed. 'In your next life you'll be on all fours if you're not careful.'

The Arab appeared to say the donkeys and sand-cart were waiting in the road, and Tony went indoors to get cameras and other paraphernalia essential to a Desert picnic. Lettice continued talking idly to Tom, who stood beside her, smoking.... The feeling of dream and reality were very strong in him at the moment. He hardly realised what the nonsense was he had said to his cousin. There was a slight sense of discomfort in him. The little, playful conversation just over had meaning in it. He missed that meaning. Somehow the comparison in his favour was disagreeable—he preferred to hear his cousin praised, but certainly not belittled. Perhaps vanity was wounded there—that his successful rival woke contempt in her was unendurable.... And he thought of his train for the first time with a vague relief.

'Birds,' she was saying, half to herself, the eyes beneath the big sun-hat looking beyond him, 'that reminds me, Tom—a dream I had. A little bird left its nest and hopped about to try all the other branches, because it thought it ought to explore them—had to, in a way. And it got into all sorts of danger, and ran fearful risks, and couldn't fly or use its wings properly,—till finally——'

She stopped, and her eyes turned full upon his own. The love in his face was plain to read, though he was not conscious of it. He waited in silence:

'Till finally it crept back up into its own nest again,' she went on, 'and found its wings lying there all the time. It had forgotten them! And it got in, felt warm and safe and cosy—and fell asleep.'

'Whereupon you woke and found it was all a dream,' said Tom. His tone, though matter-of-fact, was lower than usual, but it was firm. No sign of emotion now was visible in his face. The eyes were steady, the lips betrayed no hint. Her little dream, the way of telling it rather, per-plexed him.

'Yes,' she said, 'but I found somehow that the bird was me.' She sighed a little.

It flashed upon him suddenly that she was exhausted, wearied out; that her heart was beating with some interior stress and struggle. She seemed on the point of giving up, some long long battle in her ended. There was something she wished to say to him—he got this impression too—something she could not bring herself to say, unless he helped her, unless he asked for it. The duality was ending, perhaps fused into unity again?... The intense and burning desire to help her rose upon him, the desire to protect. And the word 'Warsaw' fled across his mind... as though it fell through the heated air into his mind... from hers.

'Tony declares,' she was saying, 'that our memories are packed away under pressure like steam in a boiler, and the dream is their safety-valve... I wonder.... He read it somewhere. It's not his own, of course. But Tony never explains—because he doesn't really know. He's flashy—not the depth we thought—the truth... Tom!'

She called his name with emphasis, as if annoyed that he showed so little interest. There was an instant's cloud upon her face; the eyes wavered, then looked away; he felt again there was disappointment somewhere in her —with himself or with Tony, he did not know.... He kept silent. He could think of nothing by way of answer—nothing appropriate, nothing safe.

She waited, keeping silent too. The Curtain was lowering, its shadow growing on the air.

'I dream so little,' he stammered at length, 'I can't say.' It enraged him that he faltered. He turned away.... Tony at that moment arrived. The cart and animals were ready, everything was collected. He announced it loudly, urging them with a certain impatience, as though they caused the delay. He stared keenly at them a moment.... They started.

CHAPTER XXXI

How trivial, yet how significant of the tension of interior forces—the careless words, the foolish little dream, the playful allusion to one man's stoop and to another's upright carriage, how easy to read, how obvious! Yet Tom, too intensely preoccupied, perhaps, with keeping his own balance, was unaware of revelation. His mind perceived the delicate change, yet attached a wrong direction to it. Perplexity and discomfort in him deepened. He was relieved when Tony interrupted; he felt glad. The shifting of values was disturbing to him. It was as though the falling Curtain halted....

The hours left to him were few; they both rushed and lingered. The afternoon seemed gone so quickly, while yet the moments dragged, each separate instant too intense with feeling to yield up its being willingly. The minutes lingered; it was the hours that rushed.

Subconsciously, it seemed, Tom counted them in his heart.... Subconsciously, too, he stated the position, as though to do so steadied him: Three persons, three friends, were off upon a picnic. At a certain moment they would turn back; at a certain moment two of them would say good-bye; at a certain moment a final train would start—his eyes would no longer see her.... It seemed impossible, unreal; it could not happen.... He could so easily prevent it. No question had been asked about his going to Cairo; it was taken for granted that he went on business and would return. He could cancel his steamer-berth, no explanation necessary, nor any asked.

But having weighed the sacrifice against the joy, he was not wanting.

They mounted their lusty donkeys; Lettice climbed into her sand-cart; the boys came clattering after them down the street of Thebes with the tea-things and the bundles of clover for the animals. Across the belt of brilliant emerald green, past clover-fields and groves of palms, they followed the ancient track towards the desert. They were on the eastern bank, the Theban Hills far behind them on the horizon. Towards the Red Sea they headed, though Tom had no notion of their direction, aware only that while they went further and further from those hills, the hills themselves somehow came ever nearer. The gaunt outline followed them; each time he looked back the shadow cast was closer than before, almost upon their heels. But for the assurance of his senses he could have believed they headed towards these yellow cliffs instead of the reverse. He could not shake off the singular impression that their weight was on his back; he felt the oppression of those ancient tombs, those crowded corridors, that hidden subterranean world. No mummy, he remembered, but believed it would one day unwind again when the soul, cleansed and justified, came back to claim it. Regeneration was inevitable. A glorious faith secure in ultimate joy!

They hurried vainly; the distance between them, instead of increasing, lessened. The hills would not let them go.

The burning atmosphere, the motionless air caused doubtless the optical illusion. The glare was blinding. Tom did not draw attention to it. He tugged his obstinate donkey into line with the slower sand-cart, riding for several minutes in silence, close beside Lettice, aware of her perfume, her flying veil almost across his eyes from time to time. Tony was some way ahead.

'Tom,' he heard suddenly, 'must you really go to Cairo to-night?'

'I'm afraid so. It's important.' But after a pause he added 'Why?' He said it because his sentence sounded otherwise suspiciously incomplete. Above all, he must seem natural. 'Why do you ask?'

The answer made him regret that extra word:

'There's something I want to tell you.'

'Very important?' He asked it laughingly, busy with the reins apparently.

'Far more important than your going to Cairo. I want your advice and help.'

'I must,' he said slowly. 'Won't it keep?' He tugged violently at the reins, though the donkey was behaving admirably.

'How long will you stay?' she asked.

'One night only, Lettice. Not longer.'

They were on soft and yellow sand by now; the desert shone with a luminous glow; Tom could not hear the sound of his donkey's hoofs, nor the crunching of the sand-cart. He heard nothing but a voice singing beside him in the burning air. But the air had grown radiant. He realised that he was beating the donkey without the slightest reason.

'When you come back, then—I'll tell you when you come back,' he heard.

And a sudden inspiration came to his assistance. 'Couldn't you write it?' he asked calmly. 'The Semiramis Hotel will find me—in case anything happened. I should have time to think it over—I like that best—if it's really so important. My mind, you know, works slowly.'

Her reply had a curious effect upon him. She needed help—his help. 'Perhaps, Tom. But one can depend so upon your judgment.'

He knew that she was watching his face. With an effort he turned to meet her gaze. He saw her against the background of the hills, whose following mass towered menacingly above her little outline. And as he looked he was suddenly transfixed, he dropped his reins, he stared without a word. Two pairs of eyes, two smiles, two human physiognomies once again met his arrested gaze. He knew them, of course, well enough by now, but never before had he caught the two expressions so vividly revealed, so distinctly marked; clear as a composite picture, one face painted in upon another that lay beneath it. There was the darker face—and there was Lettice; and each struggled for complete possession of her features. There was conflict, sharp and dreadful; one second, the gleam of cruelty flashed out, a yellow of amber in it, as though gold shone reflected faintly—the next, an anguish of tenderness, as though love brimmed her eyes with the moisture of divine compassion. The conflict was desperate, amazing, painful beyond words. Then the darker aspect slowly waned, withdrawing backwards, melting away into the shadows of the hills behind— as though it first had issued thence—as though almost it belonged there. Alive and true, yet vanquished, it faded out.... He saw at last the dear, innocent eyes of—Lettice only. It was this Lettice who had spoken.

His donkey stumbled—it was natural enough, seeing that the reins hung loose and his feet had somehow left the stirrups. Tom pitched forward heavily, saving himself and his animal from an ignominious accident just in the nick of time. There were cries and laughter. The sand-cart swerved aside at the same moment, and Tony, from a distance, came galloping back towards them.

Tom recovered his balance and told his donkey in honest English what he thought of it. 'But it was your fault, you careless boy,' cried Lettice; 'you let go the reins and whacked it at the same time. Your eyes were popping out of your head. I thought you'd seen a ghost.'

Tom glanced at her. 'I was nearly off,' he said. 'Another second and it would have been a case of "Low let me lie where the dead dog——"'

She interrupted him with surprising vehemence:

'Don't, don't, Tom. I hate it! I hate the words and the tune and everything. I won't hear it...!'

Tony came clattering up and the incident was over, ended as abruptly as begun. But, as Tom well realised, another hitch had occurred in the lowering of the Curtain. The actors, for a moment, had stood there in their normal fashion, betrayed, caught in the act, a little foolish even. It was the hand of a woman this time that delayed it.

'Did you hurt yourself anywhere, Tom?' Her question rang in his head like music for the next mile or two. He kept beside the sand-cart until they reached their destination. It was absurd—yet he could not ride in front with Tony lest some one driving behind them should notice—yes, that was the half-comical truth—notice that Tony was round-shouldered—oh, very, very slightly so—whereas his own back was straight! It was ridiculously foolish, yet pathetic. At the same time, it was poignantly dramatic....

And their destination was a deep bay of yellow sand, soft and tawny, ribbed with a series of lesser troughs the wind had scooped out to look like a shore some withdrawing ocean had left exposed below the westering sun. A solitary palm tree stood behind upon a dune.

The afternoon, the beating hotness of the air, the clouds of high, suspended sand, the stupendous sunset—as if the world caught fire and burned along the whole horizon—it was all unforgettable. The yellow sand about them blazed and shone, scorching their bare hands; the Desert was empty, silent, lonely. Only the western heavens, where the sun sank in a red mass of ominous splendour, was alive with energy. Coloured shafts mapped the vault from horizon to zenith like the spokes of a prodigious wheel of fire. Any minute the air and the sand it pressed upon might burst into a sea of flame. The furnace where the Khamsîn brewed in distant Nubia sent its warnings in advance; it was slowly travelling northward. And hence, possibly, arose the disquieting sensation that something was gathering, something that might take them unawares. The sand lay listening, waiting, watching. There was whispering among the very grains....

It was half way through tea when the first stray puffs of wind came dropping abruptly, sighing away in tiny eddies of dust beyond the circle. Three human atoms upon the huge yellow carpet, that ere long would shake itself across five hundred miles and rise, whirling, driving, suffocating all life within its folds—three human beings noted the puffs of heated air and reacted variously to the little change. Each felt, it seemed, a slight uneasiness, as though of trouble coming that was yet not entirely atmospherical. Nerves tingled. They looked into each other's faces. They looked back.

'We mustn't stay too late,' said Tony, filling a basket for the donkey-boys in their dune two hundred yards away. 'We've a long way to go.' He examined the portentous sky. 'It won't come till night,' he added, 'still—they're a bit awkward, these sandstorms, and one never knows.'

'And I've got a train to catch,' Tom mentioned, 'absurd as it sounds in a place like this.' He was scraping his lips with a handkerchief. 'I've eaten enough bread-and-sand to last me till dinner, anyhow.' He helped his cousin with the Arabs' food. 'They probably don't mind it, they're used to it.' He straightened up from his stooping posture. Lettice, he saw, was lying with a cigarette against the bank of sloping sand that curved above them. She was intently watching them. She had not spoken for some time; she looked almost drowsy; the eyelids were half closed; the cigarette smoke rose in a steady little thread that did not waver.... There was perhaps ten yards between them, but he caught the direction of her gaze, and throwing his own eyes into the same line of sight, he saw what she saw. Instinctively, he took a quick step forward— hiding Tony from her immediate view.

It was certainly curious, this desire to screen his cousin, to prevent his appearing at a disadvantage. He was impelled, at all costs and in the smallest details, to help the man she admired, to increase his value, to minimise his disabilities, however trivial. It pained him to see Tony even at a physical disadvantage; Tony must show always at his very best; and at this moment, bending over the baskets, the attitude of the shoulders was disagreeably emphasised.

Tom did not laugh, he did not even smile. Gravely, as though it were of importance, he moved forward so that Lettice should not see the detail of the rounded shoulders which, he knew, compared unfavourably with his own straighter carriage. Yet almost the next minute, when he looked back again, he saw that the cigarette had fallen from her fingers, the eyes were closed, her body had slipped into a more recumbent angle, she seemed actually asleep.

'Give a shout, Tom, and the boys will come to fetch it,' said Tony, when at length the basket was ready. He put his hands to his own mouth to coo-ee across the dunes. Tom stopped him at once. 'Hush! Lettice has dropped off,' he explained, 'you'll wake her. It's the heat. I'll carry the things over to them.' He noticed Tony's hands as he held them to his lips. And again he felt a touch of sympathy, almost pity. Had she, so observant, so discerning in her fastidious taste—had she failed to notice the small detail too?

'No, let me take it,' Tony was saying, seizing the hamper from his cousin. Tom suggested carrying it between them. They tried it, laughing and struggling together with the awkward burden, but keeping their voices low. They lost the direction too; for all the sand-dunes were alike, and the boys were hidden in a hollow. It ended in Tony going off in triumph with the basket under one arm, guided at length by the faint neighing of a donkey in the distance.

Some little time had passed, perhaps five minutes, perhaps longer, when Tom went back to the tea-place across the soft sand, stepping cautiously so as not to disturb the sleeper. And another five minutes, perhaps another ten, had slipped by before Tony's head reappeared above a neighbouring dune. A boy had come to meet him, shortening his journey.

But Fate calculated to a nicety, wasting no seconds one way or the other. There had been time—just time before Tony's return—for Tom to have stretched himself at her feet, to have lit a cigarette, and to have smoked sufficient of it for the first ash to fall. He was very careful to make no sound, even lighting the match softly inside his hat. But his hand was trembling. For Lettice slept, and in her sleep made little sounds of pain.

He watched her. There was a tiny frown between the eyebrows, the lips twitched from time to time, she moved uneasily upon the bank of sliding sand; and, as she made these little broken sounds of pain, from beneath the closed eyelids two small tears crept out upon her cheeks.

Tom stared, making no sound or movement. The tears rolled down and fell into the sand. The suffering in the face made his heart beat irregularly. Something transfixed him. She wore the expression he had seen in the London theatre. For a moment he felt terror—a terror of something coming, something going to happen. He stared, trembling, holding his breath. She was dreaming, as a person even in a three-minute sleep can dream—deeply, vividly. He waited. He had the amazing sensation that he knew what she was dreaming—that he took part in it with her almost.... Unable, finally, to restrain himself another instant, he moved—and the noise wakened her. She sighed. The eyes opened of their own accord. She stared at him in a dazed way for a moment. Then she looked over his shoulder across the desert.

'You've been asleep, Lettice,' he whispered, 'and actually dreaming—all in five minutes.'

She rubbed her eyes slowly, as though sand was in them. She stared into his face a moment before she spoke.

'Yes, I dreamed,' she answered with a little frightened sigh. 'I dreamed of you——There was a tent—the flap lifted suddenly—oh, it was so vivid! Then there was a crowd and awful drums were beating—and my river with the floating faces was there and I plunged in to save one—it was yours, Tom, yours——'

She paused for a fraction of a second, while his heart went thumping against his ribs. He did not speak. He waited.

'Then somehow you were taken from me,' she went on; 'you left me, Tom.' Her voice sank. 'And it broke my heart in two.'

'Lettice...!'

He made a sudden movement in the sand—at which moment, precisely, Tony's head appeared above the neighbouring dune, the rest of his body following it immediately.

And it seemed to Tom that his cousin came upon them out of the heart of a dream, out of the earth, out of a sandy tomb. His very existence, for those minutes, had been utterly forgotten, obliterated. He rose from the dead and came towards them over the hot, yellow desert. The distant hills—the Theban Hills above the Valley of the Kings—disgorged him. And, as once before, he looked dreadful, threatening, his great hands held out in front of him. He came gliding down the yielding slope. He caught them!

In that second—it was but the fraction of a second actually—the impression upon Tom's mind was acute and terrible. Speech and movement were not in him anywhere; he could only sit and stare, both terrified and fascinated. Between himself and Lettice stretched an interval of six feet certainly, and into this very gap, the figure of his cousin, followed and preceded by heaps of moving sand, descended now. It was towards Lettice that Tony came so swiftly gliding.

It was his cousin surely...?

He saw the big hands outspread, he saw the slightly stooping shoulders, he saw the face and eyes, the light blue eyes. But also he saw strange, unaccustomed raiment, he saw a sheet of gold, he smelt the soft breath of ambra.... And the face was dark and menacing. There were words, too, careless, playful words, uttered undoubtedly by Tony's familiar voice: 'Caught you both asleep! Well, I declare! You are a couple...!' followed by something else about its being 'time to pack up and go because the sand was coming....' Tom heard the words distinctly, but far away, tiny with curious distance; they were half smothered, half submerged, it seemed, behind an acute inner hearing that caught another set of words he could not understand—in a language he both remembered and forgot. And the deep sense of dread passed swiftly then into a blinding jealous rage; he saw red; a fury of wrath that could kill and stab and strangle rushed over him in a flood of passionate emotion. He lost control. He rushed headlong.

Seconds dragged out incredibly into minutes, as though time halted.... An intense, murderous hatred blazed in his heart.

From where he sat, both figures were above him, sheltered halfway up the long sliding slope. At the base of the yellow dune he crouched; he looked up at them. His eyes perhaps were blinded by the red tempest in his heart; or perhaps the tiny particles of flying sand drove against his eyeballs. He saw, at any rate, the figures close together, as if the man came gliding straight into her arms. He rose—

At the same moment a draught of sudden, violent wind broke with a pouring rush across the desert, and the entire crest of the undulating dune behind them rose to meet it in a single whirling eddy. As a gust of sea-wind tosses the spray into the air, this burst of scorching desert-wind drew the ridge up after it, then flung it in a blinding swirl against his face and skin.

The dune rose in a Wave of glittering yellow sand, drowning them from head to foot. He saw the glint and shimmer of the myriad particles in the sunset; he saw them drifting by the thousand, by the million through the whirling mass of it; he saw the two figures side by side above him, caught beneath the toppling crest of this bending billow that curved and broke against the fiery sky; he smelt the faint perfume of the desert underneath the hollow arch; he heard the thin, metallic grating of the countless grains in friction; he heard the palm leaves rattling; he saw two pairs of eyes… his feet went shuffling. It was The Wave—of sand.…

And the nightmare clutch laid hold upon his heart with giant pincers. The fiery red of insensate anger burst into flames, filled his throat to choking, set his paralysed muscles free with uncontrollable energy. This savage lust of murder caught him. The shuffling went faster, faster.… He turned and faced the eyes. He would kill—rather than see her touched by those great hands. It seemed he made the leap of a wild animal upon its prey.…

Fire flashed… then passed, before he knew it, from red to shining amber, from sullen crimson into purest gold, from gold to the sheen of dazzling whiteness. The change was instantaneous. His leap was arrested in mid-air. The red wrath passed amazingly, forgotten or transmuted. With a miraculous swiftness he was aware of understanding, of sympathy, of forgiveness.… The red light melted into white—the white of glory. The murder faded from his heart, replaced by a deep, deep glow of peace, of love, of infinite trust, of complete comprehension.… He accepted something marvellously. . . He forgot—himself.…

The eyes faded, the gold, the raiment, the perfume vanished, the sound died away. He no longer shuffled upon yielding sand. There was solid ground beneath his feet.… He was standing alert and upright, his arms outstretched to save—Tony from collapse upon the sliding dune. And the sandy wind drove blindingly against his face and skin.

The three of them stood side by side, holding to each other, laughing, choking, spluttering, heads bent and eyes closed tightly. Tom found his cousin's hand in his own, clutching it firmly to keep his balance, while behind himself—against his 'straight back,' he realised, even while he choked and laughed—Lettice clung for shelter. Tom, therefore, actually had leaped forward—but to protect and not to kill. He protected both of them. This time, however, it was to himself that Lettice clung, instead of to another.

The violent gust passed on its way, the flying cloud of sand subsided, settling down on everything. For a moment they stood there rubbing their eyes, shaking their clothing free; then raising their heads cautiously, they looked about them. The air was still and calm again, but in the distance, already a mile away and swiftly travelling across the luminous waste, they saw the miniature whirlwind driving furiously, leaping from ridge to ridge. It swept over the innumerable dunes, lifting the series, one crest after another, into upright waves upon a yellow shimmering sea, then scattering them in a cloud that shone and glinted against the fiery sunset. Its track was easily marked. They watched it....

Tony was the first to recover breath.

'Whew!' he cried, still spluttering, 'but that was sudden! It took me clean off my feet for a moment. I got your hand, Tom, only just in time to save myself!' He shook himself, the sand was down his back and in his hair, his shoes were full of it. 'There'll be another any minute now— another whirlwind—we'd better be starting.' He began packing up busily, shouting as he did so to the donkey-boys. 'By Jove!' he cried the next second, 'look what's happened to our dune!'

Tom, who was on his knees, helping Lettice shake her skirts free, rose to look. The high, curving bank of sand where they had sheltered had indeed changed its shape; the entire ridge had been flattened by the wind; the crest had been lifted and carried away, scattered in all directions. The wave-outline of two minutes before no longer existed, it had broken, fallen over, melted back into the surrounding sea of desert whence it rose....

'It's disappeared!' exclaimed Tom and Lettice in the same breath.

* * * *

The boys arrived with the animals and sand-cart; the baskets were quickly arranged, Tony mounted, Tom helped Lettice in. She leaned heavily on his arm and shoulder. It was in this moment's pause before the actual start that Lettice turned her head suddenly as though listening. The air, motionless again, extraordinarily heated, hung in a dull and yet transparent curtain between them and the sinking sun. The entire heavens seemed to form a sounding-board, the least vibration resonant beneath its stretch.

'Listen!' she exclaimed. She had uttered no word till now. She looked down at Tom, then looked away again.

They turned their heads in the direction where she pointed, and Tom caught a faint, distant sound as of little strokes that fell thudding on the heavy air. Tony declared he heard nothing. The sound repeated itself rapidly, but at rhythmic intervals; it was unpleasant somewhere, a hint of alarm and menace in the throbbing note—ominous as though it warned. In the pulse of the blood it seemed, like the beating of the heart, Tom thought. It came to him almost through the pressure of her hand upon his shoulder, although his ear told him it came from the horizon where the Theban Hills loomed through the coming dusk, just visible, but shadowy. The muttering died away, then ceased, but not before he suddenly recalled an early morning hour beside a mountain lake, when months ago the thud of invisible paddle-wheels had stolen upon him through the quiet air....

'A drum,' he heard Lettice murmur. 'It's a native drum in Thebes. My little dream! How the sound travels too! And how it multiplies!' She peered at Tom through half-closed eyelids. 'It must be at least a dozen miles away...!' She smiled faintly, then dropped her eyes quickly.

'Or a dozen centuries,' he replied, not knowing quite why he said it. 'And more like a thousand drums than only one!' He smiled too. For another part of him, beyond capture somehow, knew what he meant, knew also why he smiled—knew also that she knew.

'It frightens me! It's horrible. It sounds like death!' And though she whispered the words, more to herself than to the others, Tom heard each syllable.

The sound died away into the distance, and then ceased.

Then Tony, watching them both, but, unable to hear anything himself, called out again impatiently that it was time to start, that Tom had a train to catch, that any minute the real, big wind might be upon them. The hand slowly, half lingeringly, left Tom's shoulder. They started rapidly with a kind of flourish. In a thin, black line the small procession crept across the immense darkening desert, like a strip of life that drifted upon a shoreless ocean....

The sun sank down below the Libyan sands. But no awful wind descended. They reached home safely, exhausted and rather silent. The two hours seemed to Tom to have passed with a dream-like swiftness. The stars were shining as they clattered down the little Luxor street. In a dream, too, he went to the hotel to change, and fetch his bag; in a dream he stood upon the platform, held Tony's hand, held the soft hand of Lettice, said good-bye... and watched the station lights glide past as he left them standing there together, side by side.

CHAPTER XXXII

One incident, however,—trivial, yet pregnant with significant revelation,—remained vividly outside the dream. The Play behind broke through, as it were; an actor forgot his rôle, and involved another actor; for an instant the masquerade tripped up, and merged with the commonplace reality of daily life. Explicit disclosure lay in the trifling matter.

They supplied a touch of comedy, but of rather ghastly comedy, ludicrous and at the same time painful—those smart, new yellow gloves that Tony put on when he climbed into the sand-cart and took the reins. His donkey had gone lame, he abandoned it to the boys behind, he climbed in to drive with Lettice. Tom, riding beside the cart, witnessed the entire incident; he laughed as heartily as either of the others; he felt it, however, as she felt it—a new sudden spiritual proximity to her proved this to him. Both shrank—from something disagreeable and afflicting. The hands looked somehow dreadful.

For the first time Tom realised the physiognomy of hands—that hands, rather than faces, should be photographed; not merely that they seemed now so large, so spread, so ugly, but that somehow the glaring canary yellow subtly emphasised another aspect that was distasteful and unpleasant—an undesirable aspect in their owner. The cotton was atrocious. So obvious was it to Tom that he felt pity before he felt disgust. The obnoxious revelation was so palpable. He was aware that he felt ashamed—for Lettice. He stared for a moment, unable to move his eyes away. The next second, lifting his glance, he saw that she, too, had noticed it. With a flash of keen relief, he was aware that she, like himself, shrank visibly from the distressing half-sinister revelation that was betrayal.

The hands, cased in their ridiculous yellow cotton, had physiognomy. Upon the pair of them, just then, was an expression not to be denied: of furtiveness, of something sly and unreliable, a quality not to be depended on through thick and thin, able to grasp for themselves but not to hold—for others; eager to take, yet incompetent to give. The hands were selfish, mean and unprotective. It was a remarkable disclosure of innate duality hitherto concealed. Their physiognomy dropped a mask the face still wore. The hands looked straight at Lettice; they assumed a sensual leer; they grinned.

'One second,' Tony cried, 'the reins hurt my fingers,'—and had drawn from his pocket the gloves and quickly slipped them on—canary yellow—cotton!

'Oh, oh!' exclaimed Lettice, 'but how can you! It's ghastly… for a man…!' She stared a moment, as though fascinated, then turned her eyes away, flicking the whip in the air and laughing—a trifle nervously.

Why the innocent, if vulgar, scraps of clothing should have been so revealing was hard to say. That they were incongruous and out of place in the Desert was surely an inconsiderable thing, that they were possibly in bad taste was of even less account. It was something more than that. It came in a second of vivid intuition—so, at least, it seemed to Tom, and therefore perhaps to Lettice too—that he saw his cousin's soul behind the foolish detail. Tony had put his soul upon his hands—and the hands were somewhere cheap and worthless.

So difficult was it to catch the elusive thought in language, that Tom certainly used none of the adjectives that flashed unbidden across his mind; he assuredly thought neither of 'coarse,' 'untrustworthy,' nor of 'false' or 'nasty'—yet the last named came probably nearest to expressing the disquieting sensation that laid its instant pressure upon his nerves, then went its way again. It was disturbing in a very searching way; he felt uneasy for her sake. How could he leave her with the owner of those hands, the wearer of those appalling yellow cotton gloves! The laughter in him was subtle mockery. For, of course, he laughed at himself for such an absurd conclusion…. Yet, somehow, those gloves revealed the man, betrayed him mercilessly! The hands were naked—they were stained.

It was just then that her exclamation of disapproval interrupted Tom's curious sensations. It came with welcome. 'Thank Heavens!' a voice cried inside him…. 'She feels it too!'

'But my sister sent them to me,' Tony defended himself, 'sent them from London. They're the latest thing at home!' He was laughing at himself. At the same time he was shifting the responsibility as usual.

Lettice laughed with him then, though her laughter held another note that was not merriment. He felt disgust, resentment in her. There was no pity there. Tony had missed a cue—the entire Play was blocked. The 'hero' stirred contempt in place of admiration. But more—the incident confirmed, it seemed, much else that had preceded it. Her eyes were opened.

The conflict of pain and joy in Tom was most acute. His entire sacrifice—for an instant—trembled in a hair-like balance. For the capital rôle stood gravely endangered in her eyes.

'Take them off, Tony! Put them away! Hide them! I couldn't trust you to drive me with such things on your hands. A man in yellow canary cotton!'

All three laughed together, and Tom, watching the trivial incident, as he rode beside them, saw her seize one hand and pull the glove off by the fingers. It seemed she tore a mask from one side of his face—the face beneath was disfigured. The glove fell into the bottom of the cart, then caught the loose rein and was jerked out upon the sand. The next second, something of covert fury in the gesture, Tony had taken off the other and tossed it to keep company with the first. Both hands showed naked: the entire face was bare. Tom looked away. 'They are hideous rather, I admit,' exclaimed Tony. 'The donkey boys can pick them up and wear them.' And there was mortification in his tone and manner; almost—he was found out.

* * * *

It was the memory of this pregnant little incident that held persistently before Tom's mind now, as the train bore him the long night through between the desert and the river that were Egypt. The bigger crowding pictures, scenes and sentences, thronged panorama of the recent weeks, lay in hiding underneath; but it was the incident of those yellow gloves that memory tossed up for ever before his eyes. He clung to it in spite of himself. Imagination played its impish pranks. What did it portend? Removing gloves was the first act in undressing, it struck him. Tony had dressed up for the Play, the Play was over, he must put off, piece by piece, the glamour he had worn so successfully for his passionate rôle. Once off the stage, the enchantment of the limelight, the scenery, the raiment of gold that left a perfume of ambra in the air—all the assumed allurements he had borrowed must be discarded. The Tony of the Play withdrew, the real Tony stood discovered, undressed—by no means admirable. No longer on the boards, walking like a king, with the regal fascination of an older day, he would pass along the busy street unnoticed, unadorned, bereft of the high distinction that imagination, so strangely stirred, had laid upon him for a little space.... The yellow gloves lay now upon the desert sand; perhaps the whirling tempest tossed them to and fro, perhaps it buried them; perhaps the Arab boys, proud of the tinsel they mistook for gold, now wore them in their sleep, lying on beds of rushes beneath the flat-roofed houses of sun-baked clay....

This vivid detail kept the heavier memories back at first; somehow the long review of his brief Egyptian winter blocked each time against a pair of stooping shoulders and a pair of yellow cotton gloves.

During the voyage of four days, however, followed then the inevitable cruel aftermath of doubt, suspicion, jealousy he had fancied long since overthrown. A hundred incidents and details forced themselves upon him from the past—glances, gestures, phrases, such little things and yet so pregnant with delayed or undelivered meaning. The meanings rose remorselessly to the surface now.

All belonged to the first days in Egypt before he noticed anything; the mind worked backwards to their gleaning. They had escaped his attention at the time, yet the mind had registered them none the less. He did not seek their recovery, but the series offered itself, compelling him to examine one and all, demanding that he should pass judgment. He forced them back, they leaped up again on springs; the resilience was due to their life, their truth; they were not to be denied. There was no escape....

All pointed to the same conclusion: the month spent alone with Tony had worked the mischief before his own arrival—by the time he came upon the scene the new relationship was in full swing beyond her power to stop it. Heavens, he had been blind! Ceaselessly, endlessly, he made the circle of alternate pain and joy, of hope and despair, of doubt and confidences—yet the ideal in him safe beyond assault. He believed in her, he trusted, and he—hoped.

The most poignant test, however, came when port was reached and the scented land-wind met his nostrils with the—Spring. He saw the harbour with its white houses shining in the early April sunshine; the blue sea recalled a wide-shored lake among the mountains: he saw the sea-gulls, heard the lapping of the waves against the shipping....

He took the train to a little town along the coast, meaning to stay there a day or two before facing London, where the dismantling of the Brown Flat and the search for work awaited him. And there the full-blooded spring of this southern climate took him by the throat. The haze, the sweet moist air, the luscious fields, the woods and flowery roads, above all the singing birds—this biting contrast with the dry, blazing desert skies of tawny Egypt was dislocating. The fierce glare of perpetual summer seemed a nightmare he had left behind; he came back to the sweet companionship of friendly life in field and tree and flower.

The first soft shower of rain, the first long twilight, the singing of the thrushes after dark, the light in the little homestead windows—he felt such intimate kindness in it all that the tears rose to his eyes. He longed to share it with her... there was no joy in life without her.... Egypt lay behind him with its awful loneliness, its stern, forbidding emptiness, its nightmare sunsets, its cruel desert, its appalling vastness in which everything had already happened. Thebes was a single, enormous tomb; his past lay buried there; from the solemn, mournful, desolate hills he had escaped.... He emerged into a smiling land of running streams and flowers. His new life was beginning like the Spring. It gushed everywhere, reminding him of another Spring he had known among the mountains.... The 'sum of loss' he counted minute by minute, hour by hour, day by day. He began the long, long reckoning....

He felt intolerably alone. The hunger and yearning in his heart seemed more than he could bear. This beauty… without her beside him, without her to share the sweet companionship of the earth… was too much to bear. For one minute with her beside him in the meadows, picking flowers, listening to the birds, her blue veil flying in the wet mountain wind—he would have given all his life, his past, his future, everything that mind and heart held precious…. In the middle of which and at its darkest moment came the certain knowledge with a joy that broke in light and rapture on his soul—that she was beside him because she was within him…. He approached the impersonal, selfless attitude to which the attainment of an ideal alone is possible. She had been added to him….

CHAPTER XXXIII

The silence, meanwhile, was like the silence that death brings. He clung tenaciously to his ideal, yet he thought of her daily, nightly, hourly. She was really never absent from his thoughts. He starved, yet perhaps he did not know he starved.… The days grew into weeks with a grinding, dreadful slowness. He had written from the steamer, explaining briefly that he was called to England. He had written a similar line to Tony too. No answers came.

Yet the silence was full of questions. The mystery of her Egyptian infatuation remained the biggest one of all perhaps. But there were others, equally insistent. Did he really possess her in a way that made earthly companionship unnecessary? Had he lasting joy in this ideal possession? Was it true that an ideal once attained, its prototype becomes unsatisfying? Did he deceive himself? And had not her strange experience after all but ripened and completed her nature, provided something she had lacked before, and blended the Mother and the Woman into the perfect mate his dream foretold and his heart's deep instinct prophesied?

He heard many answers to these questions; his heart made one, his reason made another. It was the soft and urgent Spring, however, with its perfumed winds, its singing birds, its happy message breaking with tumultuous life—it was the Spring on those wooded Mediterranean shores that whispered the compelling truth. He needed her, he yearned. An ideal, on this earth, to retain its upward lure, must remain—an ideal. Attainment in the literal sense destroys it. His arms were hungry and his heart was desolate. Then one day he knew the happy yet unhappy feeling that she suffered too. He felt her thoughts about him like soft birds.…

And he wrote to her: 'I should just like to know that you are well—and happy.' He addressed it to the Bungalow. The same day, chance had it, he received word from her, forwarded from the Semiramis Hotel in Cairo. She wrote two lines only: 'Tom, the thing I had to tell you about was— Warsaw. It is over. As you said, it is better written, perhaps, than told. Yours, L.'

Egypt came flooding through the open window as he laid the letter down; the silence, the desert spaces, the perfume and the spell. He saw one thing clearly in that second, for he saw it in a flash. The secret of her trouble that last day in Luxor was laid bare—the knowledge that within a few hours she would be free. To Tom she could not easily tell it; delicacy, modesty, pride forbade. Her long, painful duty, faithfully fulfilled these many years, was over. Her world had altered, opened out. Values, of course, had instantly altered too; she saw what was real and what ephemeral; she looked at Tony and she looked at—himself. She could speak to

Tony—it was easier, it did not matter—but she could not so easily speak to Tom. The yellow gloves of cotton!… His heart leaped within him….

He stared out of the window across the blue Mediterranean with its dancing, white-capped waves; he saw the white houses by the harbour; he watched the whirling sea-gulls and tasted the fresh, salt air. How familiar it all was! Of her whereabouts at that moment he had no knowledge; she might be on the steamer, gazing at the same dancing waves; she might be in Warsaw or in London even; she might pass by the windows of the Brown Flat….

He turned aside, closing the window. Egypt withdrew, the glamour waned, the ancient spell seemed lifted. He thought of those Theban Hills without emotion. Yet something in him trembled; he yearned, he ached, he longed with all the longing of the Spring. He wavered—oh, deliciously…! He was glad, radiantly glad, that she had written. Only—he dared not, he could not answer….

Yet big issues are decided sometimes by paltry and ignoble influences when sturdier considerations produce no effect. It is the contrast that furnishes the magic. It was contrast, doubtless, that swayed Tom's judgment in the very direction he had decided was prohibited. His surroundings at the moment supplied the contrast, for these surroundings were petty and ignoble—they drove him by the distress of sheer disgust into the world of larger values he had known with her. Probably, he did not discover this consciously for himself: the result, in any case, was logical and obvious. Values changed suddenly for him, too, both in his outlook and his judgment.

For he was spending a few days with his widowed sister, she who had been playmate to Lettice years ago; and the conditions of her life and mind distressed him. He had seen her name in a hotel list of Mentone; he surprised her with a visit; he was received with inexplicable coldness. His tie with her was slight, her husband, a clergyman, little to his liking; he had not been near them for several years. The frigid reception, however, had a deeper cause, he felt; his curiosity was piqued.

His sister's chart of existence, indeed, was too remote from his own for true sympathy to be possible, and her married life had not improved her. They had drifted apart without openly acknowledging it. There was no quarrel, but there was a certain bitterness between them. She had a marked faiblesse, strange in one securely born, for those nominally in high places that, while disingenuous enough, jarred painfully always on her brother. God was unknown to her, although her husband preached most familiarly concerning Him. She had never seen the deity, but an Earl was a living reality, and often very useful. This banal weakness, he now found, had increased in widowhood. Tom hid his extreme distaste—and learned the astonishing reason for her coldness. It was Mrs. Haughstone. It took his breath away. He was too amazed to speak.

How clearly he understood her conduct now in Egypt! For Mrs. Haughstone had spread stories of the Bungalow, pernicious stories of an incredible kind, yet with just sufficient basis of apparent truth to render them plausible—plausible, that is, to any who were glad of an excuse to believe them against himself. These stories by a round-about way, gathering in circumstantial detail as they travelled, had reached his sister. She wished to believe them, and she did. Certain relatives, moreover, of meagre intelligence but highly placed in the social world, and consequently of great importance in her life, were remotely affected by the lurid tales. A report in full is unnecessary, but Mary held that the family honour was stained. It was an incredible imbroglio. Tom was so overwhelmed by this revelation of the jealous woman's guile, and the light it threw upon her rôle in Egypt, that he did not even trouble to defend himself. He merely felt sorry that his sister could believe such tales—and forgave her without a single word. He saw in it all another scrap of evidence that the Wave had indeed fallen, that his life everywhere, and from the most unlikely directions, was threatened, that all the most solid in the structure he had hitherto built up and leaned upon, was crumbling—and must crumble utterly—in order that it might rise secure upon fresh foundations.

He faced it, but faced it silently. He washed his hands of all concerned; he had learned their values too; he now looked forward instead of behind; that is, he forgot, and at the same time utterly—forgave.

But the effect upon him was curious. The stagnant ditch his sister lived in had the result of flinging him headlong back into the larger stream he had just left behind him; in that larger world things happened indeed, things unpleasant, cruel, mysterious, amazing—but yet not little things. The scale was vaster, horizons wider, beauty and wonder walked hand in hand with love and death. The contrast shook him; the trivial blow had this immense effect, that he yearned with redoubled passion for the region in which bigger ideals with their prototypes, however broken, existed side by side.

This yearning, and the change involved, remained subtly concealed, however. He was not properly conscious of it. Other very practical considerations, it seemed, influenced him; his money was getting low; he had luckily sublet the flat, but the question of work was becoming insistent. There was much to be faced.... A month had slipped by, it was five weeks since he had left Egypt. He decided to go to London. He telegraphed to the Club for his letters—he expected important ones—to be sent to Paris, and it was in a small high room on the top floor of a second-rate hotel across the Seine that he found them waiting for him.

It was here, in this dingy room, that he read the wondrous words. The letter had lain at his Club three days, it was dated Switzerland and the postmark was Montreux. It was in pencil, without beginning and without end; his name, the signature did not appear:

> Your little letter has come—yes, I am well, but happy I am not. I went to the Semiramis and found that you had sailed, sailed without even a good-bye. I have come here, here to familiar little Montreux by the blue lake, where we first knew the Spring together. I can't say anything, I can't explain anything. You must never ask me to explain; Egypt changed me—brought out something in me I was helpless to resist. It was something perhaps I needed. I struggled—perhaps you can guess how I struggled, perhaps you can't. I have suffered these past weeks, I believe that I have expiated something. The power that drove me is exhausted, and that is all I know. I have worked it out. I have come back. There is no blame for others—for any one; I can't explain. Your little letter has come, and so I write. Help me, oh, help me in years to find my respect again, and try to love the woman you once knew—knew here in Montreux beside the lake, long ago in our childhood days, further back still, perhaps, though where I do not know. And, Tom— tell me how you are. I must know that. Please write and tell me that. I can bear it no longer. If anything happened to you I should just turn over and die. You have been true and very big, oh, so true and big. I see it now....

Tom did not answer. He took the night train. He was just in time to catch the Simplon Express from the Gare de Lyon. He reached Montreux at seven o'clock, when the June sun was already high above the Dent du Midi and the lake a sheet of sparkling blue. He went to his old hotel. He saw the swans floating like bundles of dry paper, he saw the whirling sea-gulls, he obtained his former room. And spring was just melting into full-blown summer upon the encircling mountains.

It was still early when he had bathed and breakfasted, too early for visitors to be abroad, too early to search.... He could settle to nothing; he filled the time as best he could; he smoked and read an English newspaper that was several days old at least. His eyes took in the lines, but his mind did not take in the sense—until a familiar name caught his attention and made him keenly alert. The name was Anthony Winslowe. He remembered suddenly that Tony had never replied to his letter.... The paragraph concerning his cousin, however, dealt with another matter that sent the blood flaming to his cheeks. He was defendant in the breach of promise suit brought by a notorious London actress, then playing in a popular revue. The case had opened; the letters were already produced in court—and read. The print danced before his eyes. The letters were dated last October and November, just before Tony had come out to Egypt, and with crimson face Tom read them. It was more than distressing, it was afflicting—the letters tore an established reputation into a thousand pieces. He could not finish the report; he only prayed that another had not seen it....

It was eleven o'clock when he went out and joined the throng of people sunning themselves on the walk beside the lake. The air was sweet and fresh, there were sailing-boats upon the water, the blue mountains lifted their dazzling snow far, far into the summer sky. He leaned over the rail and watched the myriads of tiny fishes, he watched the swans, he saw the dim line of the Jura hills in the hazy distance, he heard the muffled beat of a steamer's paddle-wheels a long way off. And then, abruptly, he was aware that some one touched him; a hand in a long white glove was on his arm; there was a subtle perfume; two dark eyes looked into his; and he heard a low familiar voice:

'One day we shall find each other in a crowd.'

Tom was amazingly inarticulate. He just turned and looked down at her, moving a few inches closer as he did so. She wore a black boa; the fur touched his cheek.

'You have come back,' he said.

There was a new wonder in her face, a soft new beauty. The woman in her glowed.... He saw the suffering plainly too.

'We have both found out,' she said very low, 'found out what we are to one another.'

Tom's supply of words failed completely then. He looked at her—looked all the language in the world. And she understood. She lowered her eyes. 'I feel shy,' he thought he heard. It was murmured only. The next minute she raised her eyes again to his. He saw them dark and beautiful, tender as his mother's, true and faithful, as in his boyhood's dream of years ago. But they were now a woman's eyes.

'I never really left you, Tom...' she said with absolute conviction. 'I never could. I went aside... to fetch something—to give to you. That was all!'